ELK DR.

D1548913

Act Like It
Pretty Face
Making Up

JRL 9-19-2019

JRL -10-1-2019

DD. 4 BOOKS - FREE
10-3-2019

For Dana.
Friends then, friends now, friends always.

the austen playbook

LUCY PARKER

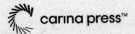

carina press™

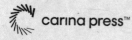

ISBN-13: 978-1-335-01622-5

The Austen Playbook

Recycling programs
for this product may
not exist in your area.

www.CarinaPress.com

Printed in U.S.A.

the
austen
playbook

Chapter One

A year ago

After twelve years of performing in the West End, Freddy Carlton had racked up her fair share of unfortunate experiences. Bitchy co-stars. Costume malfunctions. Having to stage-snog people with whom she'd had bad dates and even worse sex.

She'd never forgotten her lines during a public performance.

"Peanut, it wasn't that bad." Crossing her long legs, her older sister Sabrina pushed the basket of hot chips across the table. She'd been trying to stuff food down Freddy's throat for the past half hour. The conviction that most ills could be assuaged with carbs ran deep in their family. "You covered really well. Barely a pause."

Freddy put down her sangria and rubbed her eyes. "Yes. It really saved the day when I quoted a Bruce Springsteen song in the middle of a play set in 1945."

In the instant under the lights when her mind had just…blanked, and her stomach had dropped to her shoes, some safety valve in her brain had stepped in and supplied a line. Unfortunately, it had fixed on the last song she'd been listening to in her dressing room to wind down before curtain.

She supposed she should be thankful she hadn't trotted out a line from the second-to-last song the radio had infiltrated into her subconscious. She might have responded to her soldier lover's romantic declaration with an obscene rap.

"Oh my God." She pushed aside her glass and briefly dropped her forehead to the table. "Press night. I quoted Springsteen in front of a thousand people on press night."

She'd never really screwed up on stage before. Certainly never so bizarrely. She usually confined any major hiccups to rehearsal. She had a reputation for reliability. Affability. *Just tell Freddy where to go, what to do, who to be, and she'll do it.* She'd even throw in a smile.

Generally, the smile was genuine. She loved the stage, she loved her family, and she loved life. With the glaring exception of tonight's debacle, her career was on the up. She ought to be skipping through the streets.

Not lying awake at night, not partying too much in the extremely brief gaps between productions, and not feeling physically sick before auditions.

"People may not even have noticed." Sabrina pushed back a strand of wildly curling hair. They'd both inherited their father's ringlets, but where Freddy was dark brown, like every Carlton in recent memory, Sabs had popped out a bright redhead. An early beginning on her lifelong tendency to stand out in the crowd. "And given how shite the actual dialogue was, I thought your improvisation was a massive improvement."

"Sabrina," Akiko protested from the other side of the booth, her heavy silver jewellery glinting in the light as she shifted. Her makeup was equally sparkly, the smooth bob that curved under her chin was currently dyed cobalt blue, and she looked more like a rock star than an academic. She'd been Sabrina's best mate for over two decades, and Freddy literally couldn't remember life before her comforting presence. "I thought the script was very good." Akiko ran her fingers over the tines of her fork. She always fiddled when she was blatantly lying.

"Akiko, I love that you're a nicer person than I am, but there's politeness and there's absolute bollocks." Sabrina patted Freddy's arm. "I'm assuming that—Jesus, I can't even remember the name of tonight's play, and it was only an hour ago. Seriously, kiddo, stop beating yourself up. A forgotten line is the least of that script's worries."

"You're not being very respectful about your late grandmother's work," Akiko said, and Sabrina wrinkled her nose.

"I think enough people fawn over our infamous granny, don't you? Dad's one step away from erecting a ten-foot solid-gold statue of her on his balcony. And based on the script tonight, I'm baffled by the accolades. The 'greatest British playwright of the twentieth century'? What, were the only other plays between 1900 and 1999 written by the typewriting monkey at the zoo?"

"The play I stuttered my way through tonight is *Masquerade*." Freddy took a chip from the bowl Sabrina was waving in front of her again and bit it in half. They were venturing into territory that made boulders appear in her stomach, so she might as well pile some greasy spuds on top. "It's one of the earliest Henrietta Carlton scripts."

Their grandmother had written *Masquerade* at the age of twenty, several years before she'd hit the big time as both a playwright and an actor.

"Her writing inexperience shows in *Masquerade*.

Hugely. It's nothing like *The Velvet Room*." The script that had catapulted Henrietta into the history books. "Which I assume you've still never read." Freddy swallowed down another chip with a mouthful of sangria. The director of *Masquerade* wanted his cast to follow a healthy diet during the run. Nailing it.

"You *should* read it." Akiko swirled the melting ice in her own drink. "I'm not that keen on just paging through a script like it's a novel, but *The Velvet Room* is so poignant you forget you're reading stage directions. Your grandmother grew into a cracker of a writer."

Sabrina lifted finely threaded brows. "All that, and a brilliant actress, too. Almost seems too much talent for one person, doesn't it?" She tweaked one of Freddy's fluffing curls. "Thank God our little Frederica came along to keep the end up for this generation. Four centuries of thespians in the family, with X-factor spilling out of their Shakespearean ruffs, and it almost ended with—"

"A very talented journalist," Akiko said loyally.

"Some drunk ginger floozy from the telly?" Freddy suggested at the same time, in a tongue-in-cheek attempt to divert the stream of the conversation.

Sabrina lifted her nose. "Excuse me, baby sister. I am perfectly sober. I can hold a cocktail."

"You can hold about six in each hand at the TV Awards every year."

"Entirely different situation." Sabrina grinned. "Despite that piece of cheek, you wee shite, and even with a spot of Springsteen thrown in, I'm incredibly proud of what you can do. And I'll even bone up on *The Velvet Room*, so I'm all set for your star turn in the West End revival next year."

Freddy felt her smile fade from the inside out. Her

heart gave a hard thump of trepidation and shrivelled, and the shadow probably spread to her face. "There's no guarantee I'll get a role in it."

"Of course you will," Sabrina said, and added with sisterly affection and zero tact, "Talent aside, you're Henrietta's granddaughter. Think of the marketing opportunities. Dad's always got his eye on his investments, and this'll be a triple coup. A performance royalty from the theatre, commission from your salary, and all the media appearances he'll be able to milk out of you appearing in Grandma's *tour de force*." Her vivacious features slipped into that barbed wall of sarcasm that usually emerged when they were discussing their father. "Thanks to the offspring who *isn't* a massive disappointment, Scrooge McDuck can pour another bucket of gold coins into that vault of millions he's hoarding."

Freddy felt a tinge of colour rush into her cheeks, and that knot in her chest twisted. She put down the rest of the chip in her hand.

Akiko folded her hands on the tabletop, studying Freddy with uncomfortably shrewd dark eyes. "You do *want* a role in *The Velvet Room*, Freddy?"

"What, Henrietta's masterpiece? The Carltons' biggest claim to fame?" Sabrina waved at someone who'd just come into the pub. "Freddy's always banged on about what a good script it is. She's almost as bad as Dad on that subject. Although at least she likes it for its artistic merit, not the rewards it generates."

Akiko was still looking at Freddy.

She weighed her words. "It's an excellent play. It really does deserve all the accolades." She hadn't actually answered Akiko's question, and from her expression, it hadn't gone unnoticed. Freddy appreciated the genius of *The Velvet Room*—but did she really, honestly, want to act in it?

No. She could say it silently, privately, in her own mind, but so far she hadn't had the balls to say it aloud, even just to Sabrina.

After a moment, she lifted a shoulder. "The most likely director for the new season of *The Velvet Room* was in the audience tonight. This performance wasn't exactly a ringing endorsement, was it?"

"You were probably just nervous," Sabrina said, in a tone that suggested Freddy was eleven years old again and had just embarked on her first debut.

Incidentally, when she had debuted at eleven, she'd remembered every one of her lines.

"I'm sure press night is always terrifying," Akiko said.

Yes, it was, even after all this time. Doubly so when her family were in the front rows, as well as the dozens of critics, including the dude who'd called her "duller than a pair of safety scissors" in the *Westminster Post*.

And the scrutiny would have been high tonight, because of the family connection. By choice, Freddy wouldn't audition for any adaptations of her grandmother's works. For several reasons, one being that enough of her career had been founded on nepotism. She hadn't minded exploiting the connection in her teens, but unearned glory wore thin very quickly. With Carltons populating the theatres of London since the days of quills, bustles, and bubonic plague, she didn't need to provide extra fodder for the critics to discuss the many and varied ways she had built a career on other people's achievements.

However, her father was her manager, he did think it was good business sense to capitalise on the link, and when the casting call had gone out for *Masquerade* this season, he'd been dead set on having her in it. And she'd caved, to avoid the argument. As usual.

Akiko cleared her throat. "I'm not sure that unrelenting angst is really your thing, Freddy. I could see the natural glass-half-full sass itching to come out at every woe-laden moment."

As usual, she'd hit the nail on the head. No, weepy philosophical introspection was *not* Freddy's cup of tea, it had become increasingly apparent, and the admittedly mediocre script for *Masquerade* was so wreathed in despair and gloom that she'd had to listen to P. G. Wodehouse audiobooks in rehearsal downtime to keep up her spirits.

In that respect, *The Velvet Room* would be just as bad. It was beautifully written, but not exactly abundant with laughs.

It would, however, very likely sweep the National Theatre Awards and look bloody great on a CV.

Which, not so long ago, she'd have jotted down as item one on the priority list. Living up to the family legacy, reaching the highest salary bracket, winning countless Leading Actress awards, crossing over into film, meriting an incredibly long and detailed entry on Wikipedia— who wouldn't want that?

Who wouldn't find happiness in all of that?

She smooshed another chip into a greasy pillow between her finger and thumb.

"So, how was the show?" The question came from the next booth. The Prop & Cue was always packed to the rafters, as the closest pub to four of the major theatres, and the noise level was usually a continuous loud buzz, but every so often there was an unexpected lull. She could hear the man clearly, speaking in an attractive, melodious voice. "Where does tonight's review fall on the scale of 'could do better' to 'Jesus God, pass me the brain bleach'? Which poor sod's career is in the crapper this time?"

"It's unfortunate in some cases, but I've never trashed anyone's career."

Freddy raised her head. She knew that second voice. It was deep, with a distinctive curt resonance to it. She'd heard it just this week through her laptop speakers, while watching a Marlowe documentary on her afternoon off.

J. Ford-Griffin. Grumpiest TV presenter in the UK. And the witty wanker behind the scathing theatre reviews in the *Westminster Post*.

"If they can't pick themselves up after one person's criticism, they don't deserve another person's accolades."

She could almost see him saying it, with the same expression he wore when discussing Elizabethan tragedy. The man looked like an assassin in a war film, and would be temperamentally suited to the part.

He probably even orgasmed with a frosty stare off into the middle distance.

Although it was unfair to judge by appearances. Behind the sub-zero remarks and laser eyes, he could be a total marshmallow. Maybe he went home every night, watched *Titanic* for the hundredth time, and wept sensitively into his pet kitten.

"*Masquerade* was a pile of tedious crap when it was committed to paper, it should never have made it as far as a stage, and it's an embarrassment to Henrietta Carlton's legacy that it's still being produced. And of all the boring-as-fuck resurrections I've had to sit through, this was the worst."

Across the table, Sabrina's brows had snapped together. Freddy took a sip of her drink.

"Well, there's the first few lines set to go. The column's practically writing itself." The other voice was tinged with humour. "I hope you have *something* nice to say, my friend. People will be starting to think you're a right miserable bastard."

A snort. "That was established by the time I was old enough to talk."

Sabrina was still looking unaccountably irate. She was a protective sister, but she didn't usually go from zero to homicidal at the first hint of professional criticism.

Thoughtfully, Freddy ran her fingertip through the rings of water on the table as the nicer man asked, "Who's in it?"

"Adrian Blair, as usual blinding the audience with his veneers so they don't notice the weaknesses in his performance. When the spotlight hits his teeth, it's like looking directly into the sun."

Freddy tried to keep quiet, but a tiny squeak made it out of her throat.

"Freddy Carlton."

She'd been expecting it, but still jumped as those harsh tones spoke her name.

"I've interviewed her." The other voice again. "She's very…exuberant. Pretty. Lots of hair. Big arse. Not as striking as her sister, but much nicer."

The night just kept getting better, didn't it. And she'd just recognised that voice as well. Mystery solved as to why Sabrina had turned a curious shade of purple.

"She must be good," Nick Davenport added. He was the host of the evening chat show *The Davenport Report*, and Sabs's main professional rival. She was currently a presenter for *Sunset Britain*. Same time, different channel. No love lost. "She's in everything, isn't she?"

"She does give that impression." The reply was so dry that she could imagine wisps of steam rising from ice. "It was a surprisingly variable performance from her tonight. She fumbled a line at one point, and for some reason decided to diverge out of maudlin sentiment into classic rock. Which, to be fair, was an improvement on the actual dialogue."

Freddy glanced at Sabrina with a shade of irony.

"Even when she had her words straight, she was phoning it in. She's losing her spark. Until a few years ago, she was still getting kiddie parts, and mostly took roles in musicals and drawing-room comedy. She danced and bounced her way from curtain to curtain, it was exhausting to watch, and audiences bloody loved her. Then she aged into adult characters, switched direction into pretentious bullshit like *High Voltage*, and obviously hated every moment of it. For some reason, she's pursuing a determined line in the high-brow dramas, when she'd clearly rather be stamping about in puddles in *Singin' in the Rain*."

Carefully, Freddy set her glass on the table. She suddenly felt as if a hand had reached over and torn off her dress, leaving her sitting here naked and exposed. It was one thing for Akiko, who had known her most of her life and had always been incredibly intuitive, to see right through the real-life character she'd been playing for a long time now. It was very different to have that icy, impersonal voice slicing through all her shields and digging straight into the heart of her private thoughts and fears. Ford-Griffin had said plenty of unflattering things about her in print over the years, but she'd always been able to brush off a bad review. That was solely about her work on one distinct night, and it was often justified. Occasionally even helpful.

To her, that terse speech struck at the issue of who she was—who she'd thought she would be—as a person.

"Is that what you're going to write in the review?" Nick asked.

"That would be the tactful way of putting it."

"And the less tactful?"

"She's an overexposed, chronically confused crowd-pleaser, who's built a career riding on her family's coattails. A twirl through her grandmother's work was inevitable, and unfortunately this is probably a practice run. There's a huge revival of *The Velvet Room* coming next winter, and regardless of suitability, the surname is promotional gold." Drip, drip, went the tap of cynicism.

And realism.

"Half the world runs on nepotism," Nick pointed out.

"Agreed. Wringing her connections dry shows common sense. Which is then smashed by the complete lack of critical judgment. She either has no idea of her own strengths, or is under someone's thumb. I suspect both. You need grit to endure in this industry. If she has it, she's doing an exceptional job of hiding it."

Looking at Sabrina's expression now, Ford-Griffin should be grateful there were no lethal weapons within reach of the booth. Akiko looked torn between indignation on Freddy's behalf and alarm at the brewing thundercloud across from her.

A new group of people thankfully entered the pub then—judging by the glimpses of leotards under leggings and hoodies, it was the cast from *The Festival of Masks*—and the noise cranked up to the approximate level of monster-truck rally.

Freddy took a second to ensure that none of the turbulence in her mind leaked into her expression or words. "Put the claws away, kids. That was a short, sharp dose of painful accuracy. I have cashed in on the Carlton name and we all know it."

And he'd made a direct hit with the rest of it.

"You've also worked your tail off. What a fucking twat." Sabrina drummed her nails on the table and glowered over Freddy's head.

"Who is he?" Akiko asked curiously.

"J. Ford-Griffin. The critic for the *Westminster Post*." Freddy played with the rose in the glass on the table. She usually found flowers very soothing. Flowers and books: her happy places. "He's the guy who presents all the arts programmes on TV. Expert in the history of theatre. You know. Short-haired Lucius Malfoy. Tall. Sarcastic. Ice-blond hair. Ice in general."

Illumination dawned on Akiko's face. She was an art history professor, she'd have seen him before; he produced multiple shows on all aspects of the arts. "Oh—yes, I met him when he was filming a documentary at the British Museum. He's very…um…" Akiko always liked to pick out the best qualities in anyone she met. She was struggling. "Learned. I believe he has a PhD."

"And a mind like a snake." Sabrina made no attempt to speak quietly, so all gratitude to the boisterous dancers at the bar. "He was on the show once, and I had to interview him. Any question he didn't feel like answering, he twisted to suit himself, and I ended up looking like I had no idea what I was talking about." Sabrina looked peevish at the memory, although Freddy found it hard to imagine her sister ever feeling discomposed on camera. She'd never had a stupid professional stumble like Freddy had made tonight. "And," Sabs finished ominously, "as we can see, he's a mate of Nick Davenport's." She would probably use the same tone if she'd said, "And he likes to knock down old ladies in the supermarket."

On the charge of being uncooperative in interviews, Freddy didn't entirely blame Ford-Griffin. As much as she loved Sabrina and obviously supported her career—go team—she still had haunting memories of the one time she'd had to do a talk show interview. Incidentally, with Nick Davenport. Who was a right nosy bastard beneath the slick veneer. He'd tried to suggest she was the latest Other Woman in a co-star's train wreck of a marriage. Not likely.

A spark of amusement returned as her sister visibly simmered. "I see inter-show relations are as cordial as ever."

Sabrina said something that would send the curse-censors on her show haywire. "And see if I expend energy trying to coax a smile out of Malfoy next time they drag him on. Wanker."

"The *Westminster Post* has always been a hard sell. His column is actually extremely entertaining." When his remarks didn't hit so close to home. "He strews the insults about with such panache." Freddy wriggled out of the booth. "I'm going to get another round. Who wants?"

Akiko shook her head, but Sabrina held up her glass. "Another rum and coke, please."

It took a full minute of elbow-ducking and handbag-dodging to manoeuvre her way to the bar, where the staff were flat-out and looking harassed. She was leaning forward and trying to read the new cocktail menu when the youngest bartender, a girl with artificially grey hair, made an unwise grab for a bottle of gin on a shelf high above her head. It slipped from her grasp as she lost her balance, and Freddy shot out her hand and grabbed it. She caught it inches before it could smash right in the face and expensive jacket of the man who'd come up beside her.

There was a moment of stillness, before she flipped the bottle upright and set it carefully on the counter.

Blinking, the bartender cast a quick look over at her shoulder at her boss. "Shit. Thanks. Ever think about trying out for wicket-keeper at Lord's?"

"I'd be happy if I could just pull off that much dexterity on stage now and then. It would really—" Freddy turned to check on the target of the near-miss, and tilted her head as she finished "—widen my skill set."

Ford-Griffin, in all his towering, broad-shouldered, frosty glory, asked another bartender for two whisky-and-sodas before he looked back at her. His eyes were almost black, in stark contrast to the very pale hair, and his gaze moved coolly from the gin bottle to her face. "Nice catch. Thanks."

"Not a problem." Freddy gave her own order to the grey-haired bartender, then propped her elbow on the bar and studied him. She'd forgotten he had that nose. When he was doing his presenting work, the TV cameras didn't usually film him in profile. She suspected he didn't give a shit about his looks, but if impressions were deceptive and he spent a lot of time gazing into mirrors like his friend Davenport, he was probably grateful he had the strong jaw to balance it out. An unexpected little flutter in her stomach took her by surprise. An oxytocin hit from the walking ice cube. *Interesting life choices, body.* "Apparently I have an affinity with all sorts of small objects. Bottles. Safety scissors."

His brain didn't require even a second of internal whirring to catch on. A small glint appeared behind the emotionless observation. "If it helps, there'll be no references to predictability in the next review."

"Because I was completely rubbish tonight?"

"You weren't completely rubbish." Definite emphasis on that *completely*. He pulled the whisky-and-sodas towards him and waved his credit card over the sensor. "Comparatively, you made Adrian Blair look like he was performing in a school hall nativity." He slipped the card back into his wallet and picked up the glasses. "With the exception of the meander into Springsteen."

Freddy handed over a note for her own order and dropped the change into the tip jar. All the staff looked like they deserved a few drinks at the end of their shift. "I'll look forward to reading the review." She stuck a straw in her sangria. "Especially if you put in the part about Adrian's teeth."

He looked at her for a second and then over her head towards their respective booths. He lifted an eyebrow.

She cheers-ed him with Sabrina's rum and coke. "Nice to meet the man behind the most entertaining reviews I've ever had."

And the most discomfortingly perceptive.

Without looking back, she returned to her seat, where in the midst of Sabrina's risqué anecdote and frequent hostile glances at the next booth, she tried to forget all about J. Ford-Griffin and his insidious commentary.

And his inkwell eyes.

Chapter Two

Six months later

When his brother grinned like that, he still looked like a little kid. Eager, hopelessly optimistic, effortlessly like-able, and on the verge of yet another half-cocked scheme. Charlie was all but bouncing in his seat. It didn't bode well. He hadn't looked this excited since his grand plan to save the estate by starting a hot-air ballooning enter-prise on the north lawn.

Griff eyed him over the wide mahogany desk. He had a feeling that his day was about to get significantly worse. Tightening his grip on his phone, he turned away from Charlie's impatient wriggling and tried to keep his full attention on the call. "Henrietta Carlton rose from bit player to reigning queen of the West End stage by the age of twenty-three. She caused havoc in nightclubs from Wimbledon to Whitechapel and had affairs with some of the most powerful people in London. And before her thirtieth birthday, she'd written one of the most iconic plays of the twentieth century and permanently altered the landscape of British drama."

The studio executive at the end of the line made thoughtful noises, as if this was the first time she'd heard this pitch. Griff had delivered it three times this month alone. The process of securing funding for a film was long, frustrating, and repetitive. Investors were like police detectives interviewing suspects; they needed to hear the same story over and over before they made a decision.

The past eight years that he'd been working in television, he'd progressed from being just the figurehead they stuck in a suit and shoved in front of a camera, to having a small say in what was written on the script, to full production credits. The move from documentary production into film development was what he'd been working towards, and he'd long seen the screen potential in Henrietta Carlton's chaotic life on and off the stage, and her propulsion into unexpected literary stardom.

"The script hinges on the time when Henrietta was writing *The Velvet Room* in the countryside, but a lot of scenes will be shot in London."

Henrietta had written the play here at Highbrook, during the time she'd been heavily involved in an affair with Griff's grandfather, Sir George Ford; but for the purposes of the film, her life in London also provided dramatic scope. She'd founded the Wythburn Group in the city, a collective of actors and writers who'd occupied neighbouring party houses in Marylebone, and their exploits were legendary.

The executive babbled another stream of questions that Griff had already answered, and he bit back impatience. As fed up as he was with the red tape, he needed this backing.

He couldn't get this project off the ground without the financing, and he'd invested so much time and so many hopes into it that the prospect of failure was a kick to the gut. He could see it in his mind, what the story could be, and felt an intense frustration in not being able to immediately extract that image and cast it up onto the big screen.

And on a personal level, the film had the potential to make a healthy profit—and with Highbrook mortgaged to the roof tiles, Griff badly needed the cash infusion.

The estate had been passed down through generations of Fords since the sixteenth century, and with every handover, it grew more expensive to maintain. His grandfather had left the property to Griff in his will, because he'd anticipated the financial struggle and correctly assumed that Griff's father would just exacerbate the problem. Griff clearly recalled Sir George sitting him down on his twelfth birthday, to start preparing him to take over the reins.

Right now, he felt more like he was trying to steer a sinking ship.

The executive fired a query down the line about the "human interest" side of the film. The inevitable sex angle.

"Yes, we will be focusing on the relationship between Henrietta and George. Audiences grasp on to a love story." He couldn't totally suppress the ironic twist to his words. Love. An adulterous affair between two self-centred hedonists, which had ended abruptly after a couple of years, when his grandfather seemed to have dropped Henrietta like a hot potato for reasons unknown.

Griff was still trying to get to the bottom of that one. His grandmother's existence already cast a bad light on the relationship, so it would be better for the plot if the affair had at least ended for a more sympathetic reason than fading lust.

As he went into detail about shoot locations, his

brother stood restlessly and paced in front of the library windows. Coming over to the desk, Charlie picked up a book, put it down, accidentally knocked three more to the floor, and lifted onto the balls of his feet to stretch.

It was like trying to work with a bloody toddler in the room.

The call finally ended, with noncommittal noises from the studio. As usual. Every time there was an encouraging sign, it was dashed by further procrastination. Tossing his phone down on the desk, Griff rubbed his forehead and forced himself to focus on the more immediate problem in the room.

He turned to his brother and steeled himself. "Yes?"

In the pause that followed, he heard the distant sound of a plane flying overhead.

Now that he had the floor, Charlie seemed to be debating the best way to launch into his own pitch. Maybe that plane was his. Perhaps he'd progressed from hot-air balloons to commercial liners.

"Any advances on the film front?" Charlie asked. Ah. His favourite ploy of small talk first, horrifying scheme second.

"Some."

"Is Rupert Carlton still trying to throw a spanner in the works?"

Griff grunted. Henrietta's son was like the fucking mole in that arcade game, constantly popping out of the woodwork with ways to delay the final green light on the film. Family members were often precious about the way their relatives were represented onscreen, but in Rupert Carlton's case, Griff suspected his objections centred on the fact that he hadn't yet found a way to cash in on the project.

"*Trying* being the operative word." Looking down, he shoved aside a pile of accounts, all of which were adding up to a bleak total. The stress was a bone-deep fog, a roiling grey weight. He was tired. It was a kinetic sort of exhaustion, one setback fuelling another, each irritant turning like a cog in the mechanism.

Life was so flat-out in London right now that coming home to the country for a few days ought to be a reprieve, but the financial situation with Highbrook was rapidly becoming dire. If they wanted to avoid a forced selling-up, they had to make shrewd, long-sighted choices.

Not indulge in reckless, irresponsible flights of fantasy.

He cut short any further hedging around the point. "What are you up to?" He leaned his hip against the desk, letting it take some of his weight. He suspected he'd need the support.

Charlie cleared his throat. "I want to open The Henry." He rocked back and forth on his heels, emitting hopeful vibes.

"You want to open The Henry," Griff repeated in the most neutral tone he could muster. He rarely bothered to sugar-coat his opinions. Pandering bullshit just wasted everybody's time, but it was impossible to be too brutally blunt with Charlie. For one thing, it just bounced off his cheerful, resilient exterior.

"To the public," Charlie clarified, and Griff's gaze sliced from his eager expression to the view out the window. Beyond a wide expanse of snow-scattered grass, a turret peeked out above the trees. A leaking turret. The Henry, their boutique theatre on the far grounds, was overdue for repairs, but hardly the priority when half the estate was either dripping, squeaking, draughty, or at actual risk of falling down. The theatre was a vanity project their otherwise practical grandfather had built for Henrietta, during the period when he'd obviously been thinking with his dick, and it had never actually housed a production. At this point, it was an oversized garden shed.

"It would cost a fortune to repair it to a standard where we'd be allowed to pack two hundred people into it." Reaching for the half-empty glass on the desktop, Griff knocked back a mouthful of cognac. It felt like he'd scraped up his intestines with sandpaper. He should probably be reaching for antacids, not spirits. "Which is what you'd need to even approach breaking even on production costs. A full house. Every performance. You're not going to get two hundred people to drive all the way to rural Surrey every night. And where would they park? Flattening the south lawn with cars will just piss off the kids who ride the electric mower."

He turned around, and Charlie was grinning at him with totally unimpaired enthusiasm. Human rubber.

"Is the lecture over?" The enquiry was amiable.

Griff glanced pointedly at the sheaf of papers tucked under his brother's arm. It looked ominously like a contract. "I suspect not."

"I'm not suggesting we host a multi-night run here." Charlie waved the pages at him. "I'm talking one night, one performance. Televised live."

"Televised."

"A network has already licensed the production rights to *The Austen Playbook*." He correctly interpreted Griff's "the fuck?" expression. "It was one of the top-selling games this year. Digital mash-up of characters from different Jane Austen books, transplanted into a murder-mystery, house-party scenario. Outcome guided by the choices of the player. A mate of mine was involved in the development, and they've made a *mint* with it."

"I see the financial potential in the game. How exactly is that going to translate to a theatre adaptation?"

"One of the investors in the game is a bigwig TV executive and he's negotiated a deal to broadcast a live, audience-interactive performance of an adapted script." Charlie started flinging his hands about. Griff had noticed a correlation between the energy of his brother's hand gestures and the spectacular failure of his money-making ideas. Fortunately, the stream of unsuccessful enterprises never seemed to make the smallest chip in his self-esteem.

"Audience-interactive," he repeated with foreboding.

"The script contains multiple versions of scenes, and the audience will be able to vote through the network app on which direction the play takes as the performance goes on. So the cast will be ready with, say, three different versions of Act Two, Scene 1. And several potential endings." Charlie shoved his hands through his red hair. "It'll be fucking brilliant."

It sounded like it would be a fucking disaster.

"Who's done the script?"

"They managed to pull Steve Lemmon for it."

"Managed" to pull. Lemmon would probably have given the production team a lap dance to land the gig. Griff wouldn't hire him to write out the phone book, let alone trust him with an overly complicated, technology-dependent production. On live TV.

"And where does The Henry come into it, exactly?"

"Country-house setting, actually staged at a historic country estate. The studio ate it up. We have the facilities here to house the core cast during the rehearsal period, which, by the way, they'll pay us extra for. And there's enough accommodation in the village for the crew." Griff could see it coming even before Charlie added, "This might be just the beginning. Letting visitors tour the grounds in summer brings in a pittance, but hiring out The Henry, even parts of the main house, could be a potential goldmine. No more worries about how to fund the upkeep. It'll pay for itself at last."

His eyes were dreamy as his mind wandered off into that rosy future, where the estate wasn't a crumbling, fund-draining millstone around their necks, and pigs flew over the heads of frolicking unicorns.

"If I could just pull you back to reality for a moment," Griff said tensely, "tell me you haven't actually signed that contract yet."

Charlie shuffled one foot. "They were on a tight deadline."

Griff closed his eyes briefly, and then held out his hand for the contract. He turned over the first page.

"It'll bring in a decent whack of cash," Charlie insisted, apparently not seeing even one of the pitfalls in this situation. What else was new.

"What if the public don't vote? What if the app fails? What if the actors crumble under the enormous pressure of having to learn twelve times as many scenes as an average script and perform on a minute's notice?" Griff's eyes narrowed when he saw the way Charlie was looking at him. It suggested more incoming information that he wouldn't like.

"In order of your concerns: They will. It won't. And they won't. They're professionals," his brother said optimistically.

Pretty obvious which of them didn't regularly sit

through plays that made being stuck in London traffic jams seem like a comparatively organised and enjoyable experience.

"It could have side benefits where your career is concerned, too."

Griff managed, with a lot of effort, not to respond to that one. A script based on a video game, adapted by a gin-soaked has-been. Exactly the professional association he needed. How to lose all bargaining power in one catastrophic, very public flop.

"If you're planning to use The Henry in your film, you'll get to see it in action first, for a show that's going to be hyped to the max. Living inspiration."

Griff continued to leaf through the contract. A muscle started to tic under his mouth.

"And," Charlie said, with the air of producing his ace, "to tart up the theatre for its small-screen debut, the TV network is prepared to foot the renovation bill."

His hand stilling on the papers, Griff lifted his gaze to his brother's face, and Charlie's lips started to curve as he scented victory.

Although he'd never mastered the skill of quitting while he was ahead.

With a note of suppressed laughter, he added, "And if all else fails, it means a couple of weeks under the same roof as all the people whose work you've ripped to shreds in the *Post*. Even if the bonnets and murder and shit is a total snooze—" he grinned outright "—the possibilities for entertainment are endless."

"Lydia Bennet?" Freddy stopped trying to pull the hem of her jumper over her knees and leaned forward. Her talent agency's office was always cold, and she tended to leave these meetings with another booking she didn't want, so she usually dreaded coming.

However, it seemed to be a day for unexpected plot twists.

"It should be a dream role for you." Lisa, her agent, was turning a pen over and over between her fingers as she studied Freddy.

Lydia Bennet, *Pride and Prejudice*'s archetypal bratty little sister, who had dismal taste in men and wreaked havoc on all around her.

"If you're suggesting a temperamental similarity, I'm not overly flattered."

"You're an Austen fan, and *The Austen Playbook* is straight romantic comedy and cosy mystery, right up your street. This production is already raising a huge amount of interest. Word leaked on social media and people are here for it. The studio is predicting high ratings. It's such good exposure that even your father might be on board." Lisa's smile didn't reach her eyes.

Relations could be strained between an agent and a manager in any circumstances, but since he'd contributed half of the talent's DNA, Rupert felt that he had seniority when it came to professional decisions. Freddy had gone through three agents before she'd found Lisa four years ago, and she did not want Rupert driving this one off as well.

"Is he being difficult?" Freddy asked bluntly. This show did sound like something she'd enjoy a hell of a lot more than anything she'd done in recent memory. It also sounded like something her father would dismiss as time-wasting froth.

Lisa set the pen down on her desk and steepled her fingers. "Rupert is a very savvy manager." Tactful. Clearly only the very surface of her opinion. "The casting call is going out in six months for *The Velvet Room*." Lisa watched her narrowly.

She'd learned by rote to manufacture and hide emotion, but she couldn't stop herself reaching up to tuck the hair behind her ears. Nervous tic 101.

"He wants to see you playing Marguerite."

Marguerite, one of the most iconic characters in twentieth-century drama. The character created and first played by Henrietta. Clever, cynical, morally ambiguous Marguerite. The literary creation who walked the line between sacrifice and cunning so narrowly that when the curtain went down, the audience was divided on whether they'd witnessed the evolution of a transformative heroine or had their emotions jerked on puppet strings by a master manipulator.

One of the most difficult characters in British theatre to carry off successfully, and one of the most emotionally draining performances written into a script.

Her nails dug into her palms. "I know."

This endless run of *Masquerade* had clarified several things for Freddy, and every time she thought about doing a year-long stint in *The Velvet Room*, she ended up eating an entire family-sized bar of chocolate.

Masquerade had been forced to close last Saturday afternoon because of a fire in a nearby building, and she'd spontaneously decided to buy a last-minute ticket for the matinée of *Singin' in the Rain*. She'd loved every minute of it. She'd realised about halfway through that her feet were unconsciously tapping out the steps.

Her friend at the *Westminster Post* with the cutting comments and disturbing eyes had been quite right on press night: she *would* rather be twirling through puddles than trying to dramatic-monologue her way to a supreme National Theatre Award and the highest tier of industry cred.

At some point during the past five years, she'd become another cog in the West End machine. Constantly driving for more. Always looking to the next step. Feeling that pure, intrinsic *joy* of performing slipping through her fingers with every calculated career move.

After a moment of silence Lisa said, "Let's not get ahead of ourselves. Where's your head at right now?" She reached for the cup of tea on her desk. "Not just professionally. Full package. How are you feeling?"

Freddy turned the words over in her mind, testing them, and voiced them slowly. "I guess…at times lately… I feel like Freddy, the performing doll. With multiple people holding the strings and all pulling in different directions." She ran her thumbnail down the seam of her leggings. "I've done nothing but theatre for over twelve years. I've had no real outside interests in the past. I've never had a hobby that's completely unrelated to the job." Most of her friends were involved in the industry. So were a lot of the people she dated. She sometimes wished she had someone who just…*saw* her. Saw just the person. Not the actor, not the characters. Not the commodity. "I'm just feeling a bit boxed in."

"Do you need a complete break?" Lisa asked neutrally. "Because that's what I'm hearing."

"I don't want to stop performing. I do love it. I always have." But she wasn't sure that she wanted to live solely for it anymore. She wanted to do productions that she wholeheartedly enjoyed, she wanted a passion outside of theatre, and really—she just wanted to be happy.

She also wanted other people to be happy, and it often seemed to be an either/or choice.

She physically shook off the strain that had crept into her shoulders. "I'm making better use of my days off. Expanding my horizons." She ticked off on her fingers. "So far, art history lessons are a success, I'm surprisingly good at mug-painting, biscuit-decorating was a catastrophe but I ate the evidence, and I'm crossing all team sports off the list."

It was so simple to make small, fun changes that came with no consequences and affected her happiness only in the short-term. So complicated to make the big, permanent change that would really push her life in a new direction.

"How about developing a hankering for country walks and historic architecture?" Lisa picked up a thick sheaf of paper. "Because that's another reason I think you should take the role in *The Austen Playbook*. Which they're offering upfront. No audition required."

Apparently *everyone* saw her as Lydia material. How alarming.

"I think the role will expand your fan base considerably, and it could lead to a major professional opportunity, which we'll get to in a tick, but it's also a switch in routine that could do you a lot of good on a personal level. The show will be televised live from Highbrook Wells in Surrey, and—"

"The Henry Theatre?" Freddy looked up sharply. "It's opening to the public?" The Henry featured in the biography her father had written about her grandmother, and Freddy remembered gazing avidly at a photo of it as a little girl.

"As a one-off, at least. I don't know what the future plans are. It was built for your grandmother, wasn't it?"

"Yes. Henrietta had an affair with the owner of High-brook Wells, and he was so smitten he commissioned a boutique theatre on his lawn for her."

There were countless things that Freddy admired about her grandmother, but the affair with a married man wasn't one of them. In other circumstances, however, being given a personal theatre would be fucking epic. The most romantic thing a man had ever done for Freddy was to bring her a cheeseburger when she'd had late-night rehearsal. Which, to be fair, had really done it for her.

"The whole cast and crew will move to Highbrook Wells and the nearest village for the weeks preceding the broadcast date. You'll stay in the main house, with access to guest facilities, and rehearse directly in the theatre." Lisa tapped her fingers on the script. "You should know that Fiona Gallagher is one of the backers, and she's also just bought the UK production rights for the adaptation of Allegra Hawthorne's *Anathorn* series."

Freddy caught her breath. Allegra Hawthorne was the current It Girl of the popular fiction world. Her series of fantastical novels had stayed at number one on the Sunday lists for months on end. The books were romantic and fun, rife with intrigue and humour, and Freddy loved them. There had been rumours churning for a while that they were going to be adapted into a musical.

If there was one role in the entire scope of theatre that she'd love to win, that was it.

"When I met with Fiona this week, she expressed interest in you for a role in the show," Lisa said, and Freddy finally remembered to exhale. "She remembers your performance in *Matilda* in your teens. But she's noted that you've veered away from musicals the past few years."

Freddy pulled at a loose seam in her leggings. "Carltons are serious performers," she quoted, allowing the thick rope of irony to wrap around her words, in the privacy of the office.

"I'm not concerned with Carltons plural. I don't deny that your surname is a boon when it comes to placing you in work, but you've built goodwill with the public and your peers on your own merits. And if the lighter projects are where your heart lies…"

"When is the *Anathorn* musical likely to go into production?"

"They're moving it quickly along the pipeline. It's likely to coincide with the run of *The Velvet Room*."

Of course it was.

Everything in her life right now seemed to be arriving at a distinctive, definitive crossroads.

"I see."

That sick feeling was dragging at Freddy again, comprised largely of frustration—with the situation, and with herself. Rationally, she did realise that she wasn't obliged to follow in her family's footsteps simply because they'd eased her path for her. And…and she didn't have to fulfil the dreams that had been snatched from her father in his own career.

But when it came to actually acting on that realisation—

She visualised the hurt and disappointment she would cause, and she bottled it. Time and again.

"Fiona wants to see how your comedic timing has held up, and *The Austen Playbook* would be a good chance to dust off your skills. She'll be in the audience for the live performance, and she's notorious for making quick, instinctive decisions. If she likes what she sees…" Lisa looked at Freddy meaningfully. "It doesn't hurt to leave your options open."

Again, she waved the absolute brick of paper she was holding. "It's a win all round, as far as I'm concerned. A high-profile production, you're tailor-made for the role, and you'll get a break from London for a few weeks. At a country estate. Very lush." She grinned. "Very Austen."

Shaking off her troubled preoccupation, Freddy suddenly focused on the papers. "Hold up. What is that?"

"*The Austen Playbook* script." Lisa set it down in front of Freddy, who was surprised the desk didn't immediately collapse in a *whump* of splinters and dust.

She stared down at it, then incredulously at Lisa. "That's *one* copy of the script? It's massive. For God's sake. How long is the play? Twelve hours?"

"We arrive at the one snag." Lisa tapped a manicured finger on the topmost page. "It's an audience-interactive play."

"What does that mean? The public heckles? We bring people onstage for magic tricks?"

"Interactive with the viewing audience at home, who will be voting through the studio app on multiple-choice options for how they want the play to proceed. So you would have to learn different variations of each scene."

Freddy reached forward and flipped through a few pages. "And enact them with how much warning?"

"A few minutes, I imagine." Lisa cocked her head. "Are we daunted to the point we've lost interest?"

Freddy turned over another page, reading some of the highlighted dialogue for Lydia. A tingle of excitement was beginning to fizz in her middle.

A sense of anticipation that she hadn't felt in an age.

She still had no idea what she was going to do about her father and *The Velvet Room*, especially when the dilemma had now exploded with the addition of the *Anathorn* opportunity, but in the meantime...

It was a truth universally acknowledged that an actor in a rut must be in want of a spot of murder, mayhem, and true love.

Chapter Three

If a crew were doing establishing shots of Highbrook Wells today, it would look so impossibly lovely under the endless blue sky that cynics would assume the scene had been filmed in the tropics. In the warm light, the decrepit parts of the main house took on a charmingly lived-in appearance, the gardens smelled divine, and there were even two peacocks strutting about the lawn.

One of the avian variety. One of a more ubiquitous species.

Far from his usual habitat, a prime example of the classic Homo sapiens fuckboy, in rampant mating phase.

Paradise always did contain its share of snakes. "Dylan."

Dylan Waitely turned on hearing his name. The moment he spotted Freddy, he stood up straighter and did something that elongated his shoulders. His expression wavered between a smirk and a frown.

The struggle to remember her name was real.

They'd only debuted in the same production of *Oliver!* back in the day, played wife and husband in an eight-month run of *1553* a few years ago, and stage-snogged in front of royalty. Easily forgotten.

"It's Freddy," she said with reluctant amusement. He was an arrogant prick and a serial cheat, and if Lisa had mentioned he was cast for this, she'd have had qualms. But it was just Dylan. No point expending energy on getting annoyed with him. He never changed.

"I know who you are, Freddy." He was all injured gentlemanly charm. It would be more successful if she hadn't witnessed him getting absolutely rat-arsed at a wrap party, whipping his trousers off, and drawing a smiley-face on his willy.

Once you'd seen a bloke doodling on his dick with permanent ink, the mystique was gone.

She pushed her sleeves up and wiped the back of her wrist across her forehead. She was wearing too many layers. It had been raining and cool when she'd boarded the train in London. She hadn't expected Highbrook to exist in a sunny alternate universe, like a reverse Narnia. "I didn't realise you were doing this. What part are you playing?"

Fifty quid said it was Wickham or Willoughby. He would have to expend no effort whatsoever to play one of the sexy, unreliable rogues. He even had historical-romance hair, longish and draped artistically over one eye.

Pretty please, God, don't say Wickham. One fictional marriage to Dylan was enough for a lifetime.

He preened. "Fitzwilliam Darcy, at your service." A wink. "And I *am* at your service, babe."

"Darcy?" Freddy repeated after an extensive pause. "They've cast *you* as Darcy?"

"Jeremy Bury had it originally," Dylan said, and yes, she *had* been under the impression that Jeremy was confirmed for Darcy. She'd been stoked about it, too, because he was an absolute gent to work with.

Dylan gave his pretty fall of hair an emphatic flick. "But they've made some wise changes to the cast since the press release. Star of the show, yo."

Firstly: highly debatable. The actor playing Elizabeth, whom she sincerely hoped was still Maya Dutta, could argue for top character billing if she wanted, and not everyone considered *Pride and Prejudice* to be peak Austen, so Emma, Anne, Elinor and the rest of the primary women characters would also give him a run for his money.

And additionally: insert confused face and unintelligible exclamation here.

What a baffling choice on the part of the casting team. She wondered how it would be received by the public. Dylan was delicious to look at and he had the acting chops, but his behaviour was notorious and even the most infatuated fangirls would surely struggle to envision him as the stoic, secretly soft lover. And his ex-wife was doing the reality show circuit and her legions of fans despised him, so there was a lot of hate aimed his way on social media right now.

Freddy would go double or nothing that the voting audience opted for an unexpected plot twist in the whodunit. Darcy dead in the library. With a lead pipe.

Dylan's gaze moved over her head with the glazed change of expression that usually meant he'd spotted someone with larger breasts. He walked off with barely a murmur. She turned to see the attraction, and her stomach dropped like she was on a hundred-foot rollercoaster.

Slinking across the lawn to join the gathering cast, hips swaying, body moving with the fluidity of rippling silk, Sadie Foster gave her cat-with-the-cream smile.

Hell.

Freddy had successfully avoided working with Sadie for the past few years, which was no mean feat in the tiny inner sphere of the West End, especially when they were signed to the same agency.

She wouldn't use the word *hate*. She didn't throw that around lightly. She strongly disliked Sadie.

Strongly.

Lisa. Mate. A little heads-up on the final cast would not have gone amiss here.

Freddy pulled her phone out of her bag on the pretext of having to take a vitally important and nonexistent call, which could not be interrupted under any circumstances, and realised there were still twenty-five minutes until the scheduled cast meeting.

With this team, there were going to be enough provoking moments over the next few weeks. She wasn't racking up the first ones in the boiling heat.

She glanced uncertainly back at the main house, where a staff member had shown her to a bedroom in the left wing. Odds that she'd remember how to get back there without wandering into the wrong room and invading the Ford family's privacy? Slim. The staircases were twisty and confusing, and she'd been distracted by some very questionable carvings on the railings. Highbrook looked like a typical posh, grade-II-listed mansion on the outside, but seemed to be full of small pockets of lurid eroticism, and she no longer had any trouble imagining Henrietta and the former Ford patriarch going mad for each other. Evidently, Sir George Ford had been more of a mirrored-ceilings-and-furry-handcuffs chap than a tweeds-and-pipe man.

That was the brilliant thing about life. It was never what you expected.

Freddy walked in the direction that was instinctively tugging her closer. Any theatre felt like a second home to her, but she was itching to see this one. The Henry was divided from the house by a thick line of trees, but she could hear the sounds of construction. Lisa had said the renovations would be complete before rehearsals began, which gave them about eighteen hours to wrap things up. Considering that redoing her London flat had taken five weeks longer than the builders had estimated, she'd be seriously impressed if the construction firm had cleared out by the morning.

Coming out of the shadow of the tall oaks, she stood for a moment, admiring the theatre. Amidst the fields and trees and wildflowers, the square stone structure rose into four turrets, the exterior walls dotted with arching windows. It was as if someone had shrunk the White Tower and plunked it down in the Surrey countryside. She half expected to hear jousting and trumpets rather than hammers and drills.

It was one of the most over-the-top things she'd ever seen. Photos didn't do it justice. She *loved* it.

The entrance was still boarded up, but she found an open door behind a balustrade, and followed a winding corridor until she came back out into the sunshine in an open courtyard, and was hit with the full splendour of the stage.

It was wooden, and had been polished and varnished to a high shine. Stairs led up from the open stands in front, and ornate pillars held up the false proscenium. In her mind, she could already hear the echoes of feet stepping across the boards and projected words carrying up to the box seats above.

With her hand to her lips, she turned in a full, happy circle, taking in the atmosphere. It felt...warm. Comforting. Like good memories could be made here.

She could put up with a script the size of the *Oxford English Dictionary* and Sadie's strychnine tongue for the opportunity to perform here. Breathing in deeply, she inhaled the weirdly attractive combined scents of paint and wisteria. She closed her eyes, feeling far, far away from the creeping stresses of the city and the weight of history and expectation. She just...enjoyed.

How lucky was the Ford family, to be able to come here any time they liked.

Her momentary peace was interrupted by a crash, followed by a very creative curse that she was going to steal and use at the soonest possibility. As the distinctive voice registered, her brows shot together and then lifted.

Ford.

No way...

Walking around a column, she peeped gingerly into a small room, the function of which was undetermined. There was some sort of cage situation going on in the corner, which suggested either a menagerie or a sex cave. Either seemed feasible on this property.

And, standing on a ladder, one of her very favourite things in life, a handsome man nailing stuff.

Apparently Highbrook was now owned by Sir George's grandson, who had a reputation for being an uncompromising, despotic dickhead.

She ought to have made the connection based on that description alone.

After the initial surprise, Freddy recovered the ability to speak. "Did you accidentally take a wrong turn on your way to a meeting at the bank?" she asked politely, and the critic who had every performer in the West End shaking in their tap shoes turned his head sharply to look over his shoulder.

When he saw her, J. Ford-Griffin's lips flattened and thinned, and his whole body seemed to withdraw with an intense, deeply psychological sigh, like a doom prophet steeling for the incoming apocalypse.

Look at that, her mere presence could make a man's entire being go instantly flaccid. As superhuman powers went, she didn't really rate it up there with invisibility and flight.

"The bank?" He eyed her like she'd just arrived to repossess the property.

He could breathe easy on that one. As much as she coveted his theatre and his flowers, she had a plan for her first proper house and it didn't involve fellatio carvings on the stairs.

"I've never seen anyone do DIY in a tie." Freddy glanced at the beam he was fixing, then walked over and bent to grab another handful of nails from the bag at the foot of his stepladder. She held them up for him, and after a pause, he took one and drove it into the wood with one vigorous bang of his hammer.

"Thanks." He pulled another one from her raised hand. "The cast is here, then, are they?" His tone conjured images of empty chocolate boxes, and the aftermath of a party, and missing the bus by thirty seconds, and all of life's fleeting moments of gloom.

"Dude. You might want to dial it down a notch there. The enthusiasm is embarrassing."

He caught his finger with the hammer and swore again. She'd always thought he had a very inspiring vocabulary.

"If you're going to be rude enough to visibly grasp for patience," she said, "I would suggest keeping your eyes open. At least while you're whacking nails into a board."

Ford-Griffin shook the pain from his hand, set the hammer down on the stepladder, and swung himself down. Straightening, he moved his broad shoulders to settle his shirt back into place, and coolly adjusted the knot of his tie with a single jerk of his hand. The only concession he'd made to the heat was to roll up his sleeves, exposing muscled forearms, but there wasn't a visible bead of sweat on him. The assassin persona was firmly in place. Suave, efficient movements, immaculate clothing, and not a hint as to what was going on beneath the surface.

Freddy quite fancied the impenetrable demeanour. She could imagine several occasions when it would come in handy. For example, when dealing with co-stars who probably sashayed home at night to their coven.

He returned his hammer to the toolbox. "I'm surprised you've signed on for this shitshow."

He didn't *look* surprised. She couldn't imagine him ever looking surprised.

She bent down again to tidy the screws she'd just knocked with her foot. "This production is pure entertainment and escapism. It's fun, it's funny, it's a bit of whodunit, a bit of snogging under the stairs. It's exactly the variety of light comedy-drama that you've been suggesting is my spiritual home for the past five years." She felt sorry for his staff. They wouldn't get away with much, with Perceptive Pete here striding around. "If you're going to make judgmental comments—and I realise it's what you're paid for," she added with silky kindness, "at least be consistent with your own advice."

The pools-of-mystery eyes narrowed.

She smiled at him from her crouched position. "What's your name?" she asked suddenly.

"What do you mean, what's my name?" he said with a slight edge. "If your memory is that bad, good luck learning your lines. The script makes *War and Peace* look like a novella."

"I can't at all tell your opinion of this production. I hope the baffling fact that you're letting it be staged on your property doesn't mean I'll miss out on the joy of a written review. They're useful to have around if I'm ever in danger of developing self-esteem." She examined a strange tool with multiple prongs. "I realise we've met, but we never got around to using first names. I'm Freddy to everyone but Sadie Foster, who makes a point of using Frederica because she knows it grinds my tits. And since I've heard people call you Griff on TV, I'm assuming the 'J' in your name stands for something equally unacceptable."

Sabrina had once offered a number of suggestions on that point, the politest being Jackass. Freddy assumed the obvious eccentricities in the Ford family didn't extend as far as that.

Firmly, he removed the mystery tool from her grasp before she could follow through on her impulse to test the sharpness of the blades with her thumb. "James."

"James?" She'd expected at least a Jehoshaphat. Her hand brushed his, and she curled her fingers against the fabric of her skirt. "But you don't go by that?"

"My father's name is also James." The words still had sharp corners. "Apparently my parents didn't foresee the inconvenience. My grandfather got annoyed by the time I was six months old and started calling me Griff. It stuck." With derision, he added, "And when I was offered a column in the *Post*, the editor used the initial in my byline because I wouldn't let him slap a 'Dr.' in front of my name. He thought J. Ford-Griffin sounded credibly intellectual."

"Whereas, oddly, James Ford-Griffin sounds like both a 110-year-old antiquarian and a Mayfair playboy," she probably shouldn't have said out loud.

"Yeah, thanks for that," he said after a moment. "Unfortunately, the initial bled over into my television work."

"Should I call you Griff, then?"

"If you have to." The fervour. The passion. "Although as I will not be reviewing the show, thank fuck, I'll be steering clear as soon as I've made sure the theatre will stay intact for a few weeks."

"That's very conscientious of you."

"I own the property deeds and therefore the responsibility for anything that happens here. And as much as it would be a blessing for British theatre if a beam fell on Dylan Waitely, I'd prefer not to cop the blame for it."

She finished tidying the mess she'd made of his materials and stood up. He was closer than she'd realised and she ended up seriously invading his personal space. She shifted position so she wasn't actually breathing into his neck.

"So, your grandfather was Sir George Ford." And when she thought about it—surely her father would know that, and he could have bothered to drop it into conversation. For all his grumbling about the reviews, he'd never mentioned that the "puffed-up, short-sighted, poisonous bastard" at the *Post* was the grandson of Henrietta's lover. She nodded at their surroundings. "If this is the standard for gifts in your family, you must be very popular at Christmas."

"Your grandmother's influence must have been potent." Griff rolled his sleeves back down and cast a critical glance over whatever he'd been doing to the roof. "My grandfather was a notoriously tight old bastard before—and after—that affair."

"Maybe my father's right," Freddy said lightly, setting her fingertips to a wall beam with a gentle touch. "Henrietta is the goalpost in all aspects of life. She must have been an impressive lady."

And a daunting one. Freddy had looked up to Henrietta for as long as she could remember, but she was *almost* glad that their lifetimes hadn't coincided. She somehow didn't see her as the sort of granny who handed out sweets and hugs.

Griff's eyes flicked over her as he started to gather his tools together. "Is that the idea? To guide your career along a similar path to Henrietta's?" His tone was neutral, but she could guess at the thoughts underlying the bland façade.

"My father has always fancied the idea of producing a Henrietta 2.0." She scuffed her foot against the wooden floor. "I don't think it's going to plan."

Griff's sudden narrowed scrutiny poked at a vulnerable spot, and she gave herself a little shake and changed the subject. "I *am* surprised that you'd agree to let us perform here. Given your side gig with the *Post*, I'd have thought you'd prefer your name wasn't professionally associated with any particular production. Might look like you have financial interests swaying your reviews."

"Yes. It might."

"Not great for your reputation in general."

"No." He closed his toolbox with a distinct *click*.

"Even worse if we bomb," she added with great sympathy, and after a few more grim seconds, she saw a flicker that might have been a puny, barely there smile, but was probably muscle tension. She wondered what he looked like when he laughed.

She wondered *if* he laughed.

Slightly pointedly, he held the door open for her, and she half expected him to close it in her face once she'd passed through, but he followed her back out into the stalls.

"It's a beautiful stage." She really wanted to get up there but didn't want to fall through the floorboards if the construction team hadn't signed off on that bit yet.

"It's safe." At the creepily intuitive comment, she twisted her head to look up at Griff, and he inclined his towards the stage. "Go on up."

She almost fell up the stairs in her hasty scramble and, with an unnecessarily heavy sigh, he caught her outflung fingers and steadied her. As she reached the top and walked forward, he took several steps back and stood watching her, arms folded.

Her footsteps echoed through the resonant timber as she paced, measuring the space, looking out and up. "This is so wicked."

Her voice carried, clear as a bell. The acoustics were fab. Her smile grew.

"You have nothing to worry about," she said confidently. "We're going to sweep the ratings. Even with the more dubious casting choices."

"Waitely?"

"Amongst others." She slipped her hand over one of the pillars, tracing the intricate carvings. Sir George had restrained his personal tastes here and just decorated them with berries and fig leaves. At least—*were* those berries? "If the plan is to bugger off back to London and pretend that none of this is happening, I expect things will come off without tarnishing your reputation."

"I have every intention of avoiding The Henry, but I'm working from Highbrook for a couple of weeks."

Poor thing. The *arduousness* of having to work from your family mansion, surrounded by roses and peacocks. Weathered-but-gorgeous country estates were just wasted on some people.

"You might want to keep your door locked at night, then," Freddy said. "And check your morning coffee for traces of cyanide."

"Planning to exact revenge for the safety scissors comment after all?"

"I'm a forgiving soul, me." She grinned down at him. "Can't say the same for some of that lot out there. And it's a murder-mystery play. All the suspects gathered together for a house party. It could give someone ideas." She twirled in a circle centre-stage, enjoying the faint breeze that fluttered the hem of her skirt. "The sarcastic critic with his poison pen and scores of embittered enemies. If this was *Midsomer Murders*, you wouldn't even make it to the opening credits. If you hear the faint strains of ominous music, come find me. I'll protect you."

"I can't tell you how reassured I feel." When he set his mouth in long-suffering lines, his lips disappeared.

"Do your thoughts always bounce around your brain like a pinball game?"

"I think of it more like ten-pin bowling. Pick up an idea, chuck it at the rest, and hope for the best."

Griff looked up at her in speaking silence before he shook his head. "When you encounter my brother later, introduce yourself. You're soulmates."

Chapter Four

Freddy encountered the less scowly Ford-Griffin brother sooner than expected. When she returned to the lawn for the cast meeting, the largest circle of people had formed around Sadie and Dylan, so she gave them a wide berth and went to say hello to Maya Dutta.

Tall, with deep olive skin, high cheekbones, and an abundance of thick black hair, Maya was the Sadie antithesis in Freddy's work circle. She had a sarcastic sense of humour that made Freddy laugh, but she was often shy with strangers, one of the professional actors whose parents had originally put them in drama classes to get them talking. And she was an all-around general good egg. She had been cornered by a muscular man with red hair and laughing blue eyes, and was flushing and playing with her fringe while she slipped the occasional word into his stream of chatter. She turned to smile at Freddy with a certain amount of relief. Freddy wasn't in the least shy, but after seeing who else was in the cast, they were obviously both thinking the same thing: thank God, a friendly face.

"Hi, Freddy, how are you? Have you met Charlie? He's our resident host."

"Just think of me as the ginger, British equivalent of

Julie from *The Love Boat*," Charlie said. "At your service, here to answer any question and solve every problem." He wiggled his brows. "Day or night."

"Can you instantly recast a few principal roles?" Freddy asked, not entirely joking. Sadie was shooting malicious little peeks in their direction, and looking entirely too pleased for Freddy's peace of mind, and Dylan was staring at her boobs again.

Maya glanced over at Sadie and winced. "They didn't miss a trick casting her as Emma Woodhouse, did they? Hopefully the audience votes her into an early, grisly demise before she has to stretch her acting abilities and take Emma from insufferable meddler into an actual growth arc."

Charlie blinked. People who encountered only the quiet side of Maya were often taken by surprise when she felt at ease enough to share her full personality.

"Sadie's playing Emma?" There had obviously been a lot of last-minute swaps in the casting. On the bright side, from what Freddy had memorised of the colossal script so far, Lydia and Emma had very few scenes together.

Except in one variant of the storyline. And why did she suddenly have a sinking premonition that would be the way the vote would play out.

She clutched at her rapidly shredding optimism.

"Unfortunately, the Fleshlumpeater isn't an Austen character," Maya said, "so they couldn't *completely* typecast her."

Charlie's crack of laughter was contagious, and several heads turned curiously in their direction.

When she'd regained enough of her composure to speak without a quaver, Freddy said, "And you're still playing Elizabeth Bennet?"

"Correct, little sis." Maya grinned at her.

"You almost got to snog Jeremy Bury," Freddy said, and they both took a moment to reflect wistfully on that.

Maya glanced at Dylan. "In this instance, I reckon Elizabeth was dead-on with her response to Darcy's initial proposal. Don't let the door hit you on the way out, Fitzwilliam." She wrinkled her nose. "I hope the theatre is as adorable as promised, because this production has some serious ground to make up."

"It's amazing," Freddy murmured, her attention momentarily snagging back on the rooftop visible through the trees.

Charlie cocked his head. "Have you had a look already?"

"I—" Her mind finally caught up with Maya's brief introduction. Their host, she'd said. "I think I considerably worsened your...brother's day?" Her voice lifted on the query, and the twinkle in Charlie's eyes deepened.

"Griff busted you, did he?"

Curiously, she studied Charlie's face, cataloguing similarities and differences—there were few of the former. "Fortunately, my ego is battle-hardened where your brother is concerned. Older brother?"

"Does that really need corroboration?" Charlie spread his arms in a self-deprecating gesture. "We're an embarrassing pantomime of the dictatorial elder and feckless younger."

It wasn't difficult to deduce which of them shouldered most responsibility around here, no.

Not that she personally had a leg to stand on when it came to being a forthright, take-charge member of her own family. Grumpus over yonder could be right. She and Charlie probably had all sorts in common.

He offered immediate confirmation of that fact by producing a random roll of sweets from his pocket and offering them around. She was all for people who came with portable snacks. Maya was hailed by the assistant director as she took one, and headed in his direction, her shield of reserve back in place before she'd taken two steps.

"She's sharp," Charlie said admiringly, and offered Freddy another sweet. "I can't really imagine her as a soppy romantic heroine."

Freddy licked grains of sugar from her thumb. "I'm assuming you haven't actually read Jane Austen."

"Careful." Charlie tossed the rest of the sweets into his mouth. "Your prejudice is showing." He nudged her. "See what I did there? Prejudice?"

"It's going to be a long couple of weeks, isn't it?"

"I think your captain is summoning the troops." He nodded towards the area where people were setting up a marquee, and Freddy saw a distinctive topknot of grey curls.

Somewhere under that mountain of hair was Maf Reynolds, one-time political activist turned exceptional theatrical director. She rarely worked outside of New York these days, and her attachment to the project had been another big selling point for Freddy. Maf had been her first ever director, in the long-ago days of *Oliver!*, and she'd never forgotten the woman's ability to both coax out strength and quell bullshit.

With Maf's first words to Dylan, Freddy's afternoon took an upward curve. "Regardless of whether your wife has divorced you, if I catch you putting any particle of your anatomy near any other member of this team and it's not explicitly instructed in the script, there's going to be a short, painful meeting between you, me, and the end of this paperclip."

Maf eyeballed him for a good five seconds, then addressed the assembled cast, cutting through the hum of voices. "We'll have a first read-through tomorrow morning at nine, in the theatre. Inclusive of all scene variations. If you're not yet word-perfect, start taking your mammoth scripts to bed with you, folks, because I want everyone off-book in precisely one week. Every person here has extensive experience in live theatre or television and film, or all of the above. Very few of you will have combined the most intense aspects of all three media and performed for a public broadcast. The night of the performance will be stressful, chaotic, and if all goes well, the highlight of your working year." She slammed a hand down on one cocked hip, and the weathered dark skin around her eyes and mouth creased further into forbidding lines. "Take the rest of the day to get to know any unfamiliar faces, and if there's anyone here that you'd fancy dropping in the lake, maintain a professional distance, because I have exactly zero tolerance for actors who behave like overgrown, ego-swollen toddlers."

"Was that the typical pep talk you get in theatre?" Charlie was still hovering at Freddy's side, watching with fascination as the cast drifted into two main groups— the West End regulars and the various TV and film actors who'd been brought in as the main audience draw. Everyone was taking each other's measure with various degrees of condescension. "It sounded about as morale-boosting as being hit over the head with a two-by-four."

"It depends whether you need to be spoon-fed instructions and verbally patted on the head before you can turn in a good performance," said a silky voice, and Sadie joined them. She somehow managed to make an entrance in all situations. Even when she was just rocking up and interrupting someone else's conversation, she generated a vibe of a starlet flinging open double doors or posing at the top of a grand staircase.

She cast one brief, disparaging glance over Charlie before she dismissed him and focused her attention on Freddy. She definitely looked pleased to see her. Ominous.

"Charlie, this is Sadie Foster. Sadie, Charlie Ford-Griffin. Our host," Freddy said bluntly, and was unsurprised by the blink-and-miss-it alteration in the other woman's attitude.

Sadie's lips moved into the smile she reserved for theatre management, the press, and young men whose families owned multimillion-pound property. "Nice to meet you."

"Yeah." Charlie hadn't missed the changing dynamic, either. He'd stopped bouncing around and shifting on his feet like a child hyped on sugar. "You too. I saw you in *Oklahoma!* recently."

"Oh?" Sadie studied him through long lashes.

"Treated myself after a bad week at work." The breeziness of Charlie's voice had taken on a suspicious note. "After my brother's review, I thought it would help me put things back into perspective."

Freddy didn't make eye contact with either of them. She'd read his brother's review of that production, as well.

It was never a good sign when the first sentence contained the phrase "self-flagellation."

Sadie tossed back her glossy waves of blond hair, refrained from audibly sniffing, and looked at Freddy again. "I was so thrilled to hear that you'd signed on for this." The words were verbal syrup, slick and sweet.

"Were you." Freddy's response emerged flatly, but at least it wasn't the *"Oh, yeah?"* that tickled her throat.

"It's been *forever* since we worked together."

Three years. They'd done a short run of *From Vita to Virginia* after Freddy had finished up in *1553*. She'd been twenty at the time, and she'd come out of the experience with stress-induced shingles, something she'd previously associated with pensioners. Sadie's constant transformation from her warm, witty persona onstage to the nasty viper backstage had given Freddy mental whiplash.

"I was just thinking about you recently." The saccharine tone was turning into a purr, and Freddy had the creeping sensation of standing on a rug and feeling someone take an experimental pull at it, waiting to rip it out from under her feet. "I did a festival run of *Cymbeline* at the Globe." There was a gleam in Sadie's eyes. "Great team. It's always a pleasure when you work with such... knowledgeable people. When you've been in this business for a while, it's so fun to realise you can still learn something new. Don't you think?"

That crawling feeling was an itch at the base of Freddy's neck, sliding down her spine. "I suppose." She felt as if she was navigating a path in the dark, stepping gingerly to avoid the landmines.

"Yes." Sadie's smile widened. "I'm sure even you must find that, and you're an actor of such vast *experience*."

Annoyance was starting to fizz under the apprehension. Freddy had never had any patience for the bullshit mind games in this profession. She had no idea what Sadie thought she knew—whatever it was, she was just about hugging herself with the secret—but she'd seen too many poor puppets dancing on the other woman's strings over the years to let her slip the knot around her own neck.

She was about to say something short and rude that would probably act like lighter fluid on the situation, when Charlie shifted and spoke at her side. "Sorry to interrupt the shop talk, but I have to head out soon, so if you still want to see the library, Freddy, this would be a good time."

She felt the light squeeze of his fingers around her elbow and looked at him.

"You wanted to see our Wythburn Group first editions?" Charlie prompted, lightly, and she latched thankfully on to the rescue attempt. It was much more gracefully managed than the suggestions her own mind had rapidly offered, which ranged from four-letter words to taking Maf's unintentional suggestion and kicking Sadie into the lake.

"Are you sure you have time?"

One side of Charlie's mouth turned up. Somehow it seemed like a comradely high-five. "Never let it be said I disappointed a lady." He tucked a strong arm cosily through hers. "Sorry," he said to Sadie. "I'm going to steal her for a while."

"Oh, that's all right." Sadie infused the light comment with layers of meaning. She saved her subtlety for the stage. "Plenty of time to continue our chat."

They left her humming with self-satisfaction and headed past the rest of the chattering cast towards the main house.

"Charming girl," Charlie remarked. "I considered trying for the stage for about five minutes when I was a kid. Glad I let Griff's litany about the number of unemployed actors in London and my complete lack of follow-through push me in the direction of commerce instead. The brutality is more transparent in finance. People usually don't bother to plaster a smile over the blatant self-interest."

Freddy glanced at him, then away. "Fortunately, most people in the West End aren't like Sadie. She's in a class of her own." In the interests of honesty, she added, "She's, like, next-level talented, though. I was twelve when I worked with her for the first time, and I still remember being literally speechless with awe watching her."

"I've seen you perform. I much prefer watching you." There was no flirtation or calculated flattery in Charlie's statement. "I'm looking forward to seeing this show. I'm not into period dramas, but I went to your production of *Beauty and the Beast* years ago and you made me give a shit about dancing teacups, so I reckon I can get on board with a bit of bodice-ripping and bodies in the library." They crossed around the side of the house and he held a wooden door open for her. "Sorry, I don't express myself as well as Griff."

"But you're a hell of a lot better for my ego." Freddy stood in a cool, dimly lit hallway, breathing in the faint smell of baking bread. "Speaking of the library, I appreciate the save from Sadie's baiting and I bow to your lightning-fast ad lib, but if you don't mind, I actually *would* like to see your library."

She was still feeling unusually unsettled, and she found few things as calming as floor-to-ceiling bookcases.

A back scratch and having her neck kissed by a sexy man, maybe, but the only person on this property who was likely to oblige was Dylan, and there were not enough *nope* gifs in the world.

"I live to keep the ladies happy." Charlie gestured

down the winding passageway to their left. The interior of the house was typical of stately homes of the period: ornate, impressive, chilly, and so low-ceilinged that she could just about reach up and touch the curlicues in the joinery. "This way. If you're picturing rolling stepladders and ancient maps, I'd lower your expectations. It's not quite the Bodleian. Although my great-aunt did have a fancy for illustrated manuscripts, if you're into posh calligraphy."

As they passed an open doorway, two people came out carrying a dollhouse between them. The biggest dollhouse Freddy had ever seen. She looked enquiringly at Charlie. "Do you have kids here?"

She was trying to imagine his older brother as the doting dad of screeds of tiny, shrieking tots, and failing miserably.

Charlie held another door open for the dollhouse procession to pass through, with a word of thanks. "No. That's one of my parents' designs. A comparatively simple one, for them. Must be an early prototype."

"Your parents make dollhouses?"

"The term probably isn't grand enough. Doll estates. Towers. Castles. Entire fortified medieval towns. Think cobblers, blacksmiths, and apothecaries. Or the Parisian series—little couturiers and patisseries."

Freddy's hands rose to her cheeks of their own accord.

Charlie gave her an amused look. "Oh dear. A kindred spirit."

"Your parents design tiny working worlds? For a living?"

The glow of his smile dimmed. "I wouldn't exactly call it a living, no." He pulled open a large wooden door.

"Here we go. Highbrook Wells Library. Most likely filled with books about your gran right now."

"Why would—" Freddy cut herself off as she walked past him into the open, airy room. A massive picture window flooded the space with so much bright light that it hurt her eyes after the comparative gloom of the hallway, but she wasn't so blinded that she could overlook the icy stare coming her way from the central desk.

"Don't mind us." Charlie strolled around the dangerous vibes surrounding his brother. It was like watching a visitor to the Underworld just swan airily past Hades. "I'm just showing Freddy the library."

"I'm working." With an emphatic movement, Griff closed the file he was holding, as if she was likely to peer over his shoulder and have a good nose into his personal affairs. "As, I believed, was everyone else. Isn't that the reason a former soap opera sociopath is poking around the rose bushes?"

"Which soap opera sociopath?" Charlie peered out the window. Over his shoulder, he said, "The big cheese has put everyone on hold until tomorrow morning. And stop glowering at Freddy. She's just emerged gracefully from a run-in with a Tasmanian devil."

"A Tasmanian devil?"

"The red-lipsticked, stiletto-heeled variety."

Griff put his file down, apparently giving up on any prospect of working in peace while his brother was in the room. "Sadie Foster?"

"It's bleak if people can instantly name you based on that description." Freddy bent to examine a shelf of Austen novels. She doubted they were first editions. There'd be no reason to live in a house that was beautiful but a bit…crumbly if you had a library full of books that could fund a whole restoration. Of course, if she owned even one first-edition Austen, it would have to be pried from her frozen, comatose hands before she'd let it go, but she didn't see Griff as the type to go sentimental over material possessions. She sneaked a sideways peek at his forbidding profile. Or sentimental over anything. "I see you've got the source material on hand." She curled her fingers to prevent herself stroking the weathered spine of *Persuasion.*

She'd spoken lightly, but Griff set down the book he'd picked up from the desk and looked at her sharply. "Source material?"

"The Austens." She gestured. "The play? *The Austen Playbook?* The reason fictional murderers are fondling your petals?"

Griff changed his stance, effectively dismissing her from his attention. "Help yourself. The books are there for reading."

Charlie stopped spying on whatever was happening on the lawn and came to stand by the desk, prodding an incurious finger at a stack of old photographs, to his sibling's obvious irritation. "He thought you were talking about this lot. The intel on Henrietta and co."

Amazingly, he didn't instantly shrivel like a raisin when his brother turned his head.

"Oh. Right." Freddy stood and smoothed her skirt, her gaze on the hostile inhabitant of the room as she addressed the forthcoming one. "You mentioned Henrietta. And Wythburn Group first editions? Or was that just for Sadie's benefit?"

"I try to retain a grain of truth in my embellishments. It's more convincing." Charlie picked up one of the black-and-white snapshots. "It's for this big film Griff's working on about your grandmother and *The Velvet Room*, and that whole nutjob crowd she used to hang with. Including our grandfather, so don't worry, it's not just your relations under the microscope."

"A film?" Freddy took the photograph Charlie held out to her and looked at the beautiful lines and angles of her grandmother's face. Henrietta was smouldering up at a man who had stern eyes and a faint smile, and was clearly Sir George Ford. Looks-wise, he was a Charlie replica. As was the man in a newer portrait on the mantel, whom she assumed was Griff and Charlie's father. "The dad genes obviously run strong in your family."

"Griff excepted," Charlie said lightly. "Ma once said that if it hadn't been for the twenty-hour labour, she might have thought he'd spontaneously animated from an ice sculpture."

Freddy raised her gaze back to Griff's face. That comment could have stemmed from her own early thoughts about him, and it didn't cause so much as a flicker in his expression, but there were little arrows that only family could truly drive home.

"So, you're doing a film about Henrietta?" She turned the subject back to its original point, and Griff leaned one hip against the desk. Now, there was definitely a fleeting shade of…*something* in his look. Surprise? Or calculation?

"Haven't you heard about it? That's surprising," Charlie said.

She didn't know why. There'd never been a feature film about Henrietta, but people had always written about her and featured her in theatre documentaries. They didn't ring Freddy to tell her about it.

It was Griff who answered her unspoken query, his

eyes watchful. "Your father has been expending a lot of energy and money trying to stop the project in its tracks for the past year. And attempting to block us from using any material from his biography." He rested a hand on the familiar volume on the table.

All Her World, Rupert's great achievement, the in-depth insight into Henrietta that had won him a Reinholdt literature award. The highlight of the writing career he'd established after his own future in acting had been curtailed. The writing career that her agent thought he should concentrate on, instead of juggling his time with managing—and directing—Freddy's production portfolio.

"Apparently, he has plans in mind for a screen adaptation of his own." Griff sounded bored. "However, as a lot of his personal recollections in the book are based on the time that Henrietta stuck him with a nanny while she was writing *The Velvet Room*—"

"And vamping Grandad into building The Henry." Charlie was still nosing through photographs, and he passed Freddy one of the theatre in its early building stages, which she studied with interest. Henrietta was in this one as well, posing against the construction framework, in company with a slight woman with a dark bob, who wasn't looking at the camera, and a cocker spaniel with an overgrown coat, also not looking at the camera.

"—we already have access to a lot of similar material, including reminiscences from people who weren't snot-nosed kids at the time." Griff flipped open the cover of Rupert's prized biography and turned over a few pages. Something dismissive in the gesture raised Freddy's hackles. Her father's written voice was witty and personable; it was a good book, and it had deservedly done very well.

"He obviously doesn't trust his family history in your delicate, notoriously sensitive hands, big brother," Charlie said. "Can't imagine why, after all those glowing reviews you've given his daughter over the years."

After a few seconds in which Freddy chose to examine the chipped polish on her nails, and she couldn't hear even the slightest ruffle of movement over by the desk, Charlie compounded things by adding, "Is there a reason your dad never mentioned it? Bit weird, isn't it? Or does he have to battle off these hardnosed cultural types all the time?"

Considering that at present the relationship between Freddy and Rupert wasn't so much a strong branch of the family tree as a dry, brittle twig, it wasn't weird at all. She couldn't remember the last time they'd had a conversation about anything other than the jobs she was booking, was not booking, or should be booking. She had no idea what her father did in his spare time, who his friends were, or upon which film productions he tried to heap obstacles. And this was the first she'd heard that he wanted to do a visual adaptation of the biography.

"Two options, *little brother*." Griff's abrupt interjection bumped Freddy out of her glum reverie. She looked up and met his dark gaze. "Pipe down or clear out."

"Oops." Charlie tugged on the end of one of Freddy's curls, in a manner so reminiscent of a chastened child playing with a doll that it made her smile. Griff, on the other hand, looked even more pissed off. It was evident only in a certain tautness to his cheeks, but she figured that was the equivalent of an out-and-out scowl from another man. "Sorry. Sore point?"

She made a short movement with her head, gently

pulling away from his touch. "It's just life, isn't it? Ups and downs."

"Always best to focus on the ups." Despite his words, there was a funny note in Charlie's voice as he glanced at his brother. Freddy looked at him frowningly, but even as she blinked, that happy-go-lucky demeanour was back in place. "Very much a family affair in your case, theatre. Your dad is your manager, isn't he?" It had been a whole thirty seconds since his last tactless remark, so Charlie rushed to fill the void. "I'm surprised he signed off on you taking this role. Griff can't be his favourite person right now, so the property ought to be blacklisted by association."

Freddy tried not to tighten her fingers on the photo she'd picked up. It was the thin woman with the bobbed hair again. She was scowling out of the faded image. Actually—Griff wasn't such an outlier in his family appearance-wise after all. This lady hadn't shared the blond gene, but she had his nose, his chin, and his aura of impatience. "My father doesn't actually know I'm doing this show yet. The initial casting option fell through, so my agent back-benched the idea, and then a concrete offer came through again a few weeks ago. Dad's in New York this month for meetings, so—"

"Your head's on the chopping block as soon as his plane touches down at Heathrow?" Charlie suggested helpfully, and she winced.

She *was* in for a strongly worded lecture when Rupert got back to the UK and revisited his opinion that this production would torpedo her credibility. He emphatically didn't share her view that the world would be a sad, dull place without light entertainment.

However, since she hadn't been aware that he was involved in some sort of *High Noon* standoff with Griff, she'd expected he'd get over it. *The Austen Playbook* script was based on respected classic literature, after all. It hadn't retained as many of Jane's pearls of wisdoms as it should have, but there were a good few satirical zingers in there. And on a cynical note, Lisa was quite right: the TV ratings were predicted to be high, thanks to the screen celebs in the cast. It was also very well paid, for just a few weeks of rehearsal and one performance. Regardless of Rupert's personal tastes in drama, he had a razor-sharp business brain, and he was getting commission.

And his focus would be mostly on the upcoming audition for *The Velvet Room*.

"It'll be fine." Carefully, she passed the photographs she was holding back to Griff, and determinedly directed her mind down a less troubling path. "Can I see what you're doing with the film?"

Apparently she'd found the magic button to end his impassivity. "No, you bloody well cannot."

"Have you learned your lines yet?" Charlie didn't seem fazed by his brother's rudeness. Obviously it was an everyday event, so Freddy chose to ignore it as well. "Your director doesn't look like a lady who brooks many mistakes, and Sadie Foster looks like she'll take the first opportunity to drop you in it."

"I can handle Sadie," Freddy said, with more confidence than she felt. By nature, Sadie would prefer to taunt and play rather than divulge whatever she thought she knew and give up her new toy. In other words, she would do her best to make the next few weeks extremely unpleasant. "And I don't usually have a problem learning lines."

Things had been more stressful than usual this year, but at least she hadn't repeated the incident with the Springsteen song.

However, the multiple-choice scenes were proving a challenge. There were four voting opportunities for the audience, each with three variant scenes, but it wasn't so much the number that was tricky as the connections. When the cues could shift at any moment, there was no orderly progression to fix on.

Covertly, she watched Griff turning the pages of a folder. The sun glow was bright on his face, and as he twisted away from it, the shadows cast hollows into his cheeks and threw that interesting nose into greater prominence.

Her gaze lowered to the large studio portrait of Henrietta that Charlie had tossed carelessly down on the desk. Even in a faded, sepia-toned image, her grandmother radiated assertive ownership of her space, and the pursuit of Life with a capital L. In some ways, it was difficult to believe that Henrietta had ever been a flesh-and-blood woman. She couldn't imagine the woman in that photograph ever doubting the path she was on, or letting someone else sway her decisions.

But if anyone was likely to provide a more nuanced view of Henrietta, present the human being and not the sum of her achievements, it was Griff. There was a reason so many people watched his programmes on telly, and clearly it wasn't for the raging charisma. He had a knack of getting to the heart of a subject.

He looked up suddenly from his papers and their eyes met.

And suddenly her mouth felt dry, and she was very

aware of her heartbeat, thudding a bit too hard against the wall of her chest.

Ever so slightly, his eyes narrowed.

Just a little, her chin lifted.

Chapter Five

There was a myth that the countryside was peaceful. That might be true beyond the borders of Highbrook.

The memory of waking up in his childhood bedroom to the sound of his mad parents practicing their latest hobby on the south lawn—bowls, air rifles, paintball, insert the passion of the moment—was so fixed in Griff's mind that he still sometimes woke to revving engines outside his flat in Notting Hill and for a few seconds thought it was his mother's model airplane.

A dozen actors doing yoga on the patio at the crack of dawn were comparatively easy to ignore. He caught a few words of the motivational mantras one of them was spouting. Listening to the trite affirmations that twenty-somethings liked to emblazon across Instagram, while waving his arms and arse about before he'd even had a coffee, would not set him up for a successful day at work. It would send him quietly homicidal.

"Failure will never overtake me—"

Griff cast his eyes up and set off for his run, cutting across the lawn towards the back road through the south fields, which were blessedly free of staring, glaring, babbling people. The only nosy gaze he encountered on the route belonged to his father's old Hereford cow. He stopped to catch his breath and she *whuffed* hers over his fingers as he gently rubbed her head. Ruefully, he spread his other hand over his ribs. He was getting out of shape. Gym sessions had gone on the backburner.

With a final stroke of the cow's greying muzzle, he checked his watch and kept going, trying to ignore the invisible weight of the paperwork waiting on his desk. Another load of unexpected bills had joined the heap, and he'd had to take a temporary sabbatical from his theatre column for the *Westminster Post* just to grab a few hours of sleep each night, which meant even less income currently coming in.

His shortened breath burned grimly through his lungs as he picked up his pace. At this point, they needed both the film to come together and *The Austen Playbook* to go off without a hitch, or they were in serious danger of losing the place.

Although there could be an estate agent's placard at the gate and a bank manager nailing wooden boards across the front door, and Charlie would just make an airy comment of naïve optimism. Probably before he came up with another crackbrained scheme, lost interest halfway through, and traipsed happily back to his cocktail crowd in the City until the next time inspiration twinged. And exactly the way their parents, no matter how much they overspent, and how bad the financial situation was, always tossed out a few words about everything turning out well in the end, before they turned their backs on reality and went back to whittling tiny townsfolk out of expensive mahogany.

The sun was rising higher in the sky. It was going to be a beautiful day. The birdsong of the skylarks in the trees came from so many directions that it seemed to hang suspended in the air, like a lace of interwoven melody. It was difficult to maintain a bad mood in that setting.

Difficult, but he managed.

Aided when he turned the corner by the oldest tree on the property, an enormous, towering oak that his mother had, long ago, told him contained dozens of tiny rooms inhabited by gnomes and fairies. He'd heard her out, then offered a few short, pertinent facts on the concept of a tree trunk. Charlie had been born shortly afterwards, and she'd found a more receptive audience for her flights of imagination.

Over a quarter of a century later, the majestic old tree seemed to have picked up its first fairy, but there was nothing ethereal about her. More like a force of nature. She was sitting against the monstrous base of the tree, wearing a rainbow-striped T-shirt and incredibly short shorts, with that explosion of disorderly hair a tangle against the bark. She appeared to be trying to fix a broken lace in her left trainer.

"Oh." Freddy looked up at him through the frenetic dark mop and shoved a handful of curls out of her face. "Good morning."

"Good morning." He took in the shoe problem, knelt at her side, and reached into his pocket.

"Dear me," she said with suspicious blandness. "It's not a Mr. Collins situation, is it? I really prefer to have my breakfast before I receive unsolicited proposals."

He found one of the cable ties he'd been using to fix the broken wiring in the library this morning, inserted it through the top loops of her trainer and fastened it tightly, then glanced upwards. Her face was very close to his, and he looked straight into her sparkling eyes. There were faint dark smudges under them, but she exuded a warmth that he almost felt as a physical sensation, as if, without touching him, she was heating his own skin. That attitude of suppressed laughter was one he'd often found grating on stage, but out here in the sunshine, he felt that same sudden and strong tug of attraction he'd experienced in the library yesterday. It was like trying to bury something in the sand, only to have the wind persistently blow it back into his line of sight.

And he was still down on one knee, like he was serenading her in a fucking comic opera.

"I only propose to women I barely know on Saturdays."

"Funnily enough," she said, "I'm starting to feel like I've known you for ages. Power of the written word, I suppose. All these years of reviews, it's a bit like having a one-sided correspondence with a really crabby, judgmental pen pal."

Sticking with the theme of a one-sided conversation, he didn't bother to respond to that. He stood, and after a hesitation, reached down a hand. She took it and he pulled her firmly to her feet, then tried to let go of her.

For a person with small fingers, she had a grip like a barracuda's teeth. Freddy turned his reluctant hand over and frowned down at his knuckles. "What have you done to yourself?"

Scraped off about seven layers of skin, thanks to the endless cast of this travelling circus.

"A chance encounter with Elizabeth Bennet and a pair of pliers in the library."

"Sounds like Act Two of the play. Murder most foul under the card catalogue." Freddy was rubbing the sides of his fingers with the tips of hers. Her thoughtful face suggested she had no idea she was doing it. He looked down at where their skin touched. "You don't mean Maya Dutta went for you with a blunt instrument? She's much too nice."

"It wasn't blunt." He gestured with his scraped-up, imprisoned hand, and she released it quickly, with a murmured apology. "Apparently she lost her way trying to find the kitchen before dawn, and slammed the library door into my chair while I was cutting a wire."

"Well, I hope you didn't grump at her. She's a very sensitive person." From distracted smartarse to coolly threatening Mother Hen in one second flat. He hadn't given her enough credit in those reviews for her chameleon-like abilities.

"With no sense of direction."

"You're a little too fond of that expression. I believe you applied it to me, as well." Freddy nodded at his hand. "Did you put antiseptic on it? The pliers could have been rusty. And you should keep it covered."

"If you drop the Florence Nightingale act, I won't make any further comments about the roles you choose."

"You won't be able to if you succumb to sepsis." Freddy jogged a few steps, testing the makeshift fix on her shoe, then smiled at him. "Thanks. You're my white knight today. I do love when the day throws up an unexpected surprise before I've even had my toast."

They'd travelled at least a hundred metres before he fully realised that he'd ended up on a joint run with her.

"God, I hate running," she said as they turned at the far-most field and headed back towards the house.

"Why do it then?" He swiped the back of his arm across his forehead. "You don't seem the type to bother with anything you don't enjoy."

Freddy cut him a glance. "Other than in my career

choices, you mean?" Her breaths were coming fast and broken. "It's quick, cheap exercise, and I have to maintain a base level of fitness for the job. If it eventually gives me a bubble butt, bonus."

He managed to keep his eyes on the road ahead. Focusing on the rhythm of his own breath. Steady in, deep out.

"I tried tennis for a while, but my aim was awful. Balls flying everywhere. Besides, it was right after the director at the Southeastern Playhouse told me I wasn't thin enough to make it to the top tier, and my flatmate thought I was trying to lose weight to pacify him, so I had to stop the lessons on principle."

Griff looked at her sharply. "Who was that? Tom Michaelis? I hope you told him where to go."

"I finished out my contract like the professional I am and haven't signed one with him since." Freddy plaited her insane hair without slowing her pace. "It's all part and parcel of the industry. You don't get the perks without the bullshit."

"It's a fucking joke."

"If I decide to take one idiot's opinion to heart, I'm in the wrong business entirely."

"Was that a dig at Michaelis or at me?"

"It *does* work on multiple levels, doesn't it?"

When they reached the front lawn, the yoga disciples had gone, but the TV studio had obviously sent its advance guard to start preparations for the live broadcast. There were so many people about the place it looked like a seaside resort, and vans had left deep ruts in the grass.

"Uh-oh." Stopping at his side to catch her breath, Freddy planted her hands on her hips and surveyed the chaos and him. "You've got Too-Many-People Face, and this is only day two. Maybe you *should* respect your sanity and work from London for a week or two."

"We're in the last preliminary stages for the film before we finalise a deal. Which includes photographing locations and collating research material at Highbrook—"

"You could pay an assistant to do that."

"I could, if I wanted it done incorrectly and too slowly."

Freddy made a humming noise in her throat. "According to *London Celebrity*, control freaks are at much greater risk for arthritis, impotence, and pattern baldness. Just so you know."

"As long as you have a reliable source."

Another van pulled into the driveway, this one emblazoned with familiar branding, and his lips thinned. Leaving Freddy stretching out her hamstrings on the grass, Griff intercepted the man who emerged from the back compartment holding an enormous box. "The invoice. May I see it?"

"Morning." The deliveryman's cheerful expression survived Griff's curt demand. Yet another of life's optimists. It was far too early in the morning for them. The man leaned the box against the back door and juggled to get the form out. "Here you go. Fifty bottles of—"

"No." Griff had scanned the form in one grim sweep. "Return the whole order, thanks."

"But—" The man's protest was cut off by a bright greeting from the direction of the house, and Griff turned as his mother jogged down the front steps.

Skirting past a member of the studio crew with an absent-minded smile, Carolina Griffin joined him by the van. "Oh, good. I didn't think these would get here until Monday."

She reached for the box, and Griff put a restraining

hand on it to prevent her taking it from the deliveryman's grasp. His patience was down to a silken thread, and he didn't bother to keep the edge from his voice. "You're meant to be on a spending ban until you've used up the materials you already have. And this brand is too expensive. You were going to find alternative suppliers for the paint and fabrics."

"Were we?" Carolina was determinedly vague. "But these ones are just right. We've started a new series. Based on the Allegra Hawthorne books. They're very popular, you know. With adults, too. People will love the new houses."

Yes, they would. His parents' dollhouses—and "houses" was a broad term for the castles and cathedrals and intricately detailed worlds they created in their workshop— were pieces of art, that would likely become heirlooms if they weren't played with into disrepair. There was a waiting list of purchasers, and they always sold. Unfortunately, the high price tags were wiped out by the exorbitant sums Carolina and James spent on materials. In the last series, they'd used semi-precious jewels, handmade Nottingham lace, and Murano glass. Add in the cost of labour, and they were probably paying about fifty quid an hour for the privilege of running their business. He could see where Charlie got his financial nous.

Directing his mother far enough away from the van that they wouldn't air *every* detail of their respective bank accounts to a nationwide courier, he kept his words low and cool. "The roof needs fixing. The entire house needs rewiring. The utility bill is increasing every month. Half the place is mortgaged, and most of my assets are invested in the production company, which may or may not pay dividends. Charlie blows his disposable income on cars and nightclubs, and the trust Sir George set up is almost empty. There are no endless vaults of gold for you and Dad to dip into. If we want to keep this property, you need to pull a bank job or exercise some common sense. Either option is fine with me."

"Oh, these people are paying for the renovation costs." As usual, Carolina had selective hearing and chose to ignore ninety-percent of what he was saying. It was a technique he frequently utilised himself, and like most things in life, it was extremely irritating when the tables were turned.

"They're paying to renovate The Henry. They're not going to patch up the rest of the estate as a goodwill gesture. And as Charlie signed a profit-share contract for the rental of the space, instead of negotiating a fixed fee, any payment we receive beyond that is going to rely on strong audience engagement throughout the broadcast."

From what he'd seen of the preparation process so far, he wasn't anticipating a hefty cheque.

"Something always turns up." Carolina's gaze had turned inward, which usually meant she was mentally placing tiny artworks and papering miniature walls. "Like last year, when the plumbing went. Or was it the year before? God, wasn't that ghastly. All those cold showers. But it got sorted."

"It was three years ago. And it got sorted," he said crisply, "because I mortgaged my flat. It's taken me this long to pay it off."

"That's wonderful," his mother murmured. "You've always been so clever, Jamie. Oh, brilliant, your father's finished the new design."

She patted his arm and made a beeline for the terrace, where his father had just appeared, waving a roll of paper.

With a taut reminder that murder had unpleasant consequences, even if it would solve three of his most pressing problems, Griff turned around and almost bumped into Freddy, who had taken off her shoes and was padding barefoot towards the house.

"The patch job fell apart," she said, holding up the remains of the cable tie in one hand, "but it did the trick. Thanks again for the save." Some of the animation had faded from her face, and there was a shadow of trouble in her eyes as she darted a brief glance at his mother's departing back. She gestured with her shoes at the delivery van, where the driver was still waiting with the overpriced, unnecessary supplies and an increasing air of impatience. "Are you going to accept the shipment?"

"No, I'm not." Coolly, he steered her around the extension cord some idiot had left on the grass, before she could stand on the plug. "Eavesdropping. What *would* Jane Austen say?"

A slight smile curled Freddy's mouth. Without makeup, she still had naturally red lips and doe eyes. She ought to be racking up a stream of Disney musicals on her CV. She was adept at producing that guileless look endemic among fictional princesses and children's entertainers. "She'd probably be taking notes. Your complex character would appear in her next classic."

"As the villain, I suppose." He was already striding towards the van, but he turned back, just for a second, as her words drifted after him.

"Not sure yet," she said. "Whenever I think I know the story, you turn the page on me."

"The guy's bloody *minted* and she's already binned him once. He's at a house party with ten other birds. Just crack on with someone else, you fucking mug."

Fitzwilliam Darcy, ladies and gentlemen. Your iconic romantic hero.

"If you don't stick to the fucking script, I'm going to knock your fucking teeth in," Tarik Khan shot at Dylan. "It'll be fucking dark before we even break for lunch at this rate, arsehole."

And Captain Wentworth, such a legendary way with words. So eloquent. So achingly tender.

Freddy exchanged glances with Maya, who was looking equally fed-up, but was less likely to say so. "Can we please *all* just stick to the script?" she asked, pulling her sticky camisole away from her stomach. She was sweating like mad, and seriously regretting wearing polyester.

Everyone in the first half of Act One had been allowed on The Henry stage for a read-through, while the actors whose characters didn't come in until later scenes were having their first costume fitting. The whole cast had been enamoured by their first proper look at the theatre, to the point where even Dylan and Sadie had remained silent for about forty-five seconds. The mood hadn't lasted. It was sweltering hot, and the standing fans the crew had set up were only cooling down the people standing directly in front of them. It had taken just one stumbled line in the first ten minutes of the read for tempers to flare.

The construction crew were doing finishing touches to the mainstage arena, so the dialogue was punctuated by drills and hammers, which wasn't helping to mellow the atmosphere.

Maf had ducked outside for a few minutes to take a call, so all the kiddies in the sandpit had started throwing their toys.

"Yeah? Try it, dick," Dylan said to Tarik, ignoring Freddy's interjection.

"Oh my God," Maya muttered, rubbing her hand over her forehead. "It's like being back at school." Her angular cheeks were flushed red and she was fanning herself with a call sheet.

Freddy had tried that earlier using her script, and just about knocked herself unconscious. Each deadweight copy was probably the equivalent of an entire tree. And on current form, it was going to be performance night before they'd even managed one pass of it.

"Sit down." Maf stalked back into the stands. Barring a few frizzy curls at her temples, she looked totally unfazed by the heat. "You're not being paid this salary grade to act like snot-nosed first years at drama college. All you're required to do is plant your arse on a chair and read the lines someone has typed in a nice large font for you. If you're confused as to which part you should be reading, it's the line under the bright yellow highlighter. If that's still too difficult, see me during the lunch break and I'll give you the name of a decent neurologist."

"I think we just got pulled up in front of the headmistress," Greg Stirling murmured to Maya, who flushed and didn't answer; in the increasingly stressful atmosphere, she'd drawn into herself. Greg didn't seem to notice the lack of response. He was one of several TV actors in the cast, and so far, high-maintenance. His personal assistant was arriving by train shortly, which was fortunate, because he'd run a production assistant ragged this morning, and the girl had escaped half an hour ago and not returned. He was playing Mr. Knightley, so was meant to be secretly in love with Sadie's Emma, but clearly nobody had run a chemistry test between him and Sadie. They'd been cold and wooden with each other all morning.

With Maf keeping a firm hold on the reins, the read-through progressed, but not smoothly. There were productions when the chemistry clicked from the beginning and everyone's personality slotted into place like pieces coming together in a puzzle. And there were the rocky-road jobs, a mess of disparate methods and temperaments thrown together into a jumble, sometimes resulting in unexpected brilliance, but always bumpy.

"Good," Maf said to Freddy at one point. "But more. *More.* I wanted you for this role because you have the inner reserves to give depth to this version of Lydia. You have the substance as well as the fizz and flirtation. Find the pathos, the side the audience will connect to. She's transitioning here from the young girl she was to the adult woman she'll become. She's still vibrant, still defiant, but regret underpins her every action in these scenes. And the crossroads later, the decision she makes—or the audience makes for her—will entirely determine the outcome of her character."

Over her shoulder as she moved on, she tossed out, "Unless the public decides to give you the cyanide cocktail, in which case you're out by intermission and can have a cuppa in the green room until the curtain call."

"Which I expect you would find disappointing." Sadie made her jump. Freddy hadn't seen her coming at all. Maybe she'd started materialising out of thin air. Like a demon in a horror film, gathering in strength. "Being so very dedicated to your career."

Freddy finished winding her hair into a sweaty top-knot and turned to face her. "If you have something to say, could you put it into plain words, please, instead of floating in and out making cryptic statements? It's like being in a Greek tragedy."

Sadie's PA had been darting in periodically with blotting pads and foundation touch-ups so, fittingly, Emma Woodhouse looked a lot more pampered and put-together than any of the other women. She was also off-book already, which Freddy should appreciate for the sake of overall progress, but was petty enough to find annoying. Sadie smiled that cat-smirk again. "I'm just admiring the *energy* that some people expend for the sake of the job."

Giving up on the non-conversation, Freddy turned to move away before she was provoked into saying something that would bring the directorial wrath down on her head, but Sadie moved at the same moment. Their feet tangled, they both tried to step back, and they collided with a pillar.

Instead of grabbing on to Freddy when she felt herself falling, Sadie gave her a shove. Freddy landed on the wooden boards on her hip, which would have cut the damage short at a bruise, but apparently it was the day for painful encounters with tools. A builder had left a screwdriver beneath a stool, and the end gouged a slice out of her thigh. She squeaked and grabbed at her leg with both hands, instinctively squeezing above and below the cut to combat the sharp bite of pain. Sadie had managed to steady herself against the carved pillar and was still on her feet. Of course.

"Oh, nasty." Greg came to kneel by her, inspecting Freddy's bleeding thigh. "Might need a stitch or two."

"Good to see you're putting that fictional medical degree to use, doc." Dylan elbowed the resident soap doctor out of the way and took his turn examining the patient. He reached out, and Freddy slapped his hand away.

"I can definitely do without the grope, thank you," she said, finding her voice after the initial shock.

"I was going to check your pulse," he said, affronted.

"Is that your standard line?" Freddy shot him a look. "My pulse is fine."

Dylan grinned, and suddenly rubbed her head in a gesture that was almost brotherly. "Takes more than a minor impaling to dampen your spirit, Carlton. You're a good 'un, really."

She hissed quietly at the increased burn from the cut. Her skin was blanching white under her clenching fingers.

Maf performed a rapid assessment, decided that Freddy needed medical attention but wasn't likely to pass out, and dispatched someone to fetch the production medic.

"He's gone into the village for lunch." It was Charlie who came up the steps to the stage, his handsome, freckled face concerned. He bent over her. "You all right, Freddy?"

She found a smile for him. "Don't look so serious. Coming from you, it makes me feel like amputation is imminent. When's the medic coming back?"

"We've sent someone after him, but in the meantime I went for the next best option."

"Which is?" Her cautious query was answered when the door into the arena opened and Griff strode in, looking even stonier than he had earlier with his mother.

"Someone's had an accident?" His grim voice carried over the quiet hubbub on stage, and he must have got a reply, because he pushed through the milling cast— most of whom were complaining about when they were going to get their own lunch—and came up the steps to crouch at her side.

He was a model of efficiency, and she wouldn't have expected anything less. He moved one of her hands aside to see the wound, glanced around for the culprit—technically the screwdriver, although pain made Freddy cranky and she nearly pointed a blood-stained finger in Sadie's direction as well—and then tilted Freddy's face up. Despite the tension brewing behind his measured movements, his touch was consistently gentle.

And yes, for a moment she did think he was going to kiss her. Totally justified reaction. On the rare occasions a man moved her chin about with his fingers, he followed up with another body part. Usually but not always his tongue.

In the next instant, when she caught on to the fact he was just checking her pupils to make sure she hadn't bumped her head, or whatever the rationale behind peering into people's eyes when they'd taken a tumble, it occurred to her that if they hadn't been surrounded by two dozen of her colleagues, she probably would have kissed him back.

"You need stitches," he said, and nobody questioned it, although the diagnosis wasn't even backed up by a fictional medical degree this time. He picked Freddy up, keeping a supportive hand under her injured thigh, and stood.

Her face was suddenly very close to his, and she was looking at the teeny, tiny flecks of caramel brown in his dark eyes. He was frequently rude, definitely a Slytherin, and clearly viewed her as a sort of irritating insect who kept buzzing around his space, but there was something very reassuring about his solid warmth when she hurt. Slipping one arm about his neck for stability, she curled in, just a little, and let her forehead rest tentatively against his shoulder. She felt muscles flex and the stirring of his breath when he briefly looked down at her, but he didn't jostle her away, as she was half expecting.

"Where are you going to put her?" Charlie asked, as if she were a parcel, and Freddy opened one eye to see that he was watching them with a strange expression. Intrigued? Baffled?

"I'm taking you to the clinic in the village." Griff addressed her directly, rather than responding to his brother. "At least it's a sterile environment, and you won't end up with heatstroke. It's like a bloody sauna in here." He looked impatiently at the hovering stage manager. "Why aren't you using the ventilation system?"

There was a moment of dead silence and uniformly blank looks.

Freddy felt the movement of Griff's deep exhale. "There's a temperature control panel backstage to regulate the air on the stage. As the point of the renovations was to provide a safe workplace, it was one of the first things your construction crew fixed. If you don't want half your cast dehydrated after one day of rehearsals, I suggest you turn it on, and use the roof."

"There's a roof?" one of the riggers asked, looking up and shielding his eyes against the blinding glare.

"No, when it rains, we just turn the place into a giant paddling pool. Of course there's a roof." Exasperated, Griff said to his brother, "Next time you invite dozens of people onto the property, give them a proper debrief on how to use the space. I've got enough on my hands without actors expiring in the garden. And find out who left that screwdriver lying about."

If Sabrina had used that tone of voice on her, there would be at the very least some strong bristling, but Charlie was either the most easy-going person in the world or really had missed his calling as an actor. He simply saluted and patted Freddy on the head.

But before he ambled off to show the backstage crew how to activate the theatre's hidden comforts, she saw a momentary flicker in his eyes.

On the short drive to Highbrook village, Freddy kept one clenched fist pushed tightly against her thigh above the cut, which Griff had covered with a temporary bandage, and her eyes fixed on the scenery out the side window. "You're pretty rough on Charlie, aren't you?"

She could *feel* Griff's glance sear into her cheek. "Picked up another member of his fan club, has he?"

"Don't sneer." She turned her head and looked at him. "He's your brother, not one of us hapless peeps you're paid by the word to squash."

"Charlie's fine," Griff said dismissively. "He's unsquashable, to put it your way. And considering that the stream of hassle he causes appears to be never-ending, he couldn't care less about my opinion. I'd reserve your sympathy. Charlie will never have a problem rebounding in life. His business sense is atrocious, but his personality is his biggest asset and he knows how to use it."

"How very cynical." Freddy watched him soberly. "I don't think Charlie *uses* anything. He just is what he is— and I highly, *highly* doubt that he doesn't care about your opinion." She hesitated, wondering just how far she could push social boundaries on a subject that was none of her business, with a man she barely knew yet.

Whatever—she'd never claimed restraint in social situations, and she was in pain. "Just like you obviously care enough about your family to keep rescuing them from their bad decisions."

Griff's eyes met hers. Right now, there wasn't a hint

of warm amber; they were relentlessly, coldly obsidian.
"Do you always make extremely personal comments on
other people's relationships?"

"Quite often, yeah." Freddy rubbed the heel of her
hand up and down, trying to cut off as much sensation
as possible. "Are you jealous?"

"Of your insufferable nosiness? Not particularly."

"Of Charlie."

Griff didn't respond, but the line of his jaw could slice
through steel, and the knuckles of his left hand flexed on
the wheel as if he was imagining it was her neck.

"Because you don't need to be." Freddy returned her
attention out the window. "I'm starting to think you might
be okay. In your own way." Muttering, she added under
her breath, "If you dig down quite far."

His car was well-sprung and there was almost no road
noise, so she could hear the faint sound of his breathing,
and the way the rhythm altered for just an instant.

The GP's clinic was a beautiful stone cottage next
door to the pub—handy, if anybody drank themselves
into alcohol poisoning or weaved unsteadily into a lamp-
post. Someone had phoned ahead, and the doctor was expecting her. He was a burly, handsome man in his forties,
with sparkly eyes and a full beard. He looked more like a
mountain climber or an Antarctic explorer than a village
doc. He joked good-naturedly with Freddy while he examined her leg, and she returned the favour with a little
too much enthusiasm. Things had got so unsettling in
the car with Griff that she felt back in her comfort zone.
Light-hearted, meaningless banter.

Dr. Adams gave her a tetanus booster. As he disposed
of the needle, he looked through thick brows at Griff.
"Must be chaotic over at the estate, if you've got a TV

crew in situ and a film crew on the way. Is that still in the works? The film at Highbrook?"

"A few scenes will be at Highbrook. The majority in London." Griff was standing by the bed, looking a tad murderous. He'd been emitting increasingly dark, dangerous vibes ever since he'd laid her down on the hard plastic. "I won't ask how you know about that."

Adams grinned, undaunted. "You know how the grapevine works around here." He brought a sutures kit over to the bed. "Right. Time to be brave, I'm afraid."

Freddy had gritted her teeth through the tetanus shot, but she felt nauseated even thinking about someone sewing her like a ragdoll. She'd never had any kind of surgery, and was a baby about pain. She did have pride, though, so she gave the sexy doctor a tight smile and hid her hand under her skirt so she could wind a tight grip into the fabric.

As Adams prepared the local anaesthetic and inserted the first needle into her leg, Griff unfolded his arms, his jaw still set, and reached one hand out to her. She looked at it, and up at him, then clutched it with no further attempt to pretend she was stoic. It took three more shots to fully numb her leg, and at each pinch, she held more tightly to Griff. When the stitching began, she took one look at the neat row of thread appearing in her skin and tucked her face into her reluctant comforter's own leg.

She heard him sigh, but his free hand came down to the back of her head.

Adams mended her quickly and without fuss, bandaged her up, and gave her a couple of paracetamol.

"I'll still be able to walk, won't I?" she asked, once Griff had left to get them some takeaway sandwiches. He'd probably reached the short limit of his tolerance.

After the suture needle had hit a piece of flesh that was still partly sensate, she'd just about ground his knuckles into dust.

"I don't think I'll need to bust out a saw. You can keep the leg this time," Adams said lightly, throwing away his gloves, and she smiled more naturally.

"Walk *on* it. The rehearsal schedule for the next week is packed and if I have to tell the director I'm on bedrest, I'll probably end up back here needing treatment for attempted strangulation."

"Keep it elevated this afternoon if you can, but you should be fine to get back to your practice tomorrow morning, providing you take regular rests and the timetable doesn't involve tap dancing or combat training."

"A kiss scene and discovering a body in the library," Freddy said with a grin. "You know, shock, gasp, good hearty scream." She mimed her best silent film screech, hands clasped to her cheeks, and Adams looked amused.

"Ideal. Just think of my terrifying needlework and you'll be instantly transported to the right frame of mind." He cleared his throat. "Of course, plenty of people in these parts would be spooked by a comfort cuddle with the lord of the manor, so you obviously have infinite wells of courage."

For the first time in recent memory, Freddy could feel a blush heating her face.

Chapter Six

Griff dumped her in her bedroom on their return to High-brook, with a curt order to stay there, so she gave it a token ten minutes before she limped back to the theatre.

One of the prop team brought in a chaise longue they were going to use in the library scenes, and she finished out the read-through on that. Conveniently, it was where a significant encounter with the actor playing Wickham was going to take place, so they got in some preliminary scene blocking. And the conditions were a lot better with the roof shade pulled across and the ventilation system blasting cool air.

She was still exhausted when she tumbled into bed that night, and went to sleep with a curious, fizzy feeling uncurling deep inside.

She had no guilt about skipping her run the next morning, the bright side of having a screwdriver and a darning needle shoved into her thigh. She was fastening the straps of her favourite midi dress when her phone rang. Shoving aside a pile of discarded clothes, she unearthed it under her script, which was now tattered and marked-up and still not committed to memory.

"Hello," she said in a rush, so hasty to answer before it went to voicemail that she hadn't even noticed who was calling. With her other hand, she separated and scrunched her wet curls, shaking them out.

"If it isn't the long-lost sister." It was Sabrina. "I tried calling you three times last night. Am I in your bad books or were you busy doing high-flying, glamorous things?"

"Sorry to destroy the image," Freddy said, "but I was snoring and drooling into my pillow by nine o'clock. Long day. What's up?"

"Dad couldn't get hold of you last night, either, so he broke the habit of a lifetime and called me instead. He's winding up his wheelings and dealings in the States earlier than expected, and will be back on home turf by the end of next week. And he's been in touch with your agent."

"Fuck," Freddy said.

"Why is he so vitriolic about this show? It's not a long-term commitment. After the rehearsal period, it's one-and-done in a night, isn't it?"

Freddy sat back down on the bed to rest her leg. It was going to be another long day and she didn't want to strain the stitches. "Apparently Dad's been rumbling with Griff over a film he's making about Henrietta. Competing interests. Did you know Dad wants to do a screen adaptation of *All Her World*, because it's the first I've heard of it."

After a short silence, Sabrina said, "I think I need a dictionary translation for that entire answer. Griff?"

Freddy winced. "J. Ford-Griffin."

A longer silence. "How does the Westminster Ice King come into the picture? And since when do you call him *Griff*?"

She chose to ignore the horrified undertone. "When he isn't writing reviews and analysing Shakespeare on the telly, he moonlights as landed nobility and a budding film executive. He's Sir George Ford's grandson, he owns Highbrook, and he's here right now researching Henrietta's relationship with his grandfather. The tale of the famous playwright and her magnum opus is coming to a cinema near you."

"Was Henrietta really *that* interesting?" Sabrina had never bothered to read even the first chapter of Rupert's biography. "Outside of *The Velvet Room* phenomenon, I know she had a lot of affairs, but haven't we all."

Freddy rolled a damp curl around her fingertip. "I see you still haven't read the biography. She was pretty remarkable."

"Hmm. I'm not sure anyone can justify the fuss Dad's made over her, and the rest of the literary crowd, and now films as well. And don't get me started on having her dangled over us like some sort of golden monument—"

"No. I won't," Freddy said firmly. "What's going on with you? Interviewing anyone cool this week?"

The pause this time had a different, tense quality, and Freddy frowned, her thoughts dragged back from the impending confrontation with their father. "Sabs?"

"Work is fine." Sabrina's voice was crisp, and there was an unmistakable defensive shape to the words that put Freddy on high alert. She knew that tone. It only ever emerged when— "But since you'll have to know sometime... Ferren's back in London."

Freddy lifted a hand in a literal face-palm. Sabrina had been in an on-off-maybe-on-no-definitely-off relationship with Joe Ferren, the star of a series of high-earning action films, for about eight years. Freddy had been fifteen when she'd first been introduced to Sabs's famous boyfriend, and she'd progressed from a starstruck teenage crush to "What the fuck is my sister doing?" in the space of a month.

Their tempestuous romance had hit a wall with what seemed like a permanent crash when Sabrina had got her permanent contract on *Sunset Britain*—Ferren didn't do well sharing any sort of spotlight—and Freddy had thrown a mental carnival. He'd made himself scarce the past year working abroad, and Sabrina's overall happiness had gone on an upward climb. Freddy had hoped the unreliable shit would set up permanent camp in Hollywood.

He'd probably had a temperamental fit and been fired again.

"You're not…" Freddy trailed off apprehensively, already anticipating the frosty reaction. Sabrina's personality was ninety-five-percent rational, but Ferren always slotted into the other bit.

"We're not back together. We're just…talking."

Shit. They'd be shagging by the end of the week.

"Sabrina…"

"Peanut." The "back off" warning was flashing with full red lights. "As much as I adore you, I do not require commentary on my personal life from my baby sister."

It would be like trying to reason with a slightly patronising brick wall. Freddy sighed. "Are you still going to be calling me that when I'm eighty-five years old?"

"As I'll be a venerable old dame in my nineties by then, yes."

"Maybe even a proper dame. Famous presenters sometimes get the honour."

If they didn't derail their career and future title by making horrible decisions in their sex life.

Sabrina snorted. "Ten quid says Nick Davenport smarms his way to that one. He's probably already got a drawer full of socks and undies embroidered with 'Sir Nicholas.'"

Willing to take the easy route and keep the conversation in noncontroversial territory for now, Freddy said teasingly, "Spend a lot of time thinking about Nick's pants, do you?"

"Don't be revolting. My taste in men isn't *that* dire." Sabrina cleared her throat so pointedly that Freddy was instantly wary. "Speaking of which—"

"What?"

"My word precisely: what. Before you veered into polite small talk, you'd come over all flustered. What's going on with you and the silver-haired demon?"

"His hair isn't silver, it's just very pale blond," she said without thinking, and could visualise Sabrina's growing smile back in London. Evidently, older sisters believed they had a prerogative to meddle that was denied their *baby* siblings. "Oh, shut up."

"I haven't said anything. Your reaction is carrying the conversation for both of us. You *haven't* shagged Malfoy? He once called you so overly sweet that you were a diabetic hazard. Have some standards, Frederica."

Seriously—pot and kettle.

"I haven't shagged him." Leaning forward, Freddy rested her cheek on the quilt. "I haven't shagged *anyone*, for months. I'm sure it's bad for my health. My eczema has been flaring. It's probably sex deprivation."

"I wouldn't know."

"Smugness is not an attractive quality."

"Do you like him?" Sabrina asked, curiously, and Freddy played idly with the phone for a few seconds, giving herself time to consider her words.

"I don't know. I'm not sure how I feel about him."

She had a track record of falling into lust and crushes and infatuation with dozens of men at the drop of a hat, and emerging from each experience just as quickly and usually unscathed—but this didn't feel… It didn't feel quite like that.

"He's not your usual sort of man. Physically or in any other respect. You always seem to have a variation of the same type in tow: loud, burly, hairy, and up for a laugh."

Fair assessment of her dating history the past few years. She did tend to swipe right on certain key characteristics. "Hmm."

"But you fancy him?"

"Oh yeah," she said with feeling.

When she went downstairs—with not even a limp; thumbs up, body—the house was very quiet. Most of the cast were still in bed, since the first rehearsal call wasn't until eight. A buffet breakfast had been set up on the terrace. The caterers were keeping out of the dining areas in the house to leave them clear for the Ford-Griffins. Freddy did a full sweep of the options, chose a chocolate croissant, and took it through the woods to The Henry. She should use the spare hour to go over her lines. The deadline to be off-book was creeping ever closer, and the prospect of another Springsteen incident was haunting her.

She stood looking at the theatre in the morning light, listening to the sound of larks in the trees, and breathing deep. A hint of crispness in the air reminded her of autumn and acted on her system like a hit of caffeine.

She was looking forward to autumn—or she would be, if it weren't for the looming shadow of *The Velvet Room*. The first audition was only days away.

A bird shot out of a cluster of branches nearby with

a rustle and flap of wings, seconds before Freddy heard footsteps crunching over the gravel path through the trees. She turned, and her stomach gave one of those delicious little flutters as Griff appeared.

He had a file tucked under his arm, and a very professional-looking camera bag in his hand. His clothing looked like Savile Row and he was incredibly suave and polished and put-together for an hour when most people were still snoozing. Or getting hot and bothered under the sheets in the probable case of Dylan and whoever he'd smarmed into sharing his bed for this run.

She wasn't exactly bowled over by Griff's expression when he saw her, but there was more resignation there than "Oh, Christ, not her again." Baby steps. She might even get a smile out of him one of these days.

She finished the last bite of her croissant as he reached her. "You're getting an early start."

"I need to take some photos of source material in Henrietta's office, and I'd prefer to do it while the theatre is quiet." He was frowning at the building, but sliced his attention back to her. "You're early as well. You didn't wake up with pain, did you?"

"No, Dr. Adams's paracetamol is doing the trick, and I've got ibuprofen tucked into my bra just in case."

His brows went up at that, and his gaze went down.

She hesitated, shifting the weight of her script in her arms. She did need to get a jump on rehearsal, but… she'd been hoping to get a glimpse of the office where her grandmother had written *The Velvet Room*. Who knew, maybe she'd soak up some residual talent from the atmosphere. "Do you mind if I come in with you? I'll stay out of shot and quiet as a mouse, I promise. You won't even know I'm there."

He made a sound that wasn't quite a snort. "Somehow, I doubt that very much. Is this an attempt to install yourself as an unpaid production assistant so you can get that look at the material?"

"Just an interested observer." Freddy smiled at him, suddenly feeling a little bubble of happiness well up out of nowhere. It was a beautiful day, birds were cheeping, and a man with a majestic nose and the sensitivity of a sledgehammer was frowning at her. For this one moment in time, she had a curious, rare sense of being exactly where she was meant to be. She clung on to the feeling as if it were a balloon that could lift her up and float her away from the approaching troubles below.

"Your father will kick up hell if you show any interest in this project," Griff said, in the tone of a man who never gave a shit what other people thought of his decisions.

Mentally, Freddy wound the string of her metaphorical joy balloon around her wrist. It wasn't going to be whisked away from her, even with a sharp gust of reality. If she acted on her conviction that what her father wanted for her career was not the right path for her, then getting a sneak peek at the film research would be the least of the contention between them. "It'll be the tip of the iceberg if I make…certain other decisions soon."

Griff unlocked the door and held it open for her, and she scooted inside, then followed him as he strode purposefully towards the rear rooms. They turned down a hallway she'd never taken before. There were few windows, and the light was dim, the air a bit musty with dust.

"What other decisions?" It had been several minutes since she'd spoken, and his question was almost reluctant, with a strange vibe of unfamiliarity, as if he was going against his natural inclinations by asking.

Freddy glanced at him. He was looking straight ahead, but his head was turned slightly in her direction. "Dad wants me to audition for the new production of *The Velvet Room*." Stepping into the room he indicated and turning in an interested circle, she added, "As you predicted so unenthusiastically at The Prop & Cue last year."

Griff laid his stuff on an untidy desk that was already piled high with old books and manuscripts. "And what do you want to do?"

So matter-of-fact, just a straight question, what did she want to do, as if it were as easy as that. It *should* be as easy as that.

Still cuddling the mammoth script, she walked around the perimeter of the small room, taking in the details—the peeling wallpaper and dusty shelves. Somehow, she expected there to be something spectacular—magical—about the places where great works of art were created.

This was just a room.

She looked closer at the images on the tiled feature wall and hid a smile. Albeit a room that had been decorated according to Sir George's very particular tastes.

She didn't need to absorb the ghosts of her grandmother's ambition and conviction, anyway. She wasn't Henrietta. She was Freddy, she did know what she *wanted* to do, and the only person who could turn wistfulness into action was her.

She put down the script and sat gingerly on the edge of a rickety stool, mindful of her oath to stay out of the way. "You know Fiona Gallagher is involved with *The Austen Playbook*?"

Griff paged through a file. "She's a major financial backer."

Freddy tucked her feet into the rungs of the stool and

rested her forearms on her knees. "Fiona's just picked up the rights for the Allegra Hawthorne stage adaptation, and she's scouting me for it. I haven't done a stage spectacular or any comedy for a while, though, so she wants to see how I do with *The Austen Playbook*."

Griff set his file down. His hands were large and strong-looking. "And it's a job you want?"

Freddy tapped the back of one heel against the wooden stool leg. "Yes. It is. I'm a huge fan of Allegra Hawthorne, and it's the sort of role I love."

"It's the sort of role that made you so popular with audiences in the first place," Griff said levelly. "When you obviously feel passionate about what you're doing, your performance has a very visceral joy that affects every person in the theatre."

For a few seconds, the only sound in the room was the *tap tap tap* of Freddy's shoe against the wood. And probably the creaking sound as she tried to close her jaw after it had performed the anatomically difficult feat of dropping to the floor. "Calls me a contagious joy fairy when we're alone in a dusty backroom. Compares me to a stagnant pond in a London newspaper. Timing, my friend. It's a beautiful thing."

"My judgment in London is based on what you give in London. And for the past few years, that's been a stream of—for the most part—competent, steady, totally uninspired performances in dramas that seem to suck the life out of you."

Well. She'd always known he had the ability to cut to the chase with a few well-chosen words.

"So, what's the problem?" Griff asked, coming around to sit on the edge of the desk. "Are rehearsals off to a bad start? Other than the obvious." He nodded at her leg.

"The scene changes are going to be a challenge, and it's taking me longer than usual to get off-book. I'm a bit gun-shy about getting lines wrong now," she added ruefully.

"What did happen with *Masquerade*? You don't usually make errors like that."

Freddy lifted a shoulder. "I don't know. I just—blanked. They'd just announced the new year-long run of *The Velvet Room*, and of course my father was—is—dead set on having me in it. The definitive Carlton play. *I'd* always wanted to be in it, myself," she said slowly. "Ever since I was a little girl. Even through my early teens. I wanted to be just like Henrietta. And then—"

"And then?" Griff was regarding her very steadily, and something about his calm presence—and frankly, his no-bullshit responses—made it easy to say things to him that she never said aloud.

"My career is moving in the direction everybody expects me to follow—the classical dramas, the high-brow, serious, top-of-the-tree works that the big names in the arts discuss over champagne at posh parties. It was Henrietta's domain as an actor, and then as a writer." She bit down on the inside of her lower lip. "It would have been my father's if he hadn't been hurt."

"How did it happen?" There was an unexpected shade of gentleness in the question, and Freddy felt a sudden burn at the back of her eyes.

"It was a freak accident. I was just a toddler. My mother had died the year before. Dad was playing Iago at the Majestic, and our nanny brought me and my sister along to see him at rehearsal. A set toppled backstage, and I was standing right under it. Dad was coming offstage and he just—dove for me. I was too young to remember anything about it."

"You weren't hurt?" Griff reached forward and, just for a second, touched her hand. As he straightened, their faces passed close together, their eyes locked, and Freddy felt as if her breath was stuck in her throat.

Then he retreated, and the picture frame unfroze.

She exhaled. "N-no. No. Not even a bruise. But it badly damaged Dad's back. He couldn't walk at all for a few months, and even now he can be on his feet for only a short time before he has to rest, or he gets a lot of pain. It pretty much put paid to his career on the stage. He couldn't cope with the physical demands."

But Rupert Carlton had grown up taking the perks and prestige of his position in the West End for granted, and he had found a way to keep a foothold. First through the success of his biography on Henrietta, which had led to multiple book contracts for other members of acting royalty, and then through his daughter.

"Is that why you're forcing yourself to take roles you don't really enjoy?" Griff, as always, cut straight to the heart of the matter. "Because of a misplaced sense of guilt? Do you feel responsible for the accident?"

"In some ways," Freddy admitted. "It's hard not to feel that way, when I was the…impetus. Logically, I know it was an accident, I was a child, and it wasn't my fault, but part of the reason my father has invested in my career is because of what happened to his own, and I was a factor in that equation. I've found it difficult to look at what he's helped me achieve so far, and know he wants for me what he couldn't have for himself, and contemplate turning around and saying, 'No, ta, not for me.'" She blew out a long, frustrated breath. "But it was me, as well. I really thought that was what *I* wanted. Until I actually had a go at it, and realised I'd been much happier doing the musicals, the stage spectaculars, the comedies. I like to make people happy, I like to hear laughter and see them leave smiling and humming the songs. I *like* popular fiction of all kinds, and I think it's just as important as the lit that gets taught in class. I got to go back to my roots for the royal charity performance and it was like changing shoes and realising you've been walking around wearing the wrong size. I still enjoyed myself in a lot of those dramas—"

"I suspect you have a knack for finding some form of enjoyment in most situations," Griff said, and although the words had a sardonic ring, there was the faintest smile in his eyes.

The corners of her mouth lifted. "Parts of life are shit enough. I look for the light where I can find it. And some of those shows were great. It makes a big difference when you've got a good rapport in the cast. I had a blast doing shows like *1553* and *Becket Season*."

"And clearly loathed shows like *High Voltage*."

Freddy's smile slipped, and her stomach clenched. There were times when it had been hard to find even a thin beam of light to stand in. "No, *High Voltage* was not a high point."

Griff's eyes narrowed on her face, not missing a trick, as usual.

"Anyway," she said, determinedly bringing herself back to the present. "It's crunch time. *The Velvet Room* audition is next week. If I get that role, it'll be a year-long commitment. Likewise, if I managed to land a part in *Anathorn*, the Allegra Hawthorne show. They're expected to open around the same time. It could come down to an either/or choice, and I know which direction Dad will expect me to take."

She sat straighter on the stool. "And I know where my heart is pushing me. But it's not always that easy to go after your own happiness at the expense of someone else's." The glumness was starting to drag at her again, and she strove for a lighter note. "And sometimes it rebounds badly. Look at Lydia Bennet. Essentially, she only behaved in a way that dozens of misguided, self-centred teenagers would, and ended up stuck in eternal punishment. Although, in our play, possibly put out of her misery with a poisoned cocktail."

Which was what she needed to concentrate on in the meantime. Present preoccupations first. With a start, she checked her watch, and then relaxed. It felt like she was existing in a bubble in this room with Griff, in a curious mixed atmosphere of both warm safety and building tension, but Maf would happily produce a sharp pin and reintroduce reality if Freddy were late.

She tipped her head back to stretch out her neck. The ceiling was embedded with more of Sir George's saucy carvings. "It's nice to know I can continue my art education here," she said, with a slight wobble in her voice. "I feel like Highbrook is really going to expand my artistic horizons. I've been trying to perk things up by developing some proper outside hobbies. My online dating profile was very sparse and made me feel like a one-note person."

Griff had started setting up a tripod and looked at her over the ring light he was adjusting. "Online dating?"

"Apps. You could give them a go. You might find some like-minded misanthropes. We all have our interests."

He photographed a series of small objects—a cigarette

case, a medal, a small ceramic statue. When he removed a jewellery case from a locked safe and opened it, she couldn't resist getting up and peeking over his shoulder.

"Oh," she said, and faint lines appeared at the corners of his eyes as he came very close to forgetting himself and properly smiling.

"Were you expecting diamonds?"

"I wasn't expecting *that*." Freddy bent to get a closer look at the earrings, and what the quartz had been carved into. Even when she was in dance training and at peak flexibility, she'd never tried that position. It looked gravity-defying. "Your grandad was a right old rip under the Ye Olde Country Squire appearance, wasn't he? From the tales I've heard about the Wythburn Group, it was probably love at first sight with Henrietta."

"If you believe in it." The derision on that one all but bounced off the peeling wallpaper.

"I don't, as it happens." Freddy straightened and turned. Her body was almost touching his, and he went very still. "I believe that…*something* can happen quite fast, though. Once in a while. Maybe even just once."

When she looked into his eyes, they were wells of darkness with a flicker of warm heat. She could smell whatever he used in the shower; it was spicy and masculine, and it made her want to lean in and inhale against his neck.

He touched his fingertips to a curl at her temple. She hadn't expected him to make a move, unless it was to direct her back to the stool of silence—which had unexpectedly turned into a therapy chair—and it startled her so much that she twitched. His thumb rested, feather-light, against her cheek. Ever so slightly, just a fragment of motion, he stroked, and the shiver that went through her in response was a hard, shocking jolt.

With her nails digging into the wooden surface of the desk, Freddy rose an inch onto her toes to put their faces at a closer level. When she spoke, she was surprised her voice sounded so normal. "Do you mind if I test out something?"

His own voice was crisp, but that burn of amber was still in his eyes. "Are you asking to kiss me as a social experiment?"

"Well." Freddy tipped her head. "You *are* a pro at research."

Their eyes still locked, neither of them lowering their lashes, their breath mingled and held as she leaned forward and touched her mouth lightly to his. She didn't move for a few seconds, just feeling the sensation of his lips against hers. Then slowly, she started to kiss him, pressing softly, parting slightly. He was kissing her back while they continued to stare at each other. It was measured, cataloguing, feeling-in-the-dark—and yet, conversely, somehow the most intimate moment she'd ever had with a man. It was as if he was looking right into her, seeing something she hadn't even known was there, laid bare. Breaking her open.

And they were barely touching.

Their mouths came apart, and Freddy took a shaky breath. She tore her eyes from his and looked down as their knuckles brushed and hooked. They brought their arms up, interlocking their hands. The fingers of his right hand played with the fingers of her left. Then her gaze returned to his.

A muscle jumped in his jaw.

The second kiss was a rush of heat, urgent and hard,

his tongue in her mouth, hers in his, wetness and fire. His hands had left hers and were tangled in her hair, holding her head; her arms were around him, sliding up his back. She could feel his skin, smooth and warm. Muscles moving and shifting. Breaths jagged and snatched.

They stumbled against the desk and it knocked her away from him, so abruptly it was like tearing a page from a book, thrust from one scene into the next, a shock to the system. Gripping the wood, Freddy stood staring at Griff, breathing heavily.

His hair was a ruffled mess and his shirt had been yanked out of his belt, baring a slice of skin up his abdomen. One of her dress straps had fallen down her arm, and she didn't like to think what her own hair looked like. When she lifted a hand to smooth it, her fingers were shaking.

"Holy shit," she said, blankly.

It must have been a stunner of a kiss—the hardened critic was temporarily lost for words. He managed a sort of grunt. As he put his own clothing back to rights, Freddy was almost frightened to see that his hands weren't totally steady either.

"Results of the experiment?" A rasp in the words.

Freddy still felt jumpy, like she was darting about on molten coals even as she remained frozen to the spot by the desk. Her response was fervent. "Explosive."

Her lips felt tender, bruised from the hard pressure of his, and she rested her fingertips on them.

"I don't know why I find you so beautiful now." He'd regained control over his pitch and he said it like he was commenting on the weather, but the words fell into the silence between them with the impact of a heavy weight shattering a piece of glass.

Freddy dropped her hand and stared at him, and he turned his head. As compliments went, it was a bit back-handed, but somehow it didn't come across that way.

There was a moment of quiet breath and assessing eyes.

"I don't know why I fancy you so much," she said, with equal frankness.

"I would have thought Charlie was more your type." It was still like talking to the ice sculpture his mother had once tossed out as a comparison, but Freddy didn't make the mistake of looking at the surface.

She felt like she'd lied by omission to everyone lately, keeping so much of what she was thinking and feeling about her career to herself, but she'd at least always tried to be honest in her private life. She might be a flirt, but guile was not a weapon in her romantic arsenal. "I don't think there is a type." She swallowed and looked blindly at the surface of the desk, where the earrings were still glinting suggestively under the glow of the ring light. "Right now, I think…there's just you."

In the silence that followed, her hand clenched into a fist against the desk.

Then Griff touched her bare arm, and her cheek, just two light touches. Freddy breathed in, a long, slow inhale.

"I promised not to interrupt your work," she said on the exhale.

"Yes." A familiar note of the sardonic, which was actually a relief in the current tension. "That lasted about as long as I expected."

She cast him a look over her shoulder. "Foresaw this, did you?"

"No. This definitely wasn't the scenario I imagined."

"I expect not. After all the very gallant things you've said about me over the years. Just think, if this had happened earlier, you might have given me a better review for *Masquerade*." She reflected on that for about two seconds. "No, you wouldn't."

He snorted and said at the same moment, "No, I wouldn't."

Perversely, that made her laugh. That wash of unexpected gladness suddenly wrapped around her again, and she smiled at him. It was a bright, instinctive gesture, and it made something change in his face. "Isn't it great?"

The question just bubbled up spontaneously from that pool of happiness, and he shook his head. It wasn't a negative action. More like someone recovering from a sharp punch to the nose, actually, which she chose not to read too much into.

There was a faint smile on his usually tense mouth, and when she couldn't resist lifting up to dust another feathery kiss there, just because he felt good to touch and right now he made *her* feel good, one of his hands came up to the back of her head.

And when the door opened with only a cursory knock and his brother sailed in holding two mugs, Griff didn't behave as Freddy might have anticipated, with an instant retreat and an invisible gate slamming shut. He did lift his head and step away from her, but with no haste, and it was several seconds before his hand fell away from her hip.

Charlie was doing a deer-in-the-headlights in the doorway, gaping at them with almost ludicrous surprise.

"Is one of those for me?" Griff asked calmly, when no words seemed to be forthcoming.

Charlie looked blankly down at the mugs. "Oh. Yeah. Dad said he saw you heading outside at the arse-crack of dawn and I thought you might be ready for a coffee." He seemed to get a grip on himself and offered the other one to Freddy. "Coffee, Freddy? I haven't touched it, and

I already had two cups of tea at the house. It's got milk and sugar. I don't know how you like it."

"Like that. Thanks, if you're sure." Freddy took the mug and blew on the surface, eyeing both brothers through the steam.

"Sorry to interrupt," Charlie said, a note of amusement creeping in. "I thought you'd be buried in work, not snogging the houseguests."

"Things often take surprising turns." Freddy smiled at him. "I love life."

Creases appeared at the corners of Charlie's eyes then, and the lurking humour at their expense turned into something softer. "Yeah, I reckon you do. It's nice." His attention slid pointedly to the side. "Be nice if it rubbed off on other people, too."

"Thanks for the coffee, Charlie. Don't let us keep you."

Ignoring his brother's acerbic response, Charlie rested his hands low on his lean hips and looked around. "I haven't been in here for years." His nose wrinkled. "It smells."

"It's called dust." Somehow Griff knocked back the rest of his coffee in one go without incinerating his tongue. He put the cup aside. "It appears on surfaces when you don't have staff or your unfortunate girlfriends cleaning up after you."

"I thought the studio crew were polishing this place to a high shine to look good on camera."

"The studio crew will be keeping their tramping feet and prying eyes out of the back rooms," Griff muttered as he flipped up the camera screen and started checking through frames. "They're hardly going to include Henrietta's office in the show."

"*You* could have whisked around with a duster, since

you'll be at least replicating the space for the film. The infamous four walls where she wrote the great epic."

There were yet more aged photographs scattered across the surface of the desk. Freddy bent over them. "Who's the lady with the bobbed hair? She's in a lot of these pictures."

Charlie looked over her shoulder. "Great-Aunty Violet. Our grandfather's sister. The family black sheep. Of that generation, anyway."

"Wow," Freddy said. "Her brother had bondage statues in his strawberry patch and *she* was the family black sheep. A-plus for effort, Violet. Or did black-sheep behaviour in that generation mean she dressed in tweeds and joined the Women's Institute?"

"She had the temerity to run off to be on the stage." Charlie invested the word with all the old-school connotations of immorality. "And made a piss-poor job of it, by all accounts. The men in the family could have their fun but the women were expected to be good little girls. Our great-aunty had a habit of throwing drunken tantrums at village events, according to the old lady who used to run the sweet shop."

Griff rolled his eyes. "Which probably means she had an extra glass of mulled wine at the Christmas fête one year and refused to join in the sing-a-long. Highbrook has a history of taking dull anecdotes and inflating them into secrets that would make Bluebeard feel comparatively virtuous."

"Then she committed the ultimate blackening of the family name when she smashed her car into Tower Bridge and didn't survive to pay the damages." Charlie picked up the photo of the woman with the defiant face. "Poor Violet," he said more soberly.

"She has sad eyes," Freddy murmured.

"She was an unwanted daughter in a family that wanted another son, never had many friends, and invested everything into becoming an actor. And failed miserably at it." Griff finished organising his new shots. "She lived a short, unfulfilled life, and when she died, I suspect it was considered an inconvenience rather than a loss."

"God." Appalled, Freddy took the photograph from Charlie. "She was an actor?"

"A minor member of the Wythburn Group." Griff came to stand at her shoulder. "Very minor. I'm not surprised you haven't heard of her. Most people have either forgotten she existed, or never knew her name in the first place."

Freddy looked into Violet Ford's unhappy eyes. "I hope you're including her in your film. As a person, not a failure," she added, with a burst of fierceness, twisting so she could see him.

He was studying her rather than the photo. She couldn't read his expression at all now. "I am" was all he said.

After a moment, she turned and let her weight rest against him—and after another few breaths, she felt the stroke of his thumb against her forearm.

Chapter Seven

The worst thing about cell phones was that it was impossible to bang the receiver down on someone, a lack Sabrina was probably cursing right now. Hitting the End button really hard would just break a nail and potentially the screen. Freddy watched as the call timer stopped and her home screen reappeared. With a silent f-bomb herself, she returned the phone to her bag.

As expected, Sabrina and Ferren had progressed rapidly from "talking" to reigniting their disaster of a relationship. He'd shown up at Sabs's flat with jewellery boxes and some rehearsed speech, and her otherwise smart sister had fallen for it.

Freddy's own building stress, not aided by the fact that she still couldn't keep her lines straight, had left her more tactless than usual, and Sabrina had not appreciated her candour.

Her sister had finally lost her temper completely and snapped, "When you've had a relationship that lasts longer than an orgasm, Fred, get back to me and I might take your advice." And hung up. For a sophisticated thirty-year-old woman, who had a bad habit of still treating *Freddy* like a child, she could do a good impression of a door-slamming teenager.

Freddy rubbed at her leg as she stood up from the low brick wall in the Highbrook rose garden, where she was taking her lunch break. Two days post-screwdriver, she must be starting to heal, because the stitches were itching. She threw the rest of her sandwich on the grass for the resident peacock to find on his rounds—the feathered one, not Dylan, who had been flirting with her all morning and getting increasingly handsy. He was more likely to get a knee in his dick than a bite of her ham and cheese.

A production assistant rushed past, holding a clipboard. "Five more minutes," the harried-looking man said. He jerked his chin back in the direction of the theatre, with an exaggerated grimace. "I'd stay out here in the peace and quiet as long as possible if I were you. It's all kicking off back there."

"Oh God. What now?" The morning rehearsal had been a flat-out disaster. They'd had their first attempt at the random scene selection, with Maf acting as the voice of the viewing public and giving them four minutes' warning which version they were enacting. The whole thing had collapsed in seconds. Half the cast couldn't find their place even with their scripts right in front of their faces, and Dylan had combined the lines from two different scene variants, which had thrown everybody off completely. Freddy had delivered a very dramatic, affecting line about the death of a character who then entered from stage left, alive and well.

This was the point in rehearsals where the production always looked like an ugly old patchwork quilt, random bits thrown together and coming apart at the seams. It was usually a smoothly oiled machine by opening night, but the words "live TV" were hovering in the air like a disaster beacon. And the advent of Fiona Gallagher was hanging over the night for Freddy like a spectre. A very influential, potentially career-changing spectre.

The crew guy rolled his eyes. "The understudies have arrived and nobody knows where to put them, the Wicked Baron's people are traipsing about taking location shots for some film—" Freddy tried not to be amused "—and Greg Stirling's done a runner."

Freddy stopped casually peering around for a glimpse of the Wicked Baron, and turned sharply. "What?"

"Ostensibly," her informant said, making significant movements with his eyebrows, "he's been paged back to the soap sets in London. But—" he made a meal of looking around in all directions, and Freddy caught herself doing the same thing "—*I* heard that he's fed up working with Lady Muck over there and her demands, and can't stick it any longer."

On the terrace Sadie was sunning herself and smilingly ordering the catering staff about.

"I see."

Well, she couldn't honestly blame Greg. Sadie was in top form with this show. Freddy had been relieved that none of their scenes crossed paths this morning, but Sadie had snuck in another of her cryptic digs over morning tea. She was starting to mess with Freddy's head, making her wonder if she'd accidentally shoplifted or buried a body, or whatever dirty little secret Sadie was gleefully stroking. Ten to one, that was the whole point—just pretend you know something, and the other person winds themselves into a nervous breakdown imagining what it could be.

Anyway, Greg hadn't been the most effectual member of the cast. It was lucky he'd done a bolt with enough time for a replacement to come in and integrate properly. Fin-

gers crossed for someone who didn't keep missing his comedic timing because he was looking into a hand mirror.

As she rounded the house, a door opened, and Griff
and Charlie's father almost knocked her over.

"Oh! Heavens. So sorry." James Ford steadied them
both, then smiled vaguely at her. His greying red hair was
a dishevelled halo around his head, and his hands were
covered with ink stains. "Isn't it a beautiful morning?"

"Very. Although I think it's going to rain later."

"Oh, well. The sun always comes back out eventually,
doesn't it?" James was hopping from one foot to another.
He winked at her and actually tapped one finger to the
side of his nose. "Exciting things are afoot."

He continued busily on his way, and Freddy was left
blinking after him, feeling just the teensiest bit like Alice
after an encounter with the Mad Hatter.

She didn't know where the genes had come from that
had created Griff, but they were obviously all recessive
in James Ford.

Near the busy main entrance to The Henry, Maya was
sitting at the base of a large oak tree, her knees drawn
up to her chest and her headphones on. Not wanting to
interrupt her recharging time, Freddy lifted a hand and
was going to walk around her, but Maya pushed the headphones back to hang around her neck and stood.

"Did you hear that Greg's out?"

"One of the crew just filled me in. I hope they cast a
decent understudy."

Maya pursed her lips. "I don't like gossip."

Freddy dropped her bag. "Of course not. But?"

"First of all—my flatmate worked with Sadie recently, and apparently she's in a relationship with Lionel Grimes."

One of the most influential men in the London entertainment industry, and the other main investor bankrolling this production.

"True love, I'm sure," Freddy said, and Maya snorted.

"Especially since Sadie's also been blatantly chasing Joe Ferren for months."

When it metaphorically rained, it freaking poured, didn't it?

"For God's sake. What *is* it about Ferren? Three minutes in his company and I'd like to shove him off the nearest bridge, but half the women in London go crackers over him."

"Sadie's doing her Queen of Hearts act with this show, manoeuvring players around the board where she wants them," Maya said, obliviously continuing Freddy's Alice metaphor. "With the proviso that this is totally hearsay, and I didn't mean to overhear it, Dylan Waitely told one of the makeup girls that Sadie drove Greg out of the show."

"So I've heard. I can't say I blame him. She's annoying as shit at the best of times, even when you're not having to live with her."

"No, I mean, she, like, *had* something on him." Maya looked uncomfortable. "Dylan suggested that she was threatening him. Blackmailing him out. It sounds a bit farfetched—"

"No, it doesn't," Freddy said grimly. "Why would she want Greg out?"

"They had a thing a few years back. He broke things off, and she's hated him ever since."

"God, you just about need a labelled chart to keep track of who's slept with whom in this business."

"And you know what Sadie's like. Everyone has to dance

to her tune. You just missed Maf's announcement—guess who's arriving tomorrow to be our new Mr. Knightley?"

Immediate, appalling comprehension. That fizzy-champagne feeling she'd had in her tummy since she'd kissed Griff dissipated completely. "They haven't cast *Ferren*?"

"Got it in one." Maya pushed her fringe out of her long-lashed eyes. "Is he really that bad? I've never met him, but I do like his films."

"Another overinflated male ego. When he can be arsed and his feelings are sufficiently soothed, he's a decent actor. That's where his positive qualities end."

So much for *The Austen Playbook* being a stand-in for a holiday. A couple of relaxing weeks in the country, her sainted arse.

Her leg started to itch hideously during the early afternoon and she lifted her skirt to check it wasn't getting infected. It looked okay, just a bit red. Freddy caught Dylan staring at where her knickers were almost visible under the raised hem, and hastily shoved it back down, glaring at him. He smiled at her breezily before he slipped back into character, gazing at Maya as she sailed past him in scripted umbrage, his hand flexing into a fist as if he wanted to reach out for her.

"Okay," Maf said at about two o'clock, from her seat on the stage. She pulled a pencil from behind her ear and made a notation on her copy of the script. "Freddy, you're done here for the day."

"What?" Freddy asked, startled, as Sadie smirked in the corner. "Have I done something wrong?"

"Several things." Maf quirked a brow at her. "But nothing irredeemable. We're moving on to the court-yard scenes, and Lydia's a done duck in that version.

Enjoy your temporary murder and spend some time this afternoon with your script. I want you off-book by the weekend. Nice job today."

Considering the source, that was a top accolade, and Sadie's face dropped into sullen lines.

"By the way," Maf added as Freddy hastily grabbed her stuff, ready to make a bolt before the director could change her mind, "check your email. We're sending out the media schedule. Thanks to our head investors, we're going to end the promo circuit with full pre-show TV coverage. *Sunset Britain* and *The Davenport Report* are going to do a first-ever joint broadcast, on both channels, live from the grounds here at Highbrook before the curtain rises. Start polishing up your interview skills."

Freddy suspected her own face now made Sadie look like a beam of sunshine.

"Think of the whopping big cheque from the TV broadcast," Charlie said encouragingly, after one look at Griff's face.

"The profit share that requires a high level of audience participation through the app, and therefore people not switching off before the first ad break." Griff shoved his hand through his hair, watching as his staff tried to take location shots of The Henry, while the TV lot were weaving in and out with their own cameras. The separate crews kept getting in each other's way and fronting off like opposing gangs in a western. The sensible solution would be to put his team on hold until *The Austen Playbook* wrapped, but the meeting with network investors that would give a final nod to moving his film into full production was in less than a fortnight. "After what I saw earlier, our cut could even out at about five quid. It was more like watching the crowds at Glastonbury than a professional rehearsal. Total chaos."

"What, even your darling?" Charlie asked, provocatively, and Griff cut him a sharp glance. "How is the fair Frederica today? Still in possession of her very sharp wits, or did you snog her out of them?"

"I know it's difficult, but if you can't act your age, at least aim to rise above adolescence." Griff took the sheaf of papers his assistant handed him and flipped over the first one to check the figures. They added up to the total of needing a serious cash injection, and soon. Money. Always sodding money.

"You didn't answer the question."

Without looking up from the sums, he said, "I haven't spoken to Freddy today. I saw her for about twenty seconds on the stage."

"And?"

"And she was doing a decent job in a sea of general shite."

"Anything to add to that?"

"Steve Lemmon has done the seemingly impossible and made Lydia Bennet an even more irritating character than the original." Griff tucked the papers under his arm. Charlie was grinning at him. "Mind your own business."

"It's so weird. I wouldn't have picked it in a million years. She's such a sunny wee rocket, and you're such a bad-tempered bastard most of the time. I'd have thought you'd want to strangle her."

He did. He also wanted his hands sliding along her skin, and her irrepressible smile against his cheek, and her insane hair on his pillow. His fingers curled into a fist.

"Well," Charlie murmured, "when you retreat to your lair and start giving her the freeze-out, let me know, will you? I do a good shoulder to cry on, and I think she's a love. And she does have a very nice arse. It's so...round."

His little brother had been trying to push him into losing his cool from the moment he'd learned to walk, talk, and get in Griff's way.

For the first time in the twenty-six years since Charlie had yelled his way into the world, it worked.

When Griff turned abruptly, Charlie actually took a step back and raised his hands. "Hey. I was kidding. Mostly." The humour faded from his countenance. "Really *not* just a quickie snog in the back room, then. Jesus. Are you actually—"

"I don't know." Which really encompassed his feelings about the entire situation. Griff cleared his face of expression. He wasn't sure what he'd just presented to Charlie, but suspected it fell under the heading of homicidal.

He didn't know what she was doing to him. The physical attraction had hit him hard and early, but it was the rest that was sinking into him, changing the rules of the game.

With every nonscripted word Freddy spoke, every spontaneous move she made, she became a real person, not the half-fictional character that all human beings were to most of the world around them. He crossed paths with people every day, he worked with them, occasionally he was physically intimate with them, but in almost every case, they were and would always be a construct. Comprised of the front they put on, the curated side of themselves that they allowed to be seen in public, and his own projection and judgment, what he expected them to be and therefore what he saw. There were few people he would ever really know, see as they were and not through a hundred different filters of perception.

When he touched Freddy, when he looked into her eyes, he felt as if he was starting to see *her*. It was sexual, it was physical, but it was also the tentative stirring of a connection that he couldn't explain, couldn't put into words even in his own mind.

It was just there. And while part of him wanted to push it aside, reject the unknown, a bigger part of him felt instinctively protective. Wanted to uncover it, shelter it, lay bare the big mystery.

As Freddy had pointed out, he was a researcher by nature.

Charlie shook his head. "You really fancy her."

"Yeah," Griff said wryly, in the biggest understatement of his life. "I really fancy her."

When he walked around to where he'd parked his car on the rear sweep of driveway, he wasn't surprised to find her there. She seemed to be everywhere, either in body or flitting about his mind when he was trying to clear through the backlog of work.

What he wasn't expecting was to find her halfway up a tree.

"What the hell are you doing?" He unlocked the car, dropped his things on the backseat, and went to the base of the trunk, automatically examining the branch she was standing on, to make sure she wasn't about to make a more violent descent than intended. It seemed solid enough. Her skirt had risen high on her soft, curvy thighs, revealing a flash of lace, and a man with better manners might have averted his eyes.

"The wind earlier." Her voice came through a thick sheaf of leaves. From the neck up, she was hidden in foliage. "It blew my empty crisps bag up here."

"You decided to shin up a tree like Jack and his

beanstalk because of a crisps packet?" Griff grabbed her ankle to steady her when her trainer slipped on a patch of moss. "You've got stitches in your leg, for God's sake. And half of these trees wouldn't even bear the weight of a cat." He didn't bother to keep the bite from his voice. It was exactly the sort of irrational behaviour his parents and Charlie would accept without question.

The universe seemed determined to surround him with people who could go off half-cocked at any moment, with zero warning. Trying to anticipate and thwart their impending disasters took a lot of energy he didn't have to spare.

"Well, I couldn't leave it up there. That's littering." Thanks to Freddy's tone, *he* somehow ended up feeling reprimanded, as if he'd just advocated in favour of dumping toxic waste. "My leg's fine," she said. "It's itchy so it must be healing. And your family might let you talk them like you're Mr. Brocklehurst, but I won't. You can be as rude to me as you like in print, but I'm not into it off the clock. Knock it off."

After some quiet scrabbling and rustling above his head, she dropped back to solid ground and turned. He was standing close enough to catch her if she slipped, and she ended up pressed lightly against his body. His hands seemed to move naturally to the curves of her hips. Her skin was warm though the thin fabric of her dress, the material sticking to her in the heat.

Her fingers curled lightly against his shirt. "Charlie said you were in Henrietta's office before half past six. I think you have a problem with delegation." She moved her hands, flattening her palms against his chest. Her doe-brown eyes moved over his face, then locked on his, studying him. An increasingly familiar teasing glint appeared. "Hello."

Griff felt a crease tuck into the side of his mouth as his lips curved. "Hello."

Freddy rubbed slightly with her fingertips, and he felt her touch as a jolt from chest to groin. One tiny stroke and his breath was deepening, becoming weightier. He'd always despised not feeling in control of his surroundings or his body's reactions; it was one of the reasons he loathed flying and couldn't stand being ill.

He could imagine Freddy's reaction if she knew she was being mentally compared to a head cold.

Reason, then, would suggest that he should release his hold on her, and break hers on him.

He didn't.

"I need some parameters," Freddy said, and he wondered where her erratic thought processes were skipping off to now. "Because fair warning, I'm a chronic toucher when I'm with someone I have any kind of close relationship with. I kiss and I cuddle, and if I'm sexually attracted, I touch a lot and often don't realise I'm doing it, so if you'd rather I keep my hands to myself, you can say so."

Griff looked at her without blinking. "Do you always leave yourself this wide open?"

"No. Professionally, I've rarely been as frank as I should be. With my family, I've just sat back and avoided rocking the boat. But I've always been transparent when it comes to my private life. I just need to apply the principle to other areas," she said, her mouth briefly turning down. "Ask people what they want, say what *you* want, and it's all out on the table. Everyone knows where they are."

You could also employ a bit of subtlety, and not lay yourself bare for the world to tear strips off. There were aspects of her philosophy on life that he found appalling. "There are more effective ways to get what you want."

"Oh God, the Slytherin." Freddy coughed delicately. "So, licence to snog?" She hesitated. "For now."

Officially the strangest conversation he'd ever had with a woman, but he couldn't say he hadn't had adequate warning that Freddy was likely to throw him unexpected curveballs.

She looked up at him with a definite challenge in her gaze, but also a flicker of vulnerability. Exactly to be expected if she was going to merrily open herself up to rejection from all angles, but it hit him right in that new, growing core of protectiveness.

He cupped her cheeks and bent his head. They were staring at one another from a distance so narrow that the slightest movement would bring his lips in contact with hers. "Touch away," he said. A heartbeat, a whisper of warm breath on his mouth. "For now."

She took him at his word and brought her bare arms around his neck, pulling him forward into a kiss. There was no slow, questioning build-up this time. It was like plunging headfirst into a hot spring, enveloping heat and a rush of physical sensation that was almost suffocating in its intensity.

Wrapping his hand into the frizzy tangle of curls at the back of her neck, Griff held her in the shelter of his arm and she curved her body, angling perfectly so they came together like a couple of puzzle pieces. She opened her mouth, stroking her tongue to his, and he grunted low in his chest as his body reacted with a speed he'd thought he'd aged out of. She smiled against his cheek, and did something with her hips, rotating them into his in a teasing shimmy.

"Fuck." They were still within plain sight of the house, and that reality was rapidly sliding away from him.

"That was my signature move from the *Chicago* segment of the royal charity performance. I believe you compared it in the *Post* to a millipede being electrocuted." Freddy's voice was husky in his ear, but her laugh seemed to hit him in the chest. "Ain't irony fun?"

Then their mouths were meeting again, kissing over and over, and his hands were shaping over her back, and lower. Charlie needed to keep his opinions and his eyes to his fucking self, but he wasn't wrong about certain… attributes. It *was* round, and he was painfully hard. His hands stroked her thighs, and Freddy took his wrists and moved them back to her waist without breaking the kiss. His hold drifted back after a few seconds, and she sighed against his lips.

"Fine," she mumbled. "Keep fondling my cellulite, then."

"What?" His mouth went to her neck, lightly sucking, his hands addicted to the feel of her warmth and softness, and she shivered, an abrupt jerk, and cuddled into him.

The sound of equipment crashing to the gravel around the front of the house, and muffled voices, brought them both out of the sexual fog.

"I wonder if that was our stuff breaking or yours." Freddy leaned back against the tree, smoothing her tumbled curls out of her face with trembling hands.

"If it follows the general trend of this summer, mine." Griff fastened his belt. He hadn't even felt her tug it open. Jesus. He released a short, hard breath.

"Gee, thanks," Freddy murmured, and he looked at her.

"Not you."

She looked back at him silently, and after a moment, he checked his watch. "I need to get going. Are you late back to rehearsal?"

"No, I've been given my marching orders for the rest of the day. Maf's running the scenes where Lydia's a cyanosed corpse. Lying silently on the floor doesn't require a lot of rehearsal."

"The silent bit might require *some* practice," Griff said blandly, and Freddy aimed a light kick at his boot.

"Dick," she said. "What are you doing this afternoon?"

"I have an appointment at Mallowren Manor, about fifty minutes' east."

"It sounds like something out of *Scooby-Doo*."

"It's the estate where your grandmother met my grandfather at a house party."

They turned back towards his car, Freddy collecting her bag from a low brick wall nearby and slinging it over her shoulder. "So, what's at Mallowren Manor now?"

He opened the car door and stood leaning against the roof. "An elderly lady by the unlikely name of Wanda Wanamaker, who remembers both of them and is keen to charge us thousands of pounds to film scenes on location there."

"Are you going to?"

"From recent aerial shots, it's even more of a crumbling wreck than Highbrook, but you never know. It might turn up something."

"That's always been my philosophy. I'm sure it'll be interesting." Freddy glanced at him, the car, and then, with studied care, examined her nails. "It sounds fascinating."

Reluctant amusement was a warm tug under his ribs. "Freddy," he said, with exaggerated politeness, "would you care to come for a drive in the country?"

"Why, thank you, Griff, I'd love to." Freddy grinned at him. She waited until the car was moving before she added, "You don't mind if I run my lines on the way, do you? I'm on a short deadline to ditch the script."

He was worryingly happy to have Freddy come along for the ride.

Significantly less keen on being trapped in an enclosed space with Lydia Bennet.

They got stuck behind a tractor on the country lanes, and Griff tapped his fingers impatiently on the wheel. One of the best parts about being home was the break from London traffic jams. He was suddenly remembering the downsides of rural life.

And God, Lydia was a whiner. There was also a downside to Freddy's knack of completely inhabiting a character.

They picked up speed on the main road, although they were forced to stop at a service station to stock up on "road trip supplies" for a journey of less than an hour in decent traffic flow. He would have gambled on their survival without sustenance, but Freddy claimed to suffer from low blood sugar. He was ninety-nine-percent certain that was a blatant lie, but it wasn't a bluff he was prepared to call, so she got her Maltesers.

As a silver lining, she took a break from the script to eat.

"Why did it only last two years?" Freddy asked, when the scenery was flashing past the windows and she had a sweet tucked into the pocket of her cheek like a squirrel.

"What?" Following the nasal instructions from his GPS app, he turned into a quieter road.

She swallowed her mouthful of chocolate. "The affair between Henrietta and Sir George. All Dad's ever said—to me or in print—is that it 'ran its course,' which sounds like code for 'no idea.' If their relationship was so intense and passionate that it inspired her into writing one of the masterpieces of twentieth-century drama, and him into building her one of the most epic gifts ever— why did it end?"

Exactly what he was hoping to find out.

"There was the small inconvenience of my grand-mother," he murmured.

"Yeah, but he was married when they started the af-fair, there were children in the equation on both sides, that was all an established fact. Morality, loyalty, it doesn't seem to have bothered them overmuch while the rela-tionship was in full swing. Do you really think they just had a sudden burst of conscience at the two-year mark and called the whole thing off?"

"More likely the sexual attraction wore off and it no longer seemed worth the trouble." He heard the cynicism as he spoke, and sensed Freddy glance at him sharply.

"It does happen," she agreed after a beat, and he found her response equally unpalatable.

Freddy played with the edges of her script. "As soon as the relationship ends in the biography, that's it, Sir George is wiped from the page. Did they really never see each other again after that?"

"For my grandmother's sake, we'd hope not." His grandmother had died long before his birth, and all his father seemed to recall of her was a scathing disposition and widespread dislike of humankind. She'd evidently preferred to live in London with her dogs, rather than at Highbrook with her husband, probably with justifica-tion. "However, from a cinematic point of view, it would make for a better story if forbidden love had continued to flourish."

Once more, Griff couldn't keep back the derision that laced the words. He had a lot of respect for Henrietta's talent but reservations about her character. And with the exception of commissioning The Henry, George had been financially savvy, but any desire to follow his grandfather's path in life ended there. You didn't fuck around on your wife.

He glanced at Freddy. "Have you spoken to your father yet?"

"No, but he'll be here next week."

"To resume his campaign to get you on the playbill for *The Velvet Room*?"

"Unless he's had a complete personality transplant in New York, yes."

"And he's not going to be too impressed to find you at Highbrook."

"It's the double whammy now. I'm doing the play he called a 'frivolous butchery of classic literature,' and apparently this is enemy territory."

"How do you feel about having your father as your manager?" He phrased the question carefully. It seemed like a terrible idea, both for professional and personal reasons, but he tried to keep his opinion out of his voice. Freddy had a tendency to deflate when the topic of Rupert arose, and he didn't enjoy being the cause of her extinguished spark.

Freddy fidgeted, crossing and uncrossing her legs. "It seemed natural when I was much younger. I thought we were so close back then. The stage was like a bond between us. Even before I got my first part, Dad would take me to a matinée every weekend. We'd go out for ice cream afterwards and pick our favourite and least favourite characters." Their eyes met as a flash of amusement came into hers. "Getting my theatre critic on. If you decide to drop your column in the *Post* for good once the film takes off, I could fill your boots." The fleeting humour retreated, and she shook her head. "It's not working anymore. He's driving my agent up the wall. He's already driven more than one off completely. But…" Her voice trailed off.

But her father had projected his own ambition on to her, she felt guilt and presumably love, and the weight of both, and Rupert was fucking well milking it.

Griff turned off onto the narrow road that should lead them to Mallowren Manor. "What day's the first audition for *The Velvet Room*?"

Freddy started playing with her hair. Once or twice he'd noticed her do it on stage, always in a production where she obviously wasn't enjoying herself. That alone was a telling sign. "Tuesday."

"Are you going to go?" he asked bluntly, and she made a little sound between a gulp and an unamused laugh.

"I change my mind on that every half hour." She glanced at him. "Can you imagine me as Marguerite?"

"You could do it." A sign appeared, warning of the approaching turnoff to the estate. "And if you audition there's a very good chance you'll get it."

"Because of the family connection?"

"Partly the family connection. Also your own audience pull, and the talent to make a reasonable job of it."

"Stop with all this effusive flattery, it's making me blush."

Griff swung the car into the long winding gravel driveway. "Freddy, you know what you want. And in every other aspect of life, I expect you don't hold back in going after it."

She continued looking out the window for a few beats, then turned and looked at him with an expression that was very slightly enigmatic. "True enough."

"In plain words, you want to take charge of your own career, which is totally natural and considerably overdue, and to choose the projects that you're passionate about."

"Correct." Freddy smoothed out the packet of Maltesers, pushing the empty end into her thigh. "But—family is really important to me, too. I want a dad." The words burst out. "Not just a manager. I want a dad. The kind of dad who falls asleep in front of the TV, and gives crap presents at Christmas, and hugs me when I come over for tea. A dad who's proud of me, no matter what I do. I don't care if that's just an ideal. I don't care if I've been watching too many sitcoms. That's what I want."

They'd reached the sweeping arc at the head of the drive, and he pulled the car to a crunching stop on the gravel. When he twisted in his seat, there was a wet sheen in her eyes, and he swore.

Unbuckling their seatbelts, he hooked his arm behind her head and brought her into him. Prior to this week, he'd rarely been inclined to offer physical comfort; nor had anyone wanted it from him. She burrowed into his neck, her curls tickling his chin.

He stroked her bare arm, listening to her breathing grow steadier, and that hitch of tears fade.

"You're surprisingly good at hugs," she murmured against his skin. "For someone who probably doesn't practice much."

Or ever.

"You should give Charlie one sometime." She angled

her head to look up at him, and produced a damp grin when she saw his expression. "I'm telling you, he'd love it."

"He'd have me sectioned."

He released her and got out to open her door for her. They stood in the driveway, looking up at Mallowren Manor in all its decrepit glory. There was a bite to the air now, and grey clouds were gathering in the sky above their heads. It seemed appropriately ominous. Griff winced. Freddy's wild imagination was rubbing off on him.

"Oh my." At his side, where she leaned against his shoulder, she cleared her throat. "Is it just me, or does it even *look*—"

"Like we should have driven here in the Mystery Machine."

Chapter Eight

The resemblance of Mallowren Manor to a haunted mansion in a children's cartoon was not exactly dispelled when Griff rang the bell. The front door creaked open to reveal a very old, wizened man in a morning suit. His nose was even beakier than Griff's, and there was more hair tufting out of his ears than growing out of his head.

"We have an appointment to see Ms. Wanamaker," Griff said, with admirable composure.

"I shall see if madam can receive you." The butler had a way of overpronouncing every syllable that made his hollow, ponderous voice sound like someone rhythmically beating on a bongo.

At least it was shaking Freddy out of her embarrassing fit of the glooms. Sniffing and snuffling her problems all over Griff—God. He was probably writing her off a typical melodramatic West Ender, and wondering what the hell he'd got himself into.

It had just…temporarily got on top of her.

He really *was* surprisingly good at the comforting thing, though.

"Please follow me to the drawing room." The butler pulled the door wider. It creaked again, exactly like a sound effect tape for a C-grade horror film.

As they followed him down a dark hallway, resplendent in Gothic architecture and nineteenth-century décor, Freddy pinched hard on the end of her nose and kept her head lowered. She was *not* going to disgrace herself or Griff, or offend that poor old man's dignity.

Griff felt the jerk of her shoulder, and with the butler's back turned, he briefly covered her mouth with his cool palm as a single strangled giggle bubbled out. "I'll make you wait in the car," he threatened under his breath.

She took a deep breath, inhaling the scent of his cologne from his shirt sleeve, and composed herself.

"Or hand you over to the ghoul in the dungeon," he added in that same low, even tone, and she had to turn and smother her face into his chest before she lost all control.

By the time the oblivious butler ushered them into a drawing room that reminded her of a set for *The Addams Family*, she'd managed to remember that she was an actor. She smiled politely at him. And Griff, whose habitual stone face obviously had practical uses, accepted the offer of tea and refreshments with perfect self-possession.

While they waited to see if Wanda Wanamaker would receive them, they sat on a firm brocade couch that smelled of mothballs. Freddy now had enormous expectations for the arrival of Mallowren's owner.

"What do you think?" she murmured, keeping an eye on the door. "Miss Havisham, Lady Bracknell, or Lady Catherine de Bourgh? I need to know how to play my part. Do I go snooty and plummy to keep the end up, or am I your plucky Girl Friday? I do a decent Cockney."

"We've been here for five minutes and I'm exhausted." Griff stood up as they heard the *tip tap* of approaching heels. "One word of Cockney and you're ghoul fodder."

Ms. Wanamaker didn't disappoint, but Freddy had

been wildly off the mark. The elderly lady swept into the room on teetering stilettos, a silk caftan billowing about her like a parachute. *Grande dames* in films *wished* they could make an entrance like that.

She had violently red hair, probably thinner in texture than it looked. It had been permed and hairsprayed and backcombed into a halo about her small head. Her eyes were as black as Griff's, set deep in her angular bone structure and darting about avidly, bright with anticipation.

"The young Master Ford," she said grandly, as if she were announcing Griff's entrance at a deb ball. Freddy had to hastily press her lips together again. "Welcome, dear boy. You don't look anything like your grandfather. Why did I think you were the spitting image?"

"You're probably thinking of my younger brother," Griff said drily, as he shook her hand. There were more diamonds on her knuckles than in the jewel vaults at Buckingham Palace. Freddy wondered why she didn't sell one to fix the windows. Maybe they were costume. With a hand at Freddy's elbow, he drew her forward. "This is Freddy Carlton."

Thinly plucked crimson eyebrows shot up, and Ms. Wanamaker turned all her attention on Freddy, peering at her narrowly. "Carlton," she said sharply. "It's been a long time since I heard those surnames in the same room. You're not a relation of Henrietta? Yes," she answered herself before Freddy could. "You are. You have her eyes. Very remarkable eyes, Henrietta had. Big and brown, like a sacrificial lamb. Entirely inapt in her case." Her grip was deceptively tight for her frail appearance, her rings digging into Freddy's hand as she continued to study her. Freddy had the feeling of being slowly dissected with a scalpel. "And I suspect in yours as well. I always could recognise trouble."

"Thanks for the disclaimer on that, Master Ford," Freddy said on a low breath as they took their seats again.

"Well, she's not wrong, is she?"

"Now." Wanda, as she'd insisted they call her, folded her wrinkled hands in her lap once the butler had poured their tea. Freddy's attempt to do it for him had resulted in a sharp comment from their hostess about young people who thought their elders and betters lost all control of their faculties the moment they passed fifty. "You're making a film about Henrietta and that maudlin piece of work she foisted onto the British public."

Griff's mouth twitched. "Some people consider it upbeat compared to Henrietta's earlier work."

"Henrietta's earlier drivel," Wanda corrected. "Imagine, perfectly good trees perishing for the sake of that tripe."

"You're not distantly related to the Fords, are you, Ms. Wanamaker?" Freddy asked, and the other woman gazed at her blankly.

"No, dear. Why?"

"I just thought I heard a family resemblance for a second," Freddy said innocently, and caught Griff's expressive sidelong look. "This is where Henrietta and George met?"

"Yes," Wanda said. "I did inadvertently set that in motion. I hosted a party here one weekend, and a friend of mine brought along Henrietta and several members of that crowd she ran about with. The deviants and has-beens of Marylebone."

"I think they preferred the term Wythburn Group." Griff's insertion was mild.

Wanda's opinion of that was a snort. "*Wythburn Group.* They weren't investment bankers. They were so-called 'creatives' of varying ability, mostly using the group as a cover for their drunken escapades and bedroom shenanigans. I'm sure your film will be an enormous success. From what I see on television these days, that's all people are interested in. Sex and selfishness and blethering on about nothing."

Griff was starting to look a tiny bit peeved. Freddy was suddenly having a great time.

Grinning, she said, "I hope Henrietta and her friends didn't turn your party into a rave?"

Honestly, she'd been born in the wrong era. The contemporary club scene had nothing on what her grandma had got up to after performances.

"Certainly not," Wanda said, offended. "Although Henrietta did her best to stay in the spotlight all weekend. That girl ruled the roost. Everyone jumped to her bidding." She nodded at Griff. "I'd invited your grandfather's poor sister to the party. Sad, moping creature. My mother used to feel sorry for her. Suggested we include her on the guest list. Her family seemed grateful. Unfortunately, they didn't foresee that she'd meet Henrietta and become infatuated with the idea of the stage."

Henrietta, the idol of all aspiring actors.

"And that pompous twit George drove his sister here, took one look at that attention-seeking vamp, and the rest was—" Wanda lifted her hands meaningfully.

"History," Freddy finished.

"Appalling," Wanda corrected, pinching her lips together.

"Do you remember Violet Ford well?" Freddy asked. She knew Griff was more concerned with Henrietta and

George's affair, but the memory of his great-aunt's face was very clear in her mind. Her eyes were haunting. If Freddy and Henrietta had deceptively innocent eyes, Violet's were a mirror of the most immense pain. Even in the fading photos, it was evident.

"Oh, yes." Wanda didn't sound especially interested. Nobody seemed to have been especially interested in Violet. "She was often here for weekends after that, while the army training camp was posted nearby. Her young man used to come here to see her. From what I remember of your great-grandparents," she said to Griff, "I doubt if they would have had him in the house, had they known about him."

Griff had been doing a silent watching job, letting the talk flow around him, so he could piece out any information that might be useful. It was a skill Freddy had never mastered. At that, however, he frowned. "Her young man?"

"The chap she met abroad. Antibes? Portugal?" Wanda dismissed the matter with a shrug. "He later joined the army and they met again down here that weekend, by chance. I can't imagine Henrietta and George knew much about it, then or later. They'd have tattled straight to her parents. Expected everyone to turn a blind eye to their own indiscretions, even though they flaunted it across the county by building that conceit of a theatre, but had no problem gossiping about their fellows. They looked good together, I thought, Violet and her young man." Her tone was surprisingly tolerant, after her sharp criticism of everyone in the tale. "Pity about his family. The letters they wrote were rather lovely."

She seemed to take in their blank expressions. "I read them," she said matter-of-factly. "Violet asked if she could hide them here for safekeeping, and I found them in the old nursery after she passed. That was tragic. But she was always a reckless driver. Her family took her car off her twice because of earlier prangs, and they should have held on to it."

Freddy looked at Griff. "Did you know she had an unsuitable boyfriend?"

"No. My father remembered there being concern about the people she'd be mixing with in the theatre, but no specific name ever came up in relation to her. It was George who produced the undesirable lover." There was a glint in Griff's eyes, and Freddy lifted her brows at him.

"These shameless Carlton actresses, exercising their wiles on the poor, unsuspecting Ford nobs."

"Why do I suspect from your tone that there was a silent 'k' on that last word?"

Wanda gave them a tour of the property, becoming chattier with each dusty room they passed through and each overgrown garden they politely admired. By the time they ended back up in the room that had once been a nursery, Freddy felt she could take a decent stab at following in her father's footsteps and writing the other woman's biography, in minute detail, down to her current favourite supper. Sturgeon and peas.

She finally left them alone with a pile of old boxes and mementos related to the Wythburn Group, after Griff managed to manoeuvre her out of the room.

"Christ," he muttered, pulling a photo album from one of the boxes. "Does that woman's mouth ever stop moving? I'm surprised the butler hasn't thrown her out of the turret."

"She's lonely." Freddy had realised it before they'd reached the first flower patch. "All her stories and anecdotes were about people who've been dead for decades. She didn't mention any friends now. No relatives who visit. And I can't imagine the butler is a great conversationalist. It takes him about a month and a half to finish enunciating one sentence. I feel very sorry for her. Her way with words probably puts people off." She bit back a small spike of amusement. "I think she's recognised a kindred spirit in you. Bet she sees the son she never had."

The tarnished trophy Griff was holding made a *bang* when he set it down too heavily on the table. "Thanks for that. As I wasn't going to have enough trouble sleeping after the nightmare of the porcelain cat collection."

"For a man who grew up in a house with blowjob carvings on the library mantel, you're very judgmental of other people's décor."

Ignoring that, he said cuttingly, "And credit me with a little finesse." She'd succeeded in cracking through the shield again. She preferred the pissy Griff to the blank-wall Griff. "There have been one or two occasions when I managed to handle people's never-ending bullshit in a tactful way."

"*Have* there? Well, make sure you give me a nudge when it happens. I wouldn't want to miss that." She blew the dust from a framed photo. "Look, Henrietta's in this one." She handed it to Griff, who gave it a cursory glance. "Wanda's perspective on Henrietta wasn't quite what I'm used to hearing."

"Yeah, well, no two people will ever see or remember someone in the same way. We're all the product of other people's biases." Griff reached around to grab a stack of cardboard folders, and Freddy caught her breath at just that brief, warm press of his body. "Wanda obviously didn't like Henrietta, so she remembers all her less attractive qualities. Your father was brought up to see his mother as a role model for success, so he painted an overly rosy picture of her, and passed that view along to you. Neither is the sum total of the woman, just—pieces of her, depending on where you're standing and what angle you're seeing."

"Dad is her son. He ought to know more about her than a woman who met her a few times at house parties."

"He ought to, I agree."

"Henrietta was very talented."

"Undeniably."

"And family loyalty isn't a bad thing. We all like to believe the best of the people we love."

"Except in your father's case, I suspect there's another angle involved. Money and influence. Thanks to Henrietta, Rupert has gained a lot of both, and I imagine he foresees continuing opportunities to build on that with you."

She stiffened at that voicing of her own private thoughts, and Griff shoved his hand through his hair. It was such an uncharacteristically ruffled gesture from the master of imperturbability that it cut short any defensive retort she might have made.

"My claim of possessing tact was obviously premature." His mouth compressed. "You're such a...fundamentally positive person," he said, as if he were accusing her of a mortal sin. "I seem to be the only person who can upset you without even trying."

Freddy considered that, playing with the brown tape on the box she was trying to open. "No," she said after a moment. "There are a handful of people in my life with the power to upset me. But most of them have been in my life since I was born. You do seem to be an…anomaly in my experience, but it's not because you can make me cry."

Rain was starting to patter against the windows, which were barred. In conjunction with the grey walls and iron fixtures, it wasn't the jolliest nursery Freddy had ever seen, but it seemed to suit the sudden tension between them.

When Griff said nothing, she took a deep breath and looked into the box she'd managed to wrestle open. It was full of old notebooks and playbills, which she would usually find interesting, but right now her mind was skittering over the surface of everything. She picked up a pile of letters, absently. They were neatly folded and tied together with a ribbon, which she undid. She could hear Griff's breathing over the light *pit pat* of raindrops.

Darling Vi… The writing was faded but unmistakably masculine—a hasty, barely legible scrawl.

Her eyes focusing, Freddy unfolded the top piece of paper and turned it over to read the signature.

All love, Billy.

"I think these are the letters Wanda mentioned." She felt as if she'd intruded on Violet's privacy just reading that simple, affectionate sign-off. "Your Great-Aunt Violet and her mystery man."

It seemed to take a long time for him to appear at her side. He reached down for a letter, turned it over, and smoothed it out.

"You can't *read* it," Freddy said, and it seemed to make him more comfortable to give her his usual impatience glance.

"You're the one who endorsed making Violet a fully fledged person rather than a symbol of pathetic pathos in the film. In order to depict a person with some degree of accuracy, I'm afraid you have to get into their personal space."

"I can't see you ever letting anyone push their way into yours," she muttered.

Without looking up and with no inflection in his voice, he said, "Can't you."

After a few seconds of fidgeting, nosiness won out over her conscience, and Freddy picked up another of the letters. This was one that Violet had written to Billy. Halfway down the page, she set the rest aside and felt for the small child-size chair nearby. It was built for baby backsides, but she perched gingerly, her fingers touching the ink as she read.

And as she read, the walls of the room seemed to shrink in around her.

When she reached the final words, she sat holding it. Then she reached for the next letter and started scanning through the sentences, her frown and an odd, buzzing sensation inside her growing. Pulling her phone from her bag, she found the website for her local library and searched through the catalogue until she found the classic texts in the e-docs section. She filtered to drama, and scrolled to the C section.

She opened the script for *The Velvet Room*.

"What's the matter?" There was a rough undertone in Griff's voice, and a hint of concern in his eyes, when she lifted her head some time later, jerked out of someone else's past. He had cast aside the letter he'd been reading, and was back to going through dry-looking files.

"What?"

"You've been in a daze for almost twenty minutes. What, are they rife with the Wythburn Group's so-called deviancy?"

"No." Freddy looked at him silently. Their recent conversation was repeating in her head like a faulty audio file. She hesitated, then, carefully, she refolded the letter she was holding and returned it to the pile. "They're beautiful."

She pushed up from the chair and came back to his side, running the stack of letters through her fingers. "There was obviously a long separation, and then they met again, and they wrote to each other for months. They wrote beautiful things."

Slowly, she handed them to him. "She must have been a remarkable person. To have inspired that. And everyone seems to have written her off as a nonentity."

Griff's eyes had narrowed. "That look isn't because you've gone sentimental over someone else's love letters."

She rallied enough to retort, "Some of us do find other people's stories genuinely affecting. Isn't that fortunate for you, Mr. Filmmaker."

"Freddy."

"He's Robert."

"What?"

Freddy nodded down at the letters in his hand. "Violet's Billy. He's Robert. In *The Velvet Room*. Billy's life, his family, the things he says in these letters. They've been ripped apart and laid bare in the play. And the romantic plotline in the script between Robert and Anna—it's Billy's relationship with Violet. From what's been written and the bits and pieces people have said, I don't think the replication is quite as explicit as the characterisation of Robert, but Anna is Violet."

Griff didn't question her judgment. He gave a silent whistle—and she didn't miss the gleam that appeared in his eyes. Mr. Filmmaker coming swiftly to the surface.

A new angle to play out onscreen, and one potentially rife with human interest possibilities. "Wanda wasn't wrong, then. Henrietta wasn't shy about making use of other people's secrets."

"No. I guess not," Freddy said, and Griff suddenly put down the letters and cupped her cheeks in his palms, stroking his thumbs over the delicate skin beneath her troubled eyes.

"Freddy. Whatever you discover about Henrietta, whatever your father's actions, whatever anyone else does, it doesn't have any reflection on you. And it doesn't have to have any effect on you unless you let it."

She placed her hands over his, tracing circles on the bones of his knuckles and down to his wrists. The light scattering of hairs there were pleasantly silky, a sensual prickle that she felt in her spine as well as her fingertips. Her touch was as gentle as his, but her words were serious. "That's not how life works, though. Is it? The decisions you make always affect other people. And if it's people you care about—"

A small crease carved out between his brows. He ran his thumb over the curve of her own eyebrow, but whatever he was going to say was lost when the door opened and the butler, whom nobody had bothered to introduce yet, cleared his throat. "I did knock," the man said, with heavy, ponderous disapproval. "I was unaware that you were…consorting."

Under his minatory gaze, Freddy felt as if they'd been caught with her bra unhooked and Griff's trousers around his ankles. She was uncharacteristically embarrassed.

She was yet to see Griff properly fazed by anything, but he'd recognised her discomfort. A new hardness came into the long lines of his body, and Freddy dropped her hands to rest on his chest, pressing there lightly to try to ward off the impending ice-blast.

"A small demonstration of how you handle people's bullshit in a tactful way," she suggested, turning her head away from their critical audience to murmur, and Griff's arm went around her waist.

His hand moved, warm on her back. "For future reference, are you in the habit of remembering everything a person says and using it against them?"

Even in the slightly dazed cloud she was in, even with his frequently irascible remarks, and the looming upsets on the horizon, he had become this little thread of constant light to fix upon. Freddy looked up at him through her lashes. "I never said we didn't have *anything* in common."

A hint of an answering smile, that disappeared when he looked with cool politeness at the butler. "We lost track of time. In fact—" he turned the arm still holding Freddy to check his watch "—I have a couple more questions to ask Ms. Wanamaker, and then if she'd allow me to borrow some of her belongings here for a short time, we should be getting back."

"You may find that difficult," the butler said without expression. "The Littlebourne Fog has descended."

Somehow, everything the man said gave Freddy the feeling that they ought to be enacting this scene in black-and-white, with a cello playing ominous notes in the background.

"What's that?" she asked. "It sounds like a war helicopter."

The butler was not amused. "The weather, miss. Several times a year, the fog comes from the direction of Littlebourne Copse and envelops this part of the country.

It's unusually thick, and driving conditions are always dangerous."

Griff stalked over to the barred window, bent to look out, and swore.

"Is it heavy?" Freddy asked.

"Like trying to see through a wall of smoke. There was no mention of fog on the weather forecast."

"Nobody ever predicts the Littlebourne Fog," the butler said, with a hint of smugness.

When he'd gone, Freddy said, "I hope we're not going to be delayed too long. Because I think the next scene in the film is where you go out to the car and come back to find me chained to a table in the basement."

"Acting in a murder mystery is not having a good effect on you. I am going out to the car, to check exactly how dangerous these driving conditions are. If you're not here when I come back, I'll know where to look."

As she listened to his footsteps going down the stairs, Freddy picked up Violet and Billy's letters again, and reread the passage that was sticking in her mind the most. She was reading something into it that wasn't there. It wasn't really possible.

Was it?

That worm of disquiet was still wriggling in her stomach.

She jumped when Griff came back into the room a few minutes later, his face more thunderous than the summer storm outside.

"We're going to be delayed longer than expected. The car won't start."

Freddy dragged her mind into the current problem. "Well—fix it, then."

"I'll just pull out my toolbox and magically do that, shall I?"

"You've been doing lots of DIY around the theatre."

"Does that automatically mean I know how to fix a car?"

Oh. She'd trodden on the masculine ego. "Is there a mechanic around here?" She anticipated his response. "They wouldn't be able to get here with the fog." She blew out a breath. "Okay, so—we'll have to wait it out?"

"Short of trying to walk home, and probably ending up in Birmingham, there don't seem to be many other options."

Freddy checked the time on her phone. It was already after five. "Wanda probably wants to have her dinner soon. That's a bit awkward." She frowned. There was a text from Akiko. A delicately worded, horror-struck message about Sabrina and Ferren. She'd have to send through the latest update on that situation soon, since it looked like Ferren was about to enter from stage left. Like the villain in panto.

Hiss, boo.

"What's wrong?" For someone she'd once thought had the sensitivity of a concrete block, Griff was rapidly becoming skilful at reading her.

"My older sister is back with her ex, and her friends aren't happy about it. Neither am I."

"What's wrong with him?"

"He's Joe Ferren," she said wryly, and Griff lifted his brows.

"Hasn't he—"

"Just signed on to render Mr. Knightley completely unattractive to me forever more? Yes. Are we going to be living under the same roof? Yes. Is this summer turning out to be nothing like what I expected? Yes again." Freddy shook her head. "Never mind. One problem at a time. I suppose we'd better go and update Wanda on—"

"I've already told her. She was hovering in the driveway and pounced the moment I appeared."

"James tells me that your car won't start." Wanda sailed into the room then, and hopefully didn't hear that derisive remark. For a second, Freddy had no idea who James was. She kept forgetting Griff's real name. "The local man at the garage is a conman, but he can *probably* fix it. You won't get him out here until the weather clears, though. Life comes to a standstill around here during the fog. You'll have to stay the night."

Griff did a much better job at concealing his reaction than Freddy did.

She wiped the dismay from her face when Wanda turned back in her direction.

"I hope you're not on one of these fad diets," Wanda said with a beady look at Freddy's midsection. Freddy immediately felt like she had a waistline the approximate circumference of the Gherkin. "Arthur is making a roast dinner."

Finally, their butler friend had a name, Freddy supposed, since the only other living body she'd seen in the house was the parrot in the conservatory. She doubted it was downstairs making gravy. "We're so sorry about this. But we don't want to put you out. We'll just—"

"If you were putting me out, I would say so," Wanda said, and she probably would. She even favoured them with a smile before she bustled out "to check there were enough Brussels sprouts."

"I think she's grateful for the company," Freddy said,

and Griff propped his hands on his waist and released an annoyed breath.

"Yes. If the conman at the garage finds that the spark plugs have mysteriously disappeared, we'll know what she was doing in the driveway."

Despite everything, Freddy couldn't help smiling. "I hope you weren't this rude to her face."

"She thinks I'm very personable." He returned her stare. "What?"

"Acting lessons with Freddy. I am now demonstrating 'boggled.' This is my boggled face."

By the time Arthur served them a very delicious roast dinner in a very scary dining room, the fog had grown even thicker.

"Did you call Highbrook?" Freddy asked, trying not to keep making eye contact with the stone gargoyle head on the wall.

Griff picked up his wineglass. "I spoke to Charlie. The weather's packed up at home, too. The Littlebourne Fog has got ambitious reach today."

"Pity you weren't getting some location shots. Very atmospheric."

"Indeed. Eventful things often happen during the fog. It descended the weekend of the house party in question," Wanda said through a mouthful of potato, and added unexpectedly, "Many a love affair has begun under cover of the Littlebourne Fog."

Freddy's eyes met Griff's over a vase of poorly looking roses. He quirked a brow, and she was horrified to feel herself blush. She hadn't blushed around men since she was sixteen, and now it was becoming a regular occurrence.

Fortunately, Griff chose to exercise some tact and

changed the subject, asking Wanda the question Freddy had been wondering all day. "Why did the affair between my grandfather and Henrietta Carlton end, do you know? Who broke it off?"

"George did," Wanda said, categorically. "Henrietta was furious about it. It was probably the first time she'd ever been thwarted in something she wanted."

"So she did still want him." Griff rubbed his thumb lightly along his jaw, and Freddy could practically hear the gears whirring as he slotted new information into place. "Why did he end it?"

"I imagine the infatuation wore off enough that he got a clear glimpse of her personality. It was a clean break, by all accounts, but not a pretty one. To my knowledge—" which Freddy guessed would be extensive on any matter of scandal "—neither of them ever spoke of the other publicly again."

"That suggests something quite dramatic," Freddy said, and her voice sounded odd. She laid down her fork. "Something must have gone badly wrong."

Griff's laser attention moved to her, with a flicker of a frown.

"Probably a small nonsense that got blown out of proportion." Wanda placed an entire yam in her mouth. "George was the unforgiving type, and Henrietta was good at stirring up trouble."

Yes.

Or taking advantage of it, perhaps.

As the old house creaked and the wind blew the fog closer around them, Freddy could feel the basic roots of her life starting to tear free.

Chapter Nine

Wanda kept them up talking trivialities and plying them with brandy until close to midnight. Freddy tried a few subtle yawns, and then Griff managed, in about thirty seconds, to pack the woman off to bed in her own house and make her think it was entirely her own idea.

"I find you a fairly frightening person sometimes," she said on the landing outside the little bedroom that poor, overworked Arthur had made up for her.

Griff stood leaning against the wall of the hallway, hands tucked into his pockets, somehow still immaculate even after several trips outside. Freddy had gone out for a total of three minutes to see what it was like and had come in with a ball of frizz on her head that made her look like a shocked poodle. He'd done a bad job of concealing his amusement.

"Likewise," he said now, and the word fell into an atmosphere that had been increasingly taut ever since the comment about romantic interludes in the fog. He regarded her with a deep, dark frown in his eyes before he turned on his heel and headed for his own room.

She was still awake an hour later, lying curled up on the hard mattress, listening to the rain on the roof. It

was a sound she usually loved, but that level of soothing wasn't going to cut it in her current frame of mind.

With a sigh, she turned over, her legs tangling in the
sheet, making her feel frustrated out of proportion with
the minor annoyance. She lay for another few minutes,
hands spread on her ribcage, trying to do the deep breaths
they preached about in the yoga class that Sabrina occasionally dragged her to in Notting Hill.

Yoga was not one of her more successful hobby attempts.
She was not Zen.

In a sudden rush of movement, she threw off the covers
and reached for the dress she'd left draped over a carved
chair. Best not wander about the house in her bra and
pants. If Wanda caught her, she'd probably be disapproving of anything less than a wimple when there was A
Man in the house. Two, counting Arthur, although it was
a push to imagine anyone seeing him as A Potential Se-
ducer. Poor bloke.

Her footsteps seemed to be very loud in the hallway,
but nothing was going to drown out the snoring that she
hoped wasn't coming from Griff's room. It was like a
deep-sea drill.

Opening the door to the nursery, she turned on a lamp,
then the main ceiling light when it was still too creepy
in the shadows. She padded over to the table where Griff
had neatly divided the materials he had conned out of
Wanda on loan and was planning to pack into the car
later this morning.

She reached for the stack of letters again, and then almost jumped out of her socks when Griff's voice came
from the doorway. "I know you commit to a part, but this
might be taking the Girl Friday act too far. It's almost
two in the morning."

He came up behind her, and she startled again when she felt the warmth of bare skin. "You don't have a shirt on." She snuck a peek to see if the nakedness continued past the waist. Sadly, not.

"Sorry, am I shocking your delicate sensibilities?" He reached over her shoulder and took the letters. "Why so interested?"

Freddy hesitated, started to speak, then stopped again.

What could she say? That based on some dusty old letters, she suspected something so *wrong* had been done years ago that the secret had been buried for decades? That her entire conception of her grandmother and their family history had just twisted? That she might have just uncovered what somebody had tried very hard to hide?

She wasn't bloody Miss Marple.

He'd think it was her pinball imagination again, bouncing from one outlandish idea to another.

She hoped it was.

Griff touched a light fingertip between her brows. "You don't have to tell me, if it disturbs you that much."

She brought her hands up, clasping his forearms. He was muscled and solid, and felt like a welcome wall of reassurance right now.

Amazing, how quickly things could change. In the space of a week, her entire perception on *everything* was shifting.

"I just...need to work something out."

"I know the feeling." His eyes had a lazy, smoky look, and his jaw had developed a thin layer of stubble.

"Were you asleep?" Freddy couldn't help tracing her fingers up to his biceps. The muscles there bunched under her touch, and a very jaguar-ish glint appeared in the dark depths of his expression.

A finger ran down her back, and she shivered. "For a few minutes." His voice was turning low and purr-y. "Until someone started trying to break through a block of cement with a chainsaw."

Freddy's giggle was more of a rasp as his hand slipped around her hip, pulling her pelvis into his. "I was worried that might be you."

Another snore rattled the rooftop.

"Careful. This constant padding of my ego, I'll become unbearable."

"*Become* unbearable?" Freddy returned sweetly, and went up on her tiptoes to wrap her arms about his neck. She kissed him very lightly, testing the waters, and drew back to look into his face.

There was a warmth there, and a heat, that was yards apart from the vibes he usually put out, but it was still him. Still the sarky, difficult man she'd first spoken to in a London pub, after he'd torn verbal strips off her and left her feeling exposed and vulnerable, sitting with the people who should know her better than anyone but had failed to see what he had realised from the distance of the theatre stalls. It was perverse that she liked him so much.

And fancied him like mad.

"Snogging licence still valid?" she teased, and he kissed her in answer, hard and deep and engulfing. Once more in this room, she experienced being thrust into a dream-state, where she couldn't breathe properly, but unlike the intense dismay of her dawning realisation earlier, this was all sensation and want.

He was pushed back a few steps, and her socked feet slipped on the wooden floorboards as she stumbled closer into him. His hand gripped high on her thigh, skin on skin, and her dress must be caught somewhere around her waist.

He momentarily froze. "Stitches."

"Other leg." Her lips on his neck, unable to stop nuzzling up to his earlobe, Freddy murmured, "What if the snoring stops?"

"People over in Littlebourne Copse can get some sleep?" Griff's mouth burned a trail of kisses down to her throat, and she struggled to catch her breath, in a painful gulp.

"I mean, Wanda could wake up and she'll be in here at the first squeak."

"Do you often squeak?" he asked, and she grinned against his mouth as it returned to hers.

"Given enough inspiration, I make all sorts of noises." She felt the faint laugh move in his chest, and cupped his neck between her palms, keeping his head away from her for a second. "And we can't forget about Arthur. And possibly the parrot, if he's never in a cage."

"Freddy." Griff straightened, his hands rubbing slightly at the curve of her waist. "If you want to stop, I'd prefer you stick to your candid philosophy where intimate relationships are concerned, and say so."

Her heartbeat was a hard, fast thump in her chest, echoing the pulse of arousal. His touch made her shake, and his scent seemed to be pressed into her own clothes and skin, and she loved kissing him so much that she'd happily abandon her hobby search just to suck on his tongue at every possible moment. Her mind was a jumble right now, her body was tired and stressed and in need of release, and she wanted sex.

It was something she'd always approached kind of lightly, before and after the fact.

She'd take a guy back to her flat after a first date if she was attracted and in the mood and it was all consensual, and with one notable exception, she'd never thought much about it afterwards.

But right now—it felt like a weighty decision. Momentous, even.

She twisted her arms down and pushed her fingers through his, holding on to his hands, holding on to the patient, flickering heat of his eyes.

"What's your bed like?" She brought one of his hands to her cheek and rubbed softly against his knuckles. His grip tightened on hers. "Because mine has a lot in common with that block of cement you mentioned."

Lowering his head, he touched his lips to hers. It was a whisper-soft kiss that somehow felt like a promise, and something in her belly tightened in response.

The fizzing sense of anticipation survived the short walk back to his room, but the journey shattered some of her less-fun coiling tension, since the snoring had increased in pitch, and they had to stop by her room to get a condom from her bag because he didn't have anything, and they kept stumbling into hideous sculptural works in the dark, and the whole thing started to feel like a vaudeville skit.

After Griff had hit his knee for the second time on a decorative gargoyle, he swore vividly into Freddy's hair and stopped copping a feel until they were safely in his bedroom, with the old-fashioned key turned securely in the lock.

The wave of shyness that washed over her was utterly out of character, and she took the fastest way of dispelling it by literally throwing herself back into his arms.

He caught her with a grunt, and they ended up on the bed a bit quicker than she'd intended.

"It is soft," she said with satisfaction as he rolled on top of her and pushed the mess of curls out of her eyes. A smile twitched at her lips as she lowered her chin and looked down between their bodies. "Well…not everything."

The brief flash of his grin did more gorgeous things to her overwhelmed emotions. His body was heavy and somehow both comforting and exciting, and his definitely-not-softness was a delicious friction. Freddy arched her hips, rubbing sinuously up into him, and he released a sharp hiss of breath against her collarbone.

They lay there, kissing, hands stroking and bodies moving in small, compulsive presses, until she grew impatient and reached down, and their fingers collided on the hem of her dress. He levered himself away so they could pull it up, and she struggled to yank it over her head.

Smoothing his palm up her stomach—which was as far from flat as it had ever been thanks to her stress-eating over *The Velvet Room* audition lately, and Griff obviously couldn't care less—he kissed her again, his tongue a silky stroke against hers, retreating and then returning, teasing her. He was more playful in bed than she'd expected, and she loved it.

She couldn't stop touching him. His torso was long and his body was mostly stretches of taut muscle, but not in a super pumped-up gym way. Parts of him were softer, and areas of skin roughed into scars and the odd stretch mark, and he was real and here and *him*.

He unclipped her bra and pushed it away, and closed a warm mouth over her left nipple. Freddy shut her eyes and threaded her fingers through his hair. Her breasts weren't particularly sensitive, so having them played with never did a lot for her sexually, but the feel of his breath and the brush of his hair against her skin was lovely.

With one hand still cupping her, his thumb circling her nipple, he trailed his mouth back to her neck and nuzzled at the thin skin beneath her ear, then caught it in a gentle suckle. Her breath caught and started to quicken, and he raised his head a little, then returned his attention to the curve there, kissing and stroking. Fast learner.

Turning her head to the side to let the man work, Freddy reached down and undid the button of his trousers. Fortunately, he wasn't so meticulous that he'd bothered with a belt. She couldn't be doing with buckles right now. She pressed her hand against his erection through the fabric, and he made a muffled sound into her neck. Carefully lowering the zipper, she pushed elastic aside and wrapped her fingers around him. His whole body went tense, and his breathing was rough as he rested his cheek against her shoulder, temporarily losing focus on anything but the movement of her hand.

She stroked him once, lightly, and then firmer, testing to see what he liked. When he grunted again and turned her face to catch her mouth in a rough kiss, she thought she had an idea.

While she touched him, she slipped her free hand into her own briefs—unfortunately they were her favourite pair with the holes and tattered lace but what could you do—and started catching herself up. She broke the kiss when her head went back reflexively and hit into the mattress, and he muttered another profanity when he realised what she was doing.

That curse, however, sounded more like a heartfelt thank-you to the universe.

The leash on his control seemed to snap without warning and suddenly one of his hands was joining hers. Whatever ingenious movements he was making with his fingers, she'd take notes if her brain hadn't just shot off into orbit somewhere. She couldn't keep up her own touch, either on him or herself, and ended up just grasping on to his neck and holding on.

With a hard push of a wet, openmouthed kiss, he sat up briefly to remove the rest of their clothing—although she realised when she closed her legs about his waist that he'd forgotten her socks.

Sometimes sex was great and sometimes it was so shite it was a waste of a condom, but she was usually focused on only the mechanics and trying to bring and wring as much pleasure as possible. This was an entirely different experience.

That first thrust was the moment when she always had a jolt of hyperawareness, the objective curiousness of having part of another person inside her body. And then back to, does it feel good, are we having a good time, hopefully yes, and yay, sex.

From the first moment with Griff, it was so intensely personal. No weirdness, no awkwardness, just—right.

It was messy, it was sweaty, and a little rough towards the end—and she was totally aware that he wasn't just a person in bed with her. It was Griff she was snogging and gripping on to, Griff who was inside her, murmuring into her ear.

It was more than physical; it was a building and layering of a bond that went much deeper than that.

During the middle part, when it was slower and more

quietly sensual, and his hands were cupping her head, his kisses were deep and searching, he pulled back just for a moment to look into her eyes. She saw, in the depths of his, the same sense of wonder and trepidation that she was feeling.

Then the pulse, the *drive*, was becoming too intense for slowness, and he asked in a low rasp if she wanted to go on top, and she did squeak. With horror.

"God, no. I'm so out of condition right now I have the hip flexors of a ninety-year-old. I don't know how you're doing it."

She got her first proper laugh from him in bed, in the midst of very intense sex, and somehow that seemed right, too.

In the end, she did need more to get there, and he turned her under him, and supported her unfit hips with a strong arm while he drove into her from behind.

"Too rough?" His voice, barely comprehensible now, into her hair.

"No." Just a gasp, as she lowered her head, and gripped onto his hand where his spread fingers were braced on the mattress, holding up his weight. She reached down to touch herself again, and felt the wet slide of him, and her muscles clenched down hard and then released into seemingly endless pulsing pleasure.

She was barely aware of him tensing violently against her however long it was later, his grip on her almost painful, or how heavy he was when they both collapsed down into the mattress.

Her heart was pounding so hard it couldn't be healthy. Freddy turned her cheek against the quilt, feeling the scrape of the cotton stitches. She closed her eyes and felt back for his hand, and his fingers interlocked tightly with hers.

Eventually, he rolled over and left the bed and the room for a minute. When he came back, the mattress dipped as she felt him behind her and around her, his arm folding over her and their hands finding each other again. She could smell sweat and hear his breathing, still slowing back to normal.

The most overwhelming sense of wellbeing and safety washed over her. Not only orgasm aftermath, but *secure*. She couldn't find words beyond that.

"I think you may have underestimated yourself when you implied you weren't good at anything but acting." Griff's voice was a lazy murmur against her shoulder. "Drastically."

She barely had the energy to laugh. "Not really a talent I can write on the back of my headshot."

He kissed her neck, and she still shivered, even after all that. She turned over in his hold and her nose brushed against his. "Should I go back to my room?"

His arm flexed her closer, seemingly on reflex. "Why?"

"Possible hazard of butlers and alarming old ladies stalking the halls at dawn." She studied his face as she spread her fingers against his chest. "And a preference for sleeping alone?"

"You?" He was stroking light patterns on her back.

"Surprising nobody, I'm all for the postcoital cuddling." Delicious goose bumps broke out on her skin when his hand reached the dip at the base of her spine. "But I suspect you're not."

"Not usually. But nothing else about tonight is within my usual experience."

"But…" Her voice trailed off when he touched a knuckle to her cheek. She looked at him for a heartbeat longer, then closed her eyes again and curled into him, and felt his head come to rest against hers.

In the dark, the outside world started to exist again, and the rain continued to patter on the windows, and all the lurking problems beyond the enclosed intimacy and security of the room tried to sneak through the crack under the door and back into her mind.

She tightened her hand on Griff's.

It wasn't a censorious butler or disapproving hostess who woke them just before eight, but an unexpectedly conscientious little brother.

Charlie's current car, which looked and sounded like it should be on a Formula One track, roared into the courtyard, and broke Griff abruptly back into consciousness and momentary disorientation. He'd dropped into complete oblivion after the most intensely intimate experience of his life.

Lifting his head from the tangle of Freddy's hair, he breathed in her scent—coconut—and tensed, trying to work out what—

Another rev of a familiar engine before it cut off and a car door slammed, and he finally got his brain working. Slipping his hand down her arm in a brief caress, he disentangled their legs and rolled out of bed, striding naked to the window and looking out.

His brother was standing by the vehicle that he treated like an extortionately expensive child, looking up at the manor. Even from a distance, Griff could see the incredulity and growing amusement as Charlie took in the full Gothic splendour.

Retrieving his trousers from the floor, where Freddy had thrown them, he dressed quickly. His shirt had been removed last night before he'd gone to investigate the light footsteps creeping about the hallways, so it was in decent shape, but from the waist down he looked like he'd been dragged backwards through a bush.

Coming to sit on the edge of the bed, he looked down at where Freddy was still sleeping soundly, her hair a disaster, one hand tucked under her chin.

Wrinkled clothing was a small price to pay.

Although he could just imagine the forthcoming commentary from Charlie.

"Freddy." He ran his fingers down her cheek and then her arm, and she briefly stirred, made a small sound, and promptly went back to sleep. Griff pushed back a handful of her curls and bent to kiss her ear. "Darling." The endearment, which he'd never used in his life, slipped out with surprising ease, a low murmur straight into her ear.

Her lashes parted and she looked at him with no recognition, then a smile brightened her sleepy gaze, and he felt himself returning it.

"Good morning." She yawned and reached an arm up to hook around his neck, and he couldn't resist dropping a brief kiss on her mouth. "Why're you dressed already?" The words slurred together through another yawn.

"It's almost eight, and Charlie's just driven into the courtyard."

A single blink, and then it was like she'd been plugged in and turned on. She shot out of bed, almost shoving him aside. Folding his arms, he leaned against the tall wooden bedpost and admired the view as Freddy bent over to ferret out her dress and lingerie from under a pile of pillows.

"Oh my God. My call-time is nine-thirty today. And if Charlie's here, Wanda and Arthur are probably up. I hope they didn't hear us last night." Orgasms seemed to have an unusual effect on her. Teasing and flirtation had been replaced by flapping hands and words. "You're surprisingly loud in bed."

"*I'm* surprisingly loud? The British infantry regiments could have staged the Trooping of the Colour in the courtyard last night and you wouldn't have known a thing about it." Every muscle in Griff's body felt lax and satisfied, and it was difficult to summon the energy to care about the shite waiting back at Highbrook. No doubt the pleasant sense of lethargy had a time limit, however, and the clock was counting down. He gave it an hour at most before the stresses descended like yesterday's fog.

Considering that Charlie had driven out here at an hour of the morning when he was usually still snoring in bed, possibly about three minutes.

Freddy winced. "Do you think people *did* hear us?"

"Not even your promised squeaks could have drowned out Wanda's snoring." Griff lifted his phone from the bedside table and slipped it into his pocket. "But as it now seems to have stopped, and I doubt Charlie drove out here for a scenic trip, we'd better go down."

Freddy looked as rumpled as he did when they came out into the courtyard. Charlie was in animated conversation with Wanda, who was wearing a safari suit today and looked like an extra from a 1940s film. She was a good example of not judging people's character by their appearance, because based on her manner, most costume departments would put her in black bombazine with a chatelaine at her belt.

Although she was almost giggling under the full battery of Charlie's charm act. "Your dear brother is here to fix your car," she said to Griff. "Isn't that kind? I hope you both slept well. You obviously didn't see the garment steamer in your wardrobe."

Charlie, standing with one hip propped against his car, focused properly on Griff at that, examining him from unshaven jaw to creased legs. His intrigued gaze moved to Freddy's wrinkled dress. A small smile started to play about his mouth, and Griff looked at him warningly.

"You got up before seven in the morning to do an AA job for us?"

"From what you said, the local garage wasn't likely to do a speed fix, and our leading lady here is due on The Henry stage shortly." Charlie turned the full force of his smile on Freddy, and Griff was caught off guard by the instinctive reaction that hit him in the gut.

If he'd never been very tactile, he'd sure as hell never been possessive, but seeing Charlie flirt with Freddy shot tension through his whole body. Which was both ridiculous and bloody ungrateful, when Charlie was doing him a favour. Albeit suspiciously.

It was the similarities between them, he thought grimly, as Freddy returned Charlie's smile with breezy affection. They clearly recognised a sympathetic bond in one another. And they were a much more obvious pair. Had anyone placed a bet on Freddy becoming involved with either him or Charlie, his own odds would be comparable to a fairground pony winning the Grand National.

"You're an actress?" Wanda looked narrowly at Freddy. Her lips pursed. "I should have guessed. I suppose you have grand plans to write the next great dramatic showpiece, too. Let's hope you don't follow *too* closely in your grandmother's footsteps."

"No." That disquiet he'd noticed yesterday returned to Freddy's face. "Let's hope not."

Charlie rolled up his sleeves, retrieved a toolbox from his own car, and popped open the bonnet of Griff's. Within seconds, he was whistling. After a few notes, Griff recognised the tune as an old song about taking a girl away for a dirty weekend.

Rolling his eyes, he joined Charlie at the engine. His brother's hands were moving dexterously and surely. "Let's hear the rest of it, then."

Charlie didn't beat any further about the bush. Straightening, he wiped his hands on a grease-stained rag. "I thought you'd want to get back to Highbrook as quickly as possible."

The last of Griff's inner contentment vanished into the ether. "What's gone wrong with the theatre?"

Freddy had somehow disposed of Wanda, and she came to stand by his side. Her fingers lightly touched his elbow and he glanced down at her.

As Griff moved his thumb over her knuckles, Charlie's expression seemed to momentarily soften, but his apprehension swept straight back in.

"It's not the theatre," he said. "It's Mum and Dad."

Chapter Ten

The best sex of her life should have led to a truly epic after-glow. But even an orgasm that had blown Freddy's nerve-endings into orbit somewhere around Saturn couldn't compete with the sense of impending disaster as they neared Highbrook.

With an anxious eye on the car clock, she made an aborted attempt at running through the scenes on the schedule for today, but Griff had gone into frosty au-tomaton mode at the wheel and she didn't think he'd ap-preciate having Lydia Bennet foisted on him again. She was an acquired taste at the best of times.

"Your parents *are* all right?" she asked again into the silence. "They haven't had an accident or anything?"

"By the sounds of it, nothing has happened *to* them." The words had more edges than a Rubik's Cube. "It's what they've done that's the problem."

What they'd done became apparent the moment that Griff's car, purring like a kitten after Charlie's adept ministrations, turned into the Highbrook driveway, and Freddy saw the crane.

"Holy crap," she said faintly, when she stepped out onto the gravel. She closed the car door without looking away from the scene unfolding on the east lawn.

To the obvious dismay of bystanders from both *The Austen Playbook* crew and Griff's own production team, a whole new set of builders and some very heavy-duty machinery had arrived to join the party. They were in the beginning stages of turning a section of the Highbrook grounds into a miniature village, complete with a child-size, rideable train track.

"Village" was an understatement. Miniature city, judging by the dimensions being roped off. It wasn't *quite* Legoland, but it would make a lot of the fantasy creations that sprang up around London at Christmastime look like pound-store toy sets.

Griff's face set into dark lines as he located his parents in the crowd. He touched his hand to the base of Freddy's spine, then strode towards them. When he passed what appeared to be the structural framework of a castle, Freddy tilted her head. There was something— Oh, wow. *Not* just a village. If she was correctly identifying some of those smaller structures, what was coming together was a child-sized replica of Anathorn, the hidden city from the Allegra Hawthorne books.

Honestly, in other circumstances, she'd want to go and have an enchanted peek at the plans, but the visual reminder of the approaching audition for *Anathorn* the musical kicked nerves into her gut, and she had a rehearsal to get to. If she didn't pull off this performance in *The Austen Playbook* and impress Fiona Gallagher, there would be no future path leading to Anathorn for her, and with everything that had happened during the brief visit to Mallowren, it was going to be hard enough to concentrate as it was.

In any case, she didn't think ooh-ing and ahh-ing over the miniatures would go down well. It wasn't difficult to pick up on the vibes from Griff and Charlie. After the conversation she'd overheard between Griff and his dreamily extravagant mother, she could guess the reason for the gathering thunderclouds.

And he'd been so beautifully relaxed this morning. For about ten minutes.

"Jesus God." Charlie spoke over her shoulder. "They've actually hired a crane."

"I think it's safe to assume none of this comes cheap?"

"Even when they started with single, simple doll-houses, their cost of materials was twice the price they charged for the work. And they give away a lot to kids in need and good causes. Admirable, obviously, but…" Charlie shook his head.

"Did Griff really have to mortgage his flat once to pay for repairs on the house?" Freddy asked in a low voice, and wasn't expecting Charlie's sudden sharp turn.

"What?"

"Uh." She tucked a curl behind her ear. The nervous tic again. "I sort of overheard… I may have got it wrong."

"No." Charlie looked at the rigid lines of his brother's back as Griff cut an uncompromising path through the crowds of onlookers. All of a sudden, he looked older, that air of the Eton-and-Oxford playboy disappearing behind a grave exterior. Actually, for the first time there was a family resemblance to Griff. "Knowing Griff, I doubt if you did. He's been sliding us all out of scrapes since he was old enough to walk. The first time I can remember Mum and Dad blowing the annual budget on whatever hobby they had at the time, I was at school, and there was no ready money to pay the next term's fees. Griff emptied his savings account, talked his way into one of the most exclusive clubs in the financial district, and managed to get stock advice from the most powerful broker in London. Made enough to keep me at school for six more years. He was only a kid himself, just started at uni."

Silently, Freddy watched Griff's restrained, frustrated gestures as he spoke to his parents.

"He still invests in stocks," Charlie said. "And apparently pays for a lot more than I'd thought." When she tore her eyes from Griff, Charlie's mouth looked tight. "But it's never enough. You can only invest what you have, and the place needs a whacking big cash injection, or it's going to end up the property of the bank or some wealthy overseas tycoon, who'll use it as a summer pad a few days a year." He lifted a shoulder. "I don't know. Maybe it would be better if we just sold it."

Given Griff's general lack of sentimentality, in some ways it was surprising that the family *hadn't* just sold up. The fact that they were fighting so hard spoke volumes.

"You don't really feel that way, do you?" Freddy asked, and he shook his head once.

"No. No matter where I go, or what I do, it's home, you know? I want to think it'll still be here to come back to if I need it." His smile was a shadow of his usual cockiness. "Even when I'm a dashing old bachelor of eighty with my vintage cars and my adoring elderly girlfriends." The teasing faded. "Not that I'm doing much to keep the place in the family. One ultimately shite idea after another. I read commerce at uni because I thought, hey, look what Griff did with just a few stocks and shares. Imagine what I could do." His laugh was brief and intense with self-derision. "Bugger all, it turns out. I don't have a business brain. I'm pretty sure Griff thinks I don't have a brain at all. No wonder he thinks I'm useless."

"I'm sure that's not true."

Charlie lifted a gently mocking brow. "And I'm sure you're not biased at all."

"Oh, I am," she admitted readily. "I seem to have gone in head-first over your big brother."

"Surprising." Charlie flashed a genuine half-grin. "But I ship it."

"You give a good impression of being—" What had Griff called it? Unsquashable? "—very resilient."

"I'm an optimist and I like to have fun. I'm not a wind-up toy that just bounces around spouting happy phrases. Despite what Griff thinks, I do worry."

If he weren't several years older and delightfully ginger, she'd think she'd found a long-lost twin brother.

"I still say you're wrong about what Griff thinks, and you're bloody well not useless. I think you're just in the wrong job. Why didn't you apprentice with a mechanic or a car manufacturer? Hell, why don't you *sell* cars? Griff might have the knack of getting people to do what he wants while being incredibly rude to them, but let's face it, mate. You're the one with the sales patter."

"I'd have liked to be a mechanic." Charlie looked over his family again. "Not quite as lucrative as finance."

Since he didn't seem to be doing any great shakes in finance anyway, he might as well just do what he was good at and what made him happy, instead of sacrificing himself trying to follow in someone else's footsteps.

Hypocrisy, thy name is Freddy.

That feeling in her stomach again, like something turning over. She swallowed.

As Charlie headed over to join Griff in the stand-off with his parents, she looked at her watch, torn. She wanted to follow and offer silent support, whether it was welcome or not, but she was due at The Henry in four minutes, and none of her colleagues looked to be in a good mood.

With the amount of noise the crane was making as it set the roof on a scaled-down stone barracks, which appeared to have real gold detailing on the gates, she wasn't surprised. Rehearsals weren't going well enough for tolerance over yet more construction noise.

With a last glance back, she jogged in the opposite direction, to the path that wound through the trees to the theatre. The TV crew were doing recce outside the front entrance of The Henry, muttering about the chaos at the main house.

Inside, Maya, Sadie, and several of the other principals were already onstage, running through scene variations for the second act. Freddy did her best to smooth her crumpled dress and hoped nobody remembered she'd been wearing it yesterday. There wouldn't be time to change until the morning tea break.

Sadie was delivering one of Emma Woodhouse's monologues with her usual ease of performance, but she looked over at where Freddy stood, and her gaze immediately dropped to her clothing. Naturally, the human spyglass over there would notice every avenue of possible gossip.

It was a futile hope, given that Sadie ran a personal intelligence service that outshone MI5, but Freddy would prefer she didn't realise there was anything happening with Griff. He would give absolutely zero shits what Sadie Foster said about him—and he'd probably done her one better for snide remarks in reviews over the years—but Freddy felt irrationally protective of him. Of them.

"Fancy seeing you here, darling." A male voice spoke into her ear, and for a second an echo of memory awoke in Freddy's mind, of her sleepy rousing this morning and Griff's deeper voice murmuring that same endearment, a warm shiver on her skin.

Immediate reality intruded on dreamy recollection. She'd know that Mancunian accent anywhere. She turned. "Ferren."

She didn't bother with a polite tone. She was tired and hungry, and as much as she was enjoying playing Lydia, she'd rather still be asleep in Griff's arms right now, oblivious to everything unfolding in the waking world. And Ferren had caused enough heartache in their family for a lifetime.

Despite the drawled familiarity of his greeting, there was nothing actually lecherous in it. Ferren had many faults, but he wasn't another Dylan. He exploited his sex appeal for his career, like most people in this industry, but he didn't try to crack on with every woman he met. It was almost unfortunate—if he'd been just another fuckboy, Sabrina would have kicked him to the curb ages ago.

"If it isn't little Frederica." Typically unbothered by her attitude, he stretched in a casual, sensual motion. "How are you, pet?"

"Not happy you're here, actually." She lowered her voice in the hope he'd follow suit. People were casting them curious glances, and Sadie was watching them. Maf snapped something and Sadie returned to character, but Freddy hadn't missed that temporary transformation of Emma Woodhouse from meddling snobbery to cat-like malevolence. "Definitely not happy that you're back in Sabrina's life, or really within ten thousand miles of England, and I can't imagine you're all that stoked to be working with me, either."

Ferren ran a hand over his head. Like Sabrina, he was

a natural redhead, and the two of them were a fiery, temperamental cliché. Sabrina, however, didn't bring her quick temper into the workplace and go flying off the rails at the most minor setback.

Freddy could not, in any way, see him as an appropriate casting for Knightley, but he did have marketing pull and it was all about the pounds and pence. He was a risky proposition to have in a live broadcast. She hoped the management team knew what they were doing.

"I did have an inkling you were going to be difficult." Ferren dug in his pocket and slipped a cigarette between his lips. "But I found myself with an unexpected window in my schedule and to be brutally frank, I could do with the cash."

"Another bad weekend in Monte Carlo, was it? What happened to steering clear of the roulette wheel?"

"Lady Luck is typical of your sex. Fickle. But so very—" he winked at her, but again there was no real emotion behind the gesture; it was just a practiced routine, part of his image "—seductive."

Freddy looked back at him, unimpressed, and a small smile replaced the slick lady's man act.

"You never did let me get away with shit, did you, Fred? Even when you were just a kid, you didn't hold back when you thought I was being a dick."

"I notice it never stopped you."

"What can I say? I'm my own worst enemy."

Maf called his name from the stage, and he booped the end of Freddy's nose and sauntered off to answer the summons.

Freddy shook her head. That was the danger of Ferren. Every so often, he gave the impression of being disarmingly candid—and it went straight out the window the moment life got a little difficult, or a little dull, or someone landed a direct hit on his ego.

The scene change was called and she went to take up her position on the stage. When she reached the head of the stairs and passed under the artificial glow of the lights, Sadie grabbed her arm.

"A little word of advice, *Frederica*," she said sweetly. "I know it's your habit to be *friendly* during productions, but keep your calculating little eyes on that bastard Ford-Griffin, and steer clear of Ferren."

Had she just been called "calculating" by *Sadie Foster*? It was like being accused of eccentricity by Willy Wonka. Bloody cheek. "I would be quite happy to keep an entire continent between me and Ferren, but I think you'll find I'm not the Carlton sister who's in your way."

"Sabrina never holds his attention for long," Sadie said dismissively, and narrowly avoided having one of her own fake nails jammed into a vital artery.

Sadie could taunt Freddy as much as she liked. Just try coming after her sister.

"And have you managed to hold his attention at all?" She dropped to Sadie's own purring level for once, and was rewarded with another flash of deep malice.

Sadie tightened her grip on Freddy's wrist and pulled her closer. "Stay out of my path, or you might find I become a bit chattier around here. You never know what things can slip off your tongue."

Sadie returned to her place and resumed her scenes with Maya, who cast a concerned glance in Freddy's direction. Rubbing her arm, where the imprints of Sadie's talons were light pink crescents, Freddy made a little bit of worry space in her increasingly crowded brain to wonder again what Sadie thought she had on her.

She phoned it in during the morning rehearsal. Her mind seemed to be on a hundred things that had nothing to do with the play, and it didn't go unnoticed.

"You've got one hour and then I want you back here for the ballroom scene," Maf said when most of the cast broke to rehydrate and raid the biscuit table. "Correction. I want *Lydia* back here. You can leave Freddy in your room for the rest of the day." Briefly, she looked Freddy up and down. "A different outfit mightn't go amiss either. Long night, obviously."

Rubbing a hand over her forehead, Freddy collected her bag from the stands, intending to go straight to her room and change her dress, but in the hallway she hesitated. Then she switched directions and followed the winding corridor until the walls started to peel and the smell of dust appeared, and she left the tarted-up public part of the theatre behind.

Henrietta's office was empty, but Griff's research materials were still stacked neatly on the infamous desk where *The Velvet Room* had been born. Freddy's footsteps sounded loud in the quiet as she walked over and picked up the portrait photograph of Violet Ford. Brushing the residual dust from the surface, she looked down into those intense eyes.

She'd hoped that in the light of day, her wild thoughts yesterday would just seem ridiculous. Instead, the more she turned it over in her mind—the letters, *The Velvet Room*, Violet, Henrietta, Billy, and George—words and phrases connected like lines in a join-the-dots picture... and an ugly image was taking shape.

Violet's penetrating gaze suddenly seemed accusatory.

You're Henrietta's granddaughter. And you know. You know, you know—

A muffled voice cut through Freddy's spiralling anxiety, coming from outside in the hallway. "I think I saw her go this way, sir."

Footsteps resounded through the floorboards, and the door opened.

She looked up and stared at the man who stood there. His greying hair was a profusion of wild curls, and the deeply carved creases in his forehead and cheeks, folding around his mouth, were the result of a youth as a heavy smoker and years of chronic pain, not a life spent laughing. The aging rocker appearance hid a wily business brain. He was making no effort, however, to hide the strong disapproval.

The butterflies in her stomach went into a whirlwind.

"Hello, Dad," she said. "You're back early."

"Dad." Griff was barely holding on to his temper. He could actually feel a nerve twitching in his eyebrow. They were going to drive him up the fucking wall. Of the fucking not-*that*-miniature castle behind him. "There is no money left in the trust. There is *no money*. The estate is barely scraping by. If *The Austen Playbook* broadcast is successful, our fee will keep the place afloat for another year. If my film about Henrietta Carlton gets the go-ahead from the studio, we're good for another five years, and I hope by that time I'll have enough coals in the fire to keep things up indefinitely. But right now, there's barely enough to pay the utilities bill, let alone the mortgage. Let alone build a *fucking amusement park* in the front yard."

"It's not quite as ambitious as that, old chap," James said, totally unperturbed, his words barely audible over the noise of the bloody crane he'd hired. "But I think the local children will like it."

"The local—" Griff had to bite back any further words. He had just watched the second construction crew on the property install a gold-plated brick walkway in front of a "toy" castle the size of a van. He hadn't seen the bills yet, but to have a return on a project like this, they'd need half the kids in the county to traipse out to play with it, and would have to charge their parents twenty quid a pop at the gate.

Charlie appeared at his side then, looking uncharacteristically serious. "Uh. Griff. One of the Austen team wants a word."

The manager in charge of the theatre restoration pushed past him. "Look, I don't want to interrupt," she said brusquely, "but are you aware that a delivery lorry is stacking materials for these…dolls outside the theatre? The production will be broadcasting live shots of The Henry exterior before the performance, and it's not a good look having a load of crates propping up the walls."

"For *Christ's sake*." Griff turned to his mother, who shook her head at him with a shade of exasperation that raised his hackles even higher.

Between his family's never-ending series of bad decisions, and the advent of Freddy, this summer was seriously undermining his belief in his own temperament. He'd be stomping about throwing dramatics like the West End contingent soon.

"James, honestly. Since when have you been such a *fusser*? We just need temporary shelter in case the weather packs in again, and the south pillars of the theatre have a nice outward reach. We'll have everything installed by the end of the week, out of the way well before these people have their performance."

Griff's phone vibrated in his pocket, and he had a sudden sense of foreboding. He'd never put any credence in premonition; obviously the fantasyland around him, with all its little bubbling cauldrons and lurking dragons, was having a bad effect.

Regardless, and equally irrationally since she was just through the trees at rehearsal—and nobody was likely to call him about her in any case; he wasn't her emergency contact—his first thought was Freddy, that she was hurt again. His hand flexing around the phone, he checked the screen, ignoring the continued hum of arguing voices around him.

Not Freddy. The agent who was acting for his company in negotiations with the film studio.

He slid his thumb over the screen. "Nissa."

He'd hired her because she dispersed with tedious preliminaries and small talk, and got straight to the point. "Griff. Bad news, I'm afraid."

Rupert didn't beat about the bush. The end of his walking stick tapping against the floorboards, he made an absent-minded return of Freddy's kiss on his cheek, then levelled her with his managerial look again. "Did we, or did we not, agree that this project was unsuitable for the current path we're on? This part wouldn't have stretched your ability when you were fourteen. As your manager, Freddy, I'd appreciate being kept informed of your professional decisions if I'm out of the country, not having them dropped into conversation by your sister."

"For the path *I'm* on, *Dad*." Freddy couldn't help stressing his alternative, some might say more important title.

"I wanted to do this play, and it came at the right time for me. I needed a break from London to get my head together going forward."

Which seemed laughable, in light of everything that had happened in the sleepy old country in just a few days—including the possible upheaval of her entire future life.

"We scheduled a holiday for you in November, before the Christmas season." Rupert studied her with a shade of apprehension, as if he expected her to suddenly drop to the floor and cancel all future bookings.

"And I'm still taking my four days in Paris," Freddy said emphatically. "But I just did back-to-back performances in emotionally draining roles, and I wanted a few laughs and a bit of romance."

She'd meant scripted romance, but it was an unfortunate choice of words. Rupert's brows and teeth snapped together. "Yes. I just ran into that vile Sadie Foster, who informed me that you're zoning out in rehearsals over *James Ford-Griffin*." The derision was *dripping*.

A pleasure as always, Sadie. What a winning delight of a human being.

That unprecedented urge rose in Freddy again, to defend and protect a man who'd probably never needed—or more to the point, accepted—help from anyone in his life. She wasn't going to dismiss him even verbally, even to avoid the looming argument. "I am seeing Griff." Well, she supposed she was. They hadn't really gone into that point. They'd been too busy having sex and reading other people's letters. And when she told him about the suspicions bubbling in her mind—and if she couldn't find something to disprove the picture that was coming together, she'd have to tell him—she didn't know what would happen. "But—"

"How charming," Rupert said, with a strong edge of sarcasm. "Over dinner he can read you excerpts of the ridiculous reviews he's written."

"Oh, come on, Dad. That's his job. One of his jobs. And for the most part, those reviews were dead-on. Maybe not tactful—" the understatement of the year "—but that's partly effect for the paper. Nobody wants to read a boring review any more than they want to see a boring show." It was also just Griff's personality, but she didn't feel it necessary to add that.

Rupert didn't even seem to be listening to her. Big surprise. "A Carlton and a Ford. It's like history bloody repeating itself." Her father's walking stick scraped along the floor. "You've read *All Her World*. You know how hard it is to get to the top. You need to stay focused, keep in your mind in the game and your eye on the goal."

Most of the lecture drifted into the dust around them. Freddy's brain had zeroed in on just three words of it. The biography. Oh, fuck. *Fuck*. She hadn't even thought as far as that. *Please let me be wrong about this. Please let it be that I really am just too influenced by the play right now. Please.* "Is it true you're planning to adapt the book into a screen version? You've never mentioned it."

"There are plans in the pipeline. I didn't want to say anything until they were concrete." Her father scowled so hard that creases developed creases, and he ended up looking a bit like the Grinch. "And then that obnoxious bastard you're fawning over announced this mockery of a film he's making and threw a spanner in the works."

Freddy found that she was compulsively smoothing her hair back behind her ears. She stopped and pressed her hands against her thighs. "He's uncovering a lot of new research on Henrietta—"

"He doesn't know anything about your grandmother!" Rupert seemed to realise how sharp his voice had become, and made a visible effort to ease the atmosphere down. "Anyway, that's no longer an issue of concern. Let's concentrate on you in the meantime." He looked about them. "Christ. It's been a long time since I've been in this room."

"This is where she wrote *The Velvet Room*, isn't it? That summer?"

"Yes." Rupert's gaze ran over the huge oak desk, which was now battered around the legs and had picked up the scratches of dozens of different pens over the years; then past it, to the bookshelves, and the tiled feature wall. "This is where it was written."

He went silent, his eyes unfocused, his mind obviously back in the days of another summer, over fifty years ago.

Then suddenly, with a renewed surge of determination, he turned to Freddy. "It's obviously too late to pull out of this play now. It would be far worse for your future prospects if you gain a reputation for being unreliable. Fortunately, it's a short rehearsal period and just the one performance. We'll just have to hope this live broadcast goes without a hitch, and then we can put our full focus on the new production of *The Velvet Room*. I hope you've arranged for time off next week to come back to London for the first audition."

There was no "hope" in his voice, just pure expectation.

Freddy pulled her own gaze from the infamous writing desk. "I'm not sure I want to do it." Still hedging, but it was the first time she'd ever just come out and said that to Rupert's face.

In the seconds that followed, she could hear the tick of the clock.

"Of course you want to do it." After the initial surprise, Rupert waved her words aside, as easily dismissive as if she were still a teenager with no idea what she was doing, just going where she was told and reading the lines she was given, and enjoying herself wholeheartedly.

Freddy would still like to enjoy herself wholeheartedly—what the hell was the point, otherwise—but she'd grown out of the rest of that mindset a long time ago.

Even now, a little voice in her head was whispering that it would be easier to just do the audition, do the play, make her father proud, avoid the confrontation. And bury what she thought might be the truth, before it could bring a lot of things toppling down.

But there was another voice, a conscience voice. A self-respect voice that had taken too many blows over the past few years.

"I enjoy musical theatre, Dad," she said quietly. "I like rom-coms, and physical comedy, and all of these so-called frivolous scripts. Giving people a good time, making them happy, letting them escape for a while—that's what I think is worthwhile. I don't really care about being seen as a 'serious' actor. I don't even care if people know my name, as long as they leave the theatre feeling better than when they came in."

A muscle jumped in Rupert's jaw. "Well, regardless of whether you 'want' people to know your name, you have a name to uphold. Our family has been in the West End for over four hundred years—"

"Yes. I know they have. I love the theatre, and I'm really proud to be part of a family that's had such an impact on the way the dramatic arts have developed in London."

Freddy's voice faltered. "You know I always wanted to be like Henrietta."

"And you are," Rupert said at once, with a shade more warmth. "You've worked so hard, and your career is developing brilliantly. Your grandmother would have been very proud."

With a small, muffled half-laugh, Freddy brushed back the hair that had fallen into her face. "Yeah." She looked at him. "And you're proud of her."

The beam of weak light coming through the small side window fell directly on her father's face, so she saw the curious expression in his eyes. "Of course, I am," he said. "She was a brilliant dramatic actress. The best of her generation."

"And a groundbreaking playwright."

Rupert folded his hands over the head of his walking stick. "*The Velvet Room* cemented the Carlton name in the history books. And you're continuing the legacy." He smiled at her. "My baby girl. I can still remember seeing you up there for your stage debut. 'The most promising child actor for years,' that's what the critics said."

She'd had universally good reviews for that performance. It had been before Griff's time.

Freddy swallowed hard, because she could remember that time, too, coming off the stage to be swept into her father's arms and bounced around in triumph. And all the roles that followed, as the expectations became higher and the hugs fewer. "I'm not right for *The Velvet Room.* I think it's an amazing piece of work, but to actually act in it—it's not my sort of play at all."

"You've always underestimated your ability."

No; she'd sublimated her own wants.

"Dad—"

"I need to get back to London." Rupert glanced at his watch. "I'm meeting with Lisa after lunch."

His expression didn't bode well for friendly manager-agent relations.

"Dad."

Rupert turned at the door and gave the room a final scrutiny, glancing over the desk, fixing on the feature wall again. From a distance, the pattern on the tiles looked like Art Deco curlicues; close-up, body parts started to emerge, like a dirty Rorschach test. She hoped he didn't have his contacts in.

His eyes locked with hers. "Freddy. We have not worked this long and hard for you to throw away your potential by tap-dancing into obscurity—and early arthritis," he added drily. "Actors like your grandmother, and Cecily Redcliffe, and Cameron Savage—they didn't reach iconic status by twirling through a succession of romantic comedies. You paid your dues in the chorus; those productions were a means to an end." A muscle jumped beside his mouth. "And I have no interest in managing the career of a glorified music-hall performer. I expect you in London on Tuesday morning for the audition. Be there." He twisted too sharply and had to jerk his stick forward to keep his balance. As he hissed, she saw the pain skitter across his taut features.

Freddy swallowed on a knot of nausea.

"Is it that important to you?" She stood in the centre of the room, very still. "The Carlton legacy in the West End?"

"Yes."

One composed word that fell like a ten-ton weight.

Chapter Eleven

When her father had gone, Freddy pushed both hands through her hair, gripping it in handfuls above her ears. She released the hold and a violent breath simultaneously.

A *bang* outside rattled the ceiling light and the pornographic tiles on the wall. With another sudden surge of anxiety that made her feel like her skin was three sizes too small, she grabbed up her bag and almost ran from the theatre. She needed to be outside, in the sunshine and fresh air, away from this room and its ghosts. And she found she wanted Griff very badly. His arms, his voice, and his way of cutting through the spiralling bullshit and putting things into perspective.

Unfortunately, it was wraiths of the past inside and the forces of evil outside. She came out of the main doors and dashed headlong into Ferren, who stumbled and grabbed on to her, and they ended up in a tangle of arms and legs on the ground.

Her hair falling around their faces, Freddy tried to catch her breath, and Ferren blinked up at her. Amusement pushed out momentary surprise. "Why, Freddy, I had no idea you felt this way."

She was in no mood for this. His hands had automatically landed on her hips, and swearing under her breath,

Freddy managed to pull free of him and get back to her feet. Her dress was now a total write-off. One of them had ripped a large shred into it during the tumble. Her leg was twinging, too, and she checked the stitches.

"What happened to your leg?" Dropping the annoying jokiness, Ferren lowered his head and his hand to investigate her thigh, and right on cue, Sadie appeared on the path through the trees.

In other circumstances, with a different man, and on a day that wasn't turning to absolute shite, it would be so ridiculous it would border on funny—things going vaudeville on her again—but Freddy wasn't up for a giggle, and Sadie certainly wasn't.

Ferren made a little whistling noise when he saw the vindictive expression aimed in their direction, then went straight into self-preservation mode and hopped it. One minute he was there, the next he'd scarpered into the building, and Sadie was right up in her face, close enough for Freddy to see where she'd messed up the left wing of her eyeliner.

With that poisoned-honey voice, Sadie said, "Did I, or did I not, *just* tell you to keep your distance from Ferren?"

The phrasing was so similar to the infantilising language that Rupert had used in Henrietta's office that Freddy's temper finally unravelled. "Oh, go do one, Sadie. Ferren just took one look at you and scuttled back under a rock. Take the hint."

Sadie grabbed her arm again, and Freddy yanked it free. She was getting very tired of people pulling her in various directions. "I suggest you concentrate on your relationship with Lionel Grimes. The effort/reward ratio is better. Ferren loses most of his money in casinos and he's not big on advancing anyone's career but his own.

He might wrangle you a bit part in one of his films, but the most women get to do in those scripts is wave their cleavage about and scream during car chases."

A narrow smile spread across Sadie's face. "Are you insinuating, ever so delicately, that I have to sleep my way up the career ladder?" She shook her head. "Oh, honey. Pot and kettle."

Freddy dialled back the force of her response when a rigger walked past them. "What's that supposed to mean?"

Sadie curled her red nails, examining them with a studiedly casual air. "I mentioned, didn't I, that I just did a run of *Cymbeline*? I was working under Drew Townseville."

Freddy stiffened.

"It seems to be a popular position." Sadie looked up through her lashes. "Working under Drew." There was nothing subtle about the insinuation. "I believe you scored a job with him a few years ago. On *High Voltage*. Your first big dramatic role, wasn't it?"

"Yes," Freddy said after a pause that felt too long.

"Quite a change for you at the time." Sadie flexed her claws again. "You'd mostly been doing musicals until then, hadn't you?"

The world seemed to have narrowed to a tunnel between her and Sadie, paved with the memories she'd buried deep, and it was a shock when a new voice intruded, a production assistant calling Sadie back to rehearsal.

"I'm just coming," Sadie said sweetly. And, to Freddy: "Anything for the job."

The breeze was getting up. It blew renovation dust around Sadie as she disappeared inside, and fluttered the skirt of Freddy's dress. On autopilot, she looked down. She still needed to get changed.

It was quiet and shady on the path to the house, which existed in a bubble of calm between the chaos of people and construction at each end. As she passed the grand old oak that marked the halfway point, Freddy had a crazy vision of being able to climb into the huge knothole in the side and disappear into another world, like in Allegra Hawthorne's books. A world where parents didn't foist their own ambitions onto their children, and grandmothers were just little old ladies who handed out sherbet lemons and knitted handmade jumpers, and Sadie Fosters were shoved into cannons and fired off into space. And the revelation of secrets turned out well in the end.

Griff's parents were still on the east lawn, directing operations for their expensive flight of fancy, but there was no sign of Griff. Fleetingly, as she let herself in through the side door, Freddy covered her eyes with her hand. From physically craving his presence, she was now glad that she wouldn't have to see him just yet. She felt bruised, like every encounter in the past hour had torn away yet another raw strip of flesh.

In her room, she reached into her pocket and pulled out the Violet and Billy love letter she'd hidden there this morning, while Charlie and Griff had been nursing the car back to health.

She turned it over in her hand, then dropped it on the vanity table.

A headache was starting to spread from the base of her skull up to her temples.

She'd just pulled a silk camisole over her head and was reaching for a clean skirt when a hard gust of wind blew through the side window. The curtain snapped out like a matador's cloak, and several papers on the tabletop went flying. Even Dorothy's tornado wouldn't have moved her brick-like script, but the letter got back at her for her theft by sailing straight out through the open door onto her small balcony.

"Shit." In her cami and knickers, Freddy scrambled out onto the balcony and looked over the balustrade, then saw the paper lodged in the ivy that ran up the wall. Bracing her foot on the railings, she stretched her arm as far as she could.

Just out of reach.

Cautiously, she pushed on the next rung of the railing, testing its strength. As much as she was growing to love Highbrook, she didn't trust any part of it not to suddenly crumble. The iron seemed to be solidly bolted, so she stepped up, and, clinging to top-most railing with one hand, reached out over the abyss. It suddenly seemed vitally important to at least accomplish this. She was making a royal fuckup of enough things so far. Her fingertips touched the edge of the letter, and knocked it farther away. With a frustrated noise, she made a snatch for it, her supporting foot wobbling on the rail.

"What the *fuck* are you doing?"

It was an action replay of the situation when he'd caught her in the tree, only with the outrage meter dialled up a thousand-fold.

And thanks to Griff's impression of an angry lion, she almost toppled head-first into the patio below. At least it would have lessened the annoyance of her itchy stitches. They'd have been rather overshadowed by a broken leg and cracked skull.

Hands seized hold of her waist just as she caught hold of the letter. He hauled her back onto the comparative solidity of the balcony, and she turned into his arms.

It was not a romantic hug. He was furious. Cool, tall,

usually frostily controlled Griff had been replaced by a man with sparking eyes and too-quick breathing.

"Are you out of your mind?" he snapped, herding her back inside. "Every time I turn around, you're scrambling about like an accident-prone spider monkey. Were you not listening when we told your entire disruptive, melodramatic, pain-in-the-arse company to be careful about leaning on the railings on this side of the house? You could have broken your bloody neck."

That was it. Freddy's own leash snapped. She didn't appreciate being yelled at under any circumstances, but she'd absolutely *had it* today. She was tired of being dictated to, and censured, and judged and found wanting. She was bubbling over with troubles and she didn't know what to do about her father or the audition or the letters, and her skin felt dirty after the sucker-punch from Sadie, and—

This day had begun so bloody blissfully in the early hours of the morning, and even now she was looking at him and holy shit, the *feelings*, but the intense sexual connection between them was edged with cutting antagonism. The emotions were bleeding together and becoming a churning whirlpool in her chest. Explosion imminent. She smacked the letter she was clutching down on the bedside table and pushed the clock on top of it to weight it down.

Griff looked like he was being battered by a similarly complex mix of reactions. His temper was obviously fuelled by genuine concern—he'd run his hand over her arm and touched her hair, as if reassuring himself, against his will, that she was still intact—but he was also just pissed off in general and taking it out on her.

Well, fuck that. He wasn't the main target of her own

built-up worry and anger, either, but he'd put himself in the firing line, so—bring it.

"The only reason I almost fell was because you marched out there and screamed in my ear," she retorted, propping one hand on her hip and suddenly remembering she was wearing nothing but silk and lace.

Whatever. He'd seen her in less just a few hours ago. She was not abandoning her position on the battlefield in order to put a skirt on.

"Heard of knocking?" she added sarcastically, and his eyes narrowed.

"I did knock. Several times. You would have heard me if you hadn't been trying to throw yourself off the balcony." He swore again, every muscle in his upper body rigid with tension. "I seem to spend half my fucking life dragging someone I care about out of one reckless act after another. It only takes a second to think before you hurl yourself into—"

"I am not your parents." She *might* be warmed by that "care about" comment later, but given the rest of his little speech, probably not. "And I'm not your child or your bloody pet spaniel either, so don't talk to me like I just had my brain excised. I'm not and will never be some selfish burden in anyone's life that they have to rescue, thank you. I make my own decisions—"

"When you're not blindly following other people's in-clinations to avoid a confrontation."

"I seem to be getting over my dislike of confron-tation." Freddy curled her hands into fists. "Maybe I haven't always done the right thing." Her voice cracked slightly and she paused to take a jagged breath. "Maybe I've let people walk over me, and I've tried too hard to make everybody happy, and I've made mistakes, but at least I don't have some sort of…of God complex."

When that betraying thread of tears feathered into her fury, Griff's hand twitched, his body moving, and she instinctively knew that his instinct had been to hold. Comfort. Protect. But the anger had ignited fast and furiously, and it was still burning brightly in them both.

"If people would recognise reality when it's front of them and stop orbiting in dreamland, I wouldn't have to chase after them like a fucking nanny-goat, if that's what you're implying."

"I'm not implying anything. I'm flat-out stating that you're a control freak. I know how stressful it must be, being the guardian of this place, especially when your parents are being wilfully irresponsible, but there's someone else on the property with a vested interest."

"Charlie?" Griff made a noise in his throat that was so dismissive it infuriated her. She knew what it was like to be written off as the family flirt, the sunny one, the flaky one, good for a laugh but you wouldn't rely on them in a crisis. And Griff was short-changing himself, being a wanker about his brother and driving that distance between them when it didn't need to be there.

"Yes. Charlie. Have you actually given him the opportunity to help you? To be a support?"

"Give Charlie an inch and he runs a mile, and starts a hot-air ballooning enterprise in the backyard. My parents' genes out themselves regularly when he feels inspired to 'help.'"

"You know, if you recognised his talents, he might not feel like such a failure. He bloody worships you, and you treat him like he has the intellectual capacity of a houseplant."

"And what talents would those be?"

"I don't know, maybe the fact he fixed your car in about ten minutes flat this morning? The way he lit up like a Christmas tree when he started talking about engines and mechanics?"

"Cars are Charlie's choice of expensive hobby. And they're an even worse financial investment than my parents' miniatures." That sneer was grating on her last nerve. "You're very warm in my brother's defence. That comment about there being 'just me' didn't last long, did it?"

"Despite all evidence to the contrary, I refuse to believe that your dickhead streak runs this deep. What did you just say about recognising reality when it's right in front of you? I don't want to fuck your brother, you wanker. But I like him, and more importantly, I assume you love him, and you're both just wasting your relationship." She was breathing too shallowly, thanks to his dick remarks. "It might be exhausting cleaning up everyone's messes, but believe me, you get tired of being dictated to nonstop by people who only see what they want to see. I come from a family of personalities who think their way is the only way, and I recognise another one when I'm looking at him."

There was a sharp glint in Griff's dark, cynical eyes. "And I come from a family of dreamers, who choose to believe that the future will just work itself out, while someone else cleans up the mess."

And apparently he recognised another one when he looked at her. Freddy lifted her chin. There was truth in that, but anyone who thought that was her sum total was not what she needed. In his turn, he obviously thought she might not be what he wanted. Another sting of tears threatened, and she bit them back.

She'd never been good at holding on to temper; when she flared, it was intense and short-lived. The anger was already starting to recede, and a deep, unhappy hollowness was taking its place.

"And believe *me*," he added, with an unpleasant bite, his bastard side out in force, "I know all about your family's desire to have their own way."

Freddy looked up, trying to bring her focus back into the room and out of her head. God forbid she start *orbiting in dreamland* right in front of him. His words registered and she caught her breath. Did he think, too, that— "What?"

"Your father has finally achieved his objective." Griff had retreated deep into that hateful, impenetrable coldness. When he was like this, the man who'd been so intimate and affectionate with her in bed did seem like something from a dream. "Having pushed through his plans to adapt *All Her World* into the most biased biographical film on record, he's pulled in several favours in order to discredit me and my production company, and the studio has decided not to saturate the market. Your grandmother suddenly isn't quite interesting enough to merit both projects."

Freddy was frozen. "He wouldn't do that," she managed to get out. "How-however concerned he is with the business side of things, Dad's always had integrity. He's always made it clear to me that this industry can be brutal and—and dirty." Her voice shook hard over the words. "So it's important to do things the right way."

"Well, for someone who turns up his nose at brutal, dirty tactics," Griff said sarcastically, "he's taking to it like a duck to water. End result: unless I can push back with my own connections in London, my film is on the backburner. Not indefinitely, if I have anything to say about it, but it's certainly not going to provide the cash injection we need here any time soon."

"I'm sorry," Freddy said, after a moment, her voice strained. In the absence of anger, she was feeling naked—although her emotions seemed starker than her bare legs—but she didn't move, just kept very still. "I d-didn't know he was going to do that."

"I'm sure you didn't. If we're talking about family relationships built on mutual honesty and respect, you and your father aren't doing much better than me and Charlie, are you?"

Freddy flinched, and Griff turned away with a jerky movement and swore again, viciously, under his breath.

In the silence between them, that seemed to echo over a widening distance, her gaze went to the letter on the bedside table. "Griff—"

It was all there on her tongue; she wanted to just spill it out, all of it, everything that was nagging away at her. She *wanted* him to tell her she was being a typically melodramatic actor, looking for trouble where there was none.

But the derision in Sadie's eyes had fixed in her mind, a lingering echo of her own past regret, completely throwing her off-balance. There was probably nothing in Freddy's life that she was more ashamed of than that episode with Drew Townseville, and that shot had come unexpectedly and hit hard.

And her father's face, the implacability. The end of the road when it came to hedging and dodging, putting off the inevitable. Show up at the audition, win the role of Marguerite, or forever alter their relationship.

She couldn't stop thinking about the physical pain that had carved grooves into his face. His intense pride in his mother's achievements. In Freddy's potential.

A weight was pressing on her chest.

She was driving herself mad, turning in mental circles of "what if."

She needed to catch her breath. And this wasn't the time for this. She was due back at rehearsal shortly and needed to turn in a better performance than the shite she'd managed earlier.

After all, as Sadie would no doubt point out, with everything she'd sacrificed so far for her career—a lot of time, sleep, and sometimes self-respect—it would be a waste of effort to blow it now.

"I have to get back to rehearsal," she said. "And I have to get dressed."

Griff's mouth twisted. "Are you chucking me out?"

"Be a bit of a cheek, wouldn't it, in your own house?" Everything about this was so wrong. Freddy felt like she was having an out-of-unusually-serious-body experience, watching from afar this solemn person with her face. She wanted to be smiling, flirting, becoming exasperated because it was like trying to get a reciprocal flirtation out of a member of the Queen's Guard. Exercising her snogging licence. How had things escalated this quickly, and then fallen apart so fast? She hugged herself. "I really do need to get ready."

She saw a flicker of something she couldn't define in his expression, then he nodded once. For a few seconds, he didn't move, though, just stood looking at her, his hands shoved into his pockets. She watched the rise and fall of his chest beneath his shirt. He hadn't changed since they'd left Mallowren.

His clothing, at least. His demeanour had changed dramatically.

To be fair, so had hers.

With her arms still folded tightly, her gaze slipped down his body and lowered, and briefly, she squeezed her lashes shut. She heard him exhale, and then his footsteps as he turned. The door closed behind him.

Opening her eyes, Freddy released a shaky breath of her own, long and slow. And finished getting ready.

Her mixed-up emotions could stay in here for the rest of the day; Maf had requested Lydia, and she would get Lydia.

Who, fortunately, didn't give a shit about family expectations.

And would never worry that she'd lose a man before she'd even really had him.

Chapter Twelve

Tuesday—Three days until showtime

Biting back a stream of four-letter words that wouldn't advance his cause, Griff said a curt goodbye to the pompous prick at the broadcasting corporation and hung up. Tossing the phone aside, he rested his hip against the desk, his attention snagging on the scene outside the library window. It was Tuesday morning, the second day of tech week in the short rehearsal schedule for *The Austen Playbook*, and the core cast were emerging from breakfast and heading in the direction of The Henry. He didn't see Freddy. He'd hardly seen her at all since Friday, and the current distance between them seemed to have settled over him like a layer of ice.

It was unbelievable that of the multiple things that had hit the fan over the past few days, it was having Freddy push him away after they'd grown close so quickly that was causing the most disruption. Or he'd pushed her away. He didn't even know anymore. The scene in her bedroom seemed to have faded into a blur, from the adrenaline spike of coming in to find her dangling off that rickety balcony to the moment he'd been given his marching orders while she stood there looking utterly miserable. He'd had no intention of losing his cool when he'd gone looking for her, but he'd been pushed to the edge by the red light from the studio coming right after the confrontation with his parents. Who were still happily carrying on with their plans, with the impulse control of a couple of middle-aged toddlers, and just as much awareness of consequences. Walking in on yet another reckless action by someone he cared about, and was coming to feel incredibly protective of, had tipped the balance.

He picked up a handful of the invoices stacked on the desk. One bill after another was coming in for the miniature world that had sprung up on the lawn, the artistically beautiful, gold-plated road to bankruptcy out there. He'd worked out the budget to keep the estate running for the next couple of years: mortgage payments, staff wages, utilities, rates, repairs, the never-ending list that didn't include whatever scheme his parents would come up with next. It added up to a total so beyond their means right now it was almost laughable.

If Rupert Carlton got his way and Griff's film was shelved indefinitely, it would mean the waste of months of work, and it would put the situation with Highbrook at crisis point.

Selling up was the sensible thing to do. It was bloody ridiculous to attach so much sentimentality to crumbling brick and mortar that they drove themselves into financial ruin. But evidently, there were two subjects in life that he was incapable of approaching with a cool head. Highbrook. And the woman who'd teased, flirted, annoyed the fuck out of him, and could stop his breath in his chest when he saw her.

Some force in the universe was smirking down at him, because he'd reviewed dozens of plays during the past few years with plots grounded in characters who fell fast and hard, and he'd always scorned the idea of it happening that quickly. Past the teenage years, it was naïve to think that intense attachment after a few looks, a few touches, a single sexual encounter, was anything but infatuation that would burn out equally fast. Ironically, many of those infatuated characters he'd dissected in print had been played by Freddy.

And here they were. And the cheerful, frivolous flirt of an actor he'd criticised professionally and dismissed personally was breezily shredding every conviction he had on the subject.

Not always cheerful. His gut twisted. His first experience of Freddy had been the girl who was still so fired with enthusiasm and energy after a three-hour show that she bounced on the balls of her feet during curtain calls. He'd always found it exhausting just to watch—but after seeing her with a dark ghost in her eyes that he didn't understand, her whole bright, shining spirit dulled, and hearing the crack of tears in her voice, she could hop and skip all over the place and he'd just sit back and be profoundly grateful.

It was too soon to know what would happen between them, whether the way he felt now would survive the first hurdle—or the second, or every obstacle that arose—but he wanted to find out.

Providing she was even prepared to have dinner with him at this point, and hadn't just written him off an unfortunate one-night stand.

At least she'd tell him straight. That disconcertingly direct approach of hers when it came to situations where she wanted snogging licence. He smiled faintly, for the first time in a while.

The door opened, and Charlie stuck his head in, very tentatively. "Morning." He caught the tail end of the smile, and craned around the door, scanning the room. "No Freddy?"

"Not unless she's hiding under the desk. Which, to be fair, I wouldn't put past her if the whim struck." Pushing his hands into his pockets, Griff studied his brother.

With work on hold and Freddy mysteriously vanishing every time he got within a hundred metres of her, he'd had time to think about several things this weekend. Her blunt words about Charlie were one thing he remembered with crystal clarity from that vicious volleying of home truths and angry retaliation.

"I thought maybe you two had made it up." Charlie ventured into the room, still eyeing him a bit warily. "You don't have a face like Mr. Freeze this morning, the caterers have stopped tiptoeing when they pass the library door, and I haven't seen any weeping production assistants fleeing your path."

"Did you actually want something?"

Charlie was looking through the pile of invoices. He tucked his lips in, pressing them together, and shook his head. "Is any of this stuff returnable?"

"Since it's already been transformed into a dozen varieties of magical beast, I'm guessing not."

His brother walked over to the window. "It *is* impressive. They do have talent."

"Yes, they do." Griff joined Charlie at the window, and they both looked down at the intricately detailed miniature world below. The construction crew had got the train track working. Children would be transfixed. Pity that the youngest member of their family was twenty-six. Although he was their resident balloonist. He'd probably fancy at least one ride if he could squeeze onto a carriage. "I just wish they were the sort of artists who make use of whatever materials they have on hand, and weren't on first-name terms with luxury suppliers across Europe. I'm not denying their talent. It's their business acumen that's shite."

"Bit like me, then."

Griff turned his head. Charlie was still smiling a little as he watched the mechanics of the village below, the drawbridge of the castle lowering and lifting, the wheels of a carriage rolling over tiny pebbled stones. The bitter twist to his lips, a shade of something in his expression, were easily missed if you weren't looking. If you didn't take the time to look.

"We're all stronger in different areas," he said at last, and Charlie snorted.

"My strength certainly isn't the entrepreneurial life, is it? How many times have I tried to help and made things worse?"

Griff didn't deny the facts, but— "But you tried." Charlie turned his head sharply, and Griff managed a faint smile. Wryly, he added, "And I'm not doing any great shakes financially right now, either."

"It'll work out for the best, whatever film you make," Charlie said, propping his shoulder against the wall. It was that blind optimism based on no evidence at all, that Griff usually found totally irritating, but he said nothing this time. "I'm not just throwing out happy-happy-joy-joy statements with no basis in reality. It's faith, based on twenty-six years of knowing you. You sort things out. It's what you do."

It was Griff's mouth that twisted this time. "Not always."

"I'm not saying you're infallible." Charlie paused. "Although you give a good impression of it. I know we might have reached the end of line where Highbrook is concerned." They were both silent then, and with no planning, they each reached out and placed a hand against the carved wall of the structure that had sheltered their childhood, during times when little sense of security was to be found elsewhere. "But it'll...be okay. Whatever happens." His smile turned crooked. "You might be a bit of a bastard at times, but you're a very reassuring person to have around."

Griff shifted. Freddy might be having an alarming influence on him, but he hadn't had a personality transplant, and he was still on edge wading into sentimental territory. Gruffly, he turned the subject down a more comfortable path. "Charlie, do you want a career with cars?"

Charlie jerked, then his expression turned rueful. "The fair Freddy's been whispering in your ear, has she?"

"More like hurling verbal knives at my head. You're obviously enthusiastic about them—"

"You mean I spend too much money on them?" Charlie asked. "I don't, you know. Any car I've ever bought I've got for cheap, usually because the engine hadn't worked since 1952, and I do most of the work myself."

What had Griff always thought, that people were rarely what you projected onto them? He hadn't gone very far in applying that to the people closest to him. He pushed away from the wall and straightened. "There's a lot I haven't bothered to notice, isn't there?"

"S'all right," Charlie said, looking a shade uncomfortable himself. Then suddenly, he grinned. "Turns out you're full of surprises, as well. My stoic big bro, falling arse-over-boots for the West End's answer to Pollyanna, quick enough to make Romeo look slow on the uptake. She seems to be merrily throwing curveballs right and left. What's next for the Freddy Effect?"

Good question.

Especially since, if Griff was correct in what Freddy had risked her life to retrieve from the ivy on Friday, she'd now taken to pinching other people's love letters.

It was raining in London. Freddy stared through the car window, but rivulets of water were running down the glass so quickly it was difficult to see clearly.

"This *was* where you wanted to go?" The taxi driver's voice made her jump, and she blinked back into reality.

"Oh. Sorry." She fumbled for her purse and paid the fare. It was steep; she'd tossed and turned in bed so much last night that she'd overslept and been late leaving High-brook, and the traffic had been horrendous. If she were going to read signs into things, the universe wasn't all that keen on delivering her here in time. She could almost hear Griff snorting over that one.

She bit her lip. She hadn't spoken to him all weekend. She'd barely even seen him. Just one moment, when she'd been crossing the grass on her way back from the theatre, and she'd looked up and their eyes had met through the glass of the library window. Very filmlike. Except in a film, they might have followed up with a reconciliation scene and some passionate shagging by now. The non-fictional world was a bit shite, sometimes.

"You sure you don't want me to take you somewhere else?" The driver was getting impatient, but really, he was reading her mind. It was like the voice of her internal narrative had a deep Geordie accent.

She *did* want him to take her somewhere else. Just about anywhere, at this point.

But she'd been going back and forward on this all weekend. Go to the audition, or don't. Accept what was essentially an ultimatum, or go with her own instincts. Her own conscience. For several reasons, it would be a terrible idea to take a part in *The Velvet Room*. Only one reason to do it. And her mind kept sticking on the moment in Henrietta's office when her father's stance had faltered and he'd seem to hoist himself up by sheer pride rather than physical strength. So much had been taken away from him in the past.

She'd felt she had no choice. She owed him her loyalty. She'd had to come.

Now that she was here, though, her stomach was queasy. And her heart felt like lead.

"No," she said. "Thanks. I'm expected."

When she shut the door behind her, the car immediately pulled away, sloshing a puddle of water over the back of her legs. Not a good beginning, but then none of this felt right.

Freddy stood in the rain, feeling drips of water wiggle under the hood of her coat, looking up at the impressive frontage of the Metronome Theatre. It had fallen down a few years ago and been rebuilt super posh.

It would probably be wrong to hope it spontaneously and harmlessly collapsed again, thereby solving the immediate part of the problem for her.

Sighing, she ran lightly up the steps and pushed through the door. Pushing back her hood, she shook out her curls and handed her ID to security, who checked her name off against a list.

Her footsteps echoed as she followed the back hallway. The foyer was richly carpeted, but backstage they'd put down polished wooden floorboards. She'd performed here only once since the renovations, but it had been one of her favourite old theatres before the incident, and was now one of the nicest modern ones.

When she approached the door that opened into the stands, she heard voices, the enunciation so clear and resonant that somebody was obviously already reading lines onstage. She put her hand on the wood panelling to push it open, and sentences were suddenly audible.

"There comes a moment when the truth must out. Realisation chases away the mist of denial and self-deception, and—you know. And there's no longer a choice."

The Velvet Room. Act Two, Scene Three. Words spoken by the character of Anna.

This play—her grandmother's crowning achievement. As a child, Freddy had watched an old recording of Henrietta performing as Marguerite, and copied her movements, wrapping a tablecloth around her waist to emulate the sweeping skirt of Henrietta's ballgown.

She stood now, motionless, her palm still pressed against the wood of the door.

Griff might scorn the idea of signs, but personally, she thought it was about time she started listening to what something or somebody was trying hard to tell her.

The truth must out.

She stepped back, just as the door opened. A woman with a clipboard in her hand blinked, momentarily startled, then whipped out a pen. "Hi, there. Freddy Carlton, isn't it? You're here to audition?"

It was a rhetorical question. Actor, theatre, audition—it all followed, didn't it?

Freddy looked over the woman's shoulder, where she could see the usual scene unfolding, the bark of voices, the atmosphere that seemed to soak up both the nerves of newer performers and the ego of many established stars. She'd done this a hundred times before, sometimes for roles she really wanted, more often for roles she was strongly advised to pursue. She half expected to see her father there, but he'd made a point of not coming to her auditions since she was about fifteen, so she could fully focus. She'd been almost eighteen before she'd stopped looking into the stands and feeling his absence, still wanting her dad.

He was expecting her to report to his office shortly, with positive feedback in hand.

No longer a choice.

"No," she said to the surprised woman. "Not this time."

As she strode back the way she'd come, she tugged her phone from her bag and fired off a quick text.

Akiko's response came back in less than a minute. *At the Grantham Collections today. Meet me in the portrait room in half an hour.*

Scores of painted eyes watched from the walls of the gold-painted, high-ceilinged chamber in the centre of the Grantham Collections in Clerkenwell. The longer Freddy stared back at them as she talked, keeping her voice low in the echoing room, the more she could swear some of them were moving in their frames. The stately looking dude with all the white curls had a disapproving little smile that seemed to be growing by the second. Disconcerting.

Akiko listened to her in silence, and when Freddy stopped speaking, gave a quiet whistle. "Oh, my. You're about to toss the cat amongst the pigeons with a vengeance. Are you sure?"

"No," Freddy said glumly. "I'm not. And I hope I'm wrong."

Akiko crossed her legs, bouncing one foot in its stiletto boot. She was wearing a silk shirt and leather trousers, and looked so cool that Freddy felt like a scruffy frizzball sitting next to her in damp leggings, with her matted hair steaming. "How are you going to find out for sure?"

"I don't know." Freddy looked at the curly-haired portrait again. "If there's anyone still living who knows the facts, it's been so long that I expect they'll want them to stay buried."

Akiko followed her gaze. "General Godfrey Reynolds," she said absently, nodding at the portrait. "Highly decorated commander in the Napoleonic Wars. And responsible for the deaths of many of his soldiers, from what I've found out." Her finely arched brows compressed. "Does he remind you of anyone? It's been nagging at me for weeks."

"Dad," Freddy said abruptly. "He looks a bit like Dad."

She stood up, suddenly unable to sit still anymore, and stalked in the opposite direction, away from General Reynolds and his judgmental look. The smaller portraits in the far corner were giving off a much friendlier vibe. Akiko followed her, her heels tapping on the floorboards.

"On a lighter note, how are rehearsals going? I can't wait for the performance."

"Are you and Elise still coming to see it live?"

Akiko's wife was a sculptor, and just as much of a darling as her spouse.

"Wouldn't miss it. We'll vote too." She cleared her throat. "How's Ferren?"

"Charming everyone on the estate who's never worked with him before." Freddy tucked her hair behind her ears. "He's been at his best all weekend. An absolute delight to have around. You'd almost be fooled into thinking he's turned over a new leaf."

Akiko's snort was delicate and ladylike, but spoke volumes.

"Exactly," Freddy said. "It's only a matter of time before he goes flying off the rails. I just hope it doesn't happen until after the performance, because right now, the Ford-Griffins desperately need this show to come off. And Jesus God, I hope Sabrina isn't caught up in the crash."

"She'll be broadcasting live from the estate on Friday, won't she?"

"Yes." Freddy winced. "With Nick Davenport. Speaking of cats among the pigeons, wait for the fur and feathers to fly there. So much for a relaxing lead-up to the show. I hope they don't put anyone off. It needs to go well," she said again, and realised Akiko was smiling at her. "What?"

"You." Akiko's face was gently teasing. "Smitten kitten."

Freddy was mortified to feel her cheeks warming. Bloody Griff. He really had turned her into a blusher. "I just—want things to go well for him."

"I can see that. I think it's lovely." Akiko tugged affectionately on one of her curls. "I think *you're* lovely, and you bring so much happiness to the rest of us that if there's any justice, the world will shower it back on you soon. I suppose you've gone all in, no holds barred?"

Freddy coughed. "Um—are you asking if I've slept with him?"

"This is me you're talking to, not Sabs. I'm not that nosy. I'm talking emotions, my lovely. Are you falling for him?"

"Head-first. I suppose you're going to tell me to be cautious?"

"No. I'm not. Under that bubbly personality, you have a very good head on your shoulders, and sound instincts, and anyone who earns your affection is bound to be worthy of it." Akiko hesitated. "I know you feel like your family don't always respect your opinions, but Sabrina doesn't mean to patronise you. It's the age gap. She can't help still seeing you as her baby sister, and she worries about you where Rupert is concerned." A hint of grimness. "Her own relationship with him is so distant that I think she's afraid you'll get hurt, too."

Freddy flinched. "With some justification, I expect." She ran her gaze blindly across the portraits in front of them. "I've been a total pushover where Dad's concerned. I do know that. And I've made some bad decisions."

"Cut yourself some slack. It's been the two of you working on your career since you were eleven. It's a hard cycle to break." Akiko's voice gentled. "I know you've carried some guilt over what happened to him. Quite unnecessarily, but the mind isn't always rational. Neither is the heart."

Freddy swallowed. "If what I think *is* true, it's going to be a massive blow to him." Understatement. "And coming right after the news that I ditched the audition… I can't honestly see what things are going to be like between us from now on."

"*If* it's true, things are going to be difficult for a while.

But regardless, you can't live your life trying to fulfil whatever dream Rupert has. I think you have to do what you have to do." Akiko nudged Freddy's arm. "And it sounds like you'll have a hand to hold if you need it."

Freddy looked down at where she was holding her own hands, her fingers knotted together. "I don't know what Griff will want. He's not exactly an open book. And he's very self-sufficient."

"If he doesn't want you, he's an idiot. And based on his TV shows and columns, he's clearly not a fool. And as far as self-sufficiency goes, just because you do a good job of being by yourself, it doesn't mean you wouldn't also make a good partner. If you're a complete person in yourself, that usually makes for the best kind of partnership. Still you, but a partner-in-crime, a buddy to have your back."

Freddy smiled a little. "I've been super jealous, you know, of you and Elise this past year or so. I thought it would be so great, to have that. To know what it's like."

Akiko lifted a brow. "And what *is* it like?"

A tiny little glow of warmth amidst the tension that had sunk deep into every muscle and bone in her body. "Right now, a whole bunch of confusion, but— I think it could be the best thing ever. I—"

Her voice cut off abruptly as one of the portraits on the wall suddenly came into focus. She stared, wondering if she'd finally caved into the stress and gone crackers.

She darted forward and crouched in front of one of the lowest mounted frames. It was a moody, atmospheric depiction of a woman, her skin painted with such a luminescent light against the greyness of the background that she seemed to glow.

"Portrait of My Love," Freddy read out from the sparse plaque below the picture.

"Romantic, isn't it?" Akiko knelt at her side. "Although I always think there's something sad about it. The tones. There's a darkness. I suspect it was painted in tribute, to a love that was no longer with him in body."

Freddy touched a fingertip to the plaque. "William Gotham."

"Achieved some success as a landscape artist in the seventies," Akiko recalled from memory. "But really came into vogue as a portraitist in the eighties. He was the 'it' painter for the highest of high society. Made a mint. This piece is very different from his commission work, though. I think it's his finest portrait. I wish I knew more about the subject, but he was very private. I couldn't find much information about his life outside of his work."

"I can probably fill in some of the gaps for you," Freddy said. "That's Violet Ford."

Griff's great-aunt had been painted in profile, but Freddy had seen her hovering in the background of enough photos of Henrietta in the past week that she knew that asymmetric bob-cut, the shape of that enigmatic smile, and the unmistakable nose, the latter identical to Griff's. She tapped the etched name again.

"And this, I imagine, is her Billy."

Freddy wasn't sure exactly how she'd ended up at Tower Bridge. After she'd left Akiko and the beautiful portrait of Violet at the Grantham Collections, she'd intended to head straight back to Highbrook. She wasn't quite ready to face her father yet, and anyway, Maf had only given her leave until three o'clock.

But somehow she'd ended up asking the taxi driver to

change directions. This one was more patient with her flip-flopping decisions than the last, and just whistled cheerfully as he delivered her as close to the bridge as they could get in the traffic.

The sky was still grey and heavy, and a few more raindrops fell on Freddy's already ruffled head when she slowed her footsteps and stood at the railing, close to where Violet Ford had fatally crashed her car decades ago.

The back of her neck prickled. With a strange surge of adrenaline, Freddy spun around, and her breath caught as her eyes met Griff's.

Chapter Thirteen

Standing on Tower Bridge with his blond head darkened by rain, Griff was staring at her, equally taken aback. He recovered faster than she did. Crossing the distance between them with his long stride, he somehow managed to move them so his body was blocking most of the wind.

"Of course I'd randomly find you on Tower Bridge," he said. "I don't know why I was surprised. What are you doing here?"

"What are *you* doing here?" Freddy could do nothing but parrot his enquiry. She was at a loss for words. For God's sake—she'd been having a weird feeling all day about events slipping into motion, but it was just getting spooky now. "I didn't know you were coming up to London today."

"Likewise. I had a series of meetings about the film." That explained the suit. He always dressed smartly, but in a dress jacket he maxed out on the fanciable scale.

"How—" A horn blared, cutting her off, and the traffic noise seemed to increase in volume. "What did—" Another horn blast, and the wind whistled past them.

With a frustrated sound, she grabbed Griff's hand impulsively and started power-walking back to a less chaotic spot.

They ended up standing by a railing in a pocket of comparative calm on St. Katharine Docks.

She was wheezing. *The Austen Playbook* was a lot of fun, but it wasn't very physically demanding. With all these talky, nondancing shows lately and her lack of morning runs, she really was out of condition.

She'd have some serious work to do if Fiona Gallagher liked what she saw in the performance and cast her in the *Anathorn* musical.

If. If, if, if. Everything was an "if" right now.

"So—how did it go? Your meetings?" She studied Griff anxiously and had to catch her breath all over again when he reached out and very lightly touched the end of a curl that had gone fluffy against her cheek. He seemed surprisingly unfazed by her yanking him about like a tugboat.

His hand dropped as they looked at each other, his eyes searching hers.

"At this stage, the Henrietta film remains on the backburner." Griff pushed back the edges of his jacket to tuck his hands into his trouser pockets. "So, we move an alternative project forward."

"Do you have a Plan B?"

He cocked his head, still looking down at her penetratingly. "I always have a Plan B." A shade of Snooty Critic in the response that brought an impulsive twitch to her lips, but the tension immediately racketed back up again.

"What about Highbrook? Will it be—enough?"

"No." Fleetingly, Griff's jaw went taut, but he was very calm now. "It won't be enough. The property will go. I don't see any way around it."

"Right." Freddy's mind was whirling. She opened her mouth, closed it. Reached out to rest her fingertips against his stomach, grounding herself. She could feel the rhythm of his steady breaths. She didn't know how to say this. If—bloody *ifs* again—she was wrong, it was opening up a false avenue of hope for Griff. And if she was *right*, the implications for her own family…

He suddenly cupped her cheek, rubbing the pad of his thumb along her cheekbone. "You didn't say why you're back in the city." His voice was deep and seemed to curl around her spine. They'd drawn closer together. "Don't you have rehearsal today?"

People walking past shot them an idle, curious look, but Freddy was too worried, and too overwhelmed by being back with him, to care about onlookers.

"I organised a partial day off today in my contract." She closed her eyes briefly, and his fingers moved in a stroke against the sensitive skin of her neck. When she looked up again, a frown was starting to grow in his expression. "For my audition. For *The Velvet Room*."

His small movements, that little touch that was making her breath stutter, didn't falter, but she could sense him go very watchful. "I forgot that was today." He was emitting jaguar vibes again. "How was it?"

"I got as far as the door into the stands at the Metronome. And then I bailed."

Griff's brows shot up. "You walked out?"

"I barely walked *in*." Slowly, she reached up and slipped her fingers through his, entwining their hands. Not for an expedient dash through the streets this time. Just to have that connection, that surprising, incredible sense of wordless support. It was like being able to breathe just a little easier, having that contact back again. "You remember that line in *The Velvet Room*, when Anna says there's a moment you just *know*, and there's no choice anymore, you have to act? The truth has to come out. I reached that moment."

"And what did you know?"

Freddy lifted her gaze from her fixed study of his shirt buttons. "That I've reached the turning point where my career is concerned. Either I keep doing things I regret to try to meet my father's expectations, or I grow up and take control of my life." She bit her lip, then, on impulse, reached up and touched her mouth to the corner of his, and he turned his head so that his cheek slid against hers, moving in a gentle, thoughtful nuzzle.

She realised how hard she was gripping him, and tried to relax her tense knuckles. "There's something else… Well, a lot else, if we're talking about you and me." She was starting to babble. "But…if there's something I think has happened that's wrong, I can't just keep quiet, can I, even—" Her voice faltered, and she cleared her throat. "Even if some of the consequences won't be good."

"Freddy." Griff's own voice was very steady, but there was both concern and calculation in his eyes. She suspected he was mentally treating her like one of the medieval puzzles she'd seen him discuss on TV, examining all the angles, deciphering her. "I was an absolute bastard to you on Friday. I shouldn't have lost my temper, and I sure as hell shouldn't have taken it out on you." He traced the line of her jaw with a gentle knuckle, and then pressed his mouth briefly to the curve of her cheek under her eye. He seemed equally uncaring of anyone who might see them. "I'm sorry."

His scent and his warmth were clouding her mind, and she turned her head to catch his mouth. The kiss was hard and searching, his hair damp between her fingers as she slipped her arms around his neck, his hands making her shiver as he stroked the small of her back through the thin fabric of her short dress.

Someone wolf-whistled nearby. They broke the kiss, but their faces were still close together, Griff's nose touching hers. She shifted her hand to trace the high bridge of it, his profile bringing back the memory of Billy Gotham's painting, and the things she needed to share with him. Even if she *was* wrong. "I wasn't exactly nice to you on Friday, either."

Releasing her, Griff leaned against the railing, his eyes intent. "You've been acting strangely ever since we went to Mallowren, and I doubt very much that it's just because we're spectacularly good together in bed. What was the inciting incident in your case?"

Habit kicked in long enough that Freddy tossed him a look between her lashes. "It *was* spectacular, and I'm sure your impressive skills in the sack are enough to make anyone come over all peculiar."

The faint lines at the corners of his dark eyes deepened in amusement, but he was waiting. She sobered. "It was a two-for-one breakdown. Thanks to Sadie Foster and one of my many and worst past mistakes coming back to bite me on the arse." Actually, from what she remembered of that time with Drew Townseville and his own style in the sack, that was an unfortunately apt choice of phrase. She took a deep breath. "And the letters."

His gaze sharpened, and she could almost see the jaguar pricking up his ears. "One of which you nicked and then almost did a swan-dive into the patio trying to retrieve."

Freddy paused. "Just for future reference, I'm not sure I rate eagle eyes as an attractive quality in a man."

It was his turn to leave a barely perceptible gap in the

volley of words then, before he said, "Does that imply that I feature in your current vision of the future?" So restrained and unemotional, but his hand closed on the rail, hard.

It was all-cards-on-the-table day. And it would be quite easy to start wheezing again, from nerves this time. Just to add a real note of sexiness. "My vision of the future has been swamped in mist, like our friend the Little-bourne Fog, but…" Freddy reached out and touched him again, spreading her fingers over his ribs. "The brightest light I see right now is you." He was very still. "I don't know how you feel—and what I have to say might change things—but whatever happens, I feel very…blessed to have this." She smiled faintly. "To experience this myself, for real, and not just pretend to know what it's like by reading scripted words." Her fingers curled into a loose fist against his shirt. "I don't know what comes next, but I know it physically hurt this weekend to feel like I'd just found you, just found…it—" the only way Freddy could put it, rather helplessly "—and then be wrenched away from you. I know I pushed you away, but—"

His mouth was on hers again, his hands in her hair, holding her head so he could kiss her deeply, with the passion that flared between them so quickly, so easily. It was such a shell shock to go from the life she'd been living for years to this complete upheaval of everything she thought she'd known, that she was a bit afraid. But pressed against him, smelling the scent of his cologne, tasting his mouth, feeling his hair against her neck, she couldn't imagine not having this. Not wanting this.

If anyone whistled at them this time, neither of them heard it. They were both short of breath when Griff lifted his head, his eyes still full of heat and something else that made her chest skip and flutter.

He ran his thumbs over her cheeks again. "You're so beautiful." As he had after the first time they'd kissed, he called her that so matter-of-factly.

Freddy's instinctive, snorting disclaimer went unsaid, because he so obviously meant it. Stroking her lips, which felt plumped up and tingly—like the rest of her—she sought for the right words in response. Meaningful words.

"I fancy you like mad, too," she said, because why be romantic when you could be tremendously anticlimactic.

His mouth twitched, and that amused light sprang back into his eyes. "I did get the impression you might when you started trying to climb my body in public like you were shinning up a fireman's pole."

If he wanted her to look around in mortification, he was out of luck. She managed to keep this blush internal. "Let's hope some of your TV viewers were watching. It'll do wonders for your reputation. According to reviews of your programmes, people find you sexy but stiff-necked."

The amusement deepened. "Well, who listens to critics, anyway?"

"Oh, I don't know." Freddy looped her arms back around his neck. "Every so often, they say very lovely things."

"True things." He ran his hand over the top of her head, smoothing her curls. It was such a spontaneously affectionate gesture that it affected her even more than being found beautiful.

The way she felt about him…

Enough was enough. It felt utterly wrong to hug her fears to herself when she trusted him so implicitly.

"Griff." At the renewed seriousness in her tone, he lifted his head. "Your film on Henrietta…"

"I appreciate your encouragement on the subject," Griff said, with surprising patience, faced with what he obviously feared was another burst of optimism, "but as we don't have the funding, I think I've exhausted all current avenues where that project is concerned."

"And what if there was renewed public interest in Henrietta and *The Velvet Room*?" Freddy asked. "What if there was an entirely new angle to that story? What then?" She was barely breathing, so close was her observation of his reaction.

The quiet that followed was so heavy with meaning that her skin started prickling.

"Freddy," Griff said. "What exactly did you find in that letter?"

Her lips parted—and then, with the perfect, or imperfect, timing of everything else today, his phone rang. He ignored it, his full attention on her, but it stopped trilling for only about three seconds before another call came in.

"I think you'd better answer it," Freddy said, shifting her weight from one foot to the other, seriously on edge now. "It might be good news from your team."

With a muttered curse and a swift, piercing look at her, Griff pulled the phone out and checked the screen. "It's Charlie. Christ, what have they done now?" He swept his thumb across the screen. "Please tell me they haven't ordered something else… What?" His voice went sharp and incredulous, then his eyes closed for a moment in an obvious prayer for patience. "We're on our way back now… Freddy. She's with me… Mind your own business."

He hung up and returned the phone to his pocket, and Freddy winced. "Well?"

"The forklift that was supposed to be removing the crates stacked against the side of the theatre." Griff swore again. "It had a mechanical failure."

"What, so the crates are still there?" It was obviously more than that. Freddy wasn't sure she wanted to know. The signs for this performance turning out well were really not promising.

"That's the least of the problem. When the mechanism failed, that fucking idiot Dylan Waitely was driving, larking about with one of his mates on the crew, and he ended up driving straight into the wall."

"Oh my God." Freddy stared at him. "Are they all right?"

"They're fine. Waitely got a minor bump on the head, but I doubt if he has any viable brain cells to lose. However, we now have a forklift sticking out of a crumbled wall, and a hell of a mess."

Freddy put her hands on her hips. "Jesus. What else could go wrong?" Then, with a hasty glance up at the sky and a rap on a wooden post, "Rhetorical question!"

Griff put an arm around her, in a way that was both cosy and bossy, shepherding her down the road. "Can you come back with me now or do you have something to do first?" He looked down at her. "Do you need to see your father?"

"Oh, I expect he'll be in touch before too much time has passed," Freddy said bleakly. "No, I'll come with you now." He rubbed his thumb against the top of her arm. "I'd better make sure enough of The Henry is still standing that we can go ahead with the show on Friday. And check that Dylan and his friend are still in one piece, I suppose," she added, with what she considered a perfectly understandable lack of enthusiasm.

She'd been worried about Ferren going rogue and doing something to trash the production; she hadn't actually considered Dylan as the potential, accidental saboteur. He rarely made it through a run without breaking someone's heart, but he was usually professional enough—and had enough ego—to want the show itself to run smoothly.

This summer was turning everyone upside down.

In the car, Griff fielded constant calls through the wireless system, most of them from annoyed people back at Highbrook, while Freddy tried to study the scenes she was supposed to be rehearsing today, hoping that any disruption to the schedule would be minor.

Between two fraught phone conversations, she tapped her stylus pen against the screen of her iPad where she'd copied in her most troublesome dialogue. "By the way— what were you doing on Tower Bridge?"

Griff glanced at her as he drove. "I don't know. I had some of the old Wythburn Group photographs on my desk, and I kept focusing on Violet." He reached out a muscular arm and took her hand, threading his fingers through hers. "Probably because you wouldn't stay out of my mind, and you seem to be unusually preoccupied with my great-aunt. I had to cross the bridge for my last meeting, and I felt…drawn, somehow, to stop and see where she died. Which was ridiculous."

"Or directed by the higher forces," Freddy said, with resonant dramatic effect, playing with his fingers. She snuck a peek at him, and was rewarded with a derisive sound. Despite everything, it gave her a little bubbling spring of happiness in her tummy, being back with him, the grumpy, sexy cynic.

"Despite what my parents have done to the lawn," Griff

said, and, without looking away from the road, brought her hand to his mouth and gave her a playful nip, "we do not live in an Allegra Hawthorne novel. At least until you land yourself a role in the *Anathorn* musical. Don't be fanciful."

Freddy turned her head to look out the side window and hide her smile.

In a series of increasing disasters, it was nice to know that some things remained predictable.

Ignoring the raised eyebrows they got from some of the enormous population of people who seemed to be invading the place on a daily basis, Griff kept his fingers linked through Freddy's as they cut through the woodland path to The Henry. He'd cast his eyes up at her spiralling imagination on the way back from London, but he was currently heeding a driving, internal voice that wanted her close. Just in case.

Of what, he had no idea, but enough things had been going wrong lately that his protective instincts where she was concerned were firing off with a vengeance.

He looked down at the top of her curly head. She was still bedraggled from the rainfall, there were dark smudges under her eyes, and she looked exhausted. He could hear her muttering breathlessly to herself, and God knew what bombshell she was about to drop on his life next—and he felt so fucking blessed. She'd said it perfectly. He'd never expected to experience this. If he'd tried to imagine what it would be like he'd have been so far off, and whatever happened next, he felt he'd been astonishingly, probably undeservedly blessed.

He realised she was almost jogging to keep up with his stride, and slowed down a bit to match her normal pace.

When they emerged from the cover of the trees, The Henry came into sight, looking dour and stately under the grey, overcast sky, but otherwise normal. However, from the racket coming from the far side of the building, it wasn't difficult to locate where Waitely had decided to regress to his undoubtedly unruly childhood and joyride a forklift like it was a bloody bumper car.

Freddy's hand came up to rub at his arm as they stood surveying the damage. An entire section of the back wall had collapsed, spilling bricks and tiles out across the grass, exactly like a toddler had been playing and thrown building blocks everywhere during a tantrum. Griff could see glimpses of the interior of the back rooms, which he sincerely hoped had been empty at the moment of collision.

Charlie came out of the side door, talking to the construction foreman, who now had a few things to add to his to-do list, and immediately came over when he saw them. "It's not as bad as it looks. Hi, Freddy." He kissed her cheek and grinned unrepentantly at Griff's cocked eyebrow. "Glad to see we've moved past the hiccup in the epic love story."

"I think this could be described as another hiccup." Freddy gestured at the battered building.

"Rubbish. Barely a hitch. Don't start evolving into your boyfriend, for God's sake. If anyone's personality is going to rub off, it's meant to be the other way around." Charlie turned to address Griff in a more normal voice. "Apart from the obvious bit, the structure is still completely stable, and since the West End menagerie—" it was Freddy's turn to raise her eyebrows "—aren't using this section of the theatre, it won't disrupt the rest of the rehearsals or mean a last-minute relocation for the performance. They'll just have to do some creative skipping-over when they pan the exterior for their establishing shots. And if you're concerned about the financial side of the repairs—"

"I am."

"It was one of their conveniently insured cast members who acted like a reckless dick, so all costs to fix the damage are the responsibility of the TV network."

"Well, that's something."

"I think this is my fault." That was Freddy, and he could tell just by her voice that she was about to mess with him.

"Unless you gave Waitely the keys to the forklift and threatened him with a deadly weapon into making a break for it, I'm fairly sure it wasn't."

"I had thoughts." Every syllable was enunciated with great significance, and Charlie leaned forward, obviously prepared to be impressed. Griff managed to suppress his sigh. She was lucky she was bloody cute. "When I was hedging about going into the Metronome today, I kind of briefly hoped it might fall down again and save me the bother. And look what happened to The Henry. The universe responded."

Charlie and several eavesdropping crew members made appropriately spooked noises.

"Right," Griff said, after he'd given her the appropriate pause for her dramatic timing. "Well, when your mind has returned from its trip to never-never land, perhaps we could finish the conversation Charlie interrupted, before you have to go to rehearsal."

Charlie took a hasty step forward as Freddy moved to look closer at the worst of the damage. "Careful, Freddy, I wouldn't get too close."

Griff moved after her and slipped an arm around her waist, pulling her back against him. "You're going to turn me grey by the end of the summer."

"You're a platinum blond, Norma Jeane. You'll go white." Freddy sounded distracted. She was scanning the rise of the theatre above them. Brow creased, she bent forward again, from the curve of his arm. "Griff— I've done a lot of nosing about in this part of the theatre the past few days, and I'm officially confused. What *is* that?"

"What's what?" He lowered his head to look under the broken beam where she pointed. "It's—" He cut off, frowning as well, and found himself mimicking her movements exactly, looking up and around to orientate himself. It was a pointless move; he knew this building like the back of his hand and he could draw a map of the interior from memory.

Or he'd thought he could.

There were no windows on this side of the structure, so with the smashed-in wall, it was getting a lot more light and fresh air from the west than usual. He'd been silently grateful he'd moved most of the Wythburn Group research over to the library this weekend, even though it wasn't likely to be needed any time soon, because what they should be looking at was a brand-new, unexpectedly open view of Henrietta's old office.

But behind the crumbled wall was a tiny room, barely more than a large cupboard, which he'd never seen before in his life.

Chapter Fourteen

The figures on the tiled feature wall in Henrietta's office had one more moment to frolic in gleeful nudity, and then the sledgehammer smashed into a scene of three very happy-looking people, and ceramic body parts went flying.

Freddy and Griff both put up an arm to shield each other, and they all took a step back, out of the foreman's way.

"I hope you're sure about this, mate," the burly young guy said over his shoulder, as he lifted the sledgehammer again. "We usually try to preserve…art."

He'd just noticed the subject of the art.

"I'm sure." Griff's hand was taut on her. "Bring it down."

There was enough of the thick concrete exterior still standing that they couldn't get into the secret room from the outside, just see glimpses of it through the torn wood and broken stone, so the only way in was through the office. Thanks to the hidden compartment acting as a shield, the office itself was untouched. Earlier today, when Freddy had felt the same compulsion as Griff to head towards Tower Bridge, she'd wondered if she'd wandered into a ghost story; suddenly someone had flipped the pages and she'd ended up in a children's adventure novel. And gee whiz, kids, if there wasn't a treasure map and a smuggler or two in that room when they got through the erotica wall, she was going to be jolly disappointed.

Once it started to collapse, the feature wall came down fast. Structurally, Freddy could see it was a makeshift brick and plaster job. The space behind it was relatively shallow lengthwise, so it wasn't difficult to see why nobody had ever noticed that the tiles weren't placed directly over the exterior wall.

"Hallo," the foreman said, knocking some of the fallen bricks out of the way to clear a path. "An honest-to-goodness treasure chest. Feel like I'm in Robert Louis Stevenson." A man after her own heart. Swiping the back of his thick wrist across the drops of sweat on his forehead, he stepped back to let them past.

Freddy hung back as Griff and Charlie navigated the mess and knelt either side of a heavy-looking metal chest. It was locked, but one whack from the sledgehammer took care of that. When Griff forced the rusty hinges the rest of the way, the lid finally opened, and they all leant forward. It was starting to feel slightly comic.

"Oh," the foreman said, disappointed. "Papers." He'd clearly been hoping for doubloons. "If you don't need anything else in here, I'll get back to directing operations outside."

Griff thanked him, but he was already engrossed in the first papers he'd pulled out, crouched down on his haunches, his sleeves rolled up. Freddy did realise it was an inappropriate moment to be enjoying the sexy scholar look.

Charlie was rifling through the chest with a lot less

care. "What is it?" he asked, turning papers back and forth. They were mostly covered with faded scrawled ink. "Letters? Christ. Considering what old George felt comfortable literally plastering all over the property, anything he thought was so saucy it had to be hidden behind a mocked-up wall must be incendiary."

"It's not letters." Griff turned another page. "I'm fairly sure it's an early draft of *The Velvet Room*."

Freddy caught her breath, and all her brimming amusement over the situation faded away. She wasn't sure why she hadn't connected the dots as to what could be behind the wall, but the whole thing was just so bizarre she felt like she was spinning along in a riptide now, going where it pulled her, everything happening too quickly for thought.

"No way." Even Charlie, who didn't give a shit about the infamous play or the Wythburn Group shenanigans, sounded excited. "That's got to be worth a mint, right? Would it bring in enough for what we need?"

Freddy's gaze was fixed on Griff. She didn't miss a single emotion that crossed his face, and she saw the dawning surprise, his knife-sharp brain working rapidly. "I doubt it. But it would be worth quite a bit to literary collectors, if it was the original draft. This seems to be a copy." He flipped over another page. "The handwriting isn't Henrietta's."

"Bugger," Charlie said. "Whose writing is it? George's stenographer, on loan to his lady love?"

"I don't think so," Griff said, slowly. "It looks like—"

"Violet's writing?" Freddy spoke for the first time since they'd all crowded into the office, and Griff lowered the papers and turned on his heel to look at her, and the room seemed to grow still.

* * *

"When did you start to suspect?"

Griff stood leaning against the desk in his bedroom, one ankle tucked over the other, his hands in his pockets, and his gaze intent on her face.

Freddy curled her legs up where she sat in the middle of his big, comfortable bed. She was surrounded by pages of script and notes that they'd strewn across the covers. She'd said very little as they'd gone through it with their heads together, and Griff was Griff, he didn't waste words. His occasional, disbelieving curse had said it all.

It was all in there, the whole creative process of the play, evolving from scribbled comments about characters to intricate plot maps. All in Violet's distinctive looping handwriting with dashes instead of dots over her i's, and e's that dropped lower than any other letter in a line.

There was no longer much doubt.

"That there's a very good reason why *The Velvet Room* is light-years better than anything else Henrietta wrote? In fact, anything that Henrietta wrote, period."

It was almost nine o'clock and it was the first time they'd had a chance to talk since a production assistant had come running into Henrietta's office to tell Freddy that she was late for rehearsal and Maf was breathing fire. Charlie had looked between them, obviously confused and wanting to know what was going on, but by habit not expecting Griff to fill him in.

He'd have to know soon. Everyone would have to know.

She was so tired of feeling like she was tiptoeing around all the time. "It was the letters, the ones Violet wrote. I don't know what she was like in public, on the surface, but she poured her heart into those letters to Billy. Her personality bounces off the page. She was witty, and funny, and very acerbic."

"In other words—all the qualities critics use to describe *The Velvet Room*." Griff moved his head, stretching his neck and shoulders with a grimace. He had to be shattered. He'd spent the past few hours helping to shift rubble outside The Henry. Freddy had heard distant clattering and banging coming from the west side while she'd been on the stage, trying to look enthusiastic about kissing about the former male model who was playing Wickham. He was an insanely handsome man, basically one giant smoulder, and compared to her attraction to Griff, the chemistry between them was a damp fizz.

Maf had been firing off scene changes at them like a drill sergeant, testing their reaction time, to see if they could keep their lines straight yet.

The result hadn't been encouraging. Dylan had been in a right strop, his head bandaged and his ego chastened; Sadie was word-perfect but increasingly sharp about anyone else's mistakes; Ferren was still worryingly chirpy; and Maya had ended up on the verge of tears, neatly encapsulating everyone else's reaction.

Freddy had got through by imagining being able to sleep in Griff's arms again tonight. If he still wanted her there after this.

"The more letters you read, the more you see the similarities. You read Violet's words, her voice, and you hear the play so clearly. I kept thinking of what Wanda said, that she didn't think Henrietta knew about Violet and Billy. If Henrietta had written the script, it would have proved Wanda wrong on that point. Somehow, I can't see Wanda missing a trick where the relationship dynamics were concerned with that lot. And then in one particular letter, the one I *temporarily* borrowed," she added hastily, foreseeing his commentary on that, and the corners of his eyes briefly crinkled, "there are a few expressions Violet uses. She and Billy had a private, ongoing joke about old Victorian slang. She teased him with the phrase 'got the morbs' when he was missing her and feeling a bit down. Which is—"

"In the play." Griff let out a low whistle. "One of the most well-known playwrights in Europe. The most decorated piece of British drama in the last century. And she may not have written a bloody word of it. It's almost unbelievable."

"I've been rereading the play." Freddy realised she was actually wringing her hands, like a nervous old woman in a film. She should be as exhausted as Griff, but she felt hyped up and jittery, as if she'd been chewing on espresso beans for hours. She tried, unsuccessfully, to stop fidgeting. Several of his early reviews had made sarky comments on her excess of energy.

Really, he was lucky he was sexy.

"I can see why some people considered Marguerite to be a semi-autobiographical character," she murmured. "I never understood that, but from the picture I'm building up of my grandmother now, I reckon it's a brutally accurate portrayal of Henrietta in print. The good and the bad sides of her. If Violet started off in awe of Henrietta, she quickly saw through her—even before Grandma pinched her work and passed it off as her own."

"Christ." Griff shook his head. "Henrietta conned the entire British public."

"And kept up the deception her whole life." Freddy frowned. "I'm surprised she didn't soften the characterisation of Marguerite before she submitted the play to producers. I'm assuming *The Velvet Room* debuted after Violet passed away?"

"It opened at the old Metronome about six months after Violet's accident. And Marguerite *is* the play. I think it's justified to say she's one of the most morally complex characters in literary history. Softening her would have stripped the play of most of its impact. Henrietta may not have been a talented writer, but she was an extremely savvy actor. She would have recognised brilliance even if she couldn't produce it herself."

Freddy crossed one arm over to rub at her opposite shoulder, and Griff pushed away from the desk.

"Freddy—are you all right?"

She stopped moving, with her hand still on her shoulder. "Yes."

The bed dipped a bit as he sat on the edge of the mattress. She wasn't looking at him, but could sense him studying the part of her face he could see.

He touched the back of his finger to her cheek. "Henrietta was your idol when you were a child. Even as an adult, it's difficult to realise that somebody you admired—"

"Was a brilliant actor, a very mediocre writer, and apparently totally lacking in scruples?" She shook her head, dropping her hands to her lap. "She died before I was born, and when I started to suspect… I felt—personally betrayed." A little sound came from her chest. "Stupid."

"No." Griff's palm was warm against her neck and ear. He pulled her into him and rested his cheek against hers. "Understandable."

She tucked her fingers around his wrist. "I feel like I should be apologising to you. To your family. On behalf of mine."

"What happened in the past has nothing to do with us." Firm and decisive words, but—

"That's not true, though, is it?" Freddy pulled his arm down so she could twist to look at him. "What happened then is going to directly impact what happens now. To start with, it's probably going to be a legal nightmare. There's a lot of royalty money involved that's been directed to the wrong estate. It'll take years to sort out that mess." She hesitated. "And there's your film."

Griff had one of the sharpest minds she'd ever encountered. He would have seen the new door that had just opened, the moment he'd realised what he was holding as he crouched by his grandfather's hidden chest.

When the facts were made public, it would be a literary scandal. This was a text that was studied for university entrance exams. It made an absolute fortune in performance royalties and West End ticket sales. And it had been stolen. The observations and hopes and despair and love of the most invisible member of the Wythburn Group, ripped away and presented as coming from the brain and heart of the tabloids' favourite actress. The secret hidden for decades. An extramarital affair on one side. Heartbroken *true* lovers on the other.

A man once considered to be an unsuitable match, who'd gone on to become society's pet painter. That was tragic, that Violet had died so soon after she'd found Billy again. The letters made it clear that she wouldn't have let the fear of her family's disdain dissuade her away from him this time. And in the end, it would have resolved itself anyway. Presumably, even Griff's stodgy great-grandparents would have found the newly wealthy William Gotham eligible. It was such a waste.

And it was cinematic gold.

The entertainment business moved quickly; it struck while public fervour was at a peak. Griff's film was already far advanced in preproduction. Even with the new angle, he had it ready and waiting for a studio to snap up. Her father could do nothing to prevent it. His own project—and his treasured, critically acclaimed biography—had just been rendered obsolete.

Freddy was fairly sure that any support she gave to the Ford-Griffins from here on out would be the final straw where her relationship with her dad was concerned.

"This will change things where the studio is concerned. Won't it?"

"Yes, I expect it will." He wore a strange, preoccupied expression as he looked down into her face, a small frown etched between his brows.

Freddy took a deep breath and released it shakily. "I'm glad." Her voice was husky. "I'll be so glad if you can keep Highbrook. And you'll give Violet the recognition she should have had. You'll give her back her voice. One side of this is such a relief."

The other side was shattering.

"I thought about saying nothing." The words blurted out, and she couldn't look at him. "I saw my father stumble in Henrietta's office, and he looked so old and in so much pain, but so proud, and I couldn't bear it. The thought of having to tell him." She felt Griff make an abrupt, abbreviated movement at her side, and looked up, her misery and shame probably evident in her eyes. "I thought about keeping it buried. Which would have been so utterly *wrong*. I'm so sorry."

That weird look remained on Griff's face, but he didn't hesitate. His arms came around her and he pressed his mouth to her temple. "Freddy. Believe me, I understand the impulse to protect family." An indecipherable note to the words. "Don't look like that. I understand."

A muscle in her back was still twitching, and she moved her shoulder restlessly. Griff pushed up her top, his hand stroking, warm and strong, up her spine, and started kneading at the rock-hard tension there. It occurred to her how far they'd come in many ways, that he would even initiate this sort of intimacy. It was so good that, as the judders of emotion slowly soothed into stillness, Freddy felt herself start to go boneless, her weight sinking into him.

She could hear the light sound of his breathing in the otherwise quiet room. Without sitting up, she stretched out a hand, carefully pushed Violet's painstaking work into a pile and set it aside, then twisted against his body to circle his neck with her arms.

A different sort of shiver racked her. It was a good thing her massage therapist in London didn't have this effect on her. It seemed like, no matter what else was going on, the moment Griff touched her she felt it as a warm, almost narcotic glow in her stomach, edged with the fluttering of arousal. If she were a man, she'd soon be in danger of waving a giant flag that she was really, *really* enjoying the backrub. One of the many perks of being a woman. Willies were fun to play with, but occasionally they just seemed inconvenient. And kind of odd-looking.

She liked Griff's, though, and she had a feeling it might be equally affected by the touching. He was breathing deeper.

However, his mind, like hers, was still weighted by the underlying situation and the day's revelation. "It's fairly obvious Henrietta didn't pull this off by herself. At least after the fact."

Freddy rubbed her cheek on his shirt, an instinctive seeking of comfort, and her breath hitched when she felt the press of Griff's lips against her shoulder. His mouth moved there for a few seconds, not sexually, just gently. It was as if he'd read her mind, sensed her need. "Your grandfather helped her. Hid the evidence." She shifted as he resumed the slow rubbing, pressing his thumbs in circles over her tight muscles. "And went to quite an extreme to do it. There was basically no chance anyone was going to find Violet's drafts while he or Henrietta were still alive. Do you think he plastered over the wall with saucy tiles as a sort of double bluff? Like, everyone would look at the wall, but you'd be too distracted to even think of looking *beyond* the wall."

"No. I think the old rip just took any opportunity to exercise his tastes in home decorating. But you're right. He safeguarded that secret like Cerberus protecting the gates of the underworld. Henrietta's office was off-limits when I was small."

"He may have kept the secret, but he didn't destroy those drafts and he ended his affair with Henrietta. And never spoke to her or of her in public again. When all is said and done, Violet was his sister. And as you said—" she lifted her head "—making sacrifices for family seems to be a quality that runs strong in the Ford-Griffins."

His eyes searching hers, Griff lowered his head and rested his mouth on hers. It was more of a caress than a kiss. Freddy couldn't resist touching the tip of her tongue to his, and his palm slipped over her body to cup the curve of her shoulder. She assumed it was stage one of a campaign advancing towards her breasts.

"I can't have penetrative sex," she said against his mouth, and he nuzzled her cheek with his lovely, exuberant nose.

"Ever again, or just tonight?"

"Probably tonight and tomorrow. My pelvic muscles are really tight mid-cycle, and penetration is usually uncomfortable." She put her hands on the back of his head, feeling the softness of his hair and the warmth of his body. "Sorry."

Griff leaned back on his elbow, stroking her shoulder, tracing light circles on her chest. "You don't have to apologise for not wanting sex, for any reason. And Jesus, if it's going to be painful for you, tell me to fuck off."

"Not that I'd tell you to fuck off anyway." Freddy leaned forward and entwined her arms back around his neck. "But I said *penetrative* sex, and I emphasised. Acting lessons with Freddy, part two: following a cue."

His smile met hers before he kissed her deeply, and she made a little noise of pleasure when his fingers ran up her thigh beneath her dress. She'd already kicked off her leggings to get more comfortable. Griff brushed his knuckles very lightly across the silk between her legs. While he kissed her, he kept his hand there, making gentle movements over the fabric.

An element of mutual comfort underlay the building lust, both the giving and seeking of solace after the turmoil of the past few days.

He trailed his lips over her chin, down her jaw, and found the sensitive spot beneath her ear. He really was a fast learner.

Freddy's breath started to fracture as he slipped his hand up to her stomach and then stroked down beneath the lace band of her knickers. Her own fingers faltered on her mission to undo his buttons.

Griff kissed her neck, applying gentle suction, and then blew lightly on her; and holy crap she had a quick trigger where he was concerned. She could usually only get herself to this point so rapidly, and most of the time she needed a toy to help.

Closing her eyes, with another low sound she couldn't suppress, she put her hand over his to adjust the pressure. Her legs were starting to shake, and she inhaled sharply through her nose when the change in touch made her hips jerk upwards, pushing towards him.

The more control she took over her own enjoyment, the sexier he seemed to find it. His cheeks were streaked with a flush of red. For an instant, though, he stilled. "Am I hurting you?" His voice was a rough rasp, and in answer, Freddy tugged on his fingers, bringing them back to where it felt really…really…

With a cry, she turned abruptly into him, dislodging his hand when the tension broke in pulsing waves. Breathing as heavily as she was, Griff drew her in against his chest, his hand wrapping around her head protectively. She lay half on top of him, panting a little, her fingers clenched on the muscles of his stomach.

It had started to rain again outside, and the sound of the water hitting the roof and the balcony tiles created the most intense feeling of intimacy. She was acutely aware of even the tiniest move he made, his hands mapping the shape of her head, the length of her arm, playing with her fingers. His legs moving just a little restlessly against the covers. In these moments, just for them, there was nothing else in the world but this room. This *was* the world. Her world.

Freddy stroked his skin, feeling the prickle of hair, damp with sweat. Rubbing her cheek against his flat nipple, she turned her head and caught it in her mouth, and his fingers clenched in her hair. She smiled against the taut bud, and the quiet noise she made sounded an awful lot like a purr. His chest was much more sensitive than hers. Useful to know.

She sucked a little harder, and Griff made a sound of his own, throaty and growly. It was getting very feline in here, and Freddy loved it. With a renewed burst of energy, she sat up and swung her leg over his hips to straddle him. Reaching down to cup his head between her hands, she kissed him, hot, wild, wet, while her hips rotated and rubbed against the erection that strained his trousers.

"Fuck." Griff took hold of her waist and pulled her harder into him, guiding her movements into the rhythm he needed. The slashes of red in his cheeks had spread down his neck, and his breaths were coming out jagged and deep.

Bracing his heels, he pushed his pelvis up into her, and the intense friction started to build again. *No way.* She'd never, not this close together...

Her hands fisted on the mattress on either side of his head, Freddy pressed her forehead into his, their eyes locked together as she rocked harder, faster, almost desperately. Their mouths came back together in a clash of tongues and teeth and gasping air, and her thighs clamped down on his sides compulsively as the tension broke again.

Holyshitholyshit...

She was still trembling violently, hands, arms, legs, when his head jerked back and his jaw clenched. In the most dexterous movement Freddy had managed since the day at the pub in London when she'd caught a bottle before it could smash on him, she turned, unzipped him, and closed her mouth over the tip of his erection, wrapping her fist around him, seconds before he arched with a guttural groan.

They stayed like that until the deep, irregular expansion of Griff's ribs slowed back to a normal rhythm. The tautness seemed to drain out of his muscles, his tall frame going lax.

"God. Freddy." Her name so wreathed with feeling, his voice so rough, it was barely audible. His fingers were unsteady as they stroked over her head, threading through her hair, and gently, carefully, Freddy drew him from her mouth with a final light stroke of her thumb over the sensitive skin at the crease of his hairy thigh. He seemed to shudder with a last wave of compulsive pleasure.

Touching her fingers to her lips, she moved back to curl against him, and was immediately pulled into a tight hold. She cuddled close into the sheltering warmth of his arms, the sweat on her body cooling in the slightly chilly air. Highbrook had very efficient ventilation in summer, largely due to various cracks and holes in the walls, Freddy suspected, but it must be freezing in winter.

She might get the chance to find out, now.

She stroked Griff's chest, her gaze moving from where her fingers brushed across his body hair up to his face. He was watching her intently, still holding her, his forehead and hairline damp.

Post-orgasm lethargy had been replaced by obvious concern; she could see it in his dark eyes as he touched the back of a knuckle lightly to her cheek. Their faces were close enough that she felt the fan of his breath on her nose.

"What did you mean earlier about Sadie?" he asked unexpectedly, his voice deep and low in the lingering intimacy of the room. It still felt somehow hushed in here, significant and almost—reverent. "What's she done? Besides demonstrate every deficiency in her character on a daily basis."

At that question, the chill on Freddy's skin seemed to prickle, and she shivered. Griff rubbed his hand along her arm and stretched out for the blanket they'd knocked askew, where it lay draped at the end of the bed. Shaking it out, he tucked it around her.

"Thank you." Freddy pulled the super-soft wool under her chin. It was like a comforting hug—although not as comforting as the actual hug she got when Griff tugged her back into his arms. "It was…" She swallowed, and sensed his head turn down towards hers.

"You don't have to tell me if you'd rather not," he said quietly against her temple, and she reached up and twisted her hand into his.

"It seems she's been making a habit on this production of storing up damaging information about people. I don't know what she was holding over Greg Stirling, but she got him out to make room for Ferren, just because she fancies him."

"Charming girl," Griff said, in an inadvertent reiteration of his brother's opinion. Despite the mildness of his remark, multiple muscles went rigid against her, and he pulled the blanket back to see her face properly. "Is that little viper blackmailing you?"

From his expression, Sadie would live to regret it.

"It's not really cause for blackmail in my case. If she blabbed *my* dirty little secret all over London, it would be a five-minute scandal. After all, apparently it happens all the time in this industry." The hard edge to her words was so unlike her usual tone of speaking that she thought it shocked them both a bit.

Griff stroked her cheek, never looking away from her face.

"She's just been enjoying making little digs here and there. It's far more up her street than out-and-out blackmail, actually. I bet you a hundred quid that when she was little she was one of those nasty little shits who throw stones at cats." Freddy had to drop her gaze then. She didn't look at him when she said, "She worked with Drew Townseville recently."

"Another person who should be ostracised from the business for being a twat."

Freddy huffed out a brief, startled laugh. "Yes. He was the artistic director when I performed in *High Voltage* a few years back."

"The weakest performance of your career." The comforting thumb rubbing on her cheekbone was followed up by the theatre critic in typically blunt form. Actually, there was something perversely comforting about that, too. If he'd starting waxing poetical because of an orgasm, she'd suddenly be in bed with a stranger.

And on that note…

"Yes." She was compulsively playing with the dusting of hair on his chest. Petting the jaguar. He'd gone all watchful again. "It was the turning point. My first high-profile drama. My big move out of the child roles in *Chitty Chitty Bang Bang* and *The Addams Family* and the rest, and into Serious Theatre." She invested the phrase with full, sarcastic capitals, but her voice was hardening again. "I was eighteen. My dad was bursting with plans for my career, and the agent I had at the time was pushing as well. There was so much pressure. And I was so young then."

In actual years, she wasn't exactly on the brink of picking up a pension now, either, but that wasn't what she meant, and she thought Griff knew that.

"As soon as I started prepping for the read, it didn't feel right, and I was pretty sure I wasn't going to get it." She managed a small smile. "Everything you said in your review of that show was right, and if you thought I was shit on opening night, after weeks of rehearsal, you should have seen me at the audition."

"But you got it." Griff voiced the obvious, very calmly.

"Yes. I did get it. Even though there must have been dozens of actors who were far better suited for it. Because two nights earlier, I'd had a night out at the pub with friends. The Prop & Cue, actually," she said, with the sudden realisation of the irony. One pub, two men, two very different encounters. "And I met a man at the bar. He bought me a drink, and we got talking. He was fit and he was clever, and he made me laugh. And I went home with him."

The rain was still a steady pattering rhythm on the roof.

"I left in the morning, and I still remember him saying, with this little smile, that he'd 'see me right.' I didn't know what he meant." God, she'd been naïve, for someone who'd grown up in the industry. For all her father's faults as a manager, he had kept her very sheltered from the uglier sides of the business. "I didn't really expect to see him again. But when I showed up for the *High Voltage* audition, there he was. Drew from the bar. Drew Townseville. Artistic director."

She forged on, determined to just get this out now

and be done with it. Shove it back in the past where it belonged. "I was even more thrown off. I did my shite audition, and I was too uncomfortable to look at him. I thought he'd be finding the whole thing as awkward as I was. It turns out that I was the only ignorant person in the pub that night. He knew exactly who I was, and he thought he knew exactly what I was after. Apparently, it was a not-so-secret secret that Drew used to reserve a spot, shall we say, in his productions for an actor who wanted to go the extra mile. If you were interested, you approached him before the audition. It was a horrendous coincidence, where I was concerned. I found out later that people used to discuss Drew's *methods* behind their hands backstage all the time, but I'd always been one of the younger people in any cast before that show. People usually keep clear boundaries where the child actors are concerned. You don't bitch and gossip in front of them." Her lip curled a little. "His nickname in the West End is The Patron."

"As I suspected," Griff said, "Townseville is a piece of shit."

Freddy looked up at him, and he ran his thumb over her lower lip. The gesture made her eyes sting as she moved haltingly into the part of the story she still heartily regretted. "Drew approached me after the audition and made it clear I'd be offered the part. The underlying *why* I'd get the part was equally clear. I was horrified. I wanted to tell him where he could shove his gross, sleazy role. But then his assistant came over, and I somehow ended up outside, not sure what just happened. And—" She was silent for a moment, just breathing in and out. "And when the official offer came in, my father was so bloody proud of me. He couldn't stop talking about what a brilliant career I was going to have, how I was following in his footsteps. In Henrietta's footsteps. Which in hindsight—" She snorted. "And in the end—I took it. A role that I in no way deserved. That I inadvertently earned in bed." Once more, she couldn't make eye contact with Griff. "Drew's an undeniably brilliant director. I spent that run learning a hell of a lot, and I couldn't look at myself in the mirror."

For the tatters of her dignity, the little scoffing noise she made sounded too much like swallowed tears. "It was the first—the worst—bad decision I made, to walk a path that was being signposted by other people. And the thing is, even my career-ladder-obsessed father would have been appalled. A step too far even for him. He'd probably have knocked Drew's teeth out."

Griff's hand closed over her whitened knuckles, gently loosening her clenched fist before she could tear her skin with her own nails, and laced his fingers through hers. It was enough to help her take a calming breath.

"Drew must have told Sadie. She'd think all her Christmases had come at once. She's always hated me."

"Because you'll always be a far more talented actor than she is," Griff said very matter-of-factly, and she gave a little negative jerk of the head.

"Nobody watching rehearsal today would agree with you. I couldn't keep my lines straight with all the scene changes. She didn't screw up once."

"I'm not surprised you found it hard to concentrate today. And Sadie is a good actor, but she has her own limits. She can repeat lines and she can mimic emotion, but she'll never have the full package because she doesn't understand the characters she plays. She doesn't have the capacity to empathise with them. You might be less technically proficient in some areas, but you have heart and spirit that she won't achieve if she's still acting in forty years' time. She knows that. And instead of taking inspiration from people who have the qualities she lacks, trying to grow and improve, she just tries to eliminate the competition. She undermines your confidence and makes you doubt yourself." Griff brought their joined hands up and turned her chin so he could look directly into her eyes. "And you have no reason, ever, not to hold your head high. You're an incredibly beautiful person, by any definition of the word, and I doubt you've done anything ill-intentioned in your life."

Freddy looked at him, then bent her head and kissed his thumb. And accidentally one of her own fingers. "Who'd have thought that my harshest critic would turn out to be the person who consistently makes me feel good about myself."

"Did you talk to anyone at the time?"

"I told Sabrina. She's seven years older and she's always had a tendency to coddle me. She was furious on my behalf, but I could tell she thought, oh, Freddy's been led into a situation she doesn't want, yet again. I felt naïve enough already without having it from someone else." Her grip on Griff loosened. "I was ashamed. An experience that I thought was spontaneous and *equal* suddenly seemed dirty. And I wish I hadn't taken that job. For a number of reasons."

"You went home with Townseville because you liked him, and you wanted to. And you were eighteen years old, for God's sake, and under an enormous amount of pressure. You've done nothing to be ashamed of." In a deceptively mild voice that didn't match the bunched muscles in his arms and shoulders, he added, "Unlike that predatory fucker, who ought to have his dick cut off with a rusty saw."

Akiko's words came back to Freddy, then, about a partner-in-crime, a buddy who always had her back, and she felt her mouth tilt. "Or a pair of safety scissors." Putting a hand behind his head, she pulled him down to her and kissed him hard. "You know, if this goes on much longer, you're in serious danger of becoming my best mate."

Griff tipped her under him with a suddenness that made her squeak. When she was breathless and could do nothing but hold on to his shoulders and enjoy, he lifted his head. "Who you fancy the pants off."

"Well, that goes without saying." Freddy planted a butterfly kiss on him. "Although I thought we did spectacularly well with the pants *on*, as well."

He grinned then, that full-fledged grin that lit up his eyes and was still too rare, and their mouths met again. They lay for a long time, kissing and touching and half listening to the rain, Freddy's leg tucked companionably over Griff's hip.

She pressed her palm to his cheek. "You make me feel equal," she murmured slowly, and he rested his forehead on hers.

His hand was stroking her thigh, soothing her into a dreamy state, and their kisses were turning gentle and drowsy, when his phone rang.

No, not his phone. Hers. Her eyes opening from half-mast, Freddy let go of Griff and summoned enough motivation to feel behind her. It was wedged partly under her hip, and was lucky it hadn't gone flying across the room with their earlier activities. She tilted the screen, and her stomach dropped.

That same reaction, that same dread of facing his disappointment, no matter how old she got. "It's Dad."

Griff pushed up on an elbow, his hair mussed, and looked from the phone back to her face. "Don't answer it."

"I have to." But, miserably, she let it ring again, putting off the inevitable.

"Freddy. It's late, you're exhausted, and your rehearsals are going to hit manic mode tomorrow. There's time to have it out with your father." He held her gaze steadily, and Freddy breathed out.

"Yeah. Okay." With her thumb, she rejected the call and switched the phone to silent, and laid it on the bedside table.

When they'd turned the lights off, she lay on her side, Griff's arm a heavy weight across her waist.

She listened to his steady, deep breaths, and the tick of the beautiful little 1920s clock on his desk.

"Griff." She reached up to hold on to his wrist. "Before I found those letters, I told myself that if I cut ties with Dad professionally, it would blow over. Eventually. He has connections in the industry. He'd be able to take on more clients. And as my agent keeps pointing out, he has his writing career. But his writing career was built on the success of *All Her World*." Which now turned out to be not a factual account of how *The Velvet Room* came to be, but the accidental corroboration of an elaborate lie. "Dad's reputation could take a hit by association, especially if people think he knew. Which a lot of them will." She frowned, and Griff's arm tightened around her, his hand moving to flex compulsively on hers. "So could mine, I suppose."

Goodbye to the legacy of four centuries of successful actors; hello to the family name being synonymous with plagiarism. The fallout could go either way in her case.

On the adage of all publicity being good publicity, a bit of notoriety might not harm her chances of booking jobs. It might even give her a boost, the industry being what it was. The more familiar the public were with your name, the more tickets you sold for the management.

But as a respected theatrical biographer, Rupert was going to look either naïve or calculating. He'd profited hugely from everything that surrounded Henrietta Carlton, award-winning, history-making playwright.

And another adage tended to be true, about shooting the messenger.

"I'm going to be responsible for throwing my dad's career, his whole life, into upheaval." Again. Twenty years ago, she had been the catalyst for everything in Rupert's world changing. Now it was happening again. "I'm not sure how to tell him."

There was no question now that she'd have to. Despite that momentary falter, that surge of guilt and uncertainty, her conscience would never have stood keeping it quiet, and—

And she was realising that her loyalty to the man beside her was starting to outweigh all others.

The sheets rustled as Griff pushed up to a half-sitting position, still holding her hand. His touch was comforting—but in the thin beam of moonlight that shone through the crack in the curtains, that odd expression returned to his eyes.

It was barely dawn when Griff woke the next morning, and Freddy was still asleep, one arm slipped beneath his pillow. His arm was tucked around her, his hand pushed up under the T-shirt she'd stolen from his chest of drawers.

Gently withdrawing his hold, he sat looking down at

her. She was breathing quietly and looked peaceful and happy, her worries temporarily unable to reach her.

A thump outside the door brought his head around. Muffled footsteps paused, and then the shuffling noise continued. Something was so distinctly furtive about it that his eyes narrowed; he glanced at the time and frowned.

Swinging smoothly out of bed, he went to the door and, grimacing in case the hinges creaked and woke Freddy, pulled it open. He wasn't sure what he'd expected—a corpse to topple in on him, or a bloodstained victim dragging themselves down the hallway? *The Austen Playbook* had a lot to answer for; the whodunit atmosphere was pervading the whole bloody estate.

All he saw was a flash of movement at the end of the hallway, someone creeping back to the other bedroom wing. Freddy's room was down that corridor, with the rest of the women. It was mostly the male cast who were being housed down this end. Griff's gaze travelled five doors down, to where Dylan Waitely was sleeping; then back in the direction the mystery figure had crept. Or not sleeping, as the case appeared to be.

He wondered which poor woman had fallen victim to the line of bullshit this time. Thank God the walls in this place were about three-feet thick. If he had to hear one peep out of Waitely while he was in the throes, he'd reach the end of his tether.

He returned to bed. Freddy had turned over in her sleep and flung one arm out across his side of the mattress. A small frown tugged between her brows.

Her phone on the bedside table was still on silent, but no doubt Rupert would be trying to reach her again soon,

ready to bully her back to London and renew his efforts
to get her into *The Velvet Room*.

Very lightly, he laid his palm on her head, moving his
thumb in a feathering stroke. For a woman with such a
razor-sharp brain, she had one blind spot, and it centred
directly on her father.

In the past few months, Griff had read *All Her World*
three times, and he could recite certain passages in it
down to the last very clever phrase. The inference of
those words shone out like a beacon. And when Freddy
had got over the shock and exhaustion, and the fog of her
own misplaced guilt, she'd realise it as well.

That Rupert Carlton had to have known the true prov-
enance of *The Velvet Room* all along.

Freddy murmured something in her sleep and her hand
found his. She'd physically shook as she flagellated herself for being torn, for a passing moment, between loyalty and her own deep morality. As she ripped herself
apart trying to keep everyone happy. Trying not to hurt
anyone she loved.

Something in his chest shifted, and with his free
hand he reached for his own phone on the other table.
He scrolled through his contacts. Thanks to Rupert's ongoing campaign to be as obstructive as possible this year,
he had the man's number saved in his phone, although
he'd never had the cause or desire to text him in the past.

The message he sent was short and to the point.

*I think we need to talk about The Velvet Room. And
my great-aunt Violet.*

Chapter Fifteen

Wednesday—Two days until showtime

They were up to their ears in trouble-making scripts. Griff flicked over another page of the enormous tome on the grass beside him. Navigating the written version of *The Austen Playbook* was like trying to follow an instruction manual that had been blown about in the wind and then shoved back into a pile with no respect for page numbers. The scene variations meant that it cut abruptly in places and then skipped ahead nine or ten pages. He wasn't surprised Freddy was having trouble keeping her lines straight. He was finding it difficult just to prompt her.

"Act two, scene four, second variation," he said, feeling like the conductor of an extremely complicated symphony, and Freddy hesitated and then swung into her monologue. A snap of the fingers and he had Lydia Bennet sitting across from him—flighty, flirty, shallow, and, in Freddy's hands, bringing moments of definite and unexpected pathos.

In some ways Lydia's personality was the extreme edge of Freddy's own blithe, flirtatious side, but the character lacked her fundamental strength and generosity.

She was obviously in her element with this show, though, and enjoying the material—if they could work out where they were in it.

"I think you're doing the third variation." He flipped over another few pages, looking for the lines she was reciting. "This is the one where Wickham goes ahead with the affair with Mrs. Elton."

"Shit." Freddy sat up straighter and reached for the script. The breeze lifted the edges of the pages and fluttered the hem of her skirt. He'd met her for her lunch break on the grass at the edge of the south woodland. They were sitting facing each other at the base of a towering oak, their legs entwined at the ankles. "We're two days out from the show and I'm still not completely off-book. So much for my decisive gesture, walking out of *The Velvet Room* audition. I wouldn't rate my chances at being offered Marguerite even if I'd stayed. And I'm not exactly going to blow Fiona Gallagher away. At this rate, I'd be lucky if I got a role as third tree on the left."

"You're almost word-perfect with the lines. It's just keeping track of the bloody jumping around." He studied the page critically. "Although you can possibly play the odds on which of these variations the public is likely to vote for. I'd be surprised if they vote in any of the options that mess with the Elizabeth/Darcy love story." Running his fingertips around her ankle bone, Griff added drily, "Unless Waitely pisses everyone off so much they decide it's best that Darcy drowns in the lake."

"Dylan's much better as Darcy than I thought he'd be. Well," Freddy amended, "at least, he's nailed the pre-first-proposal, arrogant, nose-in-the-air Darcy. He's less believable as the more approachable, sacrifice-pride-for-love Darcy. I still put the possibility of him joining the fictional body count at about twenty percent." She let one of her knees fall to the side as his fingers advanced farther up her leg. "Lydia's definite whodunit bait. I give myself a fifty-percent chance of an early exit to the green room. Although I think she has a lot of built-up anger by that point and I fancy myself more in the role of unveiled murderer than poisoned corpse, so I'm hoping people vote for the third variation in the final choice. Tell your friends." She wriggled at his touch. "Actually, I'm hoping people vote, full stop."

"Yes." With everything up in the air with the film project and Rupert as yet ignoring both Freddy's calls and Griff's private message, the bills for his parents' latest extravagance were pressing and the larger the cheque from the Austen crowd, the better. "Charlie's enlisted everyone he knows to watch and vote on Friday, so that should bring in half of London."

"Fingers crossed the other half tune in for the chance to fictionally off Dylan, then." Freddy squirmed again as his fingers reached the skin at the top of her inner thigh. It was unbelievably soft, silkier than the fabric of the very brief briefs she wore. When he touched her there, she made that little purring sound in her throat that had a similar effect to a physical stroke on his own flesh. The wash of lust was a welcome release from the feeling of being constantly on edge.

Swiftly moving his hands down, Griff circled his fingers around each of her ankles and pulled. Fortunately, she'd grown up performing athletic manoeuvres in the musicals she loved, so she ended up where he'd intended. In his lap, her legs fully wrapped around his waist, and not sprawled on her back with the wind knocked out of her.

She immediately looped her arms around his neck. She was so damn affectionate, so unhesitatingly generous with her touches and her laughter; and entwined with the intense sexual attraction between them, Griff found a bone-deep comfort in her presence that he'd never experienced. Never realised he wanted. He cupped the back of her head and kissed her neck, the spot below her ear that made her hum and melt into him.

"I may not be the best person to help you rehearse," he murmured to her throat, and felt the vibration as she spoke, low and husky.

"Call it practice for the Wickham kiss in the first act."

Griff stopped kissing her neck, lifted his head, and looked at her. She'd been drawing patterns on his back, but the moment the words left her mouth, she stilled. Delicately clearing her throat, she ventured, "Er…delete last comment and insert something really sexy that doesn't mention snogging another man?"

"If you want to kill the mood so you can get back to work," Griff said, unable to hold back a smile at her comically chastened expression, "I suggest you just throw the mug of cold tea in my face."

She took his face in both hands, smacked a kiss on his mouth, and crawled back to a safe distance to reach for the script again.

"*Is* there a kiss with Wickham?" he asked idly, stretching out his legs.

"Mmm." She flipped through the pages, looking for the right scene.

"And Wickham would be the model who keeps sauntering around the grounds taking selfies, would he?"

"Sounds plausible." Finding her place, Freddy smoothed out the script and glanced up at him through her lashes.

"It's just another scripted gesture. A bit awkward the first time, and then it becomes part of the routine. About as passionate as boiling an egg."

Griff leaned back against the tree trunk and closed his eyes. "I'm sure."

"He uses too much lip balm. It's like pressing my mouth against a melted candle."

"Is it."

"He has bad breath, too."

"Good."

"And the one time I thought he was scowling at me, it turned out to be a false alarm. He had something in his eye. He just *smiles* all the time, like some sort of unhinged clown. Where's the fun in that?"

She squeaked and started to giggle when, lightning-fast, eyes still closed, he tossed a stray bread roll at her. Grinning, he lay listening to her read lines, but when her voice trailed away, and she obviously thought he'd dropped off, he cracked open an eye.

For the fifth time in the past hour, she was checking her silent phone. She'd called Rupert back this morning, and several times since, and obviously thought she was getting the silent treatment over the missed audition. Rupert switching up his usual steamroller attitude for a touch of passive-aggression.

Griff had very few good things to say about Rupert Carlton in general, and an even bigger bone to pick with him now, but he especially did not fucking like the way the man treated Freddy.

Freddy, in turn, was obviously not very impressed with his own parents' priorities.

It was going to be a bloody awkward Christmas dinner this year.

When Freddy went back to rehearsal, Griff went in search of his brother and found him in the garage, working on his latest project.

"Hey," Charlie said, frowning into a shoddy-looking engine. "How goes the production? Is it going to soar on Friday and keep us here for another Christmas?"

"Provided everybody remembers which scene they're in, we can only hope."

"I should have negotiated a fixed fee," Charlie muttered.

Griff studied the car he was working on, then looked around the garage he rarely bothered coming into. His brother had neat, labelled boxes of tools and parts, and all manner of machinery tided away. It looked like a professional workshop. "There would be no immediate cash injection coming in at all if you hadn't organised it." Then he said, "Charlie," and at the seriousness of his voice, Charlie set down a tool and reached for an oil-stained rag.

"What's going on?" he asked, wiping his hands.

Automatically, out of habit, Griff started cataloguing words in his mind, sifting through the information he should share with Charlie, the parts that were best left for him to deal with himself. No. His mouth twisted wryly. *Delegation.* Not so much acting lessons as life lessons with Freddy Carlton. Opening up to the people he cared about. Asking for help when he needed it. "There are some things you should know. About Great-Aunt Violet, and Henrietta Carlton. And the film. The gateposts just shifted radically. But there's a problem, and it's going to affect Freddy."

Charlie put down the rag and sat on a metal step. "I'm listening."

Thursday—One Day until Showtime

"Waitely!" Maf stopped pacing up and down the front of the stage like an angry tiger and turned on Dylan, who stared back at her sulkily. Whipping the pen from behind her ear, she pointed it at him. "Are you suffering from some unpleasant digestive disorder?"

His lips pinching together, Dylan propped his hands on his hips. "What?" Sweat was beading on his forehead, dripping down into his eyes. They were all feeling the heat, in more than one respect. One day left until the curtain rose and the TV cameras rolled.

"Unless you require the medic to be summoned, could we aim for haughty rather than nauseated, please?" Maf shoved her hand through her mass of grey hair, which had been so heavily moussed and sprayed that it followed the movements of her fingers and ended up sticking straight out.

Everybody was more seamless with their lines today; the prompter had to interject only once. But tempers were short and the rising pressure had joined forces with the vividly hot sun outside. The adorable, atmospheric theatre had become the choking, claustrophobic theatre. Even with the ventilation system pumping away, it was like being trapped in an oven.

Sadie smirked and fluttered her hand up to examine her nails. With a silent refrain of "What Would Griff Do?" in her head, Freddy had been determined to remain cool in the face of Sadie's continued digs, take the superior road and blank her, but she was more inclined right now to do a "What Would Rocky Balboa Do?" and just punch her in the nose.

"Freddy." Maf's tone was so censorious that for an

insane second Freddy thought the director had plucked that thought right out of her head. "I know I demanded a rounded characterisation from you, but I think you're overplaying Lydia's mental state in this scene. At this point, she's not tragically torn in her decision. She's faced few consequences of her behaviour, and the scale of her ambition might be comparatively limited, but she's prepared to be ruthless in carrying it out."

Sadie wandered past Freddy, speaking in a low voice. "Are you sure you didn't fuck Steve Lemmon, as well? It's like he tailor-made this role for you."

Summoning the last reserves of her patience, Freddy managed to keep her eyes and attention on Maf, ignoring the serpent slithering in hip-swaying circles around her. "Tone down the indecision. Got it."

She couldn't help her gaze straying to the chair in the stalls where she'd left her stuff. Her phone was on silent, but it was starting to look like her father didn't plan to call her back. Which was out of character, to say the least. He didn't make a habit of ringing her for chummy family chats, but he didn't usually ignore her, either. He'd consider that highly unprofessional behaviour between a manager and his client. She'd expected him down here in person by now, with several things to say on the subject of *The Velvet Room*.

"Right," Maf snapped. "Break for thirty minutes, before I fire someone. And Sadie, for God's sake, would you stop flowing about in circles? You look like a concussed squid."

Sadie had just flowed around Maya a couple of times, murmuring something to her. Her face took on an unflattering undertone of purple. Even she wouldn't mess with Maf, so she resorted to a sniff, followed by a meaningful look at Maya.

Who was shaking. Physically trembling.

Sharply, Freddy looked at where Sadie was slinking towards the most comfortable chair, next to the air vent, and then back at Maya, who was almost jogging towards the outside door.

Taking the steps two at a time, she grabbed her phone and followed Maya out into the sunshine, catching her up at the catering tent. She stood for a moment, watching her castmate join the line for food and reach for a plate with unsteady hands.

"I didn't think you liked shellfish," she said, as Maya piled shrimp salad on a plate.

Maya jumped so hard she dropped the serving spoon she was holding. "Oh—Freddy." She looked down at the food. "Oh. No. I'm just…" For someone who was such a brilliant actor onstage, she was absolutely rubbish at pretence as soon as she stepped out of character.

"Fetching a food plate for our lazy resident squid?" Freddy asked bluntly. "Who is a total fiend for shrimp."

Maya opened her mouth, then closed it. She swallowed.

Freddy took the plate from her before she dropped it as well, and, surveying the options, plunked on a few more spoonfuls from dishes she knew Her Majesty deemed acceptable for consumption. Then she walked over to an unoccupied bench, where they were unlikely to be overheard, and Maya automatically followed her, looking dazed. Freddy handed the full plate back. "What does Sadie have on you?"

She was just about at the end of her rope with the intrigues and skulduggery around this place. What *was* it about Highbrook? It was like the moment people entered the gates, they tumbled into some weird gameshow. Unethical Choices. *Will it be door number one, plagiarism? Does door number two and a spot of adultery tickle your fancy? No, she's going for door number three. It's black-mail, folks.*

Maya blanched. Bullseye. But under Freddy's scrutiny, her acting ability made a belated return and her expression smoothed out. Too little, too late, but clearly she didn't want Freddy's help or a sympathetic ear. Well, fair enough. It was none of Freddy's business, and God knew she had no intention of sharing her own tale of Sadie woe with Maya.

All Sadie could do was taunt Freddy, but she'd managed to turn Maya into her unpaid PA. Apparently Maya's misdemeanour, whatever it was, had worse repercussions for her if Sadie blabbed.

"Sadie asked if I'd mind, since I was coming out here anyway, and I thought it was best for cast relations to just agree," Maya said firmly, her eyes not quite meeting Freddy's.

It was true that it was better not to rock the boat at this point. No matter how much you disliked your castmates, on opening night—or only night, in this case—you left that in the wings. The production sailed or sank on the combined efforts of everyone involved.

Freddy still didn't believe a word Maya was saying. Since she wasn't going to be a hypocrite and force the issue, she just made a humming noise. "You're doing brilliantly with Elizabeth." She directed the conversation into safer territory. "You might have a Darcy who occasionally looks like he has salmonella, but people are going to love your Elizabeth."

Maya seemed to force her mind back into the present. "I hope so. *I* love how nuanced you're making Lydia. She's really coming alive in your performance."

"I hope it's going to go well," Freddy said, with a renewed flip of nerves in her stomach. With all the balls that were in the air, her attention was divided, but she was increasingly aware of how few hours were left before the cameras went live. And before Fiona Gallagher made her entrance.

"Oh God, so do I. I'm not used to having to combine camera angles with stage positioning, and I avoid interviews like the plague, so I've never actually done a live broadcast before. Have you?"

"I did the royal charity performance, but that's pre-taped. Oh." Freddy grimaced. "And I did an interview on Nick Davenport's show."

Maya's head jerked. "Right. He's coming tomorrow. And so is your sister." Talk about couples growing to look like each other; now they had a green-tinged Elizabeth as well as a sick-looking Darcy. "Um…was it scary? The interview with Nick Davenport?"

Freddy was apprehensive about the live pre-show coverage, as well, but not because she was worried about the interview segments. Sabrina was still off in fairyland about Ferren, who'd obviously snuck off to London to see her a few times this week, and nothing seemed to wind Nick up more than when the tabloids were full of pictures of Sabs and Ferren wrapped around each other in nightclubs. They each liked to remain the most high-profile. Hopeless publicity hounds, the pair of them.

Freddy felt all defensive about them making a scene on Griff's property.

She seemed to have become the dull, responsible member of the family.

"Not so much scary as irritating," she said. "I got a grilling about my personal life. Nick decided to push the line that I was shagging Dylan." Maya shot her a quick look. "God. Give me some credit. Of course I wasn't."

Something in Maya's face, some tiny change, registered, and Freddy froze in the process of weaving her sweaty hair into a plait. "Oh my God. Are *you*?" It was nosy as fuck, but the question tumbled out before she could stop it, and Maya's face flushed, deep and ruddy.

"What? No!" Her words stumbled over each other. "God, no. Don't be silly. I get enough of having to cuddle up to Dylan onstage."

Freddy stared at her suspiciously, but her attention snagged on the cars rolling up the driveway. She recognised the one in front. "Speaking of the interview segment, here comes half of the chat-show invasion. That's Sabrina."

Maya bolted. Just turned and dashed off towards the theatre, still holding Sadie's plate of food, and Freddy looked after her in astonishment. Jesus. That didn't bode well for Maya making it through her share of the interview tomorrow.

"If it isn't my baby sister, the budding TV star." Sabrina slammed her car door and advanced on Freddy, grinning. Ferren's sneak visits to London seemed to have put her in a better mood since the last time Freddy had spoken to her.

She wasn't sure how her sister had even got out of the car in her skin-tight midi skirt and sky-high heels, but she looked fab. With an envious look at Sabrina's red hair, which seemed to defy all laws of the curly-headed and never frizz, Freddy went forward to give her a hug.

Sabrina squeezed her. "How's it going? Are all signs pointing to a smash hit?"

"There've definitely been signs recently," Freddy said, stepping back. "But who knows where they're pointing? Are you here to do recce?"

"We always finalise preparations on-site if we're broadcasting outside the studio." Sabrina smoothed back a red curl and looked around. "Oh, what a beautiful place." Hands on her hips, she turned in a circle, taking everything in, then cast Freddy a wicked glance, her vivid green eyes sparkling. "You didn't forget which character you're playing and do an Elizabeth Bennet, did you? Do we mark the moment you were prepared to overlook Malfoy's faults to your first seeing his beautiful grounds here at Highbrook?"

Freddy shot her a look, and her sister grinned. "Have *The Davenport Report* team been here yet, by the way?"

"Not that I've seen."

"How slapdash and fly-by-night of them." Sabrina elevated her ski-jump nose. "I'm surprised. Davenport is such a competitive bastard that I thought he'd have been paying nightly visits to secure the best camera angles."

"Yes, it's a shame you're so retiring and bashful yourself. The way you just let him walk all over you is really tragic."

Sabrina laughed, and Freddy added, with a shade of apprehension, "You guys aren't going to rumble tomorrow, are you? We're trying to walk the line between good publicity for the show and not being overshadowed completely when you and Nick come together to film in the same location and the universe implodes."

"Fear not, little sis. I'm a professional, and he's too

vain to make himself look bad on live TV. We'll be so polite you won't know us."

"In that case, I suspect I won't."

"It's a great location. It'll make a nice change from the studio or getting blown about on the banks of the river. Dad didn't kick up too much of a stink about you doing this show against his advice, did he?"

Freddy glanced at her quickly. "Why? You haven't heard from him, have you?"

"No. But that's not unusual. He's not interested in what I'm up to." Sabrina sounded completely blasé about that, but Freddy often wondered how indifferent she really was.

"I'm sure he's proud of you."

Sabrina made a disparaging noise. "Right. That's why he's never once watched the show, didn't call to congratulate me when I was promoted to full-time, and hasn't even remembered my birthday for the past few years."

Rupert never remembered Freddy's birthday these days, either. It was only audition dates he seemed to recall with perfect accuracy.

It hadn't always been like that. *Mostly*, she had to admit, but there had been times…moments, memories…

"Remember your twelfth birthday? You were really into baking back then. You said you were going to be a famous patisserie chef when you grew up. And Dad took us to Paris for the day, and managed to get Suzette Morel to invite you into her salon." It was one of her clearest early memories. "He helped you make a cake."

Sabrina's profile was set as she stared at the house, but her lips moved in a tiny tremor before she pressed them together. "No," she said, eventually, and her tone didn't invite further reminiscence. "I don't remember that."

Freddy looked at her silently, and touched her hand. "*I'm* proud of you."

Sabrina turned her head, and her eyes warmed back to their usual green brilliance. "Likewise, Peanut."

"Sabs." Freddy hesitated. She felt she owed it to their father to tell him first what she'd discovered about Henrietta, but Sabrina had worked so hard and come so far in her career, and the potential fallout from this could affect her as well. She deserved a heads-up. "About Henrietta and *The Velvet Room*—"

Sabrina groaned. "Freddy, I read the bloody play, but I don't really want to have another cosy chat about Grandma. And I have to meet our executive producer over at the house in about—"

"You need to know this." It was Freddy's turn to cut her off, and Sabrina went immediately speculative. Out with the snarky sister, in with the journalist.

"Sounds serious."

"It is. Akiko obviously hasn't mentioned anything." She was getting flustered. When Sabs stared like that, it felt like they ought to be sitting under hot lights in a studio, cameras rolling.

"She's in on the secret, is she?" Sabrina suddenly pressed a fingertip to the spot between Freddy's brows. "You've got a fucking stress twitch. What the hell's going on?" Before Freddy could answer, she glanced hastily at her watch. "Shit, I am running short on time. Is it urgent, or can we have a proper sit-down in the weekend?"

Freddy couldn't imagine they would be taking any action until *The Austen Playbook* was safely wound up. One problem play at a time. "Okay."

At that moment, there was movement in her peripheral vision as Griff came out of the theatre and headed for the woodland path. He saw them and nodded once at Sabrina before his eyes found Freddy's and locked there. Even at a distance, the connection kicked her breath into an unsteady rhythm.

Sabrina cleared her throat loudly and Freddy jumped. "Will this mysterious discussion involve my dear Lord Disdain over there, by any chance?"

"Only indirectly." A slight stiffness was creeping over her, that protectiveness where Griff was concerned. Sabrina had made her opinion of him frank enough in the past, and Freddy doubted she was going to be singing a different tune now.

She wasn't.

After giving her another hard stare, Sabrina groaned. "Oh, God. You're sleeping with him." She shook her head. "Considering the resounding deficits of his personality, character and manners, and everything he's said about you in the past, he must be bloody amazing in bed to put that look on your face."

"Oh, he is. But that's not why I l-like him so much. And there's nothing wrong with his character or his personality." Freddy skipped over the manners aspect. She was completely lost over Griff, but she wasn't delusional. He wasn't exactly Britain's answer to Emily Post.

Sabrina hadn't missed the slight hesitation before that "L" word. The spark of concern in her eyes deepened. "You're not…getting in too deep, are you?"

Suddenly, Freddy could understand a little more why Sabrina slammed down a barrier the moment Freddy mentioned her relationship with Ferren. "Every day, I think I'm in as far as it's possible to go." She spoke slowly. "And then I find we've swum a bit farther, and I can't imagine the tide is ever going to turn." Coming back to herself, she lifted one shoulder. "Despite everything that's going wrong, in some ways I feel so lucky right now."

Sabrina tapped her nails against the plastic cover of her phone. "I don't want to be rude, but your judgment where men is concerned hasn't always been the best."

Freddy's head jerked. First of all, Sabrina could turn that accusation right around and direct it at herself. And secondly— "Are you seriously throwing what happened with Drew Townseville in my face?"

"No, of course not. You were a baby. It's not your fault that piece of shit took advantage. But you do have a track record of falling for pretty faces and words, and tumbling into infatuation with dickheads. And it never lasts. I just—don't want you to invest too much and get hurt."

Her body taut, Freddy considered her response. "I don't think there was anything wrong with testing the waters, enjoying my feelings, especially when I was younger." Her eyes met Sabrina's. "This isn't the same. It's…more." So very much more. "And if you hadn't noticed, I'm a grown woman. If I end up getting hurt, I would still never regret falling for him. I'm not going to hold back on *investing* in him just because there are no guarantees in life."

Sabrina sighed. "But *Ford-Griffin*. He's such a—"

"He's loyal, and he respects me, and he treats me well." Freddy should have left it at that, but her family insisted on believing she was incapable of making the right decisions without their input, and the frustration bubbled over. "Which is more than you can say about Ferren."

Sabrina went equally rigid. "I told you—"

"Yes, you've told me quite a lot of things about Ferren," Freddy said with a sharp edge. "And about Griff.

And I'm sorry, but our opinions differ drastically as to which of us is investing unwisely in a man who's really a bit of a shit." Once she'd started, she couldn't seem to stop. "I don't think you're in a position to make sweeping statements about—about enduring love. In the very beginning, I thought you and Ferren were like this romantic ideal, but no matter how good it might be with him at times, he treats you and everybody else like crap the moment he doesn't get his own way. He's reckless, he's selfish, he *does not care*. And I love you so much, and you're worth so much more than that."

The silence that followed was broken only by their jagged breaths. They stood staring at each other, with clenched fists.

Sabrina's eyes were bright. She parted her lips, started to say something, and then turned on her heel and walked away.

Freddy stayed there motionless on the grass for so long that the time ran out, and she had to literally sprint back to The Henry. They were using prop swords onstage today and unless she fancied decapitation by blunt blade, this wasn't the time to test Maf's patience.

The rest of rehearsal proceeded smoothly enough, but with taut undercurrents everywhere. Freddy felt as if they were all balancing on a wafer-thin high wire that could snap at any moment. Maya kept darting glances at Sadie between scenes. She definitely had the look of someone who'd done something wrong, knew she was going to be found out, and was waiting for the axe to fall.

Dylan was flirting, which was normal, and Ferren was brooding, which was alarming. If he was starting on a downward spiral, the crash was always spectacular. One day; he just had to hold it together for one more day.

Mid-afternoon, Sabrina and her team came in to see the interior of the theatre. Sabs was always careful not to cause disruption whenever she filmed on location, but several of her crew were less conscientious, and Maf gripped her hair in both hands when a cameraman crashed about with his equipment. The commotion threw Maya off her stride and she stumbled over a line, and Sadie quivered with sadistic amusement.

Sabrina and Ferren locked eyes, and Ferren's expression underwent a complete transformation. He leapt from the stage, landed at Sabrina's feet, and took her hands in his. She looked up at him between her lashes.

Freddy tightened her grip on the prop embroidery she was holding. The intensity when those two were together was undeniable. Considering Sabrina was her sister, it was a bit awkward that they absolutely radiated sexual tension.

She had once thought that it was love between them. Passionate and exciting and turbulent, but underneath, something real.

Now, having seen Akiko and Elise support and shelter each other through some very difficult times, and…and feeling the way she did herself, she thought that what was between Sabrina and Ferren was sex, and history, and mutual destruction.

When Griff came to find her after rehearsal, she was sitting outside the theatre on a wooden bench, watching the sky streak into shades of pink and orange, the trees becoming dark silhouettes against the pastel horizon. She held her phone on her lap. Lots of messages, but still nothing from her father.

Griff's hair was damp from a shower and he looked

exhausted. He sat down next to her, and put his hand over hers. Their fingers twined together.

It was very quiet for once, all the people and work and madness temporarily banished. All she could hear was the faint trill of an insect nearby.

After a moment, Freddy leaned her cheek against his shoulder, and felt his fingers tighten on hers.

Chapter Sixteen

Friday morning—Just hours to go

There was a knack to shower sex. And they didn't have it.

Freddy fell back against the wall of the stall, pushing her wet hair out of her face, giggling helplessly. Every morning this week, she'd woken up with that tense, anxious expression that sat so poorly on her naturally happy face, and it was a relief to see her laughing. Even if it had come at the expense of a mutual failed orgasm and a near drowning.

Griff propped his arm against the opposite wall and slicked back his own hair. "I'm assuming that wasn't quite what you had in mind."

"Well." Freddy grinned at him. "No. When I said 'cinematic shower sex,' the film I was thinking of wasn't *The Abyss*. I wasn't sure we were going to make it out alive at one point. I take full responsibility for blocking the drain with my foot."

"And I apologise for knocking down the faucet." Griff shook his head. They were both naked and wet, but even with a hint of bite back in the air today, his chest warmed as he looked at her.

Her cheeks were flushed and her curls were straggling

in ropes over her shoulders, and his precisely ordered life seemed to have exploded into chaos since he'd met her.

And he was so bloody in love with her.

He'd wondered if the intensity of his feelings for her could possibly last or if he'd feel differently in an hour, a day, a year.

Already, he did feel differently. As each minute passed, and the hours clustered into days, his attachment to her, the connection between them, seemed to strengthen and take root in every part of his mind and body. From those first tentative, whisper-fine threads into a knot of solid platinum.

She shivered. Still smiling a little, she crossed her arms, rubbing at the goose bumps appearing on her skin. Griff reached out and hooked a finger through one of hers. He tugged, and her smile took on that mischievous, provocative tilt. She came forward, her arms sliding around his waist. Cuddling into his body, she nuzzled her cheek against his chest in a gesture that was almost catlike, and so transparently affectionate that his heart fucking clenched.

Sliding his hand down over the soft curves of her arse, he nudged her temple with his nose. She looked up, a spark igniting in her eyes, but being so delightfully... *Freddy*, didn't just obligingly lift her mouth for his kiss. Looping one arm about his neck, she yanked him down to her and pressed her lips enthusiastically to his.

She broke the kiss long enough to lean out of the stall and snatch up another condom, and he gritted his teeth as she rolled it onto him with adept strokes that sent jolts of sensation down his legs and up his spine. Griff lifted her in a swift movement, her legs twining around his waist, his tongue delving deeply back into her mouth.

"Mmm." Freddy made a muffled sound, tilting her head to kiss the side of his mouth, his cheek, his jawbone. "I don't think I'll bother with morning runs ever again. You're much better exercise."

His laugh was ragged as his breath ran short and his blood shot southward. "As pillow talk goes, I'm not sure you'd have Shakespeare looking to his laurels."

Her reply was lost as his mouth returned to hers, and the kiss grew long and hot and drugging. Bracing Freddy against the wall, Griff held her up with his body, and her heels dug into the small of his back when he pushed slowly back inside her.

It was significantly easier with the water off.

Sex with Freddy had so far been an incredibly intense rush. This was far more relaxed, an almost leisurely build of pleasure as he stroked into her and she smoothed her fingertips over his cheeks and smiled into his eyes.

He could feel the movement of her chest, the push of her breasts against him as her breath quickened, and the quivering in the muscles of her thighs as her legs started to clench around him. Then internal muscles gripped down hard on his erection, and the rocking of her hips faltered.

She wrapped her arms tightly around his head, and he kissed her neck as the pulsing rippled through her body.

He increased the pace of his thrusts, driving his own spiralling pleasure upward, but trying to keep his movements relatively shallow, despite the urge to push and hold in deep. She'd sworn up and down that her pelvic pain had subsided, but—

His mind whited out as the pressure broke and spilled over, his nerve endings seeming to spark through his entire body. A rough sound broke from his throat, and he closed his eyes as Freddy held him close.

When he was confident enough in the stability of his arms and legs to lift his head and straighten, she adjusted the grip of her thighs over his hips, and slowly touched a finger to the centre of his chin.

He was expecting a light, cheeky comment, but her voice was solemn. "Thank you for making this week bearable for me."

His eyes searched hers, then he tucked her face back into the curve of his neck, sheltering her body with his own.

As they got dressed in the bedroom, Freddy's fingers flew as she buttoned up her dress. She was due at the theatre soon. Instead of encouraging the cast to chill out in the hours leading up to opening night, Maf Reynolds was still drilling cues into them for the different scene sequences, and her roaring had echoed around the estate this week when anyone was late. She was clearly worried about how the performance was going to come off.

"Griff." He glanced up at the alteration in Freddy's tone. A certain tension had slipped back into the set of her shoulders, and he assumed the subject in her mind had something to do with her grandmother. Even decades later, the bloody woman was still causing strife. "You've studied art history. What do you know about Billy Gotham?"

"Not a lot." He tucked his shirt into his trousers and did up his belt. "Twentieth-century portraiture isn't my area. He had a successful showing in a Royal Academy summer exhibition, attracted the notice of an influential patron, and his career took off from there. He was one of the pet society artists. And obviously became wealthy, because the boy who was born in one of the poorest streets in the East End eventually died in a home he owned in Knightsbridge."

"Alone?" Freddy asked, winding her hair into a coil on top of her head. "He never married?"

"No." Griff propped his hip against the desk. "He never married."

"Because he was still in love with Violet."

"Conjecture," Griff pointed out, and she wrinkled her nose at him. "But possibly, yes."

Not so long ago, he'd have sneered at any possibility that romantic love could be so enduring, so life-altering as that.

It no longer seemed like a notion that belonged only in fiction.

Freddy reached up to kiss him. Her mint-scented breath had just touched his skin when someone knocked on the door. She froze. "Why do I suddenly have an apprehensive feeling?"

"Because you have an overactive imagination that's proving to be contagious, and it would be best for all concerned if you put a line through whodunits on your list of future projects." He pulled open the door just as she threw a pillow at his head.

"Ahoy there, young lovers." Charlie was wearing his usual smile, but there was wariness behind it. "Sorry to break up the party," he said with a quirked brow at the pillow. "But I need a word, Griff."

Griff stepped back to let him in, but Charlie cast a glance at Freddy. "Er…in private. No offense intended, Freddy."

"None taken. I have to get to the theatre." Freddy went

up on her tiptoes and kissed Griff's cheek, her hand resting on the crook of his arm.

She shot him a smile as she went out, transparently pleased to see him and Charlie advancing to the stage of brotherly heart-to-hearts.

Unfortunately, he suspected that wasn't why his brother was here.

Once Freddy was out of earshot, he turned with raised eyebrows.

"Rupert Carlton has arrived," Charlie said. "He's waiting for you in the library."

He clenched his jaw. "Right."

"It'll work out," Charlie said, and Griff looked at him.

"That blind optimism again?"

Charlie shook his head. "That faith again."

On the first landing, they passed Sadie Foster leaning against the wall and cooing into her phone. She looked as innocent and sweet as a chocolate-box painting until her eyes lifted. She sneered at them as she continued to pour honeyed bullshit into some gullible sod's ear.

"God, she's a piece of work," Charlie muttered, and Griff glanced back at her.

She was watching them with narrowed eyes, her body language shrewd and assessing. As his cool gaze met hers, she raised her chin with clear disdain.

Downstairs, Griff paused with his hand on the library door. Charlie dropped back a few paces, a supportive presence at his back, but giving him space. An instant of silent communication passed between them, before Charlie formed a fist with his right hand and pressed it over his heart.

It was a gesture he hadn't made for years. Griff had last seen him do it when he'd been a skinny kid, standing on the paved steps leading up to his boarding school, watching Griff drive away after his visit to the headmaster's office. Griff had been eighteen then, heading into London on a mission to find enough money to pay Charlie's school fees, with no plan in mind, but a kid behind him who believed he could make anything right.

His chest momentarily tight, Griff opened the door. Rupert Carlton was standing very still in a slice of sunlight from the window, leaning on his walking stick, looking down at the Wythburn Group materials Griff had left scattered across his desk.

The older man lifted his head. Lines around his eyes spoke of physical pain and sleepless nights.

Griff closed the door behind him. "Carlton."

"Ford-Griffin." Rupert had a way of pronouncing Griff's name that pushed his mouth into a shape like he'd just smelled a rotten egg.

There was no love lost between them—and this conversation wasn't going to endear them to each other—but the fact was, this was Freddy's father. And she loved him.

Nevertheless, he couldn't quite keep the edge of sarcasm from his voice. "I see you got my message. Eventually."

Rupert closed his hand into a fist where it rested against the papers on the desk. "I believe you wanted to discuss this aborted film of yours."

"The film comes into it." Griff walked over to the bookshelves and bent down, scanning the spines, looking for the book. His own copy was still over in the office at The Henry, but he remembered there being a copy— There. Pulling it from the shelf, he joined Rupert at the desk.

He set *All Her World* down on the desk in front of its author. "But I think we'd better talk about this first, don't you?"

* * *

Sadie was tormenting Maya again. After absolutely *bouncing* onto the stage ten minutes late, with such a bubbly attitude that even the telling-off from Maf hadn't fazed her and Freddy had actually wondered if she was drunk, she'd resorted back to type.

From her position in the stands, Freddy watched with growing concern as Maya pulled at the label of her water bottle, looking close to tears. She'd never seen Maya falling apart like this. She was holding it together onstage so far, but she was a total mess between scenes. God, Sadie had a nasty streak the length of the Nile. And besides everything else, she was jeopardising the whole production by undermining cast morale, and this was going on her CV as well.

Cross-legged, Freddy reached for her own water bottle and a couple of the paracetamol tablets she had left. Her leg had almost healed, but her stress headache was thumping. Fruitlessly, she checked her phone again.

She wondered if her father was even planning to come to the performance tonight.

She heard voices as a group of people came into the rear stalls, and for a moment thought it was Griff, but when she turned, saw Charlie. He was talking to the TV crew, but as he caught her eye, he winked.

Actually—he looked a bit…furtive. Guilty, even.

Freddy frowned, swallowing down her tablets. She could hear the resonance of his voice, but not the words. He *did* have a similar voice to Griff. It was one of their few physical similarities. Otherwise, you'd never know they were related. Charlie hadn't been blessed with her favourite nose on the planet, the glorious hooked bridge Griff shared with Violet, and his smile was—

At that moment, Charlie grinned at something the head producer said to him, and Freddy stilled.

It was the most extraordinary sensation, like a veil of fog had been resting over the final piece of the puzzle, and she'd been too blind to see it. With that same buzzing feeling in her ears that she'd experienced in the old nursery at Mallowren Manor, she checked the time on her phone. Fifteen minutes until her next cue.

Long enough.

In a rush of movement, suddenly driven to just *know* all of it, she hurried across the theatre floor to the side door that led to the rear passageway. As she slipped through it, she caught a glimpse of Charlie looking startled and a bit concerned.

The back hallways were empty, and she made it to Henrietta's office without anyone stopping her for a chat or to deliver more instructions in the chaotic final lead-up to the performance.

The room felt echoing and eerie in the quiet. In the air above the shattered tile wall, little dust motes were still dancing in the dim light. Griff had left a few scattered materials on the desk, including a stack of books.

Freddy checked the spines and found the one she was looking for. His copy of *All Her World*.

Sitting down at the desk, she flipped through until she found the chapter that included Rupert's own childhood recollections of Highbrook. The weeks that he had spent here while his mother was supposedly writing *The Velvet Room*.

She had forgotten. In the shock of everything, and the confusion, and the increasing performance pressure, she'd forgotten that her father hadn't just written about

Henrietta and the creation of the play in general terms. He'd actually described—

Once she began writing, she sank into the script and didn't emerge for days. I still remember seeing her there at the desk, hand flying, ink splattering, page after page thrown into a messy pile that would later require meticulous reorganizing. And all the while, that strange little triangular smile on her face. Her expression throughout was part cynicism, part determination—and underlying it, the oddest sense of despair. Even as a child, I felt it as a chilled atmosphere that seemed to permeate the very walls.

Freddy stared down at the page, her fingers resting on two words.

As the numbness cleared, a creeping fury began to sidle in.

She slammed the cover closed, and stormed towards the door.

Outside in the drizzling rain, she passed a few people on her jog down the woodland path, but they all took one surprised look at her expression and gave her a wide berth.

When she reached the house, more cars were rolling into the driveway, and she was forced to stop briefly as the tall man emerging from an Audi hailed her in a deep voice. Fisting her hands to hold back her nervous energy, she stood still as Nick Davenport snapped open an umbrella and came to hold it over both their heads. He was broad-shouldered and long-legged, with dark skin and eyes, and his bone structure was unbelievable. He might have been carved by Michelangelo rather than sprouting from cells like other mortals. The designer of that suit should be paying him advertising commission. He was also a human fox terrier when it came to sniffing out potential stories, and one of the last people on the planet she wanted to make forced small talk with right now.

"Freddy Carlton," he said, oh so charmingly. He and Sabrina—the practiced schmoozers. They were more alike than they'd ever admit. "Nice to see you again. I hope things are on track here?"

A sound emerged from her throat that jumbled together irony and misery with a hint of hysteria, and Nick was obviously taken aback. He almost lost the trademark smile completely. "Problem?"

"Several. Excuse me." Ducking around him, Freddy dashed through the rain towards the house. She'd apologise for the rudeness later, although behind that smooth exterior Nick was ruthless and probably impervious to snubs.

Inside, she went straight to the library. Griff and Charlie had obviously finished their conversation, so she expected he'd be in there working.

She had several things to say to him. Her incredibly acute lover and budding *best mate*, who knew the research material for his film like the back of his hand.

She put her hand on the library door and stopped as voices came to her from the other side of the wood. It was déjà vu to the moment at the Metronome, standing there, listening to words that affected her profoundly. Not quite in the same way this time.

"...don't tell Freddy..." She heard Griff's deep tones distinctly, followed by an inaudible muttering from a voice slightly higher in pitch.

That she also recognised.

Her temper snapped.

Chapter Seventeen

Freddy pushed open the library door without knocking, and the two men she cared about most in the world turned their heads. They were standing by the table, with documents strewn between them, looking like a couple of wartime generals consulting on the plan of attack. Making arrangements that would affect other people's lives, behind their backs.

Ignoring Griff for the moment, since obviously none of this was a surprise to him at all, the bloody infuriating, overprotective, overbearing...*clod*, Freddy met her father's shuttered gaze. "You knew," she said. "I've been stressing for days, wondering how to break it to you. And you knew all along. You wrote *All Her World*, you profited by the story, y-you held up Henrietta to me as this shining example of a woman with drive and ambition, this goal of success—" Already her voice was cracking, the hurt warring with the anger, which only infuriated her more. These two had treated her like enough of a fucking mug without her breaking down and sobbing all over them, but she couldn't hold back the distress. "Dad. Oh, Dad. *Why* did you write the book?"

Red spots started to burn on her father's cheeks. Suddenly, as he had in Henrietta's office last week, he looked so much older.

Griff came towards her, but when she jerked away from his outstretched hand, he flinched. "Did Charlie tell you?" The question was rough with concern. "I told him I needed to—"

"Oh, you told Charlie what you'd obviously realised *straight away*, did you?" Freddy breathed in shakily, glaring at him. "Glad you're opening up to your brother and treating him like a capable adult with a brain. Wish you'd extended the same courtesy to me."

Griff's brows snapped together. "Freddy—"

"I poured my heart out to you about how worried I was about telling my father, and you didn't think to mention that it probably wasn't necessary to agonise over it. That, by the way, my dad is as much a part of the whole sodding web of lies as my script-pinching grandma and your nympho grandad."

"Freddy—" he tried again, his hand on her arm, but again she shook him off, and turned back to her father, who was watching them, a shuttered expression in his eyes.

His eyes, which were identical to hers, and to Henrietta's. The three of them connected in this bloody mess.

"Did you come here to talk to me about *The Velvet Room* audition?" Freddy shot at him, and didn't miss the way his gaze flickered over to Griff.

"No." Griff's voice was even but his face was set in tense lines. He didn't look away from her. "Your father is here because I texted him on Wednesday morning and asked him to come."

"And said nothing about it to me." Freddy swallowed. The hurt was starting to overwhelm everything else, and

Griff recognised it. Of course. Eagle Eyes over there. Perceptive as always. And apparently as much of a control freak as ever. "You realised Dad already knew the truth about Henrietta and decided to have it out with him and work out what to do behind my back. Because flighty, flirty, impulsive Freddy can't be trusted to handle it, and certainly couldn't offer any help."

A nerve pulsed beside Griff's mouth. "You're one of the strongest, brightest people I've ever met. I made the mistake of underestimating you in the past. I never will again." Some of his composure ruptured, and his words were ripped out jaggedly. "You know how I feel about you—"

"No." Freddy's voice was equally unsteady. "I don't. I *hoped* I did, but to know you said nothing all week, that you went behind my back—"

She broke off. Just yesterday, she'd spouted on so confidently to Sabrina about how Griff treated her as an equal. One of the only people in her life who did, it had seemed. And now—

Disappointment was an ache deep within her body. Somehow, Griff's actions hurt even more than the profound disillusionment of Rupert's culpability.

She looked at her father again.

If he'd known that Griff knew the truth—Griff, the nominal head of the family with a rightful claim to *The Velvet Room*, and all the money and prestige that came with it—she could see now why he'd been MIA all week.

Absent, like Violet, who had simply been allowed to fade out of existence. The amazing Invisible Woman, whom nobody could ever remember when they named the members of the Wythburn Group, who had supposedly achieved nothing, had an impact on nobody.

A woman who'd been such a biting, witty, beautiful writer that she'd penned one of the greatest dramatic works in a hundred years. A woman who'd loved and been loved so hard that a portrait painted after her death resonated off the canvas with the force of her lover's grief.

"You described Henrietta's office in the book," Freddy said quietly, and Rupert pushed a hand through his tumbled curls, an uncharacteristically uncertain gesture. "There's a poignant passage where you talk about feeling 'the oddest sense of despair' in that room. And you describe her triangular smile."

Walking forward to where he stood at the desk, she picked up one of the few close-up photographs of Violet. She turned it around so Rupert had to meet Violet's gaze. "Her triangular smile," Freddy said again. "Henrietta had a heart-shaped face, so it's a reasonable description of her smile, at a stretch. But Violet—" Griff's great-aunt had deep dimples and a cleft in her chin, and when she smiled, her lower face compressed into the distinct, carved-out lines of a triangle. "Griff's brother has that same smile." Freddy carefully set the photo down. "I read it back. That whole section where you described the actual writing process. You never once use Henrietta's name in the action sentences. It's always 'she.' You saw Violet writing the play that summer, didn't you?"

A second of silence ticked into another, and then another. It seemed an interminable time before her father answered. "Even now," he said, his gaze returning to the photo, "I can see her smile in my mind, but the rest of her face is always a blur. She seemed such a…nonentity."

The tragedy of Violet Ford's life. Fortunately, not everyone had seen her that way, and she'd died with the security and comfort of knowing herself loved. Knowing that she was strong enough to fight for that love.

"It's so hard to believe she was responsible for the brilliance of *The Velvet Room*," her father murmured, his eyes momentarily glazed, looking back into the past. Then they sharpened as his attention returned to Freddy. "Your grandmother read the draft while Violet was still alive. I heard them discussing it. She was so enthusiastic about it, was determined to star in it when Violet sold the performing rights."

Suddenly, Rupert's mouth quirked wryly. "Mam didn't recognise herself in the play." It had always been an eye-blink moment when Rupert used that term for Henrietta, the only time—*then*—that she was suddenly humanised from the glowing golden idol of Freddy's childhood to a real woman, with multiple sides to her personality, just like everyone else. "It wasn't until critics started wondering if the play was partly autobiographical that she realised how personal the satire was. She wasn't too pleased. I think she saw it as partial justification for what she'd done. Like Violet owed her something."

"When *did* she decide to take the play and pass it off as her own?" Griff cut bluntly through the pause that followed, his dark eyes still on Freddy. He'd pushed his fists into his trouser pockets, and she could see the outline of tense knuckles through the fabric.

Rupert's face hardened momentarily, but...well, the Carltons were on shaky ground in this tale, and there wasn't a lot to take umbrage about. Facts were facts. "I don't know. When we returned to London after that summer, my mother was still involved with George. He was besotted with her." Slowly, he added, "He could be very charismatic. I remember being fond of him for a while."

He shook his head. "And then, not long after, came Violet's accident. Mam came here, to Highbrook, for the funeral, and I remember when she came back she was excited. Anxious. More temperamental than usual. A few months after that, an announcement for *The Velvet Room* appeared in the papers. A new play by Henrietta Carlton, the West End's most successful actress."

"And the Wythburn Group's most rubbish writer, it seems." Griff effectively put paid to any budding sentiment. "I assume my grandfather wasn't too pleased about the new Carlton script?"

"He ended the affair." Rupert actually sounded annoyed on Henrietta's behalf, but even when Freddy had thought she'd be the one delivering the revelations about this, she'd never imagined her father would suddenly renounce Henrietta. She *was* his mother. Freddy's grandmother. The Ford-Griffins weren't the only ones with a strong instinct to protect family. That was the core of the whole problem.

"Did he never speak to her again?" she asked, and her dad made a dismissive movement.

"For all intents and purposes. Mam was never one to take rejection lightly. And she had a tendency to fixate on a particular person," Rupert said, with no awareness of irony. "She raged and stormed, but George was set in his decision. He'd keep quiet about what she'd done, but he couldn't continue their relationship. For all his infatuation with Mam, all the attention he lavished on me, he was able to walk away very easily. I saw his face when he left the flat that last day. He was like stone. It didn't upset him in the least."

"It broke him," Griff said, and Rupert's eyes cut towards him. "He was very cool-tempered and cynical."

A family gene there, then. "He was also sad. And my father once told me he could remember a time from his early childhood when George laughed a lot, seemed full of life."

"And he took all the evidence that proved it was Violet who had written the play, and bricked it up in The Henry." Freddy's hands were shaking. She knotted her fingers together. "And left the theatre to slowly go to rack and ruin."

"He didn't know about the letters, obviously." Griff's attention was focused on her, and he looked as if, with the slightest encouragement, he'd sweep Rupert forcibly out of the library and concentrate on the breach that had opened between them. For all his interest in history and the art and literature of the past, Freddy realised, Griff would always prioritise the present and the future. "I expect he would never have seen in them what you did, anyway. He doesn't seem to have looked far beneath the surface where his sister was concerned."

"Letters?" Rupert asked, at sea on that point, but Freddy didn't fill in the blanks.

The letters between Violet and Billy were so personal. It was bad enough that three nosy people at Mallowren Manor had read them, without spreading their private words any further.

"So, Henrietta knew how good the play was, and after Violet's death, she took her work."

"Whatever success she had," Rupert said, and again totally failed to see any irony, "it was never enough. She always wanted more. She always had to *be* more. She saw writing a script as the next logical step in her career. I remember her saying that people, performances, would eventually pass into memory and fade, but words would endure. But her own plays were—"

"Mediocre," said the professional critic in the room. "To put it generously."

"She couldn't accept being second-best. It had to be the top. The best. In every arena of life."

And that was the philosophy, the pressure, she'd passed on to her son. But at some point, her dad had made his own choices.

Freddy folded her arms tightly. "I can understand why George covered for her, why he'd feel split between two loyalties—" She understood that very well. "But... Dad. How could you write the biography knowing full well that the most significant part of it, the bit that readers would be most interested in, was a lie?"

Rupert's jaw was tightly clenched. Shoving his hands in his pockets, he looked at the photograph on the table, then down at the floor.

At last, when she thought he wasn't going to answer, he said quietly, "I spent my childhood in the back rooms of every theatre in London. My father was never a parent in any sense of the word bar biological fact. My mother raised me. She was always on and off the stage, always passionately throwing herself into a project—but at least she was *there*. She always came back, even if it was just for a pat on the head between scenes. If a performance went well and she came off the stage on a high, she'd shower me with attention and affection. I remember her taking me to the Savoy for ice cream after a matinée once."

As he had done for Freddy. The backs of her eyes burned.

Rupert shook his head with self-deprecation. "I realise it sounds pathetic now, but you would have had to have known your grandmother to understand how charismatic she was. There are people who just need to walk into a room, and even if they're surrounded by wealthier, more intelligent, more beautiful people, they'll still dominate. It's that rare quality of magnetism. True X-factor. She wielded an extraordinary amount of power. Everyone wanted to be around her; they all wanted to be like her."

Freddy's mouth twisted, and she saw Griff make another cut-off movement towards her. His hands were fisted at his sides.

"From an early age," Rupert said, "she told me stories about her father, our ancestors, our legacy in the theatre. For some people, it's contagious. The theatre bug." His eyes met hers. "Isn't it?"

She nodded without speaking.

"I grew up seeing it all from a child's perspective. The attention. The money. The power of having that sort of influence. And I wanted it," her father said frankly. His expression didn't change, but Freddy inwardly flinched when he added, "After my own chance on the stage ended, I didn't want to let go of that world."

"So you used your daughter to keep a foothold," Griff said very coolly, and Rupert looked at Freddy.

"Your talent was obvious from the moment you stepped foot on the stage. I knew with proper management you could become another of the great dramatic actors."

Her mouth felt dry. "And the book?"

"I was approached by a publisher. An account of Henrietta by her son, someone who had a unique, firsthand perspective on her and on that time in West End history." Rupert turned slightly then, looking away, and Freddy felt more knots forming in her stomach. To see her father,

her larger-than-life, confident father, having to behave as if he were in the dock…

Griff glanced at her. His face was carefully blank, but she could see the concern in his eyes. "You gave in to temptation," he said matter-of-factly. "Understood. And then the awards and accolades started coming in, more doors opened for you, and it was easier to rewrite history in your mind and pretend that the facts you've presented in the book are accurate. Tell yourself something enough times and I imagine it starts to feel like the truth. I'm sure you weren't too thrilled to discover your daughter was going to be spending the summer here."

"God, is that why you were so negative about me doing *The Austen Playbook*? Because you didn't want me at Highbrook, getting too close to the Ford-Griffins, in case I stumbled on your secret?" She couldn't keep the note of bitterness from her voice.

"Partly, when it comes to this particular project," Rupert admitted, being totally honest with her for the first time in her life, obviously. "Ford-Griffin has a reputation for being ruthless in his research. But I stand by everything I said. Do you know how damned excited I was when I realised that I had a child with the potential to match Henrietta's ability on the stage? And thanks to your grandmother, thanks to the book, I had enough clout to help you reach the top."

Freddy heard the ticking of the clock as if it were marking off the whirring thoughts in her mind.

"And do *you* realise," she said, and her voice fractured again, "that everything you said about your childhood with Henrietta, and everything you left shining between the lines—the pressure she piled on you, the… the propaganda about the family legacy, the *loneliness* of being a kid surrounded by busy adults… You have kept her memory alive, and you have cemented history, because you've repeated it with me. And Sabrina, who rarely even got that pat on the head between scenes once you got caught up in my career."

Rupert went slightly white.

Tick, tick, tick-tick-tick. The clock seemed to blur into one long drone of white noise.

"If I'd told the truth," he said, "everything your grandmother achieved would be wiped out. All the work we've all put in. The time, the sweat, the sacrifice. All people would remember was the scandal."

The knot in Freddy's throat was painful. "My whole life, I've wanted you to be happy. I've wanted to make you proud. But—it's wrong. What Henrietta did was wrong. Every word in that play…it's Violet. It's her story, her despair, her hope. It was her talent, and it would have been her success. And she's just been…erased." Her whole body was taut, and she could see the tension echoed in her father's stance. "Henrietta had a lot of influence on you. And you had a lot of influence on me." At that, Rupert's head came up. "You told me," Freddy said croakily, "over and over again, how important it was to have integrity in this business, to be able to stand tall and hold my head high. That at times it would test me and—" Her eyes burned. "And I'd regret it if I gave in."

She now saw that a lot of those comments had probably stirred from conscience. From guilt.

"And if I ever did feel like I'd failed you on that front…" A tear escaped, sliding down the side of her nose, and it was too much for Griff.

He obviously got the vibe that, for once, she wouldn't welcome a hug, but he stood at her side and pressed his palm against her back. And even though annoyance with him and that sense of betrayal were still tearing at her, she felt the warmth and comfort of his touch, and couldn't help leaning into it, just a little.

"I admired Henrietta so much," she said. "And I've always looked up to you. And for a long time now, I've felt…inadequate. Like I'd never manage to live up to your standards." She hesitated. "Like if I took the path that made me happy, I'd be taking something else away from you, and you'd never forgive me."

Minutely, fractionally, Rupert winced.

Freddy pressed her thumb hard under her lashes. "I love you, Dad. And I've never wanted to be the cause of you losing anything that's important to you. But all this—it's wrong."

She heard the shakiness as her father took a deep breath.

In the fraught silence, the knock on the door was as loud and startling as cannon fire.

With a swift curse, Griff strode over and pulled it open, and Charlie came in, looking apologetic. "Sorry to interrupt," he said, his eyes moving warily between Freddy and Rupert. "But there's an assistant prowling the grounds looking for Freddy and the rest of the cast who've gone AWOL, and apparently there's a very impatient director back at—"

"Shit." Freddy swung around to look at the library clock. "I have to get back."

Her father was staring out the window, a muscle ticking in his cheek, and any further words she might have found dried in her throat. She didn't know what he was going to do next. She didn't know if he'd bother staying for the performance tonight.

Just for a moment, she stood very still. Then slowly, she breathed in—deep—exhaled, and adjusted the sleeves of her dress.

She had a job to do.

Griff caught her arm as she walked past him to the door. "Freddy."

She turned her head, and whatever he saw in her expression made his grip tighten. "I fucked up." The words were rough.

"Yeah." Her voice as shaky as his, she pulled away. "You did."

Freddy left the library, her posture straight and stiff, and her entire demeanour radiated an intolerable hurt that made Griff feel like someone was driving thorns into his skin. Every instinct in his body urged him to go after her, but she was already late and so angry with him that he didn't want to throw off her concentration any more than he already had.

In seven hours' time, the *Sunset Britain* and *The Davenport Report* teams would do their live broadcast from the theatre. Then, at eight thirty, the curtain would rise on *The Austen Playbook*, with Fiona Gallagher in the audience to observe Freddy's performance.

"He told her, then?" Charlie asked in a low voice, nodding towards where Rupert stood, still looking out the window, his own shoulders held rigidly.

"She worked it out for herself," Griff said. "She's not an idiot." He shoved his hands into his pockets, the memory of her expression seared into his mind. His muscles were still tense with wanting to hold her. "Although she obviously thinks I treated her like one. I should have told her right away. She got the impression that I brought her father down here to decide alone how to handle the situation, without bothering to involve her at all."

Charlie puffed out his cheeks. "What a fucking mess, the whole thing."

Griff didn't bother to corroborate; it was stating only a plain fact.

At the window, Rupert suddenly turned. "I imagine," he said coolly, "that I'm not going to play a very flattering role in this film of yours, when it goes into production."

Griff didn't bother to soften his words. "Despite your deficiencies in that area, you're Freddy's father. It would devastate her to see your reputation destroyed, even if you did bring it on yourself. I seem to have made a good job of unintentionally hurting her, but I'd never actively do something that would harm her." He leaned against the desk. "I gave serious consideration as to whether we ought to just let the truth stay buried, and work out with Charlie and Freddy some other way—any other way— to keep Highbrook."

He didn't miss the sudden flare of hope in Rupert's eyes, but Charlie added, with a quick, grateful look at Griff for that inclusion, "But as Griff said, he's not acting alone in this, and I'm afraid I'm not quite so self-sacrificing where my home is concerned."

"And Freddy wouldn't stand for it," Griff said. "However guilty she feels about the impact on you, and however much she's had to repress these past years to live up to your expectations, she's such a fundamentally honest person. She might have been understandably tempted to keep quiet for about five seconds, but it would prey on her mind for the rest of her life that she knew the truth and had done nothing." He held Rupert's gaze, his own very direct. "And Freddy's happiness is my priority."

A multiple of emotions cycled through Rupert's expression as he held himself very still. At last, he seemed to steel his spine, in a way that exactly echoed the movement Freddy had made before she'd left, locking down her feelings because the show had to go on. "So, what do you suggest we do?"

"As Freddy has as much right to be involved in this discussion as anyone else, I suggest we hold off making any final decisions until after the performance tonight." Griff found himself walking over to the window and looking out, scanning the grounds. More chaos—Nick Davenport's crew had arrived. Fuck, he couldn't wait until this circus was over. Nick was posed under an umbrella, talking to Sadie Foster, probably trying to coax her into a better mood before the broadcast tonight. That was playing with fire; Griff had heard the roll of thunder a few minutes ago, and if lightning was imminent he wouldn't advocate standing next to the she-devil while holding a metal stick.

He finally located Freddy, already disappearing into the trees on her way back to the theatre. She was walking very quickly, and even from this distance her body language was furious.

"Fortunately," Charlie said behind him, "your daughter is not only honest, she's also kind-hearted. And if she does take pity on my socially inept brother, this whole thing becomes a family affair. Therefore, when Freddy's less distracted, I suggest we start by coming to an agreement where royalties past and future are concerned."

Turning, Griff lifted a brow. "A natural acumen for business after all?"

"Just dusting off my qualifications before I put them to use working towards opening my workshop." Charlie looked at Rupert. "I believe you're not short of a bob or two, which is lucky, because I'm afraid you're going to have to crack open the purse strings."

Rupert's mouth compressed, but he moved his head to the side in a brief jerk of assent.

"It's not solely a financial matter," Griff said grimly. "There'll be legal repercussions. And the press will seize hold of this and tear us all to shreds if they can."

Charlie sat down on the edge of the desk. "Do you think there's a risk of prosecution?"

Rupert was turning progressively paler. Griff came over to the desk. "The plagiarism was perpetrated decades ago. As far as Henrietta is concerned, there's nobody left to prosecute. And where you're concerned…" His gaze on Rupert was very cool, but to his credit, the other man didn't look away, despite how humiliating he had to be finding this situation. Having to put his fate in the hands of the enemy, so to speak. "For Freddy's sake," Griff said again, stressing the point, "I suggest we…skate over the small detail of exactly *when* you discovered the rightful playwright."

Rupert tightened his hands on his walking stick. "Not exactly honest."

"No. But if you're prepared to make amends privately," Griff said pointedly, "and Violet's work is recognised, even this belatedly, then I don't see the point of making the situation uglier than it has to be."

Rupert was silent for a moment, before he said, "I thought you'd want to throw me under the bus."

"Tempting. But—"

"But family sticks together," Charlie said, and Griff's eyes locked with his brother's.

"Christ," Rupert muttered. Then, standing up straighter,

he said, "Regardless of how we release the truth—" his voice still sounded sour "—*my* family's reputation is going to be put through the wringer."

Griff was prepared to do what he could for Rupert, but he was never going to like the man. "Then in the interests of pre-emptive damage control, we'll have to make some shrewd decisions as to how we deliver this discovery to the media, and what angle we push. Because if it breaks in the wrong way, the fallout could be fucking disastrous." Very faintly, his mouth lifted. "As your daughter would say, we'll have to get our Slytherin on."

To really cap off the shit turn to the day, the moment Freddy charged out of the house she bumped into Sadie. Their resident problem child was standing under the jutting eave that the myriad smokers in the company had commandeered, using her own break to have a cheeky cigarette. It was a terrible habit for anyone to pick up, and a disastrous one for actors who relied on their voice and stamina, but Sadie wasn't demonstrating much care for her career in general today, so who was really surprised.

"If it isn't our femme fatale," Sadie drawled, tapping a bit of ash from the end of the cigarette. With a peculiar little smile, she added, "Such a…*worthy* addition to your illustrious family," and Freddy turned, in no mood to deal with her.

"Careful. The act is slipping. You're becoming more and more unconvincing as a human being. If you give the soulless, demonic bitch full rein, even Lionel Grimes will struggle to place you in work."

Sadie lowered the cigarette and lifted her eyes to Freddy's face. There was a vivid light to her pupils.

Freddy was surprised they weren't glowing crimson. "I'd be careful what you say to me, Frederica."

"Why?" Freddy asked, with biting scorn, the latest wave of disillusionment still washing through her. Her caution about not falling out with a co-star this close to curtain went flying out into the rainy greyness. "Because you'll slither around, hissing a few words of gossip about me and Drew Townseville? I don't give a shit. You want to dig your claws into me instead of torturing Maya, who by the way, is so *good* in every respect that she makes you look like a talentless, immoral hack? Great. If it compensates for the fact that one day, nobody will even remember your name, because you're so fucking heartless you give *nothing* to people, nothing that affects them, nothing they can hold on to—then do your worst."

That glint in Sadie's eyes deepened. "Yes. Our saintly Maya." She looked Freddy up and down. "And I suppose you think your name will go down in the history books? Like your infamous grandmother?"

Muscles all over Freddy's body twitched simultaneously, and she couldn't stop herself from an abrupt flinch.

Sadie's lip curled. It was the sort of smile that a spider might give upon spotting a fly caught in her web. "Do my worst? Do you know, I believe I will. And I think, poppet, you'll find you *do* give a shit."

Chapter Eighteen

Showtime

The rain this morning had been a mild drizzle compared to the downpour tonight. It fell in a hard rhythm against the theatre roof, and sound technicians stood around in corners with morose faces, muttering about acoustics. Freddy sat in a chair in one of the makeup rooms, with her feet wrapped around the rungs and a plastic bib protecting her old-fashioned stays and petticoats. She was trying to breathe slowly and keep still.

Leo Magasiva, a makeup artist she'd worked with in the past, skilfully applied a contour shade under her chin. The makeup was lighter than usual, to adapt for the high-definition cameras that would be filming in close-up. "Am I tickling you?" he asked in his incredibly smooth, deep voice, reaching for a new brush. When he shook excess product from the bristles, his enormous biceps flexed. She'd forgotten how bloody *huge* he was, all heavily packed muscle and warm brown skin. He was a treat for the eyes, and she couldn't even be bothered to have a good perv, because her heart and mind were otherwise occupied, twirling about in love with a prat. "You're not usually this jumpy before an opening."

"Sorry. Didn't sleep well." Freddy made a renewed effort to keep still so he could start her eye makeup. It was a subtle art to make it look as if she was both well-rested and not wearing a scrap of cosmetics. Lydia might have run around with the militia, but she would have drawn the line at visible kohl liner. "It's nice to see you again. It's been a while. How's your girlfriend? And your baby?"

"A couple of troublemakers, the pair of them," said the doting boyfriend and father. Then he winked at her. "Lights of my life." Leo's dark eyes had gone very soft, and it made Freddy's heart hurt more for Griff.

Because of Maf's insistence on preparing until the last moment, she'd been in the theatre all afternoon, so she hadn't seen him, or Charlie, or her father since this morning. She was still simmering over the fact he'd gone behind her back, but— She bit down on her lip, and Leo lightly nudged her with the balm he was trying to apply.

Unlike her father, who'd lied by omission for his own ends, when it came down to it, Griff had acted the way he had to protect her.

It was still infuriating, but as the day had progressed, it had been hard to maintain the level of mad.

Unfortunately, she loved the acerbic, patronising dickhead to bits.

An assistant stuck her head into the room. "Fifteen minutes," she said, looking harassed, "and the interviews go live. Freddy, Maya, Sadie, we need you out there in ten."

Freddy looked around Leo's wide torso and met Sadie's eyes across the room. She was sitting cross-legged on a high stool, looking pretty and ringleted and impossibly sweet. Except for that scheming little tilt at the corner of her rosebud mouth.

Mockingly, Sadie lifted two fingers to her temple and saluted Freddy.

She disliked the other woman too much to ever be afraid of her—she wouldn't give her the satisfaction—but an ominous, uneasy feeling settled low in her stomach.

Her gaze shifted towards Maya, in another chair. She was in full costume already, and her fingers were in knots in her lap.

"You're creasing my base," Leo murmured, and dabbed at Freddy with a sponge. "Cheer up. It'll all be over before you know it."

She looked at Sadie and Maya again. "That's what I'm afraid of."

When the transformation into Lydia was fully complete, she stowed her water bottle in her bag and checked her phone screen out of habit. A frown flickered between her brows. There was a text from Akiko, and every word just about hummed with guilt. Sabrina had pounced on her and extracted the full story about Henrietta and *The Velvet Room*. Apparently Sabs didn't anticipate being on secret-sharing terms with Freddy any time soon.

Out in the hallway, she ran into Charlie. He surveyed her and gave a token wolf-whistle, but his eyes searched hers. "How are you doing, sweet pea?"

"I have a horrible, sinking feeling that this is going to be a total disaster."

"Jesus. You really are sounding more like Griff every day."

She bit her lip again, then rubbed at her teeth in case the faint tint of colour had rubbed off. "Where is Griff?"

"Over at the main house, schmoozing Fiona Gallagher for you," Charlie said, and she blinked.

"Excuse me?"

"This downpour has turned the west road into a muddy mire, and her car got stuck for almost half an hour. The lady was *not* in a mood to be impressed when she finally made it here, so Griff's plying her with brandy that's been in the basement since the days of Napoleon. That stuff warms you up from the gut upwards. One good gulp and all is right with the world. By the time the curtain rises, she'll be ready to put you to work for the next decade."

A little smile broke through Freddy's roiling apprehension. "*Griff* is schmoozing?"

"I know. The mind boggles. If Lady Influence is pacified, I think we can thank the cognac rather than my brother's dubious charm." Charlie's expression suddenly turned serious. "I don't think there's much he wouldn't do for you, Freddy. And it's keeping him from striding over here and forcibly demanding forgiveness, which would probably land him in the doghouse for weeks." He tucked his hands into his pockets in a way that was very reminiscent of Griff, and that ache in Freddy deepened.

Griff might be lacking in the charm department, but she wanted his matter-of-fact, reassuring, grouchy presence.

"He's trying," Charlie said, and she lifted her head. "He's had a lifetime of having to take charge and act alone. He's not used to having someone else to turn to for advice and support." He gave her a significant look. "And he's sure as hell not used to…caring about someone the way he does about you. I'm sorry, but you've endeared yourself to a bloke who's overprotective and overbearing by nature, and you'll have to deal with the consequences. But he *is* trying. With all of us."

"I know," Freddy said, quietly.

Charlie cleared his throat. "He wouldn't thank me for

interfering, but Griff didn't ask your father down here to do some sort of 'all boys together' plotting behind your back."

She stopped fiddling with the lace at her cuff. "What do you mean?"

"I agree that he should have just told you upfront. I mean, *mate*." Charlie shook his head. "My longest relationship was nine days, and even I know that you don't keep shit from your bird. But he ordered Rupert down here and basically threatened to tie him to Ma and Pa's miniature train tracks in the garden if he didn't come clean to you right away. He didn't want you tormenting yourself worrying how to break the news."

Freddy stared at him in silence, then made a frustrated sound and put her hands to her bonnet. "He's a prat."

"Yep," Charlie agreed. "But a well-intentioned prat." He hesitated. "Look, if he knew I was telling you this, I'd be train fodder as well, but when Griff gave me a heads-up about the situation, he brought up the possibility that we just keep our mouths shut. Find another way to save Highbrook and let Henrietta keep her writing laurels forevermore. Because he didn't want to do anything that would hurt you."

A rush of unexpected tears stung the backs of Freddy's eyes, and she had to blink rapidly, fanning her lashes uselessly with her hands. She had a live interview in about four minutes' time. But God—

"We can't just let it lie," she said. "I thought for a second that maybe I could. Should. But it's morally wrong, what happened, and it needs to be put right. And I'm not going to be responsible for you all losing your home when there's a chance to save it."

"My thoughts exactly." Charlie's response was emphatic. He waggled a finger between their foreheads. "We're like one mind, you and me." He coughed delicately. "I admit I applied a little more weight to your second excellent point."

A small, slightly wet laugh bubbled from Freddy's chest, and his smile turned affectionate. He studied her for a moment, and then unexpectedly, with no jokiness at all, he said, "Thanks, Freddy."

"For putting my foot down about Griff being too uncharacteristically noble for his own good?"

"No." Charlie put a hand behind her head and pressed a very fraternal kiss beneath the brim of her bonnet. "For giving me back my brother." His smile turned crooked. "He's actually *seeing* me again."

Freddy stood looking after him as he strode down the hall, her shaking hands tucked under her arms.

"Two minutes, Freddy," one of the stagehands called as she passed. The Henry was too old to have the electronic cue system that Freddy was used to in London, so it was down to old-fashioned dashing about and verbal warnings.

She moved her fists to her hips, grounding herself. Impulse and instinct demanded that she fly out into the rain and throw herself into Griff's arms, but she took her job seriously, and always had.

And there was a lot riding on this performance.

With three different TV crews in the house, she expected the stands to be unadulterated chaos, but everything seemed to be clicking over like well-oiled cogs.

On the technical side, at least.

Sabrina was standing stiffly next to Nick Davenport, and judging by her sister's body language, in about five minutes' time his head was going to be outside in the rain, detached from his body and mounted on a spike.

A man she didn't recognise paused by her side and nodded in the direction of the stand-off. "If the rumours of a merger are true, I don't want to be in the building if those two end up competing for the same job."

Freddy turned. "*Are* there rumours of a merger?"

"Oh, yeah. Buzzing's getting louder." The man grimaced. "Ever since that billionaire Lionel Grimes bought both networks, there's been talk about the evening shows being streamlined. Which probably means that either this is a trial run to see how they do working together, or—" he lifted his brows significantly "—this is a direct comparison and somebody's going to end up in the queue at the Jobcentre."

"Well, shit."

"Quite." The man's response was equally heartfelt. He nodded towards Sabrina, and Freddy's stomach flipped with renewed nerves when she saw the assistant producer of Sabrina's show beckoning. "I think that's your summons. And don't worry—if you get tongue-tied, we're switching back to the studio after the interviews wrap up here, to finish with some human-interest fluff." Her helpful confidante obviously worked for *The Davenport Report*. Nick's show ran longer than *Sunset Britain*, so *TDR* would have an extra slot to fill once Nick finished the segment here with Sabrina. "Last I heard, the second story tonight is some dog that saved a kid from drowning. That'll perk the public back up if this one's a disaster," he finished cheerfully and walked off.

After that encouragement, she felt even less confident about this, and her feet dragged as she walked over. Sadie and Maya were already standing with Sabrina, who had pointedly turned her back on Nick, with a toss of her red curls. He cast his eyes up towards the ceiling, every inch of his face lined with annoyance, and adjusted his crisp silk tie with a jerk.

"There's no need to be nervous," Sabrina was saying to Maya as Freddy approached. Her sister had a natural ease and charm with guests. Although Freddy got only an unreadable, narrowed glance. She had no idea what Sabs thought about the Henrietta situation, and her body language didn't encourage a whispered query. The lingering words of their confrontation seemed to be spaced out between them like a physical barrier.

By a natural linking of thoughts, Freddy automatically scanned the room for Ferren. No sign. She hoped he was just lingering backstage until the last minute, waiting to make a staged entrance for maximum effect. And not passed out drunk in the green room.

He had precedent.

Dylan was reclining in a seat near the stage, one boot crossed over the other, waiting for his part of the pre-show hype. When he caught her eyes on him, he gave her a swift up-and-down, and winked.

"I'm not nervous," Maya said, and immediately looked in danger of vomiting.

What the hell?

Yes, Maya struggled with shyness when she was out of character, and doing an interview as yourself was actually a very different ballgame from performing a live show, but— Seriously, if someone so much as sneezed unexpectedly right now, Elizabeth Bennet was going to do a very uncharacteristic swoon, and Sabrina and Nick would have to direct their questions around a body prone on the floor.

Freddy touched her arm. "Are you all right?" she asked in a low voice, and Maya shot her the oddest look.

It was a combination of shame, embarrassment, and apology.

"I'm really sorry," she whispered. "I wish it had never happened."

"You wish what had never happened?" Freddy was completely lost, but had to tear her attention back to the cameras when Sabrina and Nick finished their preparations and got into position.

Their backs straightened in unison and they both produced a wide smile of very white teeth. It was like someone had flicked a switch on the backs of Newscaster Barbie and Ken, and if Sabrina had heard that thought, the chance of Freddy being able to patch up their quarrel would sink to an optimistic one percent.

"It's a truth universally acknowledged that everyone loves a good whodunit. Good evening," Nick said, with that slick charm and hint of flirtation that made him popular with elderly ladies across the country, "and welcome to a very special episode of *The Davenport Report*—"

"And *Sunset Britain*." Sabrina picked up the catch effortlessly. "Coming to you live from the grounds of Highbrook Wells in rural Surrey, where we're joining forces in a network first." For an instant, her green eyes locked with Nick's brown. "For tonight only." There was a subtle emphasis on the last words.

The corner of Nick's mouth compressed as he turned easily towards the active camera. The crew moved around with silent, discreet precision. "We're here at The Henry, Highbrook's private theatre. It was built several decades ago for the playwright Henrietta Carlton, but is only now having its maiden voyage, so to speak. Final preparations are in full swing behind me for tonight's debut performance of *The Austen Playbook*, the stage adaptation of the game that went viral across the UK last year. At eight thirty tonight, the curtain behind me will rise, and people at home will pick up their phones, ready to cast their vote on the outcome of the story that unfolds."

"We have with us Elizabeth Bennet, Emma Woodhouse, and Lydia Bennet," Sabrina managed to cut in smoothly, bringing the camera back to her. "Also known as Maya Dutta, Sadie Foster, and my baby sister, Freddy Carlton."

Sabrina's baby sister managed not to roll her eyes on live television.

"It must have been a unique experience, preparing for a play when even the cast don't know which direction the plot will take?" Tactfully, Sabrina directed her first question at Sadie, giving Maya time to stop shaking. Out of view, Freddy squeezed her co-star's elbow, trying to send silent support vibes.

"Fortunately, I enjoy a challenge," Sadie said with a laugh, smoothing back one of the blond ringlets that were artfully arranged beneath her bonnet. "And I'm a massive Austen fan, so I leapt at the chance to be part of this adaptation."

Surprisingly, since it was difficult to imagine her retracting her forked tongue and curling up with a good book, that was true. Freddy happened to know that Sadie had spent an absolute fortune on a piece of memorabilia that had come up for auction last year.

"Even if it's not quite the Austen of the books," Sadie added, with a targeted little grin to make herself seem approachable and down-to-earth. "Fewer balls in the assembly room, more bodies in the library."

Nick turned towards Maya, who was darting anxious looks at Sadie. Freddy glanced between them, and added hastily, "It's been a lot of fun to rehearse." Bit of a stretch these past few days. "And we hope everyone at home will enjoy getting involved."

"If you haven't already downloaded the free studio app so you can vote during the performance, and have your say on who finds their true love and who ends up a corpse in the library," Nick said, with a flash of teeth, "we'll have instructions shortly."

"An authority on true love, are you?" Sabrina was all purring sweetness, and his smile took on an edge.

"Oh, I don't claim to be an expert." He winked at the cameras. "But I'm working on it."

Sabrina adjusted the lapel of her shirt. "I'm sure."

Suddenly, Nick looked at Freddy. "It must be quite something for you, having the opportunity to perform in the location where your grandmother, Henrietta Carlton, wrote her most famous work, *The Velvet Room*?"

Freddy stiffened. Sabrina's movements also momentarily hitched. She obviously hadn't expected that turn in the conversation, either. Apparently not a pre-prepared question.

"Um," Freddy said through a dry throat, her mind racing. "Yes. It is. I—"

"It's such a beautiful little theatre," Sabrina interjected, so efficiently it completely covered Freddy's hesitation, "that it's wonderful it's finally getting the chance to shine. And with such a prominent cast."

"Yes." A flicker of annoyance crossed Nick's handsome face. "Major names in both theatre and television. And film. I believe even our home-grown action hero, Joe Ferren, is donning a pair of breeches tonight."

The rhythm of Sabrina's breathing changed audibly, and Freddy cleared her throat. "Yes." It was her turn to step up with a diversion. Hastily, she produced the diplomatic answer that media training provided. "It's always brilliant working with actors from different media. Everyone brings different skills and experience, and this is a great ensemble. Perfect cast chemistry."

From the corner of her eye, she saw Sadie move. The other woman drew herself up, and it was so exactly reminiscent of a snake uncoiling that Freddy could swear she heard a low rattling begin. Maya seemed to sense something as well, and went as rigid as Sabrina, and that sense of impending disaster became so thick in the air that Freddy found she was holding her breath.

"Yesssss." The human serpent drew out the word thoughtfully, her eyes fixed on Freddy, who stood tensely, waiting for the attack. When it came, it was a direct hit, but in an unexpected direction. "We have had excellent chemistry." Sadie twinkled into the cameras. "You'll definitely want to tune in tonight. We've had romance blooming onstage—and off."

Maya's arm jolted against Freddy.

After a short beat of apparent surprise, Nick raised his eyebrows. "Do we have a real-life love story developing backstage?"

"Things have definitely been heating up around here." The innuendo was heavy. Sadie looped her arm companionably through Maya's, who was shaking her head. "But you'd have to ask our Elizabeth whether she's jumped from admiration to love yet." She winked as she butchered Jane Austen's words for her own bitchy purposes. "And whether matrimony is on the cards with our resident film star."

In the silence that followed, Freddy saw Ferren standing near the stage, and the expression on his face said it all. Maya looked at him desperately, and then at Sabrina. She parted her lips but couldn't seem to find any words.

Freddy's guess had been half right. Maya *had* fallen into the trap of a co-star fling. But not with Dylan.

Apparently, she could cross "fidelity" off Ferren's very short list of virtues.

Her stomach feeling hollow, Freddy saw comprehension come to Sabrina, and then what happened to her eyes. There was shock and fury, both of which she would expect from her fiery, passionate sister, but the emotion that drenched her expression was desolation. She seemed frozen, and had obviously completely forgotten about the rolling cameras and the job she was doing.

Nobody was moving. Even the crew had gone into stasis, some of them visibly confused, others latching on to the implication behind Sadie's words and avoiding making eye contact.

When Ferren turned and strode from the room, running away from the consequences as usual, the cowardly, cheating bastard, Freddy heard the small squeak of his boot sole against the wooden floorboards.

It all happened in a matter of seconds, which felt like endless minutes.

While her mind was whirring rapidly, trying to think of something to say, anything, that would patch over the horrible moment and give Sabrina the chance to recover her composure, the cavalry arrived from an unprecedented source.

Dylan—lecherous, feckless prat, and their *other* resident film star since his successful move between the stage and the big screen—got to his feet and sauntered straight into the range of the cameras. With his characteristic one-sided grin, he looped an arm around Maya, who blinked, and said to Sadie, "Giving away our secrets, Miss Woodhouse? I suppose it's to be expected, with the chronic matchmaker on the premises." He nudged Maya back into motion, and she stared at him. Then from somewhere, she found her years of experience and produced a mostly believable smile.

Nick had been looking at Sabrina's averted profile, a muscle jerking hard in his jaw, and his right hand had closed into a fist. But he recovered his professional gloss quickly. With just a shade too much jocularity, he made a comment about a real-life Elizabeth and Darcy, and Dylan tightened his arm around Maya and responded in kind. Beside them, Sadie was still looking quietly pleased with herself; despite Dylan's surprising save, the damage was done.

Sabrina's eyes, full of turmoil, met Freddy's. Because of their age difference and their father's behaviour, they'd never had the acute connection that some siblings did, an uncanny ability to communicate without words, but as she looked intently back at Sabrina, Freddy *willed* her to hang on, just get it together and get through the broadcast.

And she was so bloody proud of Sabs when she stood to her full height, cocked her hip, and smiled at Sadie. "You're playing one of the more morally ambiguous heroines in Austen's repertoire. A heroine, but also a character who causes a great deal of trouble and pain, in both the books and the script. How did you approach that dichotomy?"

After six more of the most uncomfortable minutes Freddy had ever experienced, Sabrina and Nick took the audience at home on a walking tour to see the sets, and visited backstage to give a carefully curated look at the last-minute preparations that went into a theatre production. It was basically like opening night at school, when everyone put up a show for prospective parents and pretended this state of calm, happy organisation was the status quo. The mess, the fractured tempers, and the panicking was going on in the dressing rooms, away from the cameras.

Freddy knew Sabrina well enough to see that she was going through the motions, and tonight was clearly desperate to be done with the job she loved, but to a casual onlooker, she might have got away with it.

Their segment wrapped up at half past seven, and the moment a cameraman held up his hand, signing them off and sending *The Davenport Report* to an ad break before it switched to the heroic puppy story, Sabrina dropped the fade-to-black smile and immediately shook off the hand that Nick placed on her arm.

"Sabrina," he said urgently, and she answered tautly, without looking at him.

"Be a human being for once in your life, Davenport, and keep your gloating remarks to yourself."

The skin around his eyes tightened, and Sabrina unhooked her microphone and headed towards the rear door where Ferren had scarpered. Nick seemed to hesitate for several long seconds of indecision, and then, face rigid, turned and strode outside. By the sound of it, the rain had stopped. At least the *weather* was turning out okay.

Freddy caught Sabrina up at the door.

"Sabrina—"

"Where is he?" Sabrina said between clenched teeth. Spots of red were burning through the skilful makeup on her face, which was pinched with tension and hurt.

"Probably hiding backstage until the last minute." Freddy didn't bother to hide the scorn in her voice.

Fucking, *fucking* Ferren. Thank God she had almost zero scenes with him tonight, because it would probably confuse the audience if Lydia Bennet suddenly extracted Mr. Knightley's testicles with an embroidery needle.

"Right." Sabrina pulled away from Freddy's outstretched hand. "Not now, Freddy." She vanished into the backstage corridor, the tap of her high heels a fast, furious echo.

Freddy turned, getting out of the way of the backstage crew, who had swung into quick efficiency, straightening the stands for the arrival of the in-house audience. In twenty minutes' time, the doors opened to the invited public, which would be mostly VIPs, press, and family of the cast.

Breathing in deep, she closed her eyes for a minute or two. Hell. What a night, and the onstage performance hadn't even begun yet.

Physically shaking out her arms, trying to get her bunched-up muscles moving, she took the steps up to the stage, and the young actress who was playing Harriet Smith rushed out from the wings.

"Yikes." The girl pulled an exaggerated face. "I'd steer clear of the dressing rooms. Ferren and that TV presenter are having a *hell* of a row. She just threw a half-full milk bottle at his head."

"Shit." Freddy shot forward. Sabrina wouldn't thank her for interfering—and she really needed to have her usual final scan of her lines—but... She slipped into the wings and hurried backstage. Cast members were clustered in full costume along the walls of the hallways,

avidly listening to the showdown, and exchanging meaningful, thrilled glances.

Turning the corner, Freddy came face-to-face with Maya.

"Oh God." Maya swallowed several times. "God, I'm sorry. It just…happened, the other night. He'd walked off with one of the props, and the crew were so busy, I said I'd grab it from his room, and—" She closed her eyes. "I know he's with your sister. And her face…" When her long lashes parted, they were wet with tears. "I can't tell you how much I wish… He was really upset about something, and…he was just…"

"Ferren," Freddy said. "He was just Ferren." She wavered, then touched Maya's arm. "Look, just try to keep it together, okay?" A spike of raised voices resounded through the walls. "And I'd stay away from Sabrina. In her case, the cliché about red hair and temper is totally justified."

Looking miserable, Maya headed for the green room, and Freddy gathered up her nerve to enter the fray. If Sabs had started chucking the contents of the mini fridge around, things were escalating quickly.

"What a ruckus," said a bored voice, and she turned sharply to see Sadie lounging in the doorway to the props room, examining her nails.

"Why the *fuck* did you do that? Are you *trying* to sabotage the performance?" There was no point in appealing to Sadie's finer feelings where Sabrina's and Maya's emotions were concerned; she didn't have any. She should, however, give a shit about her own production.

"Don't be melodramatic," Sadie said dismissively, straightening the lace neckline of her pink gown. "We're all professionals—"

Freddy snorted.

"And if people have been behaving like very naughty boys and girls behind the scenes, I'm sure they have enough self-control to keep their hands off each other once the curtain rises. Besides—" Sadie pushed away from the doorframe. "It was quite entertaining."

"If that was meant to get back at me, you twisted—"

"Oh, no." Sadie's smile grew. "That was just a little extra. The real fun should be starting any moment now. Enjoy the show tonight, won't you? Because it might take some time to get another one. I think you'll find that the closest you get to *Anathorn* is reading the books while you're unemployed. Fiona Gallagher is notoriously gun-shy about hiring actors with PR problems. And after all the...*effort* your family members have expended getting you to this point, too."

Freddy's nails dug into the palms of her hands as Sadie leaned in, her breath fanning Freddy's face, strong with the scent of cinnamon-flavoured chewing gum. "Next time, I suggest you keep your charming little comments to yourself."

She tapped Freddy's cheek with one finger. She'd had to remove her bright red polish, but she'd kept the long, pointed shape, and the little prick on Freddy's cheekbone acted on her nerves as violently as if Sadie had dragged her talon over a blackboard.

"And tell your boyfriend that he ought to close his library windows," Sadie finished, triumph a thick layer over every delicate feature of her face, "if he wants to keep your dirty laundry quiet. Plagiarism on a grand scale." She tilted her head. "So much for the prestigious Carltons."

It would have been an exit line worthy of Shakespeare,

if an assistant hadn't come dashing out of the props room then, holding the dagger that was going into someone's back in the first act. He yanked the door closed behind him before he sped off down the corridor, as Freddy stood frozen, her face burning with sudden heat while the rest of her went ice-cold. The latch slammed shut, and the carving hanging above the doorframe rattled— and dropped.

As Sadie was punched in the left eye by a sculptural depiction of Odysseus, complete with disproportionately large wooden willy, she made a squawking noise exactly like the peacock in the garden. *"Fuck."* With one hand cupped over her face, she glared down at the carving, which had cracked in two on the ground. "This *fucking* theatre." Her malevolent one-eyed glare turned back on Freddy, who, hopefully not using up all her acting re-serves before they got onstage, didn't allow so much as a flicker of emotion to cross her face.

Cheers, Sir George. I may have misjudged you.

"Ouch," Freddy said aloud, with sarcastic sympathy. Fighting down her spiralling panic, and with Griff's voice in her head telling her not to let Sadie see her rattled, she added solemnly, "I'd get along to makeup post-haste if I were you, Polyphemus. We're live in fifty minutes. Good thing Leo Magasiva is a whiz with the concealer."

Sadie's breasts almost popped out of her bodice with her indrawn breath, but Maf appeared in the hallway then, grey hair escaping her topknot, eyes sparking, phone to her ear. With a last vicious, muttered curse, Sadie stomped away down the corridor, which, Freddy realised with another sharp bite of apprehension, had gone very quiet. Ferren's dressing room was around the corner, and she hoped she wasn't going to find Sabrina standing over a bloodstained body. It would be better for all concerned if the murders were confined to the stage. Even if there was more than one person around here she'd personally like to skewer with Wickham's bayonet.

Her mind was whirring, Sadie's smug words tumbling around and hitting all her alarm bells. The chronic meddler had got hold of the truth about Henrietta—at least part of it—but what had she done about it?

Maf ended her call with a sharp word, stepped over Odysseus and his broken appendage without a second glance, and hit Freddy with a laser stare. "I suppose that histrionic sister of yours knows where we can find Ferren?"

"He's in his dressing room. Getting ready," Freddy added with wild, frazzled optimism. The silence was not a good sign. Either Sabrina actually *had* knocked him out, or—and please, *no*—the wily shit had managed to talk her around in about five minutes flat, and the Sabs and Ferren car crash continued. As if enough wasn't going wrong.

He had now progressed to physical infidelity. Freddy refused to believe that Sabrina would turn a blind eye to that sort of fuckery. If you were single and wanted to play the field, yay. If you chose to be in a relationship, you didn't break someone's trust. End of.

"No," Maf said with fury she wasn't even trying to suppress. "That is where he's *supposed* to be, with less than an hour until this circus beams live into living rooms across the United Kingdom. However, he's just stormed outside and vanished. I *knew* he wasn't worth the extra audience pull. He's been a selfish, unreliable little shite his entire career. And he's got fifteen minutes to get his arse back here, or he's out, and we're going on with an understudy."

"Maf!" The panicked cry came from the direction of the wings, and she turned on her heel and stalked off to put out yet another fire.

With no heed for the shape of her bonnet, Freddy took hold of each straw edge and pulled down to punctuate her despair. Disaster. At every turn, they were heading for the rocks.

Maya's dresser hurried past her, a shawl in hand, and threw Freddy a quick smile. "Audience is starting to arrive. And I see the bigwigs are already in the house. Fiona Gallagher is front and centre. Wearing *the* most amazing blazer. *Love.*"

Oh God.

For the first time in her life, Freddy wondered if she was actually going to have a preshow panic attack. Her breath was coming fast and shallow, high in her chest, and her eyes felt unfocused.

And then she turned in a blind spin of anxiety and saw Griff. His shirt and tie were crisp despite the rain earlier, his chin was closely shaved, and he was tall and calm-looking and emanated such an air of reassurance that she felt it like a physical sensation.

He came to her, sweeping her with one comprehensive look.

The costume and makeup were a barrier to hugs, but he reached for her hands. "It's going to be fine." Deep, even, *sure*. "You're prepared, you're in your element with the material, and you're going out in front of an audience of people who'll love you, in this building and right across the country. You'll be fantastic."

"Griff." Just the one word, just his name, but so much of what she was feeling was layered into that single syllable, and his eyes closed briefly.

When he opened them, his dark irises were warm with that sheen of caramel. "Freddy. This morning—I'm sorry. I'm fucking sorry."

"I know." Fleetingly, she ducked her head and lightly touched her cheek to one of his hands. "It's okay. We'll talk properly after the show. Yeah?" Her eyes searched his, and he cupped her neck with his warm palm.

"Yes."

"Griff—I'm pretty sure Sadie knows. About *The Velvet Room*."

He stiffened against her, his head lifting. "What? How?"

"She listened through an open window in the library." A few more of Freddy's stressed, stunned brain cells chugged back into gear. "She must have stood on the balcony in the next room."

"The railings out there are unstable as well." Griff's hand was still moving on her with gentling reassurance, but his expression was darkening. "Pity it didn't drop her into the courtyard. Is this one of the secrets she likes to keep close and taunt her victims with, or is she—"

"She's done something." Freddy tightened her hold on him. "I just don't know what."

As the hectic backstage noises continued around them, they stood in a little bubble of their own, Freddy acutely aware of the physical connection where their skin touched—and the invisible link that wound around them, wrapping them together in an emotion that felt irrevocable.

"Forget about her," Griff said, moving one shoulder as if he were shrugging away a persistent insect. Apt. "One thing at a time. For now—just concentrate on the show. We'll deal with the rest as it comes."

The show must go on. The ultimate theatre cliché, but one that was bred into Freddy's bones.

"Yes." Reluctantly, she released him. "And I have to find Sabrina."

"Sabrina?"

"Ferren slept with Maya the other night."

One of Griff's brows went up slightly, and Freddy could read his expressions well enough now that she blinked. "Did you *know*?"

"Before we end up on the outs again," he said firmly, "no, I didn't. Somebody was sneaking around the corridor in the early hours, however. I assumed it was Waitely's latest conquest."

"No—Dylan's turned out be something of a white knight today. Who would have thought?" She scowled. "Sadie spilled the beans during the broadcast. Sabrina's devastated, your mate Nick Davenport was no help whatsoever, and now Ferren's taken off and if nobody can find him we're going to have to sub in his understudy. Who's woefully underprepared because Ferren kept kicking up a stink about hearing someone else reading his lines."

"Is it going to come off as officious and interfering if I try to track down the cheating little pissant?"

Freddy looked at him. "No. It's going to come across as helpful and caring."

"I care," he said, and his voice was very gruff. "A fuck of a lot."

"Me too." A renewed rush of tears was clogging her throat, and her response was little more than a whisper.

Griff's eyes searched hers again, and then, with an achingly affectionate tug of one of her loose curls, he strode towards the outside door. Hand on the knob, he turned back. "Freddy, whether Ferren's there or not, and whatever else Sadie's done, you can do this."

She wound her hands into the fine muslin of her skirt, and asked the question she'd been afraid to voice. "Is my dad here?"

She read the answer in his face before he said it. "He left. I'm sorry." Griff's expression darkened, with obvious concern for her, and equally clear exasperation with her father. "I think the scene this morning was too big a hit to his pride for one day."

And his pride was apparently more important than being here for her tonight.

Wordlessly, she nodded, her chest tight.

As she moved quickly down the hallway and into the corridor where the largest dressing rooms were located, her petticoats rustled and she kept her hand pressed against the lacing over her ribs, trying to breathe evenly. After a cursory knock on Ferren's door, she pushed it open.

Initially, she thought the room was empty; then she heard the tiny muffled sound, and turned, and her heart clenched.

Sabrina—perfectly together, impossibly beautiful, vibrant Sabrina—was curled in a ball on the floor, one arm across her face. Her hair was a dishevelled mess, frizzing everywhere, as if she'd been repeatedly pulling damp fingers through the curls, and her long legs were gathered against her chest.

"Oh, Sabs." Shoving the door closed behind her, Freddy went to Sabrina's side, down on her knees, wrapping her arms about her tightly.

For four or five seconds, Sabrina went rigid, and then she broke. Her hand came up and clutched at Freddy's forearm, and she buried her face in Freddy's neck. Through her tears, she coughed out, "I'm ruining your costume."

Freddy tightened her arm where she was shielding Sabrina's head. "Shut up, Sabrina," she said, and heard a weak, wet, desolate chuckle.

They sat like that for seemingly endless, timeless minutes.

"You were right." Sabrina exhaled shakily. "About Joe."

His name was a heartbroken cry.

Freddy closed her eyes. "I didn't want to be right, Sabs."

Sabrina held her tighter. When she spoke again, her voice was still husky. "And I fucked up the show tonight. In front of fucking Davenport. Who'll probably be laughing all the way to the new presenter contract."

There was a brief knock on the door before it opened quietly. Even in these circumstances, Freddy's stomach still did a little flip when Griff came into a room. His expression softened for a moment as his gaze met hers. "Nobody's seen him," he said, a tactful eye on Sabrina, who was red-eyed and haunted-looking. "I'm afraid you're going to have to work around the understudy."

Freddy breathed out. "Right."

Sabrina's arms loosened, and moving sluggishly, she sat up, pushing her hair back. "He's walked out on the job?" She swallowed. "I suppose I shouldn't be surprised. I'm sorry, Freddy."

Griff was sorry about her father, Sabrina was sorry about Ferren; everybody was apologising for someone else's shit behaviour, and suddenly Freddy was furious.

"We don't need Ferren," she said, getting to her feet and reaching a hand down to pull Sabrina up. "Whether he's on the stage or hiding in the grounds like a cowardly, irresponsible little dick, we're going to smash it tonight. And *you* definitely don't need Ferren. Look at you. You're a rock star. You're a total babe. Fuck him."

Sabrina blinked a few times, and Griff started to smile.

"Our grandma might be the great plagiariser of the twentieth century, and our dad might have been a bloody useless parent for the past decade, but you and me, Sabs?" Propping her hands on her cinched-in waist, she lifted her brows at her sister. "Watch the new generation of Carltons bounce back. And if Sadie Foster sticks her nose in—fuck her, too."

She straightened her bonnet with a decisive jerk. Griff was outright grinning now, and Sabrina seemed momentarily lost for words.

Then, infinitesimally, a smile loosened her tense features. "Jesus, Peanut. When did you grow up on me?"

A voice in the hallway called frantically for the cast to assemble in the wings.

"Come on," Freddy said, and slipped her fingers around Griff's outstretched hand. "Let's do this."

Time to wreak havoc at the assembly ball.

And hopefully avoid the poisoned cocktail in the drawing room.

Chapter Nineteen

The public killed off Emma Woodhouse at the first opportunity. Nobody had expected the first vote to swing to the second variation, Sadie least of all. Watching from the wings as Sadie was forced to sit down at her easel in the garden set, where an unknown figure unceremoniously shot her in the back with an arrow, thus ending her entire role in the production in less than twenty minutes, Freddy didn't bother to hide her grin. Sadie usually kept up a sickly-sweet image in the media; evidently, her glee at throwing Maya under the bus on live TV hadn't gone down too well.

As Sadie passed her in the wings, her floral muslin dress splattered with Leo Magasiva's very convincing fake blood, her lips were set in a tight, thin line.

"Doesn't really pay to be a total bitch during a live broadcast," Freddy murmured, swinging her reticule. "It tends to backfire."

Sadie stopped, her hands fisting. If looks could kill, Lydia would be joining the body count right now. As it was, the vote was so far on track for Lydia to eventually emerge as the mysterious archer. If the next vote pushed forward the Elizabeth and Darcy romance, as Griff had predicted, the odds shot up that Freddy would get to go homicidal in the last scene. Fingers crossed. There would be some poetic justice in taking responsibility for Sadie's fictional demise.

Sadie's voice was a hiss. "It doesn't really pay to profit by fraud, either. That also tends to backfire."

She shoved Freddy physically out of the way as she went backstage to sulk, digging an elbow into her—and despite Freddy's surge of bravado earlier, she couldn't suppress the flicker of foreboding in her stomach as she rubbed at her arm.

Lydia threw her arms around Wickham's neck, pressing her lips to his supposedly waxy mouth.

Logically, Griff realised it was only a few seconds before Freddy released the chisel-jawed wanker and moved swiftly into the next cheeky line of dialogue, but the stage kiss seemed to linger into eternity.

What had she said? *As passionate as boiling an egg.*

Fleetingly, as the active camera focused on Wickham's smug face, Freddy gave the audience a saucy little wink. She had the room in the palm of her hand—Lydia was stealing scenes and earning unprecedented sympathy in this adaptation, although if he remembered the convoluted mess of a script correctly, she was also shaping up to emerge as the murderer—but Griff hadn't missed that she'd looked straight in his direction with that gesture. His mouth curved.

At his side, Charlie cleared his throat, low and pointedly. His brother was holding his phone on his lap, keeping track of the voting numbers as his friend the app developer sent through figures. Ignoring the teasing glint Charlie was aiming his way, Griff cocked an enquiring brow at the phone, and Charlie tilted it where he could see the screen.

Griff pursed his lips in a silent whistle. With three of four votes down, the figures were exceeding even the studio's upper predictions. The advertising revenue from the broadcast tonight would be lucrative. With his fist, he gently nudged Charlie's knee, a gesture of acknowledgment. Gratitude. Job bloody well done on his brother's part. And Freddy, who was helping carry the show through up there, despite Joe Ferren's absence and the minor hiccups caused by a flustered understudy and a very slightly off-note Maya Dutta.

God knew how long it would take to sort the legal and financial nightmare of *The Velvet Room*, especially if Rupert started dragging his feet and tried to worm out of playing his part—and Griff wouldn't put it past him—but tonight's pay cheque should clear the immediate backlog of bills.

Charlie's cheeks went a little pink, but he looked pleased. His phone was on silent, but Griff heard the vibration when it buzzed. Still smiling a little, Charlie checked the notification, and his expression altered. Frowning, he brought up another screen with quick taps of his fingers, and swore quietly.

"What's the matter?" Griff asked under his breath, with foreboding. He'd had a nagging feeling that tonight's challenges were not quite kicked to the curb.

"Stay here," Charlie whispered, checking the screen at the side of the room to make sure the camera trained on the audience wasn't doing a reaction shot. He stood quickly. "I'll check it out."

Griff stuck out his leg to prevent him vanishing and leaving it at that. "Check what out?"

Charlie's words were a quiet hiss before he hopped over Griff's foot and made a dart for the door. "My alarm system's gone off. Someone's broken into the garage."

For God's sake.

Griff shook his head, but didn't make a move after Charlie. His brother was experimenting with wireless apps and controls where his cars were concerned; he'd given Griff a rather diffident tour this afternoon in a transparent attempt to take his mind off the fight with Freddy. Chances were it was a false alarm, but either way, the countryside wasn't exactly rife with cases of grand theft auto, Charlie could handle himself, and Griff was where he needed to be.

Freddy's scene ended onstage. She was replaced with the actors playing Frederick Wentworth and Anne Elliot, and his gaze wandered to the polished carvings on the pillars around them. The camera crew had realised only this evening exactly what the carvings depicted, which had resulted in a flurry of last-minute adjustments to ensure there were no high-definition close-ups on them. One brief shot on the sculpture behind Anne's head and the studio would be hit with at least a dozen letters from the country's armchair complainers.

The audience produced a collective "aww" noise as Wentworth overacted an affecting line.

Griff had to admit, despite the weeks of upset, the endless string of problems—it was quite something to see The Henry finally coming alive.

In the front row his parents appeared to be engrossed in the play, but their heads lowered and he saw the flash of a turning page as his mother scrawled something in her ever-present notebook. His chest moved with a sigh. God knew what they were planning now.

If he woke up in a few months' time and they'd constructed a miniature Pemberley on the north lawn, he was asking Freddy how she felt about travel and boarding the next plane to New Zealand.

There was no sign of Rupert in the audience. His mouth tightened.

The man was going to come out of this situation with a more spotless reputation than he deserved. He could at least make the effort to *pretend* he gave a shit about his daughter's happiness.

Onstage, George Knightley came in, still moping about his girlfriend being used for target practice, which was frankly the least convincing reaction in the entire play. Emma Woodhouse was a divisive character at the best of times; as played by Sadie, she was so astronomically irritating that even her lover ought to privately rejoice when she was turned into a kebab.

Griff had no compunction about his satisfaction over Sadie's early exit, but he hoped she wasn't making things difficult for Freddy backstage.

They had enough to worry about where she was concerned.

As the set swung around on its oiled hinges, Freddy, Maya, and Waitely returned to the scene, and Freddy flung herself across a sofa with a sigh of dramatic exhaustion. Curling into a lethargic ball, she pitched her voice into an impressively grating whine of complaint, and Waitely's Darcy responded with a very understandable eye-roll.

Griff knew this scene. He'd listened to Freddy repeating her lines for this one for over an hour, and had occasionally unwillingly filled in the other parts for her. He could recite Maya's next line with her.

Unfortunately, as Maya froze, the camera directed at her face, beaming out live across the UK, she herself clearly couldn't remember a word of it.

Maya had forgotten her line. Her face remained blank, but Freddy had been working with her so intensely that she could see, with crystal clarity, the panic in her eyes. She had been struggling all night, obviously finding it difficult to recover from the shock of the interview. She was a good person who'd made a bad mistake, and the guilt was transparently overwhelming her. She was such an experienced actor that she'd carried it through adequately despite her distraction—but heading into the final scenes, it had apparently become too much for her.

Her fingers gripping the silk brocade beneath her, Freddy glanced at Dylan, and saw the tension come into his stance. Luckily, Darcy was still one for military posture even at this late stage in the plot.

Finally, after a few seconds that felt an absolute age, Maya's brain stumbled out of its frightened inertia and she blurted out her line. She was word-perfect.

Unfortunately, she'd just cued them into the wrong scene variation.

Freddy's follow-up line to that piece of dialogue would reference the untimely stabbing of John Willoughby. Which, in this version of the play, had not happened.

It was her turn to falter. She pushed up from the chaise longue, her ears buzzing, feeling slightly detached from her own body. She hadn't been so aware of the cameras all night, and the compulsion to turn and look directly into the lens pulsed through her, a panicked reaction.

She wondered if she was actually going to be sick. Just

to put a revolting seal on the disastrous end to an otherwise successful show.

And she'd thought it was bad when she'd started arbitrarily quoting The Boss during *Masquerade*.

Mouth dry, she found her gaze going out to the audience. Usually, with the direction of the house lighting and the way her eyes and brain worked while she was onstage, she couldn't see individual faces in the stalls. But The Henry was so much smaller than the West End theatres, and the lights were set up to illuminate the interior for the TV broadcast. Freddy knew where Griff was sitting, and she instinctively looked towards him—but her eyes locked onto the man who stood by the door to the foyer, leaning on his walking stick.

His face calm, reassuring, the long-buried experienced actor coming to the fore, Rupert held her gaze and nodded. Just once.

And Freddy took a steadying breath, turned, and lifted her nose at the unnaturally still Maya. Tossing her curls, she improvised a line for the second time in her recent stage history, this time with intention, and directed them back into the correct scene.

Still feeling as if she were existing in a surreal bubble, she read the relief in Dylan's body language and saw the flood of adrenaline return to Maya, and the energy underlying the dialogue surged.

The last twenty minutes of the play seemed to pass in a blink, as Lydia was unmasked as the murderer, and Anne Elliot proved the hero of the day, and Elizabeth and Darcy locked themselves into a passionate embrace.

They finished to a standing ovation that Freddy suspected was partly secondhand relief on the audience's part. She didn't see how anyone could have missed that momentary hitch, and it was *agony* to sit through the pause of an amnesiac actor.

But with the exception of those few fraught seconds—

"Overall," Dylan murmured at her side under cover of the applause, "not bloody bad. Nicely done, comrade. You're a trooper."

He kissed her hand, and in the audience she saw Griff lift a brow where he stood, on his feet near an inscrutable Fiona Gallagher, whom Freddy had been trying not to notice all night.

When the curtain lowered for the final time, and the "live" sign flickered off, returning Highbrook to relative privacy, away from the scrutiny of the British public, Freddy looked at Maya in silence.

Her co-star's mouth quivered, and Freddy reached out and hugged her hard.

Neither of them said anything.

Dylan placed a hand on Maya's shoulder as they walked into the wings, and for once, there wasn't one iota of lechery or flirtation in the gesture.

A lot of people really *had* grown a great deal in a few short weeks this summer.

The Highbrook effect, apparently.

In Freddy's case, she'd arrived in turmoil over her career and her relationship with her father, and her personal life had been centred on a few casual hook-ups and some mug-painting. She was returning to London fathoms deep in love. With the overly perceptive dickhead from the pub.

The dice was still rolling where her career and her dad were concerned.

Still shaking from the build-up of adrenaline, Freddy rushed through the routine backstage—stripping off her bonnet and gown in her dressing room, and doing her last costume change of the night into a black dress and heels. She left her hair and makeup as they were. She wasn't slathered with an inch-thick layer of greasepaint for once, and Leo had done a stellar job of giving her some cheekbones.

She went outside by the back door to avoid getting crushed in the throngs, and around to join the crowd out front.

Griff had agreed to let the production team hold the wrap party in the function room at the main house—for a large fee, she expected—and most people were heading for the path through the trees, which had been lit up with fairy lights tonight.

She saw him through the crowd, talking to Sabrina, who was pale but composed in the sparkle of moonlight and spotlight. Akiko and Elise were nearby, being chatted up by Dylan. There was still no sign of Ferren, the bloody rat.

Griff looked up and saw her, and even from a distance, across the heads of several dozen people, she saw the look that came into his eyes. She pressed her hands to her stomach.

"Freddy." A very familiar voice, with a very unfamiliar note in it.

Dragging her eyes from Griff's, she turned to face her father. "Dad." Rupert was standing at a slight angle, resting his weight on his hand, and purplish smudges cast shadows beneath his eyes. She had to stop herself from reaching out to offer a supporting arm; he wouldn't appreciate the reminder of his physical limitations.

"You did very well," he said suddenly. "Tonight."

"I almost lost it up there." It was habit to recount her

own weaknesses. He'd always expected her to be a solid self-critic. However good she was, she could always be better.

"But you didn't." He was holding himself very stiffly, but he didn't look away from her. "I was very proud of you."

Her breath caught in her throat. "Were you?"

A small smile moved his mouth, but an odd sadness flattened the expression in his eyes. "Very."

She did put out her hand then, hesitantly, her fingers fluttering in the night air, the moonlight glittering off the crystal ring on her pinky finger. It had been her mother's. Her father had given it to her for her eighteenth birthday. With any of the other people she loved, she would take their hand, but— "You pulled me through that glitch." She blinked away wetness from her lashes, and in her peripheral vision she saw Griff moving towards her. He'd obviously been trying to give them space, but apparently he'd reached his limit. He was firing off protective vibes now. "I felt like you were willing confidence back into me."

Rupert was looking down at her hand, where she'd reached for him and held herself back. "I was," he said, almost harshly.

She opened her mouth, but didn't get the chance to say the words that bubbled up.

What happened next was so quick and so surreal that Freddy experienced it in a series of fractured stills, like a montage of photographs in a film sequence. Even afterwards, bizarrely, her memories were all in black and white.

She heard shouting and the roar of an engine, and then swerving headlights cut through the night, zigzagging back and forth so rapidly that they created a long line of light, like a child's sparkler writing patterns in the air. The out-of-control car managed to turn, and then spun wildly again, and skidded straight towards them. It was as if she was watching a toy that someone had picked up and flung.

She heard her name—bone-deep, innate terror—from a guttural voice that she didn't initially recognise as Griff's, and then instinct kicked in and she was flinging herself at her father, knocking him towards safety. His stick hit her shin, but she felt nothing.

In a manoeuvre that was so hairline-close to hitting her it would have been too dangerous to film had this actually *been* a staged stunt, the brakes clamped down and the car stopped. Suddenly. Abruptly. And the night was so quiet and still it was almost more shocking than what had come before.

Sprawled across her father's legs, Freddy raised her head, feeling as if her neck couldn't support it, and looked into his dead-white face. His lips moved, but no words emerged.

She heard a rapid clicking sound, and realised vaguely that someone was taking photos.

In that state of what-the-absolute-fuck and why-is-my-head-floating, she saw Charlie emerge from the crowd, equally pale, and hold up his phone. "Well," he said, his voice shaking so badly he was barely comprehensible, "the remote brake system works."

Then, roughly, he yanked open the driver side door of the car, and hauled out Joe Ferren.

Freddy didn't see what happened next because Griff was down on the ground beside her, and her senses returned in a rush of sensation with the silky feel of his shirt and the warmth of his rapid breaths against her neck and the hard clutch of his hands. Inhaling in a gasp, she clung to his body, smelling the comforting, familiar scent of his hair, and felt how badly he was shaking. His palm held the back of her head, and his beautiful nose was smooshed into her throat. He was saying words there, but she heard only the timbre of his voice.

When he cupped her cheeks with hands that still shook, she had the stupid passing thought that at least her head was securely attached now, with him holding on to it, and then his mouth was on hers, and he was kissing her hard. She managed to lift arms that felt like weights, wrapping them around his neck, kissing him back just as desperately.

He tore his mouth from hers. *"Jesus Christ."* He kissed her cheeks, the bridge of her nose, her lips again. "Are you all right?" The question was forceful, demanding— and echoing with lingering horror.

"Yes?" Still bewildered, her response was more of a question than an affirmation, but he closed his eyes.

"God." He buried his mouth against her temple. "Freddy. Darling."

More than anything, it was that rare, beautiful endearment that brought her back to herself. "What happened— Dad? Dad, are you all right?"

As Griff helped her to her feet, she turned swiftly, but Sabrina and Akiko had already gone to Rupert, standing either side of him while he felt gingerly at his back. "I'm fine." He looked as shocked as she felt. "Freddy— *Christ.* You could have been hit. You shouldn't have—"

Pieces of recollection came back to Freddy, the memory of him tensing against her, and she shuddered, holding tightly to Griff. "I could feel you about to push me out of the way," she said, her breath hitching. "Again. I couldn't let you be hurt again because of me."

Her father's face changed, the shock of the near miss overtaken by realisation, and almost...shame. "Freddy. Baby girl. Whatever else I—I've done, surely you've never thought that I blamed you for what happened at the Majestic?"

Before she could answer, Ferren came stumbling forward, rubbing at his ruffled hair. His beard was growing in, and he looked typically handsome and romantic— and, by the looks that surrounded him, he was a dead man walking. "What the fuck," he muttered, "is wrong with that car?"

"What's *wrong* with that car," Charlie snapped, "is that it's completely wired for an experimental remote system. You can't access half the controls right now without the app."

Ferren scowled. "Well, how was I supposed to know that?"

"You were supposed to not fucking break into my garage and steal it, and almost mow down my brother's girlfriend, you utter fucking twat."

Very belatedly, Ferren addressed Freddy and Rupert. "Sorry." He scrubbed his hand over his head again. "You two all right?"

Freddy felt Griff's body tense in the instant before her cool, contained critic lunged at Ferren, and her past jaguar comparisons no longer seemed amusing. He looked absolutely livid.

"You piece of shit." Griff's fist knotted in the front of Ferren's shirt and he yanked him forward, and that was the impetus for Freddy to recover her wits completely.

There were plenty of witnesses around and several

journalists still avidly filming, and if he broke Ferren's jaw, the biggest drama queen in British film would inevitably press charges.

"Griff." She jumped towards him, but Charlie was already there, dragging him off.

"Mate, I get it, but you're going to end up under arrest." He spoke hastily, right in his brother's ear, and when Griff tried to tug free, took a different tack. "Freddy needs you."

Breathing hard, Griff stilled and turned to look at her again. Freddy was actually feeling not too bad now, but she immediately tried to look in need of immense support. From the flash of reluctant amusement that crossed Griff's face, it wasn't convincing at all, but it succeeded in calming him down enough that he stepped away from Ferren.

Coming back to her, he pulled her into his arms and pressed his mouth against her hair. "Okay," he said. "I'm not going to hit him."

Ferren committed the last in a series of enormous errors of judgment then, and sneered.

"But I am," Sabrina said, and slammed her fist into his nose.

The camera flashes accelerated.

As her presumably *ex*-boyfriend went down to his knees, swearing and trying to stem the blood with his sleeve, she hissed and shook out her hand. *"Fuck*, that hurt."

When Ferren stumbled back to his feet, he looked like he'd just come out of makeup for the climactic scene of every film he'd ever made. He was sweaty and blood-stained, and swelling was already starting to appear, but in this instance he wasn't the triumphing hero.

He took a few steps towards Sabrina, extending a hand towards her. "Sabs. Please."

Freddy tensed, but Sabrina didn't hesitate. "Call for your car," she said, her voice flat. "And go back to London. I'll have anything you left at my flat sent over."

He didn't move, his gaze fixed on her, his jaw jerking. "Sabrina. I'm sorry."

A hint of fire returned to Sabrina's eyes then. "For years of messing me about? For fucking your co-star? Or for almost hitting my family with a stolen car? *Get out*, Joe."

Everybody around them was quiet. Freddy could hear breaths and rustling, but nobody spoke.

When Ferren turned on his heel and left, Sabrina closed her eyes.

"Well, we can't say we weren't warned." Charlie's voice was refreshingly normal above her ear as he tried to alleviate the tension. "Invite the West End over and the drama is inevitable."

Freddy looked at her father, who was watching Sabrina with a conflicted expression. "Are you sure you're okay, Dad?"

Rupert made a dismissive gesture with his stick. "I'll do a heat treatment on my back and it'll be right as— Well. Right as it ever is."

Her feelings must have shown on her face because, with a decisive movement, he reached out and took her hand. "Freddy. What happened twenty years ago was an accident. An unfortunate *accident*. I—" His throat moved. "I do have a lot of regrets and…bitterness about the circumstances and the consequences, but none of that was ever directed at you. I would do it again in a heartbeat." Muscles twitched around his eyes. "I didn't intend to make you unhappy. I didn't ever intend that."

Behind her back, Freddy reached out her free hand and felt Griff's fingers close around it firmly.

"And yet you've made such a bang-up job of it." Sabrina's words were heavily caustic. Her green eyes sparked as she looked at their father. "For years, you've tried to control Freddy, and you've made me feel like nothing I did was worth anything, and all this time, you've been living this massive lie—"

"Sabrina," Freddy cut in warningly, her eyes on the tabloid reporters present. Her sister was shaking with residual shock and adrenaline—so was Freddy—and had lost her professional caution, and right now she looked capable of relaying the whole story to everyone present.

"I'm afraid it's a little late to be discreet," a new voice said ominously, and Freddy turned as her agent joined them.

Lisa was holding an iPad, and she flipped it around to show them the screen.

Freddy took one look at the headline and her heart dropped towards her toes.

Chapter Twenty

In the Highbrook library, away from the crowds and noise in the reception room, Sabrina scanned through the latest news article, and spots of red burned bright in her high cheekbones. "That *fucking*—" She seemed to be beyond words.

No mystery about the subject of her ire. Sadie might have blabbed, but it was Nick Davenport who'd chosen to sneak outside The Henry after the pre-show interview and broadcast the revelation about Henrietta and *The Velvet Room*. An exclusive scoop for *The Davenport Report*.

Apparently the story of the Great British Plagiariser was more newsworthy than the life-saving puppy.

While Freddy had been onstage, thoroughly enjoying herself as Lydia, her reputation, and Sabrina's, and certainly Rupert's, had been systematically trashed in the media, and it was spreading like wildfire. She didn't know exactly what Nick had said in his initial report, but the online outlets were strongly implying that all three of them had been complicit in the con. Ironically, it seemed to have given a massive boost to *The Austen Playbook* viewership. Small silver linings.

Freddy looked over Sabrina's shoulder as a photograph

of her and Griff kissing appeared. She winced. Speculation was running rampant.

"I'll kill him," Sabrina said between her teeth. "That treacherous, selfish—"

"Get in line." At Freddy's side, Griff looked equally furious. Nick was a friend of his, Freddy recollected belatedly, her mind chugging back into gear, and this situation heavily involved Griff's family as well.

Nick had broadcasted it to the nation, in the least sympathetic light possible, while on Griff's property.

She laid her hand on Griff's stomach, spreading her fingers there, and his arm tightened around her shoulders.

"Before anyone breaks out the cyanide," Lisa said briskly from her position perched on the edge of the desk, "I suggest we move into damage control. Quickly."

There was a sudden tap on the door, and Akiko pushed it open, her pretty face troubled. "Sorry, guys, but there's a lady here who wants to speak to Fred—"

The lady in question pushed firmly past her, and Freddy tensed against Griff.

"Forgive the intrusion," Fiona Gallagher said, surveying the occupants of the room. "But I have to get back to London and I think it's best we wrap this up quickly."

Not an auspicious opening. A sick feeling started to roil between Freddy's ribs.

"I won't beat about the bush. I don't care to dwell on disappointments." Fiona's attention flickered over to Lisa before she focused on Freddy. "Ms. Carlton. Lisa will have told you that we're in the process of casting for the first run of *Anathorn*. I had high hopes for you in the role of Quinn."

Had.

Freddy's hand closed into a fist against Griff's ribs,

and his own fingers came up to cover hers, warm and strong.

"I'm afraid I won't be pursuing that possibility."

Cool, collected words that hit her like a physical blow.

"We'll be strongly refuting the allegation that Freddy was complicit in this...incident," Lisa said, her voice as brisk as Fiona's, "and an unsubstantiated rumour is hardly cause to bar her from auditioning."

Fiona coughed, a discreet clearing of her throat. "You'll recall that when Allegra's first novel was published, a member of her family made a claim that was later proven to be false, that the initial idea for the series had been his. Allegra is retaining a great deal of control over this adaptation, and she won't want the latest literary scandal associated with this production. Her own situation would inevitably be raked up in the press."

To Freddy, with the first faint hint of sympathy, she said, "You did a very good job tonight, but I'm sorry, I won't be considering you for *Anathorn*."

"Fiona—" Lisa sounded furious, but Fiona lifted a hand.

"It's not open for discussion." She firmly blocked Lisa's move towards her, and her demeanour was closed-off and adamant as she left the room.

When the door had closed behind her, Sabrina slipped her hand into Freddy's and squeezed. "This is ridiculous," she snapped. "You haven't done anything wrong. Why should you be penalised? It's so unfair."

Freddy let herself feel the intensity of her disappointment, then determinedly, she shoved it down. She straightened her shoulders. "There'll be other productions." Her eyes met Griff's. "Still feel blessed," she whispered. "No matter what."

Her breath went shallow at the depth of feeling in his usually inscrutable face.

"But that's the role you want." Rupert spoke for the first time since they'd come back to the house. He'd been sitting on the couch looking a hundred years old, seeming to retreat further and further into himself with every passing word, but he stood now.

Stood tall. He suddenly smacked down the end of his stick, and the bang as it connected with the wooden floor echoed through the room.

"You're right," he said to Sabrina. "It is unfair. And enough is enough." His jaw moved sideways in a nervous gesture, but his eyes didn't waver from her. "I believe you're going up against Davenport in this studio merger. You're in contention for the headline role?"

"I was," Sabrina said coolly. "As he's now informed the whole of Britain that I knowingly profited from fraud, I'll be lucky if I end up with any job at all."

The footage of her punching Ferren in the nose wouldn't aid the cause, either.

"You're going to get the job you want." Rupert came forward. Freddy realised how much effort he was expending to walk without a limp. He held his head high, and there was a dignity to his body language that had been missing since she'd first confronted him, in this room, over his dishonesty. "And so should Freddy. You've both worked incredibly hard for your careers, and you deserve your success. I won't let you suffer for your grandmother's mistakes." His chin rose just a little farther. "Or for the choices I made wilfully."

Sabrina looked understandably sceptical. "And what exactly do you intend to do about it?"

"You get your biggest audience share on Monday nights." Rupert still spoke steadily. "Yes?"

"Yes." Everything about Sabrina screamed hostility. "I'm surprised you know that."

"I've been…deficient where you're concerned." He shaped the words tautly. "But I do care, Sabrina." His jaw worked again. "And more to the point, I watch."

Sabrina lifted her head.

"You're an excellent presenter. Charismatic. Personable. Honest." His voice wrapped ironically around that one, intensely self-condemning. "The public has a good deal of trust in you."

"They did." The sardonic edge was strong in Sabrina's reply, as well.

"On Monday night, you go live with the truth. The whole story." He was very pale. "*We* go live. You set the record straight—and you take back the upper hand from Davenport."

Freddy was still holding on to Griff, and as her arms flexed around him instinctively, she felt his body shift. "The truth?" he queried, the heel of his hand rubbing against the small of her back. "Are you referring to the PR-friendly, edited version of the truth?"

"Everything. Violet. Henrietta. And my own role in it." Rupert looked squarely at Freddy and Sabrina. "And more importantly—your roles in it. Or lack thereof."

His face and body were very still, but his hands were shaking on the handle of his stick.

Oh, Dad.

"I hate to throw cold water on the grand gesture." Charlie suddenly spoke up from his armchair by the bookcase, where he was sitting with a pensive face, one long leg bent and propped on his opposite knee. "But you won't be able to wipe off all the muck with one interview. People prefer to believe the worst."

"True." Lisa stroked her thumb along her chin, her eyes narrowed. "But both Freddy and Sabrina are popular with their audiences. And they're very media-savvy. I think if we play this right, we can push a lot of sympathy back on their side."

And paint her father as the villain of the piece.

"I don't think—" Freddy began, and Rupert cut her off, gently but firmly.

"Freddy. You were right." He reached out hesitantly, and she took his hand. "It was wrong, baby. All of it. And it's time to put it right."

She looked at him, troubled, and his grip tightened. "It's time, Fred."

Somehow, she thought he was referring to more than the situation with *The Velvet Room*.

After a few more breaths, they let each other go.

"It sucks about that audition," Charlie said sympathetically, and Freddy felt Griff's mouth dust against her temple again.

As she struggled with a complex mix of emotions, her gaze slipped around the perimeter of the library, taking her usual weird solace just from the sight of the books—and stopped on the object in the corner. One of James and Carolina's smaller *Anathorn* structures had proved vulnerable to the rain, and had been moved in here this afternoon.

It was, very fittingly, a stage, where marketplace magicians showed off their spells to potential purchasers.

She stared at it for so long that Griff nudged her.

She glanced at him. Then she lifted a brow at Sabrina. "What did I say earlier?" she said, and a tiny smile started to lift the corners of her eyes. "Watch the Carltons bounce back."

The *Sunset Britain* studio buzzed with noise and anticipation. The rivalry between this show and *The Davenport Report* was not limited to the presenters. Sabrina was popular with the crew, and everybody was furious about what *TDR* had done so covertly on Friday. It was a battle of the ratings, and Freddy strongly suspected that on this occasion, *SB* was going to crush the competition.

She watched proudly as Sabrina stood with the producer, conferring over a clipboard. Every red curl was perfectly in place, her sister's makeup was immaculate, and her demeanour was that of a lioness ready to fight.

Nick Davenport probably thought Sadie had handed him the golden ticket where the new presenter role was concerned. He was about to hit a major setback.

Freddy's smile faded slightly as her gaze moved to her father, who was waiting tensely off set, standing alone, not moving.

Instinctively, she looked around for Griff. He'd texted twenty minutes ago, stuck in traffic, but he should be here any moment. He and Sabrina were equally unenthused about doing another interview together, but they'd all agreed that it was wise if he joined them for the broadcast. A public display of unity between the Carlton and Ford families. It also wouldn't hurt to push the relationship angle between Griff and Freddy, Sabrina had added, ignoring Griff's scowl. "People are always more interested in sex than theft."

"Freddy Carlton?" The voice behind Freddy was soft and almost delicate, definitely not Griff's deep, sardonic tones, and when she turned, for a second she thought it was coming from a child.

The girl who'd just come into the studio was small, with thin arms and legs, a pointed, freckled face and enormous hazel eyes, and she looked about fifteen. However, Freddy had seen that face numerous times on the back covers of her favourite books.

Allegra Hawthorne was young, but she wasn't a child. And from the determined light in her eyes and the firm set of her chin, she looked like a woman who knew her own mind.

"You're Freddy Carlton," she said again, a statement of fact, not a query, and Freddy blinked out of her preoccupation.

"Yes, I am. And you're Allegra Hawthorne." Whom she'd been planning to track down in a couple of days if she didn't receive a reply to her email, but had not been expecting to see here tonight. "Were you...looking for me?"

Coming closer, Allegra pulled her handbag from her shoulder and opened it. "I've just been doing an interview upstairs with Greta French." She made a face. "It was like trying to claw my way out of a spider's web, avoiding her nosier questions. And the makeup guy mentioned you were here tonight."

Digging around inside her bag, she pulled out a sheaf of papers and held them up.

It was a computer print-out of the images Freddy had sent her over the weekend, after Charlie had managed to track down Allegra's email address in about half an hour. He was a very useful person to have around.

The pictures were a beautifully photographed—if she did say so herself—catalogue of James and Carolina's miniature *Anathorn*, from the full spectacle to the tiniest details.

"It's wonderful," Allegra said simply, a pink flush warming her pale face as she looked at the pictures again. "I adore it. I can't believe someone would take so much trouble over something I've written; it's still very surreal. It's like they've pulled my dreams right out of my head and turned them into reality. And I definitely want it for the show."

Freddy released the breath she was holding. "Good."

"I also want *you* for the show." Allegra grinned suddenly as Freddy made an audible surprised squeak.

It had been a long shot, but she'd hoped that maybe, just maybe, she'd be able to win back the opportunity to audition. She hadn't thought—

"Ballsy, to include the audition tape with your email." Allegra saluted Freddy with a flick of her fingers to her forehead. "Exactly the sort of thing Quinn would do in the books, in fact."

"I love her," Freddy said sincerely. "I *get* her."

"Yes, I think you would." Allegra was studying her. It was disconcerting, such insightful eyes in such a baby face, but Freddy was the last person who would underestimate someone in that respect. "I'll talk to the team."

A crew member called out across the studio. Five minutes until they went live and laid out their family secrets before the nation.

Freddy hesitated. "Fiona Gallagher ruled me out of the running for a reason. You'll know…about my grandmother."

The entire world seemed to know about Henrietta Carlton at this point.

Henrietta had wanted enduring fame, but this probably wasn't what she'd intended.

"And I believe you had a…um, situation yourself with your first manuscript that I expect you'd rather forget." Freddy tried to put it tactfully.

Shadows flickered over Allegra's face as she looked across the studio at Sabrina, and then at Rupert, before that shrewd hazel gaze returned to Freddy. "I know what it's like to take a public fall because of someone else's mistake. And I know what it takes to rise above it. In my head, you're my Quinn. I'll throw my backing behind you."

Freddy couldn't find the right words. Eventually, she just said, "Thank you."

As Sabrina waved Freddy over, Allegra turned at the studio door. "The miniatures— They're fantastic as they are, but we'll need more. A lot more. Do you think the artists—"

Drily, Freddy said, "If you need extravagance and excess, you've come to the right place."

An assistant bustled around her with a powder brush, removing the sweat that had sprung up on her forehead during the past few extraordinary, exhilarating minutes, and Freddy joined Sabrina and her father on the studio couch.

As she smoothed her skirt repeatedly and then tucked her nervously fidgeting hands under her knees, she looked at Rupert. "Are you sure about this, Dad?"

Sabrina looked at him sharply. It was blatant that she still half suspected him of playing a game. Their relationship was even more fractured than the difficult bond between Rupert and Freddy, and it wasn't going to be magically transformed.

Rupert swallowed visibly and had to clear his throat a

few times, but quiet determination threaded his features. "I'm sure. Let's put the record straight."

The screens behind them switched on, and two large portrait photographs appeared. Henrietta's vivid, confident, beautiful face stared defiantly from one; Violet's haunted, reserved expression filled the other.

"Where's Griff—" Sabrina hissed, but he came into the room at that moment, with about ten seconds to spare, not looking in the least sweaty or harried. His expression, Freddy noted fondly, was set at his highest level of implacable don't-fuck-with-me.

Brushing aside the advancing makeup artist with a brief word, he joined them, sitting beside Freddy and taking her hand.

"Don't rush or anything," Sabrina muttered, and he lifted a brow, then bent his head so his mouth was right next to Freddy's ear and out of range of the microphones.

"All right?"

She knotted her fingers through his. "You don't think this will make things worse?" The last-minute apprehension came out in a whisper.

His grip tightened reassuringly on hers, and unexpectedly, faint lines of amusement appeared around his eyes. "Chin up, darling. Nobody handles a PR crisis like a Slytherin."

She repressed a startled huff of laughter as a camera swung around, the crew hushed, and a woman in a cap raised her hand, counting them in with her fingers.

The red light beamed out.

Sabrina's practiced smile was absent tonight. She looked down the camera, directly into the invisible faces of their critics across the country, and nodded, as if acknowledging their right to suspect, to judge, to condemn.

"Fame. Romance. Tragedy. Betrayal. This is the tale of two women, two *families*, and one of this country's greatest works of literature. Revelations over the past few days have been an enormous shock to me, and I know that many of you are equally bewildered."

Smart opening. It had always been one of Sabrina's strengths as a presenter, that natural, approachable warmth, her ability to establish a rapport with her audience.

"Even those of us who don't regularly attend the theatre—and I admit that I don't spend as much time in the West End as I should, given that I have a stage star in the family—" Sabrina's smile was rueful and appealing "—most of us will be familiar with *The Velvet Room* from the English curriculum at school. What I didn't know, and what almost nobody has known all these years, is that the story behind the writing of that play is more dramatic, more passionate—" her smile flickered and faded "—and more hurtful than the words in the script. Mistakes have been made, and a very talented woman has been robbed of her voice, and I hope…" She turned her head and looked at Rupert, in a mannerism that was, to Freddy, less calculated than the rest of the rehearsed performance. She heard her father exhale slowly as Sabrina finished quietly, "I hope tonight we can start to right some wrongs."

Rupert left after the broadcast, looking drained and small, and Freddy stood with Sabrina, watching him go.

"How much trouble do you think he'll be in?" she asked, and felt her sister tense against her.

"Not as much as he probably deserves." That expression that only hardened her features where their father—

or Nick Davenport—was concerned faded into a smile as she hooked one arm about Freddy's neck in a hug. "Nice job, Pea—" She stopped herself. "Freddy."

Freddy found herself smiling back. "You can still call me Peanut, you egg. Just try to remember that I'm not six."

"You're a star." Sabrina raised her brows. "Speaking of which—was that Allegra Hawthorne I saw earlier? Do you have news?"

"Not yet. But I have hopes." Freddy cleared her throat. "And where do you think you're placed now in the great race of the headliners?"

"Davenport's not going to take it out without a fight. Put it that way."

"To be fair," Freddy said warily, "I don't think he knew what was going to happen during the broadcast. With Ferren." She brought him into it with reservations; it was going to be a raw subject for a long while, and the slice of pain that went across Sabrina's face was explicit.

"Maybe not," Sabrina said after a moment. "Didn't stop him going ahead with his little plot afterwards, though, did it?"

"No. It didn't." Across the room, Griff ended his conversation with the producer, who seemed to be a friend of his, and Freddy found a stupid smile widening across her face.

Sabrina sighed, and when Freddy dragged her eyes back to her sister, Sabs was looking at her with affectionate exasperation. "At least not *all* of his mates are knobs," she said, inclining her head towards the two men before she headed for the dressing room. "And he's got the brilliant taste to be utterly infatuated with you, so there's definitely hope for the wanker."

As she left the studio, her longs legs moving effortlessly in her high heels, hips swishing, she gave Griff a small nod.

He tilted his head in absent acknowledgment, but his eyes and attention were fixed on Freddy, and as they met in the middle of the studio, she looked up at him, and his face turned down to hers. It was smudged with tiredness, lined with the residual strain of the past few days—weeks—and just looked so…unmistakably *hers*.

"What's that look for?" he asked with a hint of amusement, brushing a curl from her face.

She brought her palms up and rested them on his chest. "I suddenly felt alarmingly possessive."

"I know the feeling." His hands closed warmly over hers and rubbed her fingers in the slight chill of the air. "I believe I handle it with a little less subtlety than you do."

With a swift tug on his shirt, ignoring the scattered crew around them, she pulled him down and pressed her mouth to his, and he kissed her back deeply, his tongue stroking hers. It wasn't a hard, groping snog—although those were fun too; it was slow, and dreamy, and loving.

Pulling away to catch her breath, Freddy leaned her forehead against his chin. "We'll learn how to do it together," she murmured. "I've never been in real love before."

She heard and felt Griff's uneven breath. He lifted his head. "In love?"

"Utterly. I suspect irrevocably. Even unconditionally, since even when you're being kind of a dick, I'm still completely mad about you." Freddy considered. "I should have seen it coming. That first night we spoke at The Prop & Cue, you made me go all fluttery inside.

Logically, I should have wanted to knee you in the balls. I was doomed."

He touched a fingertip to the curl at her temple, an echo of his gesture in the moments before they'd kissed for the first time. "I love you." Something in the way he said the words made her wonder if he'd ever said them before.

Her hands tightened on him, that immense gratitude and profound *wonder* flooding her. "Proper in love?"

His smile spread from his eyes to the rest of his face. "Proper in love."

When he kissed her again, she said against his mouth, "Still duller than a pair of safety scissors, Griffin?"

His chest moved abruptly with his laugh. "I will retract one single statement from my past reviews. I had no idea what I was in for."

Epilogue

Four months later

The show had finished almost thirty minutes ago, but the foyer of the Majestic was still packed with people. They clustered around the perimeters of the huge Baroque space, bending and pointing at every small detail as tiny mechanical figures moved behind little bevelled windows. Miniature carriages rattled over real paving stones, and dragons flew from the roof of the gold-plated castle, their wings fluttering in the air, duochrome scales glittering in shades of purple and green as they hit the light from the enormous Christmas tree nearby. As the clock struck the hour, a door opened and the beautiful little train puffed out.

Freddy and Allegra had been right in their plan for the miniatures; the display brought the public flocking. Carolina Griffin and James Ford's expanded design had people queuing to get inside the theatre as early as nine o'clock in the morning. It was one of the most popular holiday attractions in the West End this year. And thanks to Griff's and her father's combined negotiating skills, his parents had sold it to the *Anathorn* musical for a sum that had totally exceeded Freddy's expectations.

Let it be pointed out, however, that while the Slytherins in the bunch had jacked up the price, it had taken a Hufflepuff to spot the obvious opportunity.

Squeezing around a group of chattering people with a murmured apology, she had to stop briefly to pose for photos, then pulled on her wool coat as she kept moving. She was running late. She exchanged smiles with a couple of younger girls from the chorus, who were standing with a group of their family and friends. As she edged past, listening to the clacking of the train wheels and the lovely sound of a child laughing with pure joy, one of the girls said in a hushed, apprehensive voice, "Shit. Isn't that the bastard from TV who does the reviews for the *Post*?"

The reply was equally horrified. "It *is*. And I messed up my steps tonight." The last was a wail.

"God, he even *looks* scary."

Not bothering to hide her grin, Freddy just about skipped around the last obstacle between them, and saw him standing near the door. Tall and handsome, his blond head uncovered, his hands tucked into his trouser pockets, Griff turned—and a smile lit up his cool, intimidating face.

He pulled his hands from his pockets just in time; he knew her well. As she catapulted happily into his arms, Freddy boosted herself with her forearms on his shoulders and pressed her nose against his cheek. "Hello," she said, and kissed the side of his nose.

He held her a few inches off the ground while he gave her a kiss in return, much harder and longer, on her mouth. "Hello."

The chorus girls were watching them with identical gapes. Apparently they'd missed all the furore four months ago after the *Sunset Britain* interview. Sabrina had been right; the literary world was going to be picking apart the salacious details of *The Velvet Room* affair for a long time to come, but the notoriously icy J. Ford-Griffin's love life had held the attention of the general public for a lot longer than the fraud.

"Come on," Freddy said, grinning as her toes touched the ground. She tucked her hand into the crook of the arm he offered. "You're scaring the littlies. And I want to see this surprise you've got for me."

"How do you know I've got a surprise?"

"Charlie let it slip when he called about Christmas." As Griff cast his eyes up in complete exasperation, she shrugged. "It's all right. He wouldn't tell me any details. I sensed a present on the horizon and stopped trying."

"Not *exactly* a present." Griff ushered her towards the door. In the car he turned on the heater for her and edged into the manic December traffic. It would probably take about three years to get wherever they were going, but at least at this time of year the Christmas lights made the traffic jams a bit prettier.

She was studying a mechanical window display that was nowhere near as impressive as James and Carolina's work when Griff took her hand, linking his fingers through hers. "How was the show?"

"Awesome. I love it so much."

Those crinkles she loved were at the corners of his eyes as he slowed to a stop again. "I know. And it shows."

He was flat-out at the moment with the film—and the next two projects he had in the pipeline—but he was doing his column again, and he'd been sent to review *Anathorn* on opening night two weeks ago, despite the ragingly obvious conflict of interest.

Which had not noticeably inhibited him.

She examined her nails. "I will at some point get over the totally unnecessary comment on my solo. I was off-key for *one* word, and I do not *purr*." Anticipating his quick grin, she added primly, "In public."

"I believe I used the phrase 'otherwise excellent.'"

"I was somewhat pacified." Freddy looked at him. "Everyone absolutely loves your parents' art." There was no other term for it, especially after James and Carolina had gleefully accept the brief to develop it further. It was beautiful work. Expensive, but beautiful.

They'd had multiple commissions since, which her father had proved unsurprisingly adept at wrangling. Despite his history with the Ford family and the very different personalities involved, he got on unexpectedly well with Griff's parents.

He loathed Griff, and the feeling was mutual, but she couldn't expect to have everything in life. And regardless—

"I really appreciate you getting Dad involved. He needed the distraction."

Rupert had avoided criminal prosecution, but his writing career had been ripped to shreds in the aftermath of the confession. And he'd voluntarily resigned as her manager, to Lisa's transparent joy, and Freddy's own private relief.

Griff lifted a shoulder. "When it comes down to it, he's a savvy businessman. He's already got them a dozen commissions. And let's be honest. That move with the suppliers might not have been completely transparent, but it was fucking genius."

As Charlie had once pointed out, James and Carolina, for all their faults, had very soft hearts where charitable causes were concerned. It was Rupert who'd quickly found the solution to their overspending. He'd enlisted Charlie and his endless stream of contacts to find local suppliers who could do with a helping hand and didn't charge the earth. He'd then embellished every one of the suppliers' hard-luck stories, and, Freddy suspected, just blatantly made one up where none existed. Griff's parents had been extremely affected. End result: overseas couriers were making far fewer deliveries in rural Surrey.

Griff indicated and turned left, and she rubbed a circle in the condensation on the window. "Griff, where are we going?"

"We're paying a visit."

When the car rolled to a stop in a quiet residential street ten minutes later, Freddy looked hesitantly out at the stone terrace house. She hoped he wasn't moving to Whitechapel, because they lived two streets apart in Notting Hill, and it was extremely convenient just being able to jog back to her place in the morning if she'd forgotten something.

"Have you bought it? Is that the surprise?" She tried to sound enthusiastic.

"It's not for sale." Griff got out and came around to open her door for her. "The owner's family have lived here since the early part of the twentieth century—although when times got tough, her family once took in paying guests." He gestured with his chin at the upper floors. "Including former soldiers turned struggling artists."

Oh.

Freddy pushed the door shut behind her and her lips parted as she gazed upward, from tiled doorstep to the window boxes on the third floor. "Was this Billy Gotham's house?"

Griff put a gentle hand on her back as they walked up

to the spotlight-lit front door, which was painted a sunny shade of yellow, a cheery note in the gloom of the night. "The owner got in touch after she saw Billy mentioned in an article about the film. She was a young child when he lived here, and she still remembers him. And Violet."

Freddy glanced at her watch. "It's very late to call on someone."

"She works nights. Her shift starts at one o'clock, but we'll be home by then." Griff reached for the knocker. "And apparently we need a full moon for this."

"How mysterious. And lycanthropic."

Half a minute after his polite tap, the door was pulled open by a middle-aged woman with very kind eyes. "Mr. Ford-Griffin," she said. "How nice to see you again." She smiled at Freddy. "And this must be Miss Carlton. I'm Helen Abernathy."

She stepped back to let them into the brightly tiled little hallway. "Do come in. It's a foul night." Closing the door behind them, she looked at Griff. "The room in question is on the third floor. The door on the left. It's still more or less as it was then." She lifted her shoulders. "Somehow I've never been able to bring myself to change it. I'll let you go up by yourselves. I think it's best experienced for the first time in private."

"Thank you," Griff said, and stepped back to let Freddy past, inclining his head towards the stairs.

Curiously, slightly apprehensively, Freddy started up, looking over her shoulder. "Why are we creeping around someone else's house at almost midnight?" She found herself whispering in the quiet. It was spooky wandering around any darkened house in the middle of the night, let alone a complete stranger's.

"There's something here that Helen thought we'd like to see."

There were two doors on the top floor, and Freddy hesitated, looking back at Griff.

"If there are werewolves," he said solemnly, "I'll protect you."

She was smiling when she pushed the left door open and walked into the room beyond—and stopped.

"Oh."

It was all she could say.

Griff came to stand beside her, and they stood in silence. Just looking.

It was a cosy little room, a *romantic* little room, with a desk and comfortable arm chairs, and books everywhere. A narrow bed was pushed against the wall. Just the right size for two people to have to curl up close. It was the sort of room that she'd love to have in a house of her own one day.

But her imagination wouldn't have stretched to anything quite like this.

The renowned portrait artist had been a multi-faceted talent. During his time living here, Billy Gotham had painted the walls, from floor to ceiling, with the most beautiful murals—combining figures and cascading floral patterns and curlicues, rich gold and jewel-toned imagery. He'd turned the whole room into a walk-in illuminated manuscript.

"Violet collected illuminated manuscripts." Griff tucked his hands back into his pockets as he turned, taking in the full effect, and Freddy remembered that small cluster of books in the Highbrook library.

As he spoke, the moon came out from behind a cloud. And as the silvery light hit the walls, it seemed to sink into what Freddy realised were countless embedded fibres, and the entire scape of murals suddenly gained the illusion of a rich, plush texture that defied the crumbling plaster beyond. She could swear that if she reached out her palm, she'd feel the smooth nap of fabric rather than the cold rasp of paint.

The Velvet Room.

Her gaze fell on the small snapshot on the mantel. Walking over, she picked it up, already suspecting what she would see.

Violet stood beside a young man with messy hair, a pleasant face, and dancing eyes. The dark bob of her hair was familiar, the nose was *very* familiar, but here there were no hidden shadows and the gaze that looked out of the picture was happy.

Griff's hand came to rest on Freddy's hip.

Setting the photograph back in place, she reached into her bag and felt for the folded piece of paper that was still safely tucked into her planner. Carefully, she tucked Violet and Billy's letter behind the snapshot.

"Thank you for not completely vilifying Henrietta in the film script," she said quietly, and turned to look up at Griff.

"In Violet and Billy's story, Henrietta was the antagonist." Griff smoothed back Freddy's hair, his touch very gentle. "And she made some extremely questionable choices. But she wasn't a villain. It's the same with everyone, isn't it? We're all a hundred different things at once. A different person to everyone who knows us. And there are very few people we'll ever love and trust enough to let them have—well, as much of the whole of ourselves as another person *can* know."

Their hands twisted together.

Her words were still barely a thread of sound when she said, "I think you let me know you."

"Yes." His brief response was a murmur against her mouth as he kissed her.

The easy passion between them flared hot and...well, hard, and Freddy dragged enough of her mind back to remember where they were. "I think we'd better hit the pause button until we get home," she muttered into the kiss.

He lifted his head with a muffled sound. "Stop pushing your hips into me, then."

Teasing, she gave him one last nudge with her pelvis. "'Is that a ring in your pocket or are you just happy to see me?'"

It was a direct quote from Anathorn, and she expected Griff to recognise it.

She did not expect *every* muscle in his body to go stiff.

Pulling away, frowning, she looked up into his face, and her breath caught. "Oh my God. Oh my God."

"Freddy. *Jesus*." Griff rested his hands on his hips and glowered down at her. For the most part, he was a dedicated film producer now, but at this moment: full-on Grumpy Critic in the house. "There's candlelight and champagne waiting at home. I was not planning to ask you in an attic. Albeit a very nicely decorated attic."

"Oh my God." She'd turned into a stuck record, and her hand went to her mouth as, with an enormously resigned expression, he reached into his pocket and pulled out a light blue, appropriately velvet box. When he opened it, the moonlight had something else to sparkle on.

And it was fucking *huge*.

"Frederica Carlton."

"Well, that's not a good start, is it?"

"For fuck's sake, Freddy." Griff looked more annoyed than ever.

"Better." Finally managing to draw in a deep, shaking breath, Freddy shoved her left hand at him, and he caught it automatically.

"There was a little more to come."

"Oh, sorry." She started to pull her hand away, but he held on, and reluctantly, his grin broke through.

He shook his head, then cupped the back of hers and tugged her up on her tiptoes to smack a hard kiss on her mouth. "Oh, fuck it. I love you like hell, you brilliant, beautiful, exasperating woman." Her eyes stung when she realised that the hand holding the ring box was ever so slightly unsteady. "You're the light of my life, and I can't imagine a future without your infuriating presence front and centre."

Freddy held on to his wrist, shaking much harder than he was.

The hand on her head moved to her cheek, and Griff's thumb rubbed gently. "Marry me?"

Her response was very simple. "Yes, please."

He kissed her again, then broke away to press his lips to the sensitive spot on her neck, where he spoke in a tone so ardent and husky that she didn't initially register the words. "We'll bring it full circle. You can walk down the aisle to Springsteen."

He twisted away from the swift movement of her foot, and she remembered that she'd once wondered what he would look like when he laughed.

Diamonds in the moonlight had nothing on it.

* * * * *

Author Note

This book contains a number of fictionalised elements, including but not limited to Highbrook Wells, Mallowren Manor, the Wythburn Group, the play and game version of *The Austen Playbook*, and *The Velvet Room* and all the trouble it caused.

Acknowledgments

As always, I'm so profoundly grateful for the constant support and encouragement I received while I was writing this book.

To my editor, Deborah Nemeth, my agent, Elaine Spencer, and the entire team at Carina Press—thank you so much for your expertise, professionalism, and kindness.

To the family and friends who talked me through the low points, let me talk through the plot tangles (special mention to my very patient mum!), and kept me going— I love you all so much and I couldn't have done it without you.

To my community online, who inspire me every day and make me feel better about the world in general—all the hugs. You're amazing.

And to Remus, the furriest member of our family— you made everything brighter and we'll love you forever.

Chapter One

Almost every night, between nine and ten past, Lainie Graham passionately kissed her ex-boyfriend. She was then gruesomely dead by ten o'clock, stabbed through the neck by a jealous rival. If she was scheduled to perform in the weekend matinee, that was a minimum of six uncomfortable kisses a week. More, if the director called an extra rehearsal or the alternate actor was ill. Or if Will was being a prat backstage and she was slow to duck.

It was an odd situation, being paid to publicly snog the man who, offstage, had discarded her like a stray sock. From the perspective of a broken relationship, the theatre came up trumps in the awkward stakes. A television or film actor might have to make stage love to someone they despised, but they didn't have to play the same scene on repeat for an eight-month run.

From her position in the wings, Lainie watched Will and Chloe Wayne run through the penultimate scene. Chloe was practically vibrating with sexual tension, which wasn't so much in character as it was her default setting.

Will was breathing in the wrong places during his monologue; it was throwing off his pacing. She waited, and—

"Farmer!" boomed the director from his seat in the
front row. Alexander Bennett's balding head was gleaming
with sweat under the houselights. He'd been lounging in his
chair but now dropped any pretence of indifference, jerking forward to glare at the stage. "You're blocking a scene,
not swimming the bloody breaststroke. Stop bobbing your
head about and breathe through your damn nose."

A familiar sulky expression transformed Will's even
features. He looked like a spoilt, genetically blessed
schoolboy. He was professional enough to smooth out
the instinctive scowl and resume his speech, but with an
air of resentment that didn't improve his performance.
This was the moment of triumph for his character and
right now the conquering knight sounded as if he would
rather put down his sword and go for a pint.

Will had been off his game since the previous night,
when he'd flubbed a line in the opening act. He was a
gifted actor. An unfaithful toerag, but a talented actor.
He rarely made mistakes—and could cover them better
than most—but from the moment he'd stumbled over his
cue, the additional rehearsal had been inevitable. Bennett
sought perfection in every arena of his life, which was
why he was on to his fifth marriage and all the principals had been dragged out of bed on their morning off.

Most of the principals, Lainie amended silently. Their
brooding Byron had, as usual, done as he pleased. Bennett had looked almost apoplectic when Richard Troy
had sauntered in twenty minutes late, so that explosion
was still coming. If possible, he preferred to roar in his
private office, where his Tony Award was prominently

displayed on the desk. It was a sort of visual aid on the journey from stripped ego to abject apology.

Although a repentant Richard Troy was about as likely as a winged pig, and he could match Bennett's prized trophy and raise him two more.

Onstage, Chloe collapsed into a graceful swoon, which was Richard's cue for the final act. He pushed off the wall on the opposite side of the wings and flicked an invisible speck from his spotless shirt. Then he entered from stage left and whisked the spotlight from Will and Chloe with insulting ease, taking control of the scene with barely a twitch of his eyelid.

Four months into the run of *The Cavalier's Tribute*, it was still an undeniable privilege to watch him act.

Unfortunately, Richard's stage charisma was comparable to the interior of the historic Metronome Theatre. At night, under the houselights, the Metronome was pure magic, a charged atmosphere of class and old-world glamour. In the unforgiving light of day, it looked tired and a bit sordid, like an aging diva caught without her war paint and glitter.

And when the curtain came down and the skin of the character was shed, Richard Troy was an intolerable prick.

Will was halfway through the most long-winded of his speeches. It was Lainie's least favourite moment in an otherwise excellent play. Will's character, theoretically the protagonist, became momentarily far less sympathetic than Richard's undeniable villain. She still couldn't tell if it was an intentional ambiguity on the part of the playwright, perhaps a reflection that humanity is never cast in shades of black and white, or if it was just poor writing. The critic in the *Guardian* had thought the latter.

Richard was taunting Will now, baiting him with both

words and snide glances, and looking as if he was enjoying himself a little too much. Will drew himself up, and his face took on an expression of intense self-righteousness.

Lainie winced. It was, down to the half sneer, the exact same face he made in bed.

She really wished she didn't know that.

"Ever worry it's going to create some sort of cosmic imbalance?" asked a voice at her elbow, and she turned to smile at Meghan Hanley, her dresser. "Having both of them in one building? If you toss in most of the management, I think we may be exceeding the recommended bastard quota." Meghan raised a silvery eyebrow as she watched the denouement of the play. "They both have swords, and neither of them takes the opportunity for a quick jab. What a waste."

"Please. A pair of blind, arthritic nuns would do better in a swordfight. Richard has probably never charged anything heavier than a credit card, and Will has the hand-eye coordination of an earthworm."

She was admittedly still a little bitter. Although not in the least heartbroken. Only a very silly schoolgirl would consider Will Farmer to be the love of her life, and that delusion would only last until she'd actually met him. But Lainie had not relished being dumped by the trashiest section of *London Celebrity*. The tabloid had taken great pleasure in informing her, and the rest of the rag-reading world, that Will was now seeing the estranged wife of a footballer—who in turn had been cheated on by her husband with a former *Big Brother* contestant. It was an endless sordid cycle.

The article had helpfully included a paparazzi shot of her from about three months ago, when she'd left the theatre and been caught midsneeze. *Farmer's co-star and*

*ousted lover Elaine Graham dissolves into angry tears
outside the Metronome.*

Brilliant.

The journo, to use the term loosely, had also com-
plimented her on retaining her appetite in the face of
such humiliation—insert shot of her eating chips at
Glastonbury—with a cunning little system of arrows
to indicate a possible baby bump.

Her dad had phoned her, offering to deliver Will's
balls on a platter.

Margaret Ward, the assistant stage manager, paused to
join the unofficial critics' circle. She pushed back her po-
nytail with a paint-splattered hand and watched Richard.
His voice was pure, plummy Eton and Oxford—not so
much as a stumbled syllable in his case. Will looked sour.

Richard drew his sword, striding forward to stand
under the false proscenium. Margaret glanced up at the
wooden arch. "Do you ever wish it would just accidentally drop on his head?"

Yes.

"He hasn't *quite* driven me to homicidal impulses yet."
Lainie recalled the Tuesday night performance, when
she'd bumped into Richard outside his dressing room. She
had apologised. He had made a misogynistic remark at a
volume totally out of proportion to a minor elbow jostle.

The media constantly speculated as to why he was
still single. Mind-boggling.

"Yet," she repeated grimly.

"By the way," Margaret said, as she glanced at her
clipboard and flagged a lighting change, "Bob wants to
see you in his office in about ten minutes."

Lainie turned in surprise. "Bob does? Why?"

Her mind instantly went into panic mode, flicking

back over the past week. With the exception of touching
His Majesty's sacred arm for about two seconds—and
she wouldn't put it past Richard to lay a complaint about
that—she couldn't think of any reason for a summons
to the stage manager's office. As a rule, Robert Carson
viewed his actors as so many figureheads. They were
useful for pulling out at cocktail parties and generating
social media buzz, but operated beneath his general notice unless they did something wrong. Bob preferred to
concentrate on the bottom line, and the bottom line in
question was located at the end of his bank statement.

Margaret shrugged. "He didn't say. He's been in a bad
mood all day, though," she warned, and Lainie sighed.

"I could have been in bed right now," she mused wistfully. "With a cream cheese bagel and a completely trashy
book. Bloody Will."

On the flip side, she could also still have been in bed
with Will, enjoying the taste of his morning breath and
a lecture on her questionable tastes in literature. From
the man who still thought *To Kill a Mockingbird* was a
nonfiction guide for the huntin', shootin' and fishin' set.

Life could really only improve.

On that cheering thought, she made her way out of the
wings and backstage into the rabbit's warren of tunnel-
ling hallways that led to the staff offices. The floors and
walls creaked as she went, as if the theatre were quietly
grumbling under its breath. Despite the occasional sticking door handle and an insidious smell of damp, she liked
the decrepit old lady. The Metronome was one of the oldest theatres in the West End. They might not have decent
seating and fancy automated loos, but they had history.
Legendary actors had walked these halls.

"And Edmund Kean probably thought the place was

an absolute dump as well," had been Meghan's opinion on that subject.

Historical opinion was divided on the original seventeenth-century use of the Metronome. Debate raged in textbooks as to whether it had been a parliamentary annex or a high-class brothel. Lainie couldn't see that it really mattered. It would likely have been frequented by the same men in either instance.

Personally, she voted for the brothel. It would add a bit of spice to the inevitable haunting rumours. Much more interesting to have a randy ghost who had succumbed midcoitus than an overworked civil servant who had died of boredom midpaperwork.

Aware that Bob's idea of "in ten minutes" could be loosely translated as "right now," she headed straight for his office, which was one of the few rooms at the front of the theatre and had a view looking out over the busy road. Her memories of the room were associated with foot shuffling, mild sweating and a fervent wish to be outside amid an anonymous throng of shoppers and tourists heading for Oxford Street.

"Enter," called a voice at her knock, and she took the opportunity to roll her eyes before she opened the door.

Her most convincing fake smile was firmly in place by the time she walked inside, but it faltered when she saw the two women standing with Bob.

"Good. Elaine," Bob said briskly. He was wearing his usual incorrectly buttoned shirt. Every day it was a different button. Same shirt, apparently, but different button. He *had* to be doing it on purpose. "You remember Lynette Stern and Patricia Bligh."

Naturally, Lainie remembered Lynette and Pat. She saw them every week, usually from a safe distance. An uneasy prickling sensation was beginning to uncurl at the base of her neck. She greeted Pat with a mild unconcern she didn't feel, and returned Lynette's nod. She couldn't imagine why the tall sharp-nosed blonde was here for this obviously less-than-impromptu meeting. She would have thought her more likely to be passed out in a mental health spa. Or just sobbing in a remote corner. Lynette Stern was Richard Troy's agent, and she had Lainie's sincere sympathies. Every time she saw the woman, there was a new line on her forehead.

It was Pat Bligh's presence that gave Lainie serious pause. Pat was the Metronome's PR manager. She ruled over their collective public image with an iron hand and very little sense of humour. And woe betide anyone who was trending for unfortunate reasons on Twitter.

What the hell had she done?

She was biting on her thumbnail. It was a habit she had successfully kicked at school, and she forced herself to stop now, clasping her hands tightly together. She had been in a running panic this morning to get to the Tube on time, and now she wished she'd taken time to check her Google alerts.

Nude photos? Not unless someone had wired her shower. Even as an infant, she had disliked being naked. She usually broke speed records in changing her clothes.

She blanched. *Unless Will had taken...*

In which case she was going to hit the stage and make short work of borrowing Richard's sword, and Will was going to find himself minus two of his favourite accessories.

"Sit down, Elaine," Bob said, his expression unreadable. Reluctantly, she obeyed the order—Bob didn't do invitations—and chose the most uncomfortable chair in the room, as if in a pre-emptive admittance of guilt.

Get a grip.

"I'll come right to the point." Bob sat on the edge of the wide mahogany desk and gestured the other women to sit down with an impatient wiggle of his index finger. Reaching for the iPad on his blotter, he flipped it open and keyed in the password. "I presume you've seen this."

He held the iPad in front of Lainie's face and she blinked, trying to bring the screen into focus. She could feel the heavy pulse of her heartbeat, but dread dwindled into confusion when she saw the news item. *London Celebrity* had struck again, but she wasn't the latest offering for the sacrificial pit after all.

It appeared that Richard had dined out last night. The fact that he'd entered into a shouting match with a notable chef and decided to launch a full-scale offensive on the tableware seemed about right. She took a closer look at the lead photograph. Of *course* his paparazzi shots were that flattering. No piggy-looking eyes and double chins for Richard Troy. He probably didn't *have* a bad angle.

God, he was irritating.

She shrugged, and three sets of pursed lips tightened. "Well," she said hastily, trying to recover her ground, "it's unfortunate, but…"

"But Richard does this kind of shit all the time," was probably not the answer they were looking for.

And what exactly did this have to do with her? Surely they weren't expecting her to cough up for his damages bill. The spoon in baby Richard Troy's mouth had been diamond-encrusted platinum. He was old family money, a millionaire multiple times over. He could pay for his own damn broken Meissen. If he had a propensity for throwing public temper tantrums and hurling objects about the room, his management team should have restricted him to eating at McDonald's. There was only so much damage he could do with paper wrappers and plastic forks.

"It's getting to be more than *unfortunate*," Lynette said, in such an ominous tone that Lainie decided to keep her opinions to herself on that score.

Pat at last broke her simmering silence. "There have been eight separate incidents in this month alone." Three strands of blond hair had come loose from her exquisitely arranged chignon. For most women, that would be a barely noticeable dishevelment. Lainie's own hair tended to collapse with a resigned sigh the moment she turned away from the mirror. For Pat, three unpinned locks was a shocking state of disarray. "It's only the second week of October."

Lainie thought that even Richard should fear that particular tone of voice from this woman. She flinched on his behalf.

"Any publicity is good publicity. Isn't that the idea?" She glanced warily from one mutinous face to the next. It was an identical expression, replicated thrice over. A sort of incredulous outrage, as if the whole class were being punished for the sins of one naughty child.

Apt, really. If one considered the personalities involved.

"To a point." Bob's nostrils flared. She couldn't help noticing that a trim wouldn't go astray there. "Which Troy has now exceeded." He gave her a filthy look that suggested she was personally responsible for Richard's behaviour. God forbid.

"Men in particular," he went on, stating the loathsome truth, "are given a fair amount of leeway in the public eye. A certain reputation for devilry, a habit of thumbing one's nose at the establishment, sowing one's wild oats..." He paused, looking hard at her, and Lainie hoped that her facial expression read "listening." As opposed to "nauseated." He sounded like a 1950s summary of the ideal man's man. Which had been despicably sexist sixty years ago and had not improved since.

"However," Bob continued, and the word came down like a sledgehammer, "there is a line at which a likable bad boy becomes a nasty entitled bastard whom the public would rather see hung out to dry in the street than pay to watch prance about a stage in his bloomers. And when somebody starts abusing their fans, making an absolute arse of themselves in public places, and alienating the people who paid for their bloody Ferrari, they may consider that line *crossed*."

Lainie wondered if an actual "Hallelujah" chorus had appeared in the doorway, or if it was just the sound of her own glee.

She still had no idea why she was the privileged audience to this character assassination, but she warmly appreciated it. Surely, though, they weren't...

"Are you *firing* him?" Her voice squeaked as if she had uttered the most outrageous profanity. Voiced the great unspoken. The mere suggestion of firing Richard Troy was the theatrical equivalent of hollering "Voldemort!" in the halls of Hogwarts. He-Who-Shall-Not-Be-Missed.

Still...

She wondered if it would be mean-spirited to cross her fingers.

Bob's return look was disappointingly exasperated. "Of course we're not firing him. It would cost an absolute bloody fortune to break his contract."

"And I suggest you don't attempt it." Lynette sounded steely.

"Besides," Bob said grudgingly, "nobody is denying that he's a decent actor, when he confines his histrionics to the script."

That was a typical Bob-ism. Pure understatement. Richard Troy had made the cover of *Time* magazine the previous year. The extravagantly handsome headshot had been accompanied by an article lauding him as a talent surpassing Olivier, and only two critics had been appalled.

"And if he conducted his outbursts with a bit of discretion," Bob said, as if they were discussing a string of irregular liaisons, "then we wouldn't be having this discussion. But Troy's deplorable public image is beginning to affect ticket sales. The management is not pleased."

Lainie couldn't match his awe of a bunch of walking wallets in suits, but she echoed the general feeling of dismay. If the management weren't pleased, Bob would make everyone else's life an utter misery until their mood improved.

"I'm not sure what this has to do with me," she said warily.

"If ticket sales are down, it's everybody's problem," Lynette said pompously, and Pat looked at her impatiently.

"We need some good publicity for Richard." She folded her arms and subjected Lainie to an intense scrutiny, which wavered into scepticism. "The general consensus is so overwhelmingly negative that he's in danger of falling victim to a hate campaign in the press. People might flock to see a subject of scandal, but they won't fork over hard-earned cash to watch someone they wholeheartedly despise. Not in this competitive market. At least not since it became socially unacceptable to heave rotten vegetables at the stage," she added with a brief, taut smile.

Lainie allowed herself three seconds to fantasize about that.

"How badly have sales dropped?" she asked, wondering if she ought to be contacting her agent. She had a third audition lined up for a period drama that was due to begin shooting early next year, but if there was a chance the play might actually fold...

An internationally acclaimed West End production, brought down by Richard Troy's foot-stamping sulks. Unbelievable.

"We're down fourteen percent on last month," Bob said, and she bit her lip. "We're not going bust." He sounded a bit put out at having to lessen his grievance. "It would take a pipe bomb as well as Richard's presence onstage before there was any real threat of that. But we've had to paper the house four nights running this month, and we opened to a six-week waiting list. This play has another four months to run, and we want to end on a high. Not in a damp fizzle of insulted fans and critics."

Lainie was silent for a moment. It was news to her that management were giving out free tickets in order to fill empty seats. "Well, excuse the stupidity, but I'm still not sure what you expect me to do about it. Ask him nicely to be a good boy and pull up his socks? Three guesses as to the outcome."

The tension zapped back into her spine when Bob and Pat exchanged a glance.

Pat seemed to be debating her approach. Eventually, she commented almost casually, "Ticket sales at the Palladium have gone up ten percent in the last three months."

Lainie snorted. "I know. Since Jack Trenton lost his last remaining brain cell after rehab and hooked up with Sadie Foster."

Or, as she was affectionately known in the world of musical theatre, the She-Devil of Soho. Lainie had known Sadie since they were in their late teens. They had been at drama school together. She had been short-listed against her for a role in a community theatre production of *42nd Street*, and had found shards of broken glass in the toes of her tap shoes. Fortunately before she'd put them on.

She was so preoccupied with a short-lived trip down a murky memory lane that she missed the implication.

"Quite." Pat's left eyebrow rose behind the lens of her glasses. She was now leaning on the edge of Bob's desk, her blunt, fuchsia-painted nails tapping a jaunty little medley on the surface. "And the only genuine buzz of excitement Richard has generated in the past month was when *London Celebrity* printed photos of the two of you attending the Bollinger party together." She again stared at Lainie, as if she was examining her limb by limb in an attempt to discover her appeal, and was coming up short.

The penny had dropped. With the clattering, appalling clamour of an anvil.

Don't miss
Act Like It *by Lucy Parker.*

*Available now wherever
Carina Press ebooks are sold.*

www.CarinaPress.com

Get 4 FREE REWARDS!

We'll send you 2 FREE Books plus 2 FREE Mystery Gifts.

FREE Value Over **$20**

Both the **Romance** and **Suspense** collections feature compelling novels written by many of today's bestselling authors.

YES! Please send me 2 FREE novels from the Essential Romance or Essential Suspense Collection and my 2 FREE gifts (gifts are worth about $10 retail). After receiving them, if I don't wish to receive any more books, I can return the shipping statement marked "cancel." If I don't cancel, I will receive 4 brand-new novels every month and be billed just $6.99 each in the U.S. or $7.24 each in Canada. That's a savings of at least 13% off the cover price. It's quite a bargain! Shipping and handling is just 50¢ per book in the U.S. and $1.25 per book in Canada.* I understand that accepting the 2 free books and gifts places me under no obligation to buy anything. I can always return a shipment and cancel at any time. The free books and gifts are mine to keep no matter what I decide.

Choose one: ☐ **Essential Romance**
(194/394 MDN GNNP)
☐ **Essential Suspense**
(191/391 MDN GNNP)

Name (please print)

Address   Apt. #

City   State/Province   Zip/Postal Code

Mail to the Reader Service:
IN U.S.A.: P.O. Box 1341, Buffalo, NY 14240-8531
IN CANADA: P.O. Box 603, Fort Erie, Ontario L2A 5X3

Want to try 2 free books from another series! Call 1-800-873-8635 or visit www.ReaderService.com.

Get 4 FREE REWARDS!

We'll send you 2 FREE Books plus 2 FREE Mystery Gifts.

Harlequin® Desire books feature heroes who have it all: wealth, status, incredible good looks... everything but the right woman.

FREE
Value Over
$20